The Last To Die

by

Graham K. Strickland

To Kelly
For the Cause
Graham K. Strickland
July 18, 2004

The Last To Die

by

Graham K. Strickland

Jarrett Press & Publications
Book Publishers Since 1994

Published December, 2000

The Last To Die - (first edition)
Copyright © 2001 by Graham K. Strickland.

All rights reserved. Printed in the United States of America. Except as permitted under the United States Copyright Act of 1976 no part of this publication may be reproduced or distributed in any form or by any means, or stored in a database or retrieval system, without the prior written permission of the publisher, except by a reviewer, who may quote brief passages in a review. Published by Jarrett Press & Publications, Inc. 2805 Spring Forest Rd, Suite 201, Raleigh, NC 27616.

Cover art by Larry Arnold
Editing by Melissa Saas - Wake Forest, NC
Maps by Mari Jones
Final edit by William Carrington - Durham, NC

Library of Congress Catalog Card Number: 00-134355
Strickland, Graham K., 1940 -
          The Last To Die

ISBN   1-888701-27-7 (paper)

Book Cover
From the original <u>SERIES GRAY</u>. Colorwheel Sales presents
"The Struggle at Battery Wagner" by South Carolina artist Larry Arnold

Copies of this book may be obtained from
Rd, Suite 201, Raleigh, NC 27616.
Phone orders and information requests sho

Graham K. Strickland

588 Eastwood Drive

Asheboro, NC 27205

E-Mail: gkstrick@yahoo.com

BIOGRAPHY

Graham Kent Strickland was born in 1940 at Fayetteville, N.C. He was reared in the eastern part of Cumberland County, the path traveled by Sherman's Army some seventy-five years earlier. Growing up in this area stimulated an interest in finding the facts of the past and resulted in a degree in history from UNC-Chapel Hill. His military experience came as a member of a howitzer battery in the U. S. Marine Corps reserve.

A real estate appraiser by occupation, Strickland has had free-lance articles published in several well known magazines. It was the research for his article, "The Search for Thomas" which appeared in the November 1986 issue of The State magazine that formed the basis for this novel.

Other than a year as a teacher, history has never been his occupation but it has always been Strickland's hobby and practically all non-fishing vacations have included either stops at historical sites or searching for relics with his metal detector. In fact, almost all of the battle sites mentioned in this novel have been visited by the author in an effort to be as historically accurate as possible. He now makes his home in Asheboro, N. C. where he is a real estate appraiser for Randolph County.

ACKNOWLEDGMENTS

How do you write your first book? You certainly don't do it without the help of a lot of people. Many people deserve my thanks. Diane Mitchem and Joyce Oliver read each chapter as I wrote it and kept convincing me that I was really writing a book that was readable. My grammar coach was Clara Strickland, the wife of my cousin Trent, who is responsible for the red marks on my manuscript. They also furnished needed advice for my composition. Annette Jackson did the proof reading and some editing for me. Debra Hill and Amanda Fields also critiqued some chapters.

Since it was my intent to write a historically accurate novel, I have included a bibliography of sources I have used. However, after several decades of reading and research, I still had to rely on the advice of experts in certain areas. Mr. Sion Harrington of the North Carolina Archives and History Department was very helpful explaining the troop movements pertaining to the battles of Averasboro and Bentonville. Mr. Ray Flowers, a member of the staff at Fort Fisher helped with details of that battle.

There would not have been a book without the information provided by Mr. George Fluhr of Pike County, Pennsylvania. It was he who finally filled in the information gaps about the Shohola train wreck, which up to that time had received almost no mention in Civil War writings.

PREFACE

It took my family one-hundred and twenty five years to find the facts which I have included in this book. Maybe the wives were told some details by returning Confederate comrades, but in my lifetime there were only vague stories about battles in Virginia, some soldiers from home being captured, and a train wreck. Armed with only these references, I began a search for my Civil War ancestors which has taken more than two decades. They were part of the non-slave holding small farmers who made up the vast majority of the Confederate Army and whose story has never been fully told. They were members of the 51st North Carolina Regiment, Clingman's Brigade, Hoke's Division. They fought at Battery Wagner in Charleston Harbor, several major battles in Virginia, and at Bentonville in eastern North Carolina. Many of these encounters have never been the subjects of any novels of which I am aware.

As I gathered facts about these men and women, I realized I would need to tell the historical background of the battles and events they experienced and which I describe. For that reason it might be difficult at times to determine if I am a story teller or a historian. I try to be both. I want to explain why battles were fought where they occurred and how the lives of these people were drastically changed by the decisions of Presidents and Generals. This book has a distinct Southern flavor to its point of view and to paraphrase a popular song of that time: "I don't want no pardon for anything I've wrote." I hope you enjoy The Last to Die.

Graham K. Strickland

CONTENTS

DEDICATION

To my wife Judy

"Who challenged me to begin this work,
and encouraged me until I finished it."

CHAPTER 1
Rumors of War

There are some years in history when great events are destined to occur. In these years mighty forces come together with such power that the lives of individuals are changed irrevocably. They are picked up and carried away as with water running down hill or an avalanche of snow. They have no control as to where they will eventually land. Such a year was 1861.

In the election of 1860, Abraham Lincoln ran for president on the Republican ticket. He had promised that if elected he would stop the spread of slavery into the territories. This would mean that when the territories became states their Senators would vote with the North. The South would have no way to stop the hated tariffs on cotton since they would now be outvoted in the Senate. Even though the Republicans were not on the ballot in many southern states, Lincoln won the election. This was the last straw for South Carolina and in December of 1860 she seceded from the Union.

North Carolina had remained loyal to the Union through all these occurrences. The population of the state was made up of small farmers who had flooded in during the periods of European unrest which had occurred during the 1700's. There were Germans in the Piedmont section of the state who lived side by side with an amalgamation of people from the British Isles who called themselves Scotch-Irish.

The English had filtered in from Virginia and South

11

Carolina and laid claim to the rich bottom land of the Coastal Plains. The failed Jacobite rebellion in Scotland in 1745 had sent the Scottish Highlanders flooding up the Cape Fear River Valley for two hundred miles. The children and grandchildren of the immigrants were beginning to enjoy some degree of prosperity.

The Cape Fear River was navigable by larger boats up to the town of Fayetteville in Cumberland County. From there, smaller boats hauled freight twenty miles upriver to Averasboro. Several miles east of this river port rises a tributary of the Cape Fear named the South River. This river bottom is thick with cypress and gum trees and the tannic acid from the cypress knees turns its water black. This river flows into the Cape Fear above Wilmington and eventually reaches the Atlantic Ocean. The land between these rivers is rich and productive and the people who lived on this land were industrious. They were mainly small, non-slaveholding, farmers who grew cotton and tobacco and tapped the longleaf pines for the turpentine which made the state the leading producer of naval stores in the world.

On the seventh day of March of 1861, a happy group of these people made their way along the wagon wheel ruts which sufficed as a road toward Fayetteville. Thomas Strickland and Susan Gay were going to be married by the justice of the peace that afternoon.

Thomas was driving a wagon pulled by a mule used to pulling plows and harrows in sandy fields. He was a rugged, broad shouldered man who had worked hard all of his life, but still managed to maintain a good sense of humor. He was reared across the river in Sampson County but moved to Cumberland as a young teenager. He had worked as a laborer on the river docks, and in the hot, sandy cotton fields and the turpentine woods between the two rivers. He had saved enough money to buy ten acres of land, cut the timber and built a comfortable two room house with a large fireplace. All he needed now was a wife.

Susan's family had moved into the area from Smithfield. Her parents had worked as ferry tenders on the Cape Fear River where the Clinton road met the river. A new bridge had made the ferry useless and sent her father to work in the turpentine woods. She had worked as a domestic for one of the wealthier families upriver and had met Thomas there. She rode beside him on the wagon seat holding on to his burly arm as if he might yet escape before they got to Fayetteville. She could not have been any happier at this moment and saw no reason why her happiness would not last forever.

She and Thomas had never learned how to read. All they knew of the impending crisis was what they were told by friends. Three days earlier, it had appeared in the <u>Fayetteville Observer</u> that Abraham Lincoln had become the sixteenth president of the United States. On that same day, the national flag of the Confederate States of America was hoisted over the capital building in Montgomery, Alabama.

The third member of the wedding party was Thomas' best friend Sam Morgan. Sam was a young farmer who owned a considerable amount of rich bottom land. His family was wealthy for the area because his great-grandfather had received a land grant from King George II for his service in putting down the Jacobite rebellion in Scotland. Sam's grandfather and father had expanded the holdings and because there were never more than two heirs upon the death of these men, Sam owned more than one hundred acres. Most of the cleared land was used for the growing of cotton and the remainder grew the pine trees which he tapped for turpentine.

Sam's father, John, had kept a family of black tenants to work on his farm which lay adjacent to Sam's property. John had freed the slaves he had owned ten years before. One of these men and his family had chosen to remain on the property and help raise the crops by supplying the labor for a share of the harvest. After the death of his father, Sam had inherited his property and saw no reason to change this arrangement. Sam was married to the daughter of another farmer from Robeson County whom he had met while studying at an academy down there. His wife, Betty, had chosen to stay at home while Sam rode his horse to Fayetteville to sign as the witness to Thomas and Susan's marriage ceremony.

The March wind made a whistling sound as it came through the longleaf pines which grew in the white, sandy soil

13

beside the road. Sam almost had to yell as he teased Thomas, "I don't suppose you two would listen if I tried to talk ya'll out of what you are about to do."

Thomas replied with a laugh, "I reckon it's too late for that. Besides, nobody was able to tell you anything, were they?"

"That's right," added Susan, "besides, if you didn't have Betty to keep you straightened out, you wouldn't be worth a durn for nothing."

"Damn right," added Thomas.

"What in the world are ya'll talking about"? Questioned Sam. "I'm one of the most dependable people you would ever hope to meet."

"I'm not saying you ain't," Susan replied. "But if it weren't for your having a good wife like Betty, you would spend too much time drinking likker and running them coon dogs of yours till all hours of the night."

"Thomas helps me run them dogs. You ain't going to make him give it up are you"? asked Sam.

"Oh no," she answered. "He's going to need to get out some and I reckon we can use the meat. But I aim to be such a good wife, he ain't going to want to be away much." Susan snuggled up a little closer to her intended, her long red hair blowing in the breeze.

"I guess you still want me to witness your ceremony after all," Sam concluded.

"I never had any other thought," Thomas said with a big grin on his face.

As the procession wound through the low, flat pine forests on the east side of the Cape Fear, the Goldsboro road they were traveling intersected at the nine milepost of the Northern Plank Road from Fayetteville. This plank road went to Averasboro and continued on to Raleigh some seventy miles to the north. At this junction, a large broad shouldered black man had stopped to rest. He was Moses Hawkins, a free man who was well known to Sam Morgan and his friends. During his days as a slave, he had been owned by the Graham family who had a plantation upriver near the Bluff Church.

For more than a century this bluff had been the only

place in this flat country where homesick Scottish Highlander immigrants could stand on one piece of ground and look down on another. He had attended the church with the Grahams, sitting in the balcony with the rest of the slaves, listening to the same sermon as the white landowners who sat on the first floor. Moses had been made a household servant by the Grahams. One night flames from the cook fire had ignited soot in the flue and had spread from the cooking area attic to the main part of the house. Moses saw the glow in the sky and had run to the house in time to rescue the three Graham children from the upstairs. He had been given his freedom by the grateful family, but had remained on their farm as a hired hand.

He had stayed in the area mainly because of his affection for a pretty young black girl named Spicey, who was a member of the family that lived on Sam's land. Moses stood up as Sam and his friends approached.

"Hello there, Moses," greeted Sam. "Where are you heading"?

"Hello mistuh Sam, mistuh Thomas, miss Susan," Moses greeted, nodding in their direction. "I'm going to Fayetteville to catch me a ride on some wagon heading north up the Salem plank road."

"We are going that way. Climb up in the back of the wagon if you want a ride." Thomas offered.

"Much obliged," said Moses as he tossed on the burlap fertilizer sack which held his clothes, ham meat and biscuits he had packed for his journey. He seated himself with his back against the front seat. Riding in the back of a springless wagon was not going to be comfortable but it was better than walking, he reasoned.

"Did I understand you to say you are leaving home and going north," Sam asked? "What's got into you?"

"It's not so much what's got into me as it is what's got into the rest of the folks," Moses answered. "I know it's another country across the state line in South Carolina. I hear they is still arguing over dat fort down there. There is going to be a war. You can feel it coming."

"Naw there ain't," countered Thomas. "We ain't so dumb that we can't work things out."

15

"I ain't taking that chance," Moses replied. "There ain't many rights I got now as a free man. If this state goes out and joins them Confederates, I might not have any. I'm gittin' out while I can."

"You be careful crossing state lines," cautioned Sam, "I understand some states have strict laws about freed men entering from other states."

"I know about all that. They ain't going to know when I do it," Moses explained. "Don't forget that black folks have ways of goin north. I'll get to Boston all right." Moses realized that he had just inadvertently given away his destination. While he trusted the white men he was talking with, the less known about his plan the better. He knew of the many dangers he faced and in case of unforeseen trouble with slave hunters, he had a small pistol tucked away in the middle of his belongings sack.

"What about Spicey," asked Susan?" I thought for sure you two would get together one day."

"Now ain't the time for that, Miz Susan. Since the law won't let us git married like white folks, the best we can hope for is for me to come back one day when things is better," Moses replied.

"Moses, I might be doing the same thing if I were in your place," said Sam," but I don't think North Carolina will go out. We ain't got all that much in common with those big cotton growin' states."

"That may be true," Moses countered, "but just the other day I heared Mistuh Graham arguin' with a visitor who had stopped by to talk and he says if Virginia goes out, there ain't nothing for this state to do but go wif em. North Carolina ain't goin to send troops against South Carolina and won't let anybody else's troops cross this state to do it either. No suh, that's what they both says."

"Is that what's got you all riled up," Sam asked? "What else did they talk about?"

"They was talking about callin some convention in Raleigh. Mistuh Graham didn't want to do it, but the visitor was tryin' to change his mind. I was workin' there in the yard and could hear everything they said," Moses explained.

16

"Mistuh Graham says that the only reason for the convention is to vote to go out of the Union. They ain't goin' to meet just to discuss things."

"Can't you men talk about anything but politics and all," Susan asked? "This is my weddin' day and me and Thomas aim to start a union, not get out of one. There ain't one of us that's going to stop anything that's goin to happen anyhow. Let's talk about something else."

In respect to the bride-to-be's wishes, the men changed the subject to farming, fishing, hound dogs and coon hunting. Soon, the covered bridge over the Cape Fear River and the Clinton road junction came into view. The traffic was light on this particular day and the bridge crossing was made without meeting any other wagons. The terrain slopes upward from the river for a half a mile until the road comes to the Old Market House in the center of Fayetteville. The Cumberland County courthouse lay one block south and it was here Thomas and Sam tied their animals to the hitching post at the curb of the wooden street.

"Much obliged again for the ride," Moses said as he gathered his belongings and jumped down to the ground. "Maybe I'll see ya'll again one day."

"You take care of yourself and don't forget what I said about crossin' state lines," Sam cautioned. "I hope things work out for you."

"I'll be all right. I'll appreciate any help you can give Spicey and her family if things go bad," Moses answered.

"Don't you worry none about that," Thomas said as Susan nodded her agreement.

"That's right," Sam said emphatically, "I'll bet we'll need them as bad as they'll need us."

Moses turned and headed toward the center of town. He walked west down the plank road, which stretched from Fayetteville to the towns of Salem and Winston near the foothills of the mountains, rounded the market house and was lost from sight,

The office of the justice of the peace was located in a wooden building near the court house. Thomas and Sam had previously signed the marriage bonds which then authorized

17

any minister or justice of the peace to perform the ceremony. One of the employees at the court house was Lewis Hobson, a mutual friend of Thomas' and Sam's who had grown up a few miles south of Averasboro. He greeted them as they walked into his office.

"Whatta-ya say boys? How're you Miss Susan? he greeted. "I've been expectin' to see ya'll around for several days now."

"What do you mean?" asked Sam. "I didn't know the law was lookin' us."

"It ain't yet?" Hobson joked back. "It's just that the waitin' period is up on these marriage bonds and most folks usually get married then. Let me fill out this license for you and ya'll be set."

"Thank you!" Thomas said. "While you're doin that, how about catching us up on all the war talk."

"Ain't much changed." Hobson responded. "They're still arguin'about Fort Sumter that the Yankees occupied illegally."

"You think they'll fight over it?" asked Thomas.

"Yes I do and North Carolina will go out with the rest of the South," Hobson said, glancing up at the wedding party. "We've just formed us an artillery unit up near home called the Black River Tigers, and we've got two cannons to drill with. You fellers want to join? We're lookin' for good men."

"No they don't!" Susan said emphatically. "This is my weddin' day, not some day that war's declared. Please hurry up with them papers." The men thought it better not to discuss the possibility of war any longer.

Since getting married has always been much easier than getting unmarried, the ceremony was quickly performed by the Justice of the Peace and the friends began to retrace their route back to their homes.

Along the road leading down to the river lies a parade ground which was the drill field of the town's militia group, the Campbelltown Rifles. Sam paused to watch them go through the manual of arms with their old flintlock rifles and War of 1812 uniforms. He had always been interested in military history and had done some reading about the battles of

18

the Napoleonic wars. As he watched, the unit finished its drill and then made an attack upon an imaginary enemy. The front rank advanced with fixed bayonets to the staccato sound of the drum. The rear rank advanced with shouldered arms so an exploding shell would not send their bayoneted rifles onto the back of a friend in the front rank. "Better them than me," Sam thought as he nudged his horse into a trot to catch up with his friends.

After he had crossed back over the river, Sam coaxed the horse into a trot in order to catch Thomas' wagon which was further up the road than Sam had thought. "Did you have fun watching them practice for war," Susan teased?

"Yes, I did," Sam answered. "I have read some about Napoleon's campaigns and you know something? They still fight battles the same way. One side lines up and attacks the other side which tries to shoot em down. It looks like there ought to be a better way."

"Well there ain't," Thomas said, "and you won't ever be able to change it unless you get to be a general or something one day."

"No chance of that," Sam said. "I don't plan to ever leave this part of the country. I reckon I have to be satisfied with what I am."

At the junction of the Goldsboro road where they had picked up Moses earlier in the day, Sam left the newlyweds. "I'd better see if I can get home before dark. I got some chores to attend to," he lied. " Besides, ya'll don't need me around no more."

"Thanks for standing up for me," Thomas shouted as Sam nudged his horse into a canter. "We'll see you around."

"You can count on that," Sam shouted back with a sly grin on his face. Sam's rush to get to his home near Graham's Bridge was not due to the need to feed his livestock or to chop wood for the cookfire. Even though he would do these things, he had to get ready for a southern tradition called a shivaree. This was a custom where the friends of the groom would gather outside the dwelling of a newly married couple and fire guns and make other disturbing noises on the wedding night, no doubt endearing themselves to the otherwise happy couple.

Sam lived a half mile to the east of Thomas at the end of a long sandy path which turned off the main road. About a hundred yards down this wagon path stood a large home with a front porch good for sitting and rocking shaded with large oak trees. In the front yard stood the well with the community gourd dipper. The house had been built by Sam's father and it was well known that a thirsty traveler could always get a cool drink of water from the Morgan well. Sam and his horse came trotting up to the well just as Betty came out to get water to cook supper with. Sam drew some water to give to the horse first then turned around and kissed his wife hello. The Morgan's oldest son, William, came running out of the house and started pulling on his father's coattail.

"What'd ya bring me Daddy, what'd ya bring me," he yelled. Sam pulled a small sack of horehound candy out of his pocket and handed it to the boy which he accepted eagerly. Sam had bought it in Fayetteville after the wedding knowing he must not return home empty handed.

"What do you say to your father?" Betty reminded.

"Thank you, Daddy," the boy yelled as he ran back into the house with his treasure. William was six years old and didn't have to share with anyone since his year old brother, Rufus, was not yet aware such things existed.

"Did ya'll get the job done," Betty asked, referring to the wedding?

"We sure did," Sam replied. "It's now official. We now have a married couple as neighbors living across the branch from us."

Betty drew another bucket up from the well, poured Sam a drink in the gourd and handed it to him. "I suppose you and your friends are going to serenade Thomas and Susan tonight," she inquired.

"We surely are," Sam said emphatically. "You remember what Thomas did to us. I thought I'd never catch that possum he put in our window that night."

"I can still see you running around the house trying to catch that thing with just the light from the fireplace ," laughed Betty. "After what he did, I guess you owe him one. I do hope that now that both of ya'll are married that maybe

20

you two will grow up a little."

Sam playfully slapped Betty on her rump and said, "I might not be as much fun if I grew up."

"Stop that," Betty snapped, faking sternness. "You just have time to feed up before dark. I'll have supper waiting for you when you get through." Sam obeyed because underneath his dark haired wife's exceptional beauty lay a confidence which made him want to carry out her wishes.

Sam led his horse to the stable and gave him some oats. There were also hogs to feed and a cow to milk and some firewood to split up for the cooking fire. These were things which had to be done every day in good weather and bad, so Sam ungrudgingly did them.

After supper, Sam and Betty sat rocking on their front porch and watched two figures approaching down the path from the main road in the gathering darkness. One of them was Sam's cousin Neil who lived across the South River in Sampson County. The other was his friend Dougal McKay whose family owned the farm on road across from Neil's family's farm. These two men were Sam's and Thomas' hunting and fishing buddies and had walked over to participate in the shivaree. Neil owned some of the best coon hunting hound dogs in that part of the country, and when they teamed with Sam's long legged mongrels on a cold winters night the raccoon population suffered.

Dougal had just turned twenty two years old and was somewhat younger than his friends. He had dark curly hair and possessed the good looks that caused the girls at church to go out of their way to speak to and be noticed by him. He was a crack shot with a rifle and usually was the one to dispatch the coon when the dogs had treed. He had brought with him an ancient muzzle loader which had an unusually loud report, and was the very thing for startling newlyweds.

As the pair drew near to the house, Sam's two dogs howled joyfully as they went out to greet them. When these men came over at night, it usually meant a hunt. "Evening, gentlemen," Sam greeted.

"Howdy, Sam," Neil returned. "Hello, Miz Betty" he continued, addressing Sam's wife with Southern respect.

"How are you boys doing", she responded. "Are ya'll going to make this night miserable for our new neighbors"?

"Actually, Miz Betty," Dougal began, "we feel like it's our duty to conduct a proper shivaree for ol' Thomas."

"That's certainly the truth," added Sam. "You know he would feel like he had no friends if we didn't do something." The three men then joined in mischievous laughter to show their agreement.

"I hope ya'll not be too rough," she begged. "Just make sure you can still be friends later."

In some of the rougher shivarees, the groom would actually be captured and tied to a tree and left there through the wedding night. This one would be tame by comparison. The three friends built their customary hunting fire out of sight of Thomas' cabin and about twice every hour they would sneak up near the dwelling and throw rocks and pine cones up on the roof. Every hour or so, some one would fire Dougal's musket up near the house. All through the early evening, a resin coated string was pulled through a hole in a dried gourd. This made a wailing noise akin to the legendary cry of the banshee, who made its noise across the moors of the British Isles, a place the ancestors of these friends were not much more than a century removed.

Most of the time was spent around the fire, warming themselves from the early March chill and sampling the moonshine jug Neil always seemed to bring along. Sam's hound dogs wandered around puzzled because nobody was starting the hunt. Occasionally one of them would bay at the moon out of boredom.

"Hey Sam," Neil yelled to make himself heard above the crackling of the fire, "what is the latest news from Charleston?"

"A paper came yesterday and there didn't seem to be much change," Sam replied. "After they wouldn't let that ship bring supplies to the fort, they have been doing a lot of talking. It doesn't seem like they are accomplishing much. I don't see what the fuss is anyway. The government has already given up several forts along the Gulf coast and one at Savannah. Why is Fort Sumter different? Anyhow, if the fort can't be supplied, the troops can't stay there forever. It's just a matter of time."

"Shoot," Neil said, almost disappointedly, "I think they ought to go ahead and kick the Yankees out and be done with it. They try to stick their nose in our business all the time."

"What on Earth are you talking about, boy?" Sam countered. "You are talking about a war which ain't even necessary. All anybody with gnat brains has to do is wait and the garrison will leave the fort. Besides, North Carolina is still part of the United States."

"Well, I'm getting ready just the same." Neil announced, "I've been drilling with the South River Rangers for the past six months."

"That just makes me feel a whole hell of a lot safer," laughed Sam. "Anyhow, your daddy is still around to take care of your farm in case you go traipsin off to war. Mine ain't. Pass me that there jug, boys." The jug was passed and Sam took a big swig that caused him to wrinkle his face as the burning liquid passed down his throat. He then reached for a jar of water and drunk deeply from it, "chasing" the whiskey. He stomped his right foot three times on the ground as he spun around in a circle. Then he groaned as if he were dying and then said, "Damn, that's good likker!" Looking around to continue the conversation, he asked, "What do you think about the war situation, Dougal?"

"Ya'll just going to have to fight any war that comes without me," Dougal replied. "I'd just break too many hearts if I went off and got myself shot. Hey, you bout through with that jug?."

The talk went on till midnight when the friends decided that shivareeing on a cold March night with a now empty jug just wasn't worth their time. Neil and Dougal headed back down to the river and Sam headed home with two confused hound dogs. There would be some hurting heads behind the plow tomorrow.

March is the month that the farm land between the rivers is broken up with bottom plows to get ready for planting. In April, the cotton is planted along with the gardens which provide the bountiful summer feasts of those who till the black soil. It was on the twelfth day of this month, when the

23

white dogwoods were in full bloom along the Cape Fear River, that a Confederate gunner fired his mortar in Charleston. The shell reached the top of its arc in the predawn hours, its path marked by a trail of smoke from its glowing fuse. It began its slow seeming decent until it burst like a deadly flower over the parapets of Fort Sumter. At this signal the other artillery batteries ringing the harbor began a general bombardment of the fort.

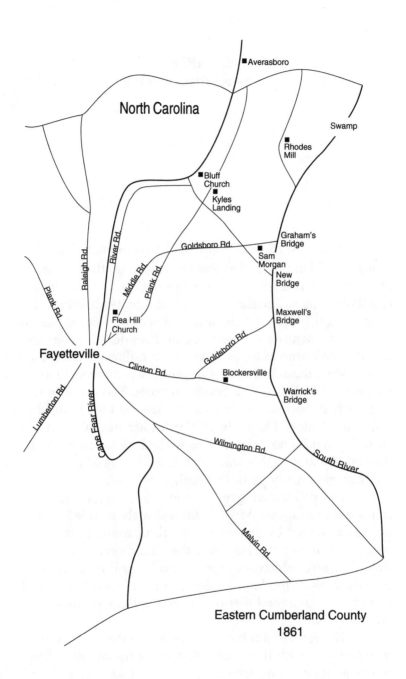

North Carolina

■ Averasboro

Swamp

■ Rhodes Mill

■ Bluff Church
■ Kyles Landing

Graham's Bridge

Goldsboro Rd.

■ Sam Morgan

New Bridge

Raleigh Rd.

River Rd.

Middle Rd.

Plank Rd.

Plank Rd.

Maxwell's Bridge

■ Flea Hill Church

Fayetteville

Clinton Rd.

Goldsboro Rd.

Blockersville ■

Warrick's Bridge

Lumberton Rd.

Cape Fear River

Wilmington Rd.

South River

Melvin Rd.

Eastern Cumberland County
1861

25

CHAPTER 2
Neuse River Bridge

Abraham Lincoln contended that no state had the right to leave the Union. In that line of reasoning, the Confederate States of America was not a foreign nation, but a collection of rebellious states. The flag of the United States had been fired upon at Fort Sumter by the armed forces of these states; therefore, armed insurrection had begun. President Lincoln, in his capacity as commander-in-chief of the military, issued a call for seventy-five thousand troops to put down this rebellion as well as a naval blockade of all Southern ports. The result of this request had the immediate effect of driving four more states out of the Union. The reply of North Carolina's Governor Ellis was, "...I can be no party to this wicked violation of the laws of the country and to this war upon the liberties of a free people. You can get no troops from North Carolina."

The pro-Union sympathy in the remaining southern states eroded rapidly. Virginia immediately seceded and was quickly followed by Tennessee. North Carolina at this point could do nothing else but leave the Union and join her sister states, a move which was applauded by wildly cheering crowds in all of the larger cities. Arkansas soon followed. It would now take total war by the Federal Government to end this rebellion.

The fertile land between the rivers does not wait for men to finish with their politics. April is the month when cotton is planted and tobacco plants are taken from their beds and transplanted in the fields. Any late planting must be done by May. In the middle of that month, Thomas had driven his mule and wagon to Fayetteville accompanied by Sam. They were going to buy some cotton seed and fertilizer for the late planting. As they got halfway between the river bridge and the market house it became obvious that something exciting was going on. Men and women lined the streets to such an extent that some of the stores were closed. Thomas was able to hitch his mule in front of the store where they would buy their supplies and walk inside with Sam.

"What's all the excitement about?" Thomas asked the clerk. "I ain't never seen people this riled up."

"Ya'll must be from out in the county else you would have heard. The Lafayette Rifles and the Cambelltown Rifles are being called up to state service and are leaving for Raleigh," explained the clerk. "Just day before yesterday, them and the Fayetteville Light Infantry marched over to the arsenal and took it over clean as a whistle. They got gunsmiths over there right now changing the flintlock rifles to take percussion cap firings. It sure looks like there's going to be some fighting to be done," he said, almost unable to control his excitement.

"What are the troops going to Raleigh for?" Sam questioned. "The Capitol isn't in danger is it?"

"Naw, the Governor is going to use them to help form the first state regiment. He might even send them up into Virginia if they need help up there. "Listen! Here they come now!" he shouted.

Everyone rushed outside to see the troops march past. They looked quite efficient in their ordered ranks, with polished brass and new percussion cap rifles taken from the arsenal. The band played "The Girl I Left Behind Me," and "The Bonnie Blue Flag." The crowd went wild when it cut loose with "Dixie." Ladies waved their handkerchiefs while the men cheered and waved their hats in the wildest public show of emotion ever witnessed by the two country boys. For a state, very pro-Union before Lincoln's call for troops, North Carolina would now enthusiastically cast her lot with the Confederacy. The voting on the official Ordinance of Secession would come later, but the fact was that the voting could go only one way because North Carolina was a Southern state and would live and die as such. The troops marched to the Market House where they listened to a patriotic speech. Rail service had not yet reached Fayetteville, so the soldiers crossed the river, turned north and began the march toward Raleigh.

Thomas and Sam reentered the store, bought the seed and fertilizer, loaded the wagon and headed for home. The mule traveled at a slower pace due to the added weight, so Thomas held the reins loose and let the animal travel at his own pace. They crossed the bridge over the Cape Fear and left Fayetteville on the other side of the river, still buzzing with excitement. The friends traveled in silence along the plank road past Flea Hill Church, thoughtful over what they had just seen.

Thomas finally broke the silence. "Ya know, Sam, I've never thought I had anything to fear from the old Stars and Stripes. I can't seem to git used to it becoming our enemy. What do you think has caused all this mess?"

"It all has to do with the way we have been treated," Sam replied. "The Yankees have used taxes on cotton to raise the national budget for years, at least that's what I read in the paper. They tax our cotton going out and then coming back in as finished goods. The South gets outvoted in the Congress all the time."

"You mean the plants from these seeds we're hauling are going to cause a war? " Thomas asked.

"Probably as much as a plant ever has," Sam added. "In the case of states rights', there is only one way to look at it. The states got together after the Revolution and created the Federal Government. Now, is the thing the states created more powerful than the states which created it. We don't think so in the South. And then there is the issue of slavery. A lot of people think it ought to be ended down here as well as in the North. My Daddy didn't like the idea of breaking up families so he kept all of the slaves he owned together before he set 'em free. He freed ol' Cairo when I was a boy and now James and Lonnie still live there on my place with their families. You knew they were Cairo's sons, didn't you?"

"I figgered they were, though nobody ain't never told me," Thomas replied.

28

Sam continued. "The Yankees don't make a profit out of slavery so they think it ought to be ended down here. I went to New York once and you ought to see some of the children they work in their factories. They hardly pay them nothing and work 'em to death. I treat the people on my farm better than that and Daddy treated 'ol Cairo better than that when he owned him. They ought to clean up their own house before they start worrying about what we do down here."

"What are you going to do if there is a war?" asked Thomas.

"I'm not going to do anything about it till I'm made to," Sam quickly answered. "Me with a wife and two kids and trying to run this farm. I sure ain't going out looking for no war. It's going to have to find me."

The two friends returned home and planted their crops. As Spring changed to Summer, it looked like it would be a good crop year. However, events occurring in other parts of the country would soon make Sam's words prophetic.

Neil had gone down to Clinton and enlisted in a Sampson County company, making good his boast to Sam he made around the fire the night of Thomas' shivaree. The night before he left, he and Sam had sat rocking on the front porch remembering the good times and working on a jug. Neil was eager to get in on the adventure because he feared the war might end too quickly if he didn't. Sam, on the other hand, sadly felt that a good chapter in their lives was ending. He was fearful of what the coming chapter would bring.

In July of 1861, two unprepared armies met at Bull Run Creek near Manassas, Virginia. The Confederate Army won this first encounter. However, for nearly a year after this initial victory, the Southern forces would know nothing but defeat.

Sam eagerly read each newspaper as soon as they arrived for news of the war, but they seemed to tell only of fresh disasters. In August, the Union Navy came to the coast of North Carolina and in six months controlled the eastern part of the state from Elizabeth City to Beaufort including the town of New Bern. The loss of Fort Donelson and Fort Henry resulted in the Union occupation of western Tennessee.

As 1862 arrived, Admiral Farragut fought his way past

the Confederate forts at the mouth of the Mississippi River and now Yankee cannons ruled New Orleans, the largest city in the South. In Virginia, a Federal army of 120,000 men was on the outskirts of Richmond. It soon became obvious to Sam that the rebellion would have a very short life unless a large army could be raised.

While all of this had been happening, one crop had been harvested and another had been planted on the farms between the rivers. Susan was pregnant and would deliver her and Thomas' first child in the fall. They had been married slightly more than a year.

Thomas had been working especially hard because of the coming addition to his family. He was plowing the day he heard the news that would mean his own involvement in the war. Charles Guy and Uriah Bass were the ones who told him. These two men lived with their parents down on the banks of South River. They grew the food they ate in small gardens and raised a few head of livestock. The rest of their diet was caught in the river or shot out of the trees. When these two were hunting in the woods, the bark of a squirrel or the switch of its furry tail most often sealed the animal's doom.

Thomas stopped his mule at the end of the field where the road passed. "How ya doin, boys," he greeted. "What ya'll been up to?"

"I reckon we done signed up to join Jeff Davis' army, "Uriah bragged, a touch of pride in his voice. "This war has gone long enough, so we decided to go ahead and enlist and win the war and git it over with."

"Yeah," Charles added. "Anyhow, it is join up now or git conscripted and that means you as well as us. What are you planning to do, Thomas?"

"I've spent the last several days looking at this mule's rear. What are ya'll talking about? When did this all happen?" Thomas inquired.

"Just yesterday," Uriah announced. "Ol Jeff Davis is calling everybody over eighteen into the army. There is a company being formed in this area so we joined up to be able to serve together. You ought to join up too."

"It sounds like I might have to," answered Thomas.

"What ever happens, me and Sam will probably go together."

Uriah and Charles walked on down the road while Thomas finished breaking his ground. He finished at the far end of the field away from the road. He unhooked the mule's trace chains from the singletree and hooked them around the hanes which fastened around the mule collar. He led the animal to the stable, poured him some water and left four ears of corn in the feedbox. He was greatly disturbed about the news and had to talk to Sam. Thomas crossed the creek which separated his land from the Morgan land and walked up to the house where Sam was sitting on the porch reading the paper.

There was no greeting this time and no small talk. Thomas asked the question which was on his mind. "What have you read about this here Conscription Act, Sam?"

"I'm afraid it is all true," Sam answered. "I've been reading for some time that it could happen and now it has. It don't look like we can win this war unless everybody that can fight joins up."

"What's going to happen to our crops?" worried Thomas. "This could ruin me with a baby on the way."

"I've been working this out," comforted Sam. "This company will be mustered in on the 23rd of April in Wilmington and we can join up now and still get our planting done before we leave. James and Lonnie can raise the crop and we can pay them a percentage of the harvest. That's the fair way to do it so we'll just plant more garden crops and less tobacco and cotton. Your baby won't come till after we've gone so Susan can move in with Betty. They'll be good company for each other."

Thomas was elated. "Sam, you are going to be President one day. I might have known you would have it all figured out."

"We can help each other out where we are going and our wives can do the same. If they can't get along, Susan can move back home after the baby is born," Sam added.

Thomas was encouraged by Sam's plan but he didn't feel real happy as he made his way across the creek back to his house. All of the plans he and Susan had made were rapidly becoming unraveled. Susan had just hung a skillet of spoon bread in the fireplace to cook when Thomas entered the house. Without a word he walked over to her and wrapped his arms around her waist, pulled her to him and gently kissed her. "What's the matter, darling?" she asked. "I can tell something is wrong."

"Let's go out on the porch where it's cool," he said. "We need to talk about some things."

They held hands as they walked out to the rough bench on the front porch and sat down. "Susan, I've got to go to war. Everybody over eighteen who can fight is being called up and that can only mean we are losing"

"Oh, no!" she exclaimed. "Just when we were getting this place in decent shape and with a baby on the way."

"Susan, if I'd known things were going to happen like this, I would have never married you no matter how much I loved you," he said, almost tearfully. "I never imagined I'd be anywhere else but by your side when our first child was born."

"Now you hush that," she responded. "The only thing you and I have ever known is hard work, and since we've been married we have at least been working toward something for ourselves. We can't control the future no more than we can control them making you go to war. No matter what's going to happen, I don't have no regrets about this past year. It's been the happiest year of my life and I wouldn't trade it for nothin."

"You don't know how good that makes me feel," Thomas said. "I feel the same way. I just don't like to not take care of my responsibilities, but in a way it is my responsibility to fight. Anyhow, with a son on the way, my name will go on no matter what happens to me. Name him Thomas if it's a boy. You name it what you want if it's a girl. I'll think up a second name before I leave."

"When will that be?" she asked. "How much time do we have?"

"The company that's being formed will be mustered in on April 23rd." Thomas answered. "Anybody that don't join up will be conscripted anyhow. Let me tell you about what Sam has offered."

About this same time, Sam and Betty were having a similar conversation. Betty would have a large responsibility left on her, but there was no other choice. She had grown fond of Susan, the wife of her husband's best friend. She listened as Sam explained what he had proposed to Sam.

The wives agreed to the plan. The planting was finished and James and Lonnie were excited about the opportunity for extra income. Sam and Thomas left home the third week of April in 1862. The only thing of value Sam owned that didn't help him make a living was his father's gold watch which he left with Betty.

Thomas told Susan as he left, "If it's a boy, name him Thomas Jackson Strickland after me and Stonewall." He lifted her up by the waist until their eyes were even and gave her a long, warm good-bye kiss. Then with a half smile, he turned and walked down the path to the main road where Sam waited. Thomas reached the road and turned and waved good-bye. Then, they were gone.

All the men from between the rivers who had enlisted made their way to Fayetteville where they began the march which would take them to Wilmington. The fact that these and many other companies of green troops were sent to Wilmington was by design. Since the loss of Norfolk to the Union forces, Wilmington was the northern most port city still open to the Confederates. It was the one city in North Carolina which had been given sufficient arms with which to defend itself because it was now the most important city in the South. New Orleans had been lost and the Confederacy survived. Norfolk fell and the South fought on. But now if Wilmington were lost, the armies of Lee and Jackson in Virginia could not be supplied. Great battles might still be fought, but they would be fought far to the south of Virginia where any defeat of Confederate forces could be fatal.

Eighty-two men were mustered into Captain Hector McKethan's company on the 23rd of April, 1862 at Camp Holmes, near Wilmington. This unit would become Company I of the Fifty-First North Carolina Regiment. Joining the men from Cumberland and Sampson counties would be men from the Cape Fear Valley region down to the river's mouth at Smithville.(Southport)

The troops had been issued uniforms and were storing

them in a corner of their tents which were lined up in rows. These rows seemed to stretch forever and made the camp a tent city.

"Damndest thing I ever saw," Uriah Bass complained to his friends. "They give us six times as many socks as they do trousers."

"That can only mean one thing," Charles Guy chimed in. "They aim to march us to death."

"Listen to all this complaining," Thomas added. "These guys were the first ones to join."

"Why didn't ya'll join the Cavalry?" chided Sam. "Then you could ride."

"I still can't figure why you didn't, Sam." Dougal said. "You know you have to bring your own horse and none of us ain't got one 'cept you."

"My horse is too old for the cavalry," Sam replied. "Besides, I had to come along to keep the Yankees from gettin you guys."

The five friends were in the same squad in the 2nd platoon of Company I. Practically all of their waking hours were spent drilling - Squad drill, Company drill, and Battalion drill. Sam was getting to understand the methods of the Lafayette Rifles he had seen drilling in Fayetteville. Advance in a straight line with your left elbow touching the elbow of the man on your left. If the pressure on your left elbow was removed, it should mean that the man on your left had been shot or, heaven forbid, had run. Death was preferable to dishonor to many men of this era. When a soldier fell, the man in the second rank would step up to take his place.

Lieutenant George Garrison was in command of the 2nd platoon. He had been a cotton merchant in his father's company in Wilmington before the war. He was a good officer and had a sincere care for the welfare of his men.

In July the regiment was moved to Camp Mears located on Wrightsville Sound. This was good for the men because they were able to supplement their diet with seafood when they were able to catch it. It was also bad because Lt. Garrison liked to march them in the beach sand for ten miles or so south toward Fort Fisher and then back. He wanted to make sure his men were ready for any forced march circumstances might require.

On one particular day in August the march had begun as usual. The griping and complaining was led by Uriah and Charles and was made worse by the fact that they were getting wet. A line of squalls with heavy rain was moving through the area and thirty miles to he north the blockade runner Judith was approaching Topsail Island. When the vessel sailed from Bermuda, the captain had hoped to reach the area at night but an easterly wind had shortened the time of arrival. He had planned to hide behind the island until dark before making his run to Wilmington but now a tailor made cover had been provided by nature. He could sail down the coast, hidden by the squalls. He quickly made a decision and gave orders to set a course to the south and stoke the boilers for maximum speed.

A little more than two hours later, Company I was trudging along the beach under the watchful eye of Lt. Garrison. They were getting close to the Union blockading squadron and sometimes one of these ships would send a shell toward a large body of troops. Suddenly, "Pom", "Pom" with a frightening echo was heard from the ocean. Even though most had never heard it before, all knew what it was - cannon fire. "Take cover," the officers and enlisted all yelled at the same time. The five friends ran up the dunes and dived under a clump of yaupon trees, not caring if any snakes were in the area. A man can be snake-bit and live, but a Yankee cannon ball kills quickly.

From this vantage point, the company witnessed an exciting spectacle. The Judith came bursting out of the squall line with her flag flying and gray smoke belching from her boilers from the hot burning British anthracite coal. Her giant side wheels were sending up large sheets of water as they dug into each swell. The Union gunboats rapidly closed in but their aim was greatly affected by the rough seas just as the Captain of the Judith had figured. The unarmed blockade runner had used deception to get this far, but now the surprise was gone. It would live or die by its speed.

It was a race for life or death to the cover of the guns of Fort Fisher. This fort possessed the finest rifled cannons in the

Confederacy and one of them fired a shot which splashed a hundred yards in front of the runner to show where safety lay. The captain of a blockade runner had to make a decision as to whether he could make it to the fort or if he would have to beach his vessel if his path was blocked and at least salvage the cargo. The splash in the water from the exploding shell also told the pursuing Union vessels that if they passed that point, the chance of getting shot through the boiler was very good. The Judith would win this race. The blockaders suddenly became aware of their approaching peril and turned back out to sea. As the ship passed into the protection of the fort, the men of Company I stood up and cheered. It was not coincidental that the next week they were issued .58 caliber Enfield rifles of British manufacture. Now trained and armed, the 51st was combined with the 8th, 31st, and 61st North Carolina Regiments to form a brigade under the command of Brigadier General Thomas L. Clingman.

News from home was good for Thomas and Sam. Thomas was the father of a son who had been named as he had instructed and it looked like another good crop year. Sam had received the news in a letter from Betty.

If possession of the town of Wilmington was vital to the continued existence of the Confederacy, the Wilmington and Weldon Railroad which carried the munitions to Virginia was no less so. The capture of New Bern by the Union forces had given them a base in eastern North Carolina from where they could threaten this rail line.

In mid-December of 1862, the 51st was marched to the rail station where it was loaded on boxcars pulled by a wood burning locomotive which slowly labored out of Wilmington and headed north. "I don't like the looks of this," Sam said with a concerned scowl on his face. "We are sure being sent somewhere in a hurry. Every time we've changed camps, we've taken our time about it."

"Where do you think we are going, Sam?" Thomas asked. "Do you reckon we're being sent to Virginia?"

"Naw, I don't think so," Sam replied. "They loaded us up real fast on this train. I figure there is a fire up this railroad somewhere we got to put out."

"Where all does this railroad go?" Uriah inquired. "I know it ends up in Richmond."

"It goes through Goldsboro and then to Weldon in this state," answered Sam. "There are a few small stops in between."

"Then it could be anywhere," Dougal McKay surmised. "Anyhow, I'm going to get me some sleep before we git there." He stretched out on the hay covered floor of the boxcar and laid his head on his blanketroll. He soon discovered he couldn't sleep because of the clacking of the metal wheels of the rail joints.

Sam was right. There was a fire to be put out and it was at Goldsboro. In conjunction with General Burnside's winter campaign against Lee's army at Fredricksburg, Virginia, Union General John G. Foster had marched westward from New Bern with an army of over ten thousand. His sheer weight of numbers had pushed aside the Confederates at Kinston and now he was heading on to damage the railroad at Goldsboro. The most vulnerable part of the railroad was the wooden bridge across the Neuse River. The Yankee army was advancing up the south side of the river and was approaching the bridge from the east just as the troop train stopped one mile south of Mount Olive Station. A raiding party of Yankee cavalry had torn up the tracks leaving the train still several miles from the bridge. The Southern officers began barking orders, "Company formation, guide on me, right face, double time, march!"

The regiment began its march at a near trot. As they passed through Mount Olive Station a crowd made up of women and old men lined the street to cheer their rescuers. A particularly pretty girl was waving her handkerchief at the soldiers as they marched by. This was a perfect opportunity for Dougal McKay who took off his cap and waved back. This caused the girl to give an extra wave and a smile in his direction. "Hey, boys," he said, "I think I just fell in love."

"I think you are crazy," Uriah kidded. "That girl was smiling at me."

"Not a chance," Dougal countered, "when she could have me for the asking."

"Any girl could have you for the asking," added Sam.

"I heard you are stringing four or five along up and down the river."

"I think that this one could be special," Dougal said. "Maybe I will get a chance to make her acquaintance when we pass back through."

Thomas wasn't in a jovial mood and didn't enter in the conversation. He was thinking about his wife and new son he had never seen and wondering if she would be mourning him after this rapidly approaching battle.

When Civil War armies met in combat, the gun fire from the advance pickets sounded like a popping sound from the distance. As more troops became involved, the popping changed to a rattling noise. When totally engaged, the sound of the firing became a continuous roar which was clearly audible to the men of the 51st as they trotted in formation toward the sound, their lungs aching from the cold air and exertion. The 52nd North Carolina from Pettigrew's Brigade had already been joined by the 8th North Carolina from Clingman's Brigade and was in a heavy fire fight in front of the wooden railroad bridge. The arrival of the 51st raised their numbers to two thousand as they formed a two line firing position.

Thomas raised his new rifle to fire it in anger for the first time as the Yankees advanced. "Front rank, FIRE! Second rank, FIRE! Independent, fire at will," came the command. He marked a blue clad target with his front sight and squeezed the trigger. The noise of the regiment firing at once was so loud Thomas didn't hear his rifle discharge. Only the recoil into his shoulder told him that his weapon had fired, but the cloud of smoke from the black powder kept him from seeing if he had hit his target.

If General Clingman's men were inflicting casualties, they were taking them as well. A minnie ball fired from a rifle makes a sickening "thwuck" sound as it strikes human flesh. The frequency of this sound along with the screams of the wounded soon told the commander that the cost of holding this position would be too great. Just as the command for the regiments to take cover in the woods to their right was being obeyed, Lt. Garrison came up to Sam.

"Morgan, I need five sharpshooters to keep the Yankees

38

from burning that bridge. Pick four more men and make it hot for them," he ordered, motioning toward some large fallen trees. Sam didn't have to ask for volunteers because when he looked at his four friends, they all nodded at him in a show of support.

Sam positioned his men behind a large fallen oak tree fifty yards in front of the new position. "Dougal, you're the best shot so you take the first Yankee that runs toward that bridge. Charles, you take the next one and I'll be third, then Thomas, then Uriah," Sam commanded. No sooner had Sam finished speaking than a Union soldier burst from his lines carrying a small bucket of coal oil. The Union army was three hundred yards from the bridge and if they advanced closer, they would expose themselves to an enfilading fire down their lines from the two Confederate regiments in the woods. It would take a heroic effort for the soldier to reach the bridge. Dougal McKay squeezed off a shot and the man pitched forward and lay where he fell. Another Yankee sprang from his lines as his comrades cheered him on. Charles fired and missed. Sam took careful aim and gently squeezed the trigger. His shot missed the man but smashed the bucket he was carrying and sent it flying. This time two men started the dash and drew the attention of Thomas and Uriah. Their shots both hit their targets and knocked them down. Both Yankees got up and limped back to safety slightly wounded.

The Federal commander now began a bombardment of the bridge with his artillery and almost immediately had the structure ablaze. Sam noticed that another battery had swung around and was preparing to send some excitement his way. "Let's get back to the regiment," he commanded, "We can't do nothing more here." The five rebels raced back to the regiment's position and arrived there as the first shells began landing at the oak tree they had just left. "Well done, Morgan," said Lt. Garrison, "You did all you could and exercised the proper judgment by not exposing your men to further danger." Sam's leadership ability had been noticed.

The bridge was burning furiously when General Foster ordered his troops to return to New Bern, even though he had scored one of the greatest tactical victories of the war. He could have captured Goldsboro and placed his army on the Wilmington and Weldon Railroad and stopped supplies from the blockade runners from getting to Lee's army. With reinforcement, he could have enveloped Wilmington from the north and made Fort Fisher a useless pile of sand. But he had heard of Lee's crushing defeat of Burnside at Fredricksburg, so he withdrew. Two weeks later, Confederate engineers had replaced the railroad bridge. Once again, the tools of war flowed freely from Wilmington to Lee's Army just as if the Battle of Neuse River Bridge had never been fought.

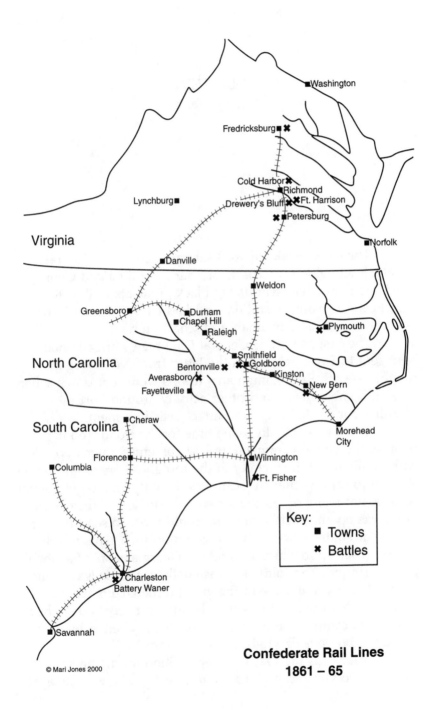

Washington

Fredricksburg ■✖

Cold Harbor ✖
Lynchburg ■   Richmond ■
Drewery's Bluff ✖✖ Ft. Harrison
✖ Petersburg

Virginia   ■ Norfolk

■ Danville

Weldon ■

Greensboro ■   Durham ■
■ Chapel Hill
Raleigh ■   ✖ Plymouth

North Carolina   Smithfield ■
Bentonville ✖ ■ Goldboro
Averasboro ✖   ■ Kinston
Fayetteville ■   ■ New Bern ✖

South Carolina   Cheraw ■

Morehead
City ■

Florence ■   Wilmington ■
■ Columbia   ✖ Ft. Fisher

Key:
■ Towns
✖ Battles

✖ Charleston
Battery Waner

■ Savannah

Confederate Rail Lines
1861 – 65

© Mari Jones 2000

41

CHAPTER 3
Battery Wagner

The early weeks of 1863 saw an increase of Federal naval activity along the coasts of South Carolina and Georgia. The Union navy had sent its big black gunboats to Port Royal, near Beaufort, South Carolina, and had captured a base for operations against Savannah and Charleston.

The 51st as part of General Clingman's brigade had been sent to Savannah, when the letter from Neil Morgan caught up with Sam. Clingman's troops were sent down when a naval bombardment and other activity around Fort McAllister indicated a ground attack was imminent.

There was actually some time for the troops to kill because the Union commanders had contented themselves with bombarding the vicinity of the fort and there would be no attempt to capture the city. Sam was the only one to get a letter because not many of his friends could read, and if they could there was no one back home who could write to send them a letter. The soldiers were lounging around their tents which had been set up for them by grateful Georgians on a Savannah parade ground. The soldiers occasionally got some leave time to visit the city and some of the grateful merchants would accept the North Carolina script the men carried. Today, they were all in camp when the mail came. Sam yelled at his friends, "You boys like to hear a letter from Neil?"

Uriah was the first to accept. "Shore nuff," he answered." Do you reckon he's found that fight he was always talking about?"

"I'll bet he has if he is with Jackson like I heared," said Dougal. "What's he say, Sam?"
The letter began:

"Dear Sam, I seat myself down and take pen in hand to write these few lines and hope when they reach you that you are well and safe. My mother got your company and regiment from your folks which I was glad to find out. I think the Lord must have something special in mind for me since in his mercy he has let me live this past year. They put me in Co. H, 20th Regiment and then sent us to Richmond to join the command of General D. H. Hill. This was about the time when General Lee took command of the army. The Yankees had a huge army coming up the river about twice our size. General Lee sent us across the river to join Stonewall Jackson's army. We were in attacks for seven days in a row and drove the Yankees away from Richmond. Our division stayed around the city in case the Yankees came back while General Lee took the army back up to the battleground at Manassas and whipped the Yankees again there. In September we marched up north to rejoin the main army. We were attached to Longstreet's corp. We dug in, in front of one of the passes on South Mountain which the Yankees were trying to take. I fired my rifle till it was too hot for me to touch. We finally gave way and fought a big battle near Sharpsburg. I think we were still in Maryland. Anyhow, the Potomac River was at our backs and the Yankees nearly broke our lines but A. P. Hill's men got there just in time from Harpers Ferry to help us stop them. I don't think we whipped the Yankees this time but they didn't whip us neither. The next battle was at Fredricksburg, right before Christmas. There was a big snow and it was still real cold. Our brigade was back from the lines and we didn't fight much but the Yankee shells came over the lines and bursted around us. Most of the Yankee attacks came on our left against our men who were behind the stone wall. I didn't see this but a boy from Fayetteville who used to sell us seed and fertilizer who is in the 24th North Carolina says there are five acres of dead Yankees in front of that wall. That's where he was during the battle. I accidently met him after the battle and he told me this. He says he knows you. No more news at this time. You write me when you can. I am in Company 'H, 20th North Carolina, Rodes Brigade. We are still attached to Gen. Jackson's army. He leads us down some rough roads but there is always victory at the end.

Your cousin Neal Morgan

"Damn!" Uriah swore. "It looks like Neil has got himself into a mess of fightin'. He always did say that's what he wanted to do."

"I don't think Neil or any of the rest of us had any idea just how terrible a thing war is," Sam stated. "We've had a taste of it, but nothing like he has seen."

"I"ll tell ya'll about something that happened at that fight at the Neuse bridge we were in," Charles said. "After it was all over, I noticed that my britches were wet. I must have peed in them but I don't remember doing it. I've never been so scared in all my life. You acted like it didn't bother you none, Sam. Were you scared?"

"Scared'ern Hell." Sam replied. "I was scared in that one and I'll be scared in the next one. It's kind of funny that as much as we have talked about that battle, none of us has admitted how scared we were until now."

"I wonder if you get scareder in a big battle," Uriah mused. "I don't think I'll be as scared in the next one as I was in the first one. I sort of got calmed down after I started shootin'."

"Well, I ain't going to admit how scared I was," said Thomas. "Anyhow, it was real good to hear from Neil and find out he's all right. You know, when this war is over, I think I'll learn to read and write. It would be nice to let Susan know how things are where I'm at. I just ain't never had a chance to learn to or a reason to need to. Is it real hard, Sam? Do you reckon I could learn?"

"Why yes, you can certainly learn to if I did. It's really not that complicated and I can help you start learning the alphabet if we get any spare time around here," Sam offered.

Sam was sincere in his offer but the spare time was not to be forth coming. The regiment was soon moved back to Charleston, and from there to a camp on Topsail Sound above Wilmington. Several of the companies of the 51st checked a Union raid on the railroad near Warsaw, N.C., and captured several prisoners. The men of Clingman's Brigade were being used to react to Federal raids along the coasts of the Carolinas.

In July of 1863, a major engagement was developing around Charleston. Since this city was called "the cradle of the rebellion" by the North, much effort was expended throughout the war toward its capture. The Confederates were just as determined not to let it fall. The Union Navy earlier in the year had sailed their ironclads and monitors into Charleston harbor to blast the Rebel forts into submission. Unlike New Orleans, where the city was defenseless after the Union frigates sailed past the forts, these war ships sailed into a cul-de-sac of cannon fire which sent them scurrying back across the bar to safety. They would now attempt to take the city by seige.

The men of the 51st were very perplexed as they boarded the train for the movement to Charleston. The camp at Topsail had been a healthy one. In addition to a good water supply, the men had been able to suppliment their diet with the large number of rabbits in the area. It was with much reluctance that they left.

"I hadn't never rid on a train before I got in this here army," Thomas complained. "When this war is over I plan to ride on one to some place I want to go."

"I bet this is the way you go to Hell," Uriah added. "When you die the Devil picks you up in a train like this one and you just ride forever breathin smoke and getting cinders in your eyes."

"Yeah," Sam responded, "and you got to go so bad you're bout to bust."

The box car roared with the laughter of the soldiers as the train left Wilmington in the distance. The railroad turned inland and crossed the state line into South Carolina. The troops tried to get some rest since sleep was nearly impossible with all the noise, smoke and cinders. Several hours of jolting and jarring passed and the train sounded its whistle as the town of Florence loomed up ahead. The engineer brought his engine to a gradual halt in front of the water tank as the train crew scurried about to get ready to take on wood and water.

The soldiers were allowed to stretch their legs and refresh themselves while the train was stopped. The stop offered other opportunities to Dougal McKay. The young bachelor always had an eye out for pretty girls and one of the prettiest he had ever seen was walking down the street a half block away. Her dark brown curls hung out from beneath her sun bonnet and she carried a basket which looked to Dougal like it held some kind of food. She had a bubbly personality and spoke to all the ladies and old men she passed on the street.

"Hey, boys, "Dougal said, "I bet you I can get me some of what's in that basket." Having stated his intentions, he sprinted a half block behind the buildings which faced the street, came up an ally and out on the main throughfare. He would now meet the girl, walking toward her as nonchalantly as possible. As they met, he made eye contact with her and gave her a half smile which she did not return. He walked on a few steps, then turned suddenly and said, "Oh, Miss."

The girl stopped and looked back over her shoulder as Dougal walked up to her. "Ma'am," he began, "I just had to speak to you because you look so much like my sister, but now I see you are a lot prettier than she is."

The girl had been ready with her usual rebuffs she had used on the many soldiers she always encountered when one of the troop trains stopped. This time she had been caught offguard by the compliment and this was an extremely hand-some young soldier. "I-I don't think we've been properly introduced, sir," she stammered.

"I know we haven't and please don't think I act like this all the time around a proper lady like you. It's just that I haven't been home in over a year, and when I saw you I just had to speak to you. Besides, I might never come back through

Florence again," Dougal said, hoping he might accidently say something that would gain the favor of this lovely young girl.

"And just why should that be a concern of mine?" she responded giving him her haughtest toss of her head.

"It's just that here lately when they load us up and send us off like this, there's some Yankee's to be fought somewhere," he explained.

"Oh!" she exclaimed, "I don't mean I'm not concerned about the safety of one of our soldiers, but it's not proper for me to be seen talking to strangers, especially a soldier carrying a rifle like you are. Maybe I can do something for our war effort. Do you like sweet potatoes? That's what I've got in this basket."

"Lawdy, ma'am, I've not had anything that good to eat since I joined the army," Dougal said hopefully.

"Well, you wait right here and I'll get you some cooked ones. I just took Mrs. Grantham some butter beans and she gave me some sweet potatoes. We already had plenty of them. It's for the war effort, you understand, and not a reward for your freshness, Mr. soldier, whose name I don't even know." As she spoke, she wheeled suddenly and started walking up the street.

"It's Dougal," he shouted after her. "My name is Dougal McKay."

This time when she looked back over her shoulder, she gave him a half smile which was meant for just a tiny bit of encouragement. The voluptousness of her figure was even more encouragement as he watched her enter a white two story house which had the usual front porch with the rocking chairs. She came back in less than a minute carrying six sweet potatoes wrapped in newspaper. "Here," she said, as she handed them to him. "Share these with your friends. The only thing we've got plenty of since the war started is sweet potatoes."

"Thanks for your kindness," Dougal said. "You are truly an angel and a beautiful one at that."

"Now you hush that," she scolded. "The Devil's goin to get you for lying before the Yankees have a chance to."

The blast of the train whistle ended the conversation as

Dougal tucked the sweet potatoes and got ready to run to the train. "I don't know your name. Please tell me your name," he pleaded.

"It's Sarah McLain, if you must know." she answered, still doing nothing to indicate she was enjoying this meeting.

"Well, Miss McLain," Dougal said with a sly smile, "I consider that we have been properly introduced and after we get through whipping them Yankees and come back through Florence, I aim to knock on the door of that white house on Evans Street and tell your mother that I have come to call on her daughter."

He turned and ran toward the train as the engine made a big puff and the wheels started turning. Dougal had left in such a hurry he had not even seen Sarah's pretended smerk of annoyance. As he ran along beside the boxcar, he handed his rifle to Thomas and the sweet potatoes to Sam. Two other members of his squad grabbed his arms and swung him on board.

"It looks like you made out all right," Uriah said when he saw the food Dougal had gotten for them.

"Lawdy, boys, I think I'm in love!," exclaimed Dougal. "I just got those taters from the prettiest girl I've ever seen."

"I thought that girl at Mount Olive Station was the prettiest you had ever laid eyes on," Charles kidded.

"That she was until I met Miss Sarah McLain" answered Dougal. "You can bet that if I don't get shot where we're going, I am going to look that young lady up when we pass through Florence again."

"I like her fer these taters and I ain't seen her yet," Uriah added as he cut and divided the sweet potatoes among the squad. "You know something," he continued, "this just might be the perfect food. They are good hot or cold, you can eat them cooked or raw, and it takes them a long time to spoil."

"I don't reckon I'm going to give mine much of a chance to go bad," Sam said. His sentiment was agreed to by all the hungry Rebels, and soon, the potatoes were eaten and the brief stop in Florence was forgotten by all but Dougal McKay.

In a few more hours, the train began to slow down as it

approached the station at Charleston. This country was becoming very familiar to the men of Clingman's Brigade who were actually glad to leave the train and march somewhere. Some of their previous camps near the city had been malaria ridden and they expected more of the same. However, this was to be a very different visit to Charleston for these Rebel soldiers.

Instead of marching to a campground to spend the night, the Brigade was marched to a parade ground where they were awaited by the commanding General of the coastal defenses of the Carolinas, General Pierre Beauregard. After the Battle of Bull Run, this officer had been one of the South's best known leaders, but he had a difference of opinion with Jefferson Davis after the Battle of Shiloh and had been relegated to this obscure command. As soon as he arrived, the Yankees did also, and the South was indeed fortunate to have a commander of his ability at Charleston when they did. He was a good military engineer and harbor defences were made formidable against attack from the sea, but the Union Army meant to test them from the land also.

General Beauregard was a Creole from Louisiana, short of stature with a short beard and thin mustache. He was well aware of the psycology of command and after reviewing the North Carolina troops, pronounced them "Veterans." Clingman's Brigade had not suffered many casualties up to this point and Beauregard aimed to use the well manned regiments of Clingman at the place most likely to be attacked by the Federals - Battery Wagner, on Morris Island. This island has a long, narrow strip of solid beach which runs parallel to the shipping channel leading into the harbor. The western part is swampy and virtually unusable. The Yankees planned to leapfrog from Folly Island and advance northward to take Battery Wagner. From there they could fire their seige guns at Fort Sumter only a mile away. Beauregard was just as determined that this would not happen.

Battery Wagner was rapidly becoming the most bombarded place in the history of warfare. In addition to the land based artillery, angry Monitors steamed back and forth off the beach, shelling the fort. The Confederate defenders spent a week on duty inside of Battery Wagner before being relieved.

The changing of the defenders had to be done at night by necessity. The 51st and part of the 31st regiment would be the first troops from Clingman's Brigade to man the fort. The steamer which shuttled the troops to their new duty stations could take four companies at a time, so three trips were necessary. As the troops passed the ominous hulk of Fort Sumter in the late night fog, there were many who prayed that the fort's defenders had been told that those passing under her guns were friends.

The steamer pulled up at the dock on Morris Island and unloaded Company I where a company of the Georgia regiment was waiting to be relieved. "What outfit you fellers from?" a Georgia soldier asked Thomas as his unit trudged by in the deep sand.

"51st North Carolina," he replied. "Got any advice for us on how to stay alive on this here hell hole?"

"Yeah," the Georgian replied, "don't let the shells bewilder you when they are coming toward you. Those Monitors like to skip their shells along the water, and we lost some men who watched them too long and then couldn't git to cover when they exploded above the fort. Just remember, they are firing them things at you to kill you. There are other things your officers will tell you about, but nobody told us about that."

"Much obliged," Thomas responded. "I hope ya'll get some good duty now."

"It can't be no worse than this," the soldier said . "Good luck to you."

The regiment trudged through the deep sand to the interior of Battery Wagner where they bedded down to salvage what they could of the night's sleep. The land face of the fort was two hundred yards wide with artillery positions in the middle. As it neared the ocean, it turned at a sharp right angle to the left to protect against an asault from the sea. For the next week, the defence of the fort would be the responsibility of Clingman's men aided by the Charleston Battalion and some artillery units from South Carolina and Georgia.

Most of the infantry would spend the daylight hours in the reinforced area of the fort called the bombproof. The logs of the Palmetto tree covered with sand had protected the cannons which helped the South Carolinians defeat the British fleet in 1775. Not suprisingly, Battery Wagner was constructed by the same method with large logs covered with sand offering overhead protection from the huge projectiles crashing down from above. Sam's squad would not receive this protection.

Lt. Garrison had sent for Sam to report to him in the parade ground of the fort. Sam walked over to meet the officer as the first light of the sun begun to show itself over the ocean. "You sent for me, Sir?" Sam asked.

"Yes, Morgan," the Lieutanant replied. "You are now a Corporal. That was excellent work you did at Goldsboro and since we have been ordered to furnish a team of sharpshooters, I'm putting you in charge. Pick the five best shots from your squad and go over to the armorer and trade your rifles for British Whitworths with globe sights. Find a position in the dunes west of the fort and see if you can pick off some Yankees who might get careless and show themselves in our front. Any questions?"

"Yes, Sir," Sam said, overwhelmed by the officer's words. "I have several. I appreciate the promotion, but I don't know anything about being a sharpshooter."

"None of us do at this point, but we have to learn fast," the Lieutenant replied. "You did good work at the bridge with the men you picked and you only need to add one more. The rifles have been sighted in by the Georgia boys who were using them, so all you need to do is load and take your positions. You might want to make sure your shirts and hats are a color near like the sand. There are going to be some Yankees on the other side who are going to be shooting at you."

"I'll do my best, sir," Sam said with a salute. "I reckon that me and my friends are pretty good shots."

"Also," the Lieutenant added, "if we are faced with an attack by infantry, get your Enfields back and join your company to repel it. When we are relieved, turn the Whitworths in for the next garrison to use. That will be all."

Sam made his way back to the company and informed his four friends that they had been chosen for some specialized work. The other man he chose for the duty was Daniel Gra-

ham who came from up above the Bluff Church back in
Cumberland County, and who was also good with a rifle. The
men drew their weapons, ate a meager breakfast of hardtack,
and took their positions in the sandy dunes. The brilliant
sunshine of the new day indicated it was going to be a hot one.
The Yankee gunners were going to make certain of it.

Some of the Georgia defenders had served previously in
the fort and had suffered at the hands of sharpshooters who
occupied a two story house located about two hundred yards
from Battery Wagner. The line of sight from the upper story
windows covered part of Wagner's interior. The troops usually
avoided walking across this area, but on this day a careless
soldier was shot through the head by one of the Union marks-
men in the house.

Sam's squad had settled in among the dunes and was
looking through its rifle sights at the Federal fortifications.
"Wowee, it's just like having a telescope on top of your rifle,"
Uriah said in amazement.

"It sure is," responded Sam. "I guess it's time for us to
put them to work. Mark you a target and be sure to keep your
own heads down."

The concentration of the sharpshooters was broken by
the arrival of five soldiers from the Georgia regiment who came
up behind them carrying a can of oil and kindling wood.
"When ya'll hear us shootin, keep those Yankees busy in the
upstairs window of that house," one of them said.

"I haven't got any orders about any attack," Sam said.
"Is this all of you?"

"Yes it is," the soldier responded, "and we ain't zackly
got no orders neither. We just got tired of seeing our friends git
killed by them bastards in that house. Remember, give us time
to sneak up on 'em and you start shootin when you hear us."

The Georgians disappeared behind the dune line and
entered the marshy growth to the right.

"Dougal, when you hear them begin shootin, see if you
can drop that Yankee in the upper right window, Sam ordered. "Thomas, you take the one in the left. Uriah, you and
Charles back up Dougal if he misses and me and Daniel will
back up Thomas. It must be two hundred yards so allow for a

little dropage. I don't think there is enough wind to worry about."

In about ten minutes it seemed that the Georgia boys should be ready to begin their attack. "Mark your targets and get ready," Sam ordered. Suddenly, a volley of fire was heard from the direction of the house. The Union sharpshooter in the upper right window stood up and leaned out to see what kind of unexpected attack was coming from the sound side of the house. Dougal's shot hit him in the shoulder and dropped him to the ground. Another Yankee rushed to the left window just as Thomas fired. The man fell back and was not seen again. The sound of the high pitched Rebel yell was heard from the house as smoke started curling upwards from the structure. Now a Yankee patrol was running from their lines toward the house to help out their comrades, but it was too late. The fire was blazing out of control, sending a large black plume of smoke upward in the windless sky. Sam and his men fired at the advancing Federals as the guns from Battery Wagner fired at the Union trenches. This action brought its own response from the Union cannons. What had started as an unordered attack was turning into a major artillery duel.

Sam and his squad were elated when they saw the Georgians emege from the marsh. All five had made it back. As they lay in the shelter of the dunes, panting for breath with the shells passing overhead, one of the exhausted attackers finally spoke. "Whoever shot them two Yankees in the upstairs winders saved some of us from gittin shot."

"Were they both killed?" Thomas asked.

"The one that fell out got carried away so we don't really know. The one upstairs was all bloody. I went up there to set the fire and I drug him out so he wouldn't burn. I think he was dead," one of the Georgians volunteered.

Thomas was saddened by this description of the man he had shot. He wondered if the man had a family to mourn him. What was his name, where was he from? Would they have been friends if they had met in different circumstances? Thomas would spend the rest of the day in thoughtful remorse, but the violent actions of the coming months would not often allow the luxury of such reflections.

After fifteen minutes of rest behind the dunes, the Georgians knew that it was time to return to the fort. "Well, boys," one of them said, "I reckon it's time for us to go take our medicine."

"Yeah," another agreed. "I don't expect no brass band to welcome us." Upon their return to the fort, the men were arrested for their unordered attack and court-martialed. At the hearing, it was determined by General Taliaferro, the fort commander, that the men had actually corrected a situation which had been overlooked by the officers. All charges were dropped.

The duty on Morris Island was terrible for the defenders of Battery Wagner. An attack had to be prepared for at any time and the artillary fire from the fleet and land forts fell with monotinous regularity. Food and water had to be brought in under the cover of darkness. The cook for Company I was a middle aged Scotsman named Neil McMillan who owned a large farm down on Brown Swamp and farmed it with his large family. Because of his age he had been exempted from most of the combat training and made the company cook. All of the men respectfully called him Mister Mack.

At most of the other camps he had occasionally been able to come up with some fresh pork or beef to feed the troops and when he did he made it well known and expected to be praised for it. He usually made a kind of soupy stew with the leftovers. It was at this this duty station that the pork and beef became scarcer, but still the soupy stew was occasionally served. When asked what kind of meat the stew contained his stock answer was, "Did it make you sick?" When the questioner answered no, Mister Mac would would say, "Then don't ask." It was suspected that the fare included crows, seagulls and perhaps even buzzards. Eventually, nobody did even bother to ask. The troops respected him and it was joked by the men in Company I that theirs was the only cook who bothered to dip the maggots out of the soup when they floated to the top. Such was the difficulty of manning Battery Wagner.

The morning of July 18, 1863, dawned like any other. The sun came up over the the ocean to the east and the Yankees continued their constant shelling from their forty-one land based guns. Sam, as usual, led his squad of sharpshooters out in the dunes to begin their deadly work.

Since the repulse of the Union ironclads attack against Charleston's forts in April, the Federals had been gathering their forces to capture the city by land. In early July, they made the crossing from Folly Island over to the southern part of Morris Island. From there an advance and capture of Battery Wagner and Battery Gregg at the northern part of the island would put their artillery in point blank range of Fort Sumter as well as the remaining forts in the harbor. An attack on Battery Wagner before the arrival of Clingman's men had been easily repulsed by the Confederates, but since that time, the Yankees had shelled Battery Wagner mercilessly during the daylight hours.

Sam and his men were glad to be outside the fort and not have to be stuffed into the hot, stinking bombproof. On this day about noon, five Monitors and five gunboats took their position in front of the fort where they were soon joined by the "New Ironsides", the flagship of the fleet and at that time the most powerful warship on Earth. These vessels teamed with the land based morters and artillery to send a shell into Battery Wagner every three seconds for eight hours. When shells fired long from the fleet passed over Wagner and started landing in the dunes around Sam and his men, they beat a hasty retreat for the safety of the fort and its bombproof.

The squad entered the bombproof at a dead run after dodging shells the entire way. As his eyes became acclimated to the darkness after the bright sunlight of the dunes, Charles noticed a man standing nearby who was not dressed in any kind of uniform. Instead, he was making rapid marks with a pencil on a sketch pad, doing a drawing of some kind "Hey, feller, what outfit are you with?" Charles asked the man.

"I'm a war correspondant from London," the man answered. "I'm going to sketch and report on what is to occur here today."

"You mean you don't even have to be here?" Charles asked, incredulously. "Can't you watch just as easily from Charleston?"

"Oh, I wouldn't miss it for the world, ol' boy," the man

replied. "You chaps are putting on a splendid show, just splendid."

The conversation was short due to the difficulty talking over the sound of the exploding shells outside. Charles turned away, shaking his head. This was the last place on Earth he would be if he didn't have to.

The bombardment continued for eight hours during which the conditions inside the bombproof became almost unbearable. As the day progressed, the inside temperature exceeded one hundred degrees. The men were short on rations and the water supply was almost non-existant. By necessity, the hospital was located in the bombproof and the screams of the men wounded from the shelling was unnerving to the soldiers who knew they were to soon face an infantry attack.

Union General Quincy Gilmore looked through his field glasses at the bombardment falling on Battery Wagner. He had sighted the Union guns which had reduced Fort Pulaski at Savannah and he had no doubt that he would do the same to this fort. He had six thousand troops to send at the fort's thirteen hundred defenders. It was time. With a nod of his head, he started a sequence of comands which sent the Union infantry forward.

But Battery Wagner was not a masonry fort. It was constructed mostly of sand and most of the exploding shells did little but rearrange the sand which cushioned their impact. The nine thousand shells fired at the fort had caused around thirty casualties among the defenders. Many of the heavy guns in the fort had been dismounted to save them from destruction, and Wagner had made little attempt to reply to the bombardment, their commander preferring to save his ammunition for the land attack which he knew would follow. As the bombardment ended and the attackers were forming, the roll of drums ordered the Confederate defenders out of the bombproofs and up to the parapets. The 51st responded, almost eagerly.

The Union Brigade advancing up the beach as night fell was led by the 54th Massachusetts, a regiment of black soldiers eager to prove their worth. Their commander, Colonel Robert Shaw, a white abolitionist from Boston, was leading them into history. As they advanced in the gathering darkness, one of the soldiers to the left of Sam shouted, "Look, those are black troops they are attacking us with."

Lt. Garrison looked at the advancing columns with his fieldglasses and determined that what the soldier said was true. "Has ol Abe done run out of white Yankees to fight us with?" another soldier remarked.

The Lieutenant responded, "Look! Whatever you might think of these troops advancing on us, they looked trained, they are armed, and they are coming here to kill you. You had better be ready to defend this position."

A cheer from his men indicated this was indeed the case. Because of the racial feelings of the time, his men were actually insulted to be attacked by the black regiment.

The Lieutenant put his hand on Sam's shoulder and said, "Corporal Morgan, I want you to spread your squad up the length of the company. Tell them not to shoot when we fire our volleys. I want them to pick off any stragglers who might not be hit when they try to come up the wall. We can't let any Yankees into these positions. Do you understand?"

"Yes, Sir!" Sam answered and began to position his squad. He explained the orders to each soldier as he was posted along the line.

The advance of the 54th Massachusetts was being impeded by the topography of the beach. The path of their assault was narrow to begin with and they were forced to march in massed column file. The island reached its narrowest point in front of Battery Wagner and spring storms had eroded two thirds of the land the Federals thought they had at their disposal over which to launch their attack. When the men on the right of the column began to wade knee high in the ocean, Col. Shaw veered his attack to the left. This was unfortunate for the attackers since they had been heading for an unprotected part of the fort. The 31st North Carolina had been in a part of the fort which had been blasted by the heavy Naval guns. Their officers were having a difficult time getting them to leave the bombproof and defend their part of the parapets.

The shift in the Federal attack sent them toward the 51st North Carolina who confidently waited for them behind the defenses. The guns of Fort Johnston on James Island began to send grape and canister shot into the massed Union troops. Battery Gregg began firing over the top of Wagner, adding its support. The Massachusetts Regiment charged into a water filled moat directly in front of the 51st. A brilliant flash of light illuminated the night sky as six hundred rifles fired the first volley from the waiting Confederates and evaporated the front of the attacking force. Colonel Shaw was not hit but crossed the moat and charged up the sandy slope yelling encouragement to his men. When he reached the top, a Confederate rifleman shot him through the heart.

The Confederates did not have time to remount their cannons before the attack so one of the Georgia artillery units lit the fuses of its cannon balls by hand and rolled them into the moat. The horrified Federal troops could only watch as the shells rolled in upon them and exploded around their ankles.

A lone black soldier came charging up as Thomas put him in his sights as best he could in the darkness, occasionally lighted by explosions and flares. He squeezed his trigger finger but felt no recoil, just the snap of the weapon's hammer. "Misfire," he thought. "Must be a bad cap." He jumped up and prepared to meet his enemy with a bayonet thrust but the sand gave way under the man's feet and Thomas's thrust missed. The man righted himself as Thomas prepared to come back with his rifle butt. Instead, both men froze. Thomas was staring into the face of Moses Hawkins. They had last seen each other on the way to Fayetteville the day Thomas was married, but this was no time for reunions.

"Get down from here, you damn fool," Thomas yelled as he pushed at Moses with his rifle butt. He had meant to shove the black soldier back into the moat by hitting him in the shoulder, but instead the heavy butted weapon caught Moses in the face and split it from his left eye to his cheekbone and sent him tumbling backwards.

To stand on this parapet for very long meant death, so Thomas dived back on his belly toward his trench as he heard the zing of bullets passing through the space his body had occupied moments before. He had no desire to kill Moses and for the rest of the battle would fire to the left of where the struggle had taken place.

Other Union regiments were attacking Battery Wagner and meeting much the same fate as the 54th Massachusetts. However, the 48th New York and the 6th Connecticut did succeed in getting inside the fort and atop the bombproof and giving a good account of themselves. When the second wave of attackers arrived in the darkness, they had to climb over a tangle of bodies from the first wave. Thinking the troops in front of them were Rebels, they fired into the backs of their own men. Being shot at by the defenders in their front and their attacking friends in the back, the Yankees fell in heaps.

The Confederate cannons had been remounted and were waiting for the second wave which they mowed down by companies. Survivors from the first attack had begun drifting back to tell of the massacre occurring in front of the fort. General Gilmore, hearing of this, ordered the third attack canceled. The Confederates shifted troops from the west end of the fort to the east to contain the breakthrough. When reinforcements from the 32rd Georgia arrived, the battle mercifully ended with the capture of the surviving Yankees who were still in the fort.

Sam was trying to round up his squad in the pre-dawn darkness. They had been spread out on Lt. Garrison's orders and Sam was anxiously searching to see if they were still alive. Charles and Dougal had found each other and were elated to find Sam unhurt. Thomas, Uriah and Daniel Graham were all peering down into the moat where the heaps of mangled bodies lay.

"Sam," Thomas exclaimed, "I saw Moses Hawkins."

"The Devil you say," Sam answered. "Where? Was he with that black bunch.?"

"I hit him with my rifle butt and he fell back down there," Thomas said, motioning toward the moat.

"Well, keep your heads down," Sam cautioned. Somebody down there might have a loaded rifle. We'll look for him in the morning." He saw the white bandage in the darkness as he looked toward Uriah. "What happened to you, boy? I just now noticed that bandage."

"I either got hit in the face with some shrapnel or a spent bullet. I don't know which," he answered. "I'm just thankful it didn't hit any bones."

"I'm just glad it didn't mess up that pretty face of his none," Charles kidded. Almost immediately he realized how close his friend had come to death and added, "I shore thank the Lord none of us got hurt no worse than that."

"We all have a lot to be thankful for this night," Daniel added. Nobody disagreed.

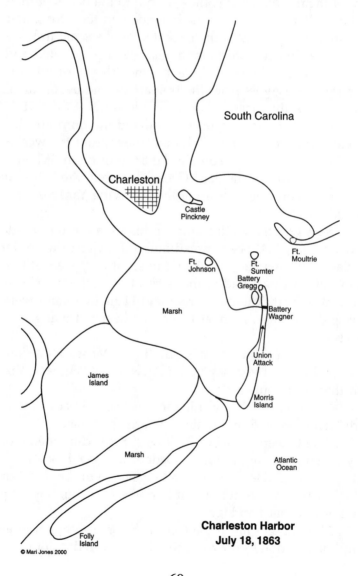

Charleston Harbor
July 18, 1863

© Mari Jones 2000

60

Chapter 4
Charleston

For the rest of the night, sporadic small arms fire was heard from the parapets of Battery Wagner, intermingled with an occasional load of grape shot fired at an unseen enemy. The exhausted defenders were ready for the third attack, but it never came. The moans of the wounded and the dying added to the eeriness of the night. As the sun of a Sunday morning rose in the summer sky, a scene of unspeakable horror was revealed. The men who had been killed by rifle fire lay stiff in the weird and unnatural positions in which they had died. Other bodies had been blown apart by artillery and were spread hideously over the landscape. The bodies of those who had been killed in the surf floated up on the beach on one wave only to be carried back by the next one.

Some movement could be seen inside the fort in the early morning light as repairs were being made and Yankee prisoners were being herded to the rear. The Union Army had suffered more than fifteen hundred casualties while the Rebels had lost one tenth that number. If there were no other consequences of the battle, it insured that Charleston would be Rebel for another year or two.

The Federals, under a flag of truce, had received permission to retrieve their wounded and bury their dead. Rebel details were removing the shoes from the Union dead for their own use. A small group from the 51st was searching through the bodies in the moat.

"He ain't down here," Thomas said conclusively. "I've done looked at all those bodies over there and I know that was the spot I saw him land."

"Maybe it wasn't him that you saw," Daniel Graham responded. "I know it would have been hard for me to recognize anybody last night."

"Both of us stopped for a second when we saw each other, so it had to be him," Thomas argued. "He used to work for some of your folks, Daniel, so you would recognize him."

"That I would," Daniel agreed. "We used to set trot lines in the Cape Fear River together. We would set 'em in the evening and take the catfish off in the morning."

"Well," concluded Sam, "it can only mean that he wasn't hurt bad and got away."

"That don't displeasure me none," said Thomas. "I'm glad he got away."

Sam added, "We need to see if the Lieutenant wants us to get our sniper rifles back and get back in the dunes."

"Do you think the Yankees will attack again, Sam?" Daniel asked.

"No I don't," Sam answered. "They wouldn't fare any better than they did last night. I imagine they will try to wait us out and dig some siege trenches."

The men climbed back into the fort and got ready to resume the dull monotony of their duty on Morris Island. But, to their delight, the exhausted men of the 51st were relieved and sent back to Charleston. The people of the city were excited that the Union attack on Battery Wagner had been smashed, but an aura of gloom hung over the Confederacy. The news from the West was bad. The city of Vicksburg had fallen to General Grant's siege and now Yankee gunboats controlled the entire Mississippi River. The news from the east was worse.

The early reports from Pennsylvania had told of a Confederate victory with the army withdrawing in good order. Later reports had admitted that Lee did not deliver the knockout blow he had been seeking. As casualty figures came flowing in to the newspapers, it was becoming clear that a Confederate disaster had occurred at Gettysburg. The confidence most

Southerners had in eventual victory was beginning to melt away.

It was about this time that another letter from Neal arrived. Sam brought the letter back to his tent to read it. It began:

Dear Cousin Sam,

I seat myself down and take pen in hand to write you a few lines and hope you are well when this letter comes to hand. I have been in the greatest victory our army has won so far. The Yankees had twice our number and came across the river west of Fredricksburg. I was part of the troops that Gen. Jackson marched thirteen miles around the Yankees right flank. He spent an hour getting everybody into place. When he gave the order to move up, we hit the Yankees with an attack four men deep and a mile long which drove the deer before us as well as the Yankees. The fighting was terrible but we won a great victory. You remember Evander Page who had that bunch of children on the farm down the river from us. When we was forming up for the attack me and Carson Pope saw him up on the front rank. We asked if one of us could take his place us not having wives or children or nothing. He cussed us out and said that he would do his duty and for us to do ourn. After the battle ended the next day we noticed he was missing. We found him at a place called Hazle Grove. He had been killed by grapeshot and tore up pretty bad. I shore feel sorry for all them kids of his. You no doubt have heard of Gen. Jackson being wounded. I hope he gits well soon since we can't afford to lose him and I hear we might go back north soon. If we can whip the Yankees up there, we can take Washington and win this war. You should be thankful there ain't much fighting where you are. Write when you can.

Your Cousin Neil Morgan.

Sam threw the letter on the ground of his tent. It was

almost like reading the last chapter of a book before reading the beginning. Everyone knew the ending. Stonewall Jackson had died and without him, Lee had been defeated at Gettysburg. Sam could only wonder if Neal had survived the bloody battle. He felt some remorse that he hadn't answered Neal's first letter. He needed to write and let him know he had survived the assault on Battery Wagner and that there was fighting here. But most of all, he had to write Betty to tell her how much he loved and appreciated her. She could tell all the families of his friends that they too had survived. He sat himself down, took pen in hand, and began to write.

Charles and Uriah were looking some excitement. The strain of their week at Battery Wagner had been terrible and these two young men needed to blow off some steam. The 51st and the other troops who had defended Wagner had been given two days off and Charleston was the largest city most of them had ever visited. The coming forty-eight hours were going to be wild.

After a week of trying to stay alive on Morris Island, merely taking a bath and putting on clean clothes was a luxury.

"If you don't hurry, our passes are going to be used up before we even git to town," Charles scolded at Uriah.

"Just keep your shirt on," he answered. "I reckon it ain't going to take some sharpie more than an hour or two to have all of your money in his pocket once you git there."

"You mean her pocket," said Charles.

"You'd better be careful in a place like this," cautioned Uriah. "I hear you can catch some things there ain't no cure for. You ever heard of the clap or the French pox? Places like this is where you catch 'em. It ain't like you are with some girl down by the river who ain't never been nowhere and wants to find out how things work. Some of the diseases you have around a seaport like this here come from all over the world and ain't even got no name."

"Look," Charles said, acting annoyed. "I don't reckon I need nobody to look after me. I'm old enough to vote and buy my own likker." The fact was that Uriah had changed Charles' mind about his original intentions.

Charleston was a port city before the blockade and there were many establishments which catered to the thirsts and pleasures of off-duty sailors. Since the blockade, the number of sailors visiting the port had decreased but their places had been taken by the thousands of soldiers and artillerymen who now protected the city. The bars and bawdy houses in the part of town left to them were doing a thriving business. This was the part of town in which Charles and Uriah found themselves. It was a cobblestone street full of brightly lit, noisy, two story houses with lots of soldiers going in and out. Some served food, but in all of them a thirsty man could find something to drink.

"What do you want to do first?" Charles asked. "I could use some decent food and I sure am thirsty."

Uriah walked up to the front of one of the watering holes and looked at a list of prices. "What do you mean first?" he answered. "Unless they pay you a Hell of a lot more than they pay me, we ain't got enough to do more than have a few drinks."

"Well, I reckon we ought to do that at least," Charles quickly decided. "I've sure missed all the jugs we used to work on back home."

"Yeah, and in these places a drink costs almost as much as a jug does back home," Uriah observed.

"It's almost like our money is gittin to where it won't hardly buy nothing," Charles added. "Let's find the best lit place to drink in."

"We'll do that," Uriah agreed. "What do you think of that one over there?"

"I like it, let's give it a try," his friend answered.

The two country boys walked up on a wide front porch and entered a large crowded room filled with soldiers sitting around the tables and a bar on the back wall. A piano player with a banjo accompanist was playing in the corner. They sat down at a vacant table where they were immediately visited by a waitress in a low cut red dress. "What'll you boys have?" she asked cheerfully.

"Bring us some whisky with some water for a chaser," Uriah ordered confidently.

"Certainly, boys," she said with a smile. "You probably won't need the water. The whisky's watered down enough already," the woman said with a melodious laugh.

She stepped toward the bar with a swirl of her skirt and quickly returned with the order. "That's thirty cents apiece, boys."

"Hey," Uriah protested, "that sign said twenty cents for whisky."

"That was last weeks prices," their waitress replied. "Things are so wild around here that nobody has had time to change it. Anyhow, you can't buy it cheaper nowhere else."

The pair reluctantly paid for their drinks and started downing them. "You know something?" Charles asked. "When I was out there on the island, I tried to imagine just how good the first drink was going to taste when I finally got one."

"I was wondering if I was ever going to have a chance to git a drink again, what with all them there Yankee shells flying around," Uriah responded. "The thought just struck me that we don't know if we are going to live long enough to ever come back to town again, so we might as well go ahead and spend all this money."

"It shore ain't going to do us no good when we are dead," Charles agreed. "We might as well drink it up."

That is exactly what the two friends proceeded to do. As the night wore on and their funds got lower, another lady approached their table. She was wearing a long black skirt with a red satin blouse which she amply filled. She was wearing heavy makeup and smelled highly of French perfume. "May I bring you boys another drink?" she asked.

"Certainly, Ma'am," they both answered at the same time, somewhat flattered that they had been noticed.

Knowing what they had been drinking, the woman soon returned with their drinks and sat down with them. "Where are ya'll from, boys?" she asked, starting the conversation.

"North Carolina. We are with the 51st Regiment," Uriah answered.

"Oh!" she exclaimed. "That is the regiment that fought

so bravely against the Yankees at Battery Wagner. We Charlestonians owe so much to you brave boys."

"We are a tough outfit and we did give the Yankees a good whipping," Charles agreed. "We'll do it again if we git the chance."

The woman looked at him and said, "I'd like to take you upstairs and show our appreciation. I can make you forget about that battle and any other problems you have. For you, I'll make it only twenty dollars."

"I shore would like to, Ma'am, but I'm married and I love my wife," Charles lied, thinking about Uriah's warning.

The woman stood up and bent over from the waist, letting her blouse fall open just enough to show Charles more cleavage than he had ever seen in his inexperienced life. "Has your wife got anything like this?" she inquired.

Charles' resistance vanished like a puff of smoke and Uriah's warning was quickly forgotten. "Lordy, Ma'am!" he exclaimed as he stood up. "My cow ain't got nothing like that!" He reached into his pocket and pulled out his remaining money. The silver coins and Confederate currency had been spent early in the evening, and now all he had was North Carolina script, small denomination paper money issued by the state.

The woman picked up one of the notes and asked in an annoyed voice, "Is this what you aim to pay me and to buy those drinks with?"

"Why, yes," Charles replied. "It's money, ain't it?"

"Not down here it ain't," she retorted. "Hey, George, I think we got a problem here."

A short stocky black haired man, wearing a purple shirt, came out from behind the bar. "What's the matter, Maggie?" he asked.

"These soldiers aim to pay for those drinks with that stuff. I thought you ought to know," she said.

"What's wrong with our money?" Uriah asked, since he was down to state script also.

"Look, son," the bartender said. "I ain't seen the gold in the North Carolina treasury to back up this garbage and neither have you. Until I do, I ain't even using this stuff to paper an outhouse wall with. I was born at night, but it wasn't last night. I'll have Theodore to show you gents the door." He nodded to a large black man who had stood almost hidden in the shadows. The man got up from his stool and started walking toward them.

"We don't need no help finding the damn door," Uriah swore. "We'll just take our business somewhere else." He and Charles stood up and started toward the door, almost reeling as the full effects of the alcohol hit them. Uriah turned and shouted back, "The next time I see a Yankee, I ain't going to shoot him, no sir-ee. I'm going to shake his hand and give him your address."

"Good," the man retorted, "Maybe he'll have some gold pieces instead of worthless paper." He carefully picked up the two glasses of whiskey and took them back to the bar to sell to someone else.

"Ain't that one heck of a note," Charles complained. "We come down here to help defend them and they won't even take our money."

"It just occurred to me that this States Rights stuff we're supposed to be fighting for has a few details that still need working out," Uriah said.

"Damn right! I agree," Charles concurred as the two friends walked out into the street and staggered off in the direction of camp.

While the single men had spent the night carousing in "dens of iniquity," the married men had spent their free time relaxing and writing letters if they could. Sam and Thomas had always considered themselves to be indestructible, but after the fierce fighting they had experienced, they had now realized they were indeed mortal. No matter how skillfully they became at the art of war, they never knew whether they were in some enemy's sights or a cannon ball fired a mile away would explode at their feet. Sam had always tried to let his wife know how special she was to him, but now he was putting it all on paper. He never before realized how many pages that would take.

Thomas, on the other hand, had many of the same thoughts, but was unable to write them down. Because of this,

68

he vowed that this would become his first priority when he got the time between battles. He had to be content with telling Sam what to write to Betty so that she could convey it to Susan. He missed her terribly and wanted to hold his son, whom he had never seen.

Daniel missed his family up on the Cape Fear but was not too worried about them. He knew that his large family of younger brothers and uncles would maintain his farm and feed his family. He had no doubts that he would one day return and resume the life that he had left.

Dougal McKay was in a dither. The fight at Battery Wagner had convinced him that his life should have some direction to it and from now on it would. He had lived his life as if he would be young and handsome forever. He had called socially on many of the young ladies who lived between the rivers, but the relationships had been one sided. He had no intention of being tied down by any girl. It had now occurred to him that no one other than his family would have mourned him for very long if he had been killed at Wagner. In fact, since he had no children and had never built anything, there was nothing to show that he had ever been on the face of the Earth. It was the morning of their second off-duty day that Dougal knocked on the front of Sam's tent. "You in there, Sam? Can I talk to you?" he called.

"Sure, come on in," Sam answered. "I'm just finishing a letter to Neal. You know, I've been aiming to answer his letter for weeks on end. Now, I don't even know if he's alive. What are you doing hanging around camp? I thought you of all people would be in town. You sick or something?"

"Sam, do you believe in love at first sight?" Dougal asked with a touch of embarrassment.

"Yep, you're sick all right," Sam answered with a chuckle. "Is it that girl from Florence?"

"Sam, I just can't seem to get her out of my mind. I don't really even know her or anything about her," Dougal explained.

"Dougal, these feelings might not be permanent," Sam advised. "Getting shot at makes you have some strange emotions. I know I'm writing some mighty long letters home and to

Neal because I want to tell them every thought I ever had. Do you feel something like that?"

"Sort of." Dougal answered. "I just realized that I ain't never done nothing worth a damn in my whole life. I just looked to have a good time and thought the next day would be better than the last."

"You might actually be showing some signs of growing up," Sam said with a laugh. "You never did plan to fish and hunt and drink likker all your life, did you?"

"I never had no plans for nothing," Dougal complained. "If I disappeared off the face of the Earth, nobody but my folks would know I was gone."

"I reckon you're more valuable than that," Sam comforted. "Is that why you came to see me, just to tell me this?"

"Sam, I want you to write a letter for me. You met Betty there where you went to school. You wrote her some letters, didn't you?" Dougal asked.

"Yes I did, lots of them, but I wrote them about me. I can't tell her what's in your heart. You got to do that and you got to be honest about it." Sam continued, "If you win her affections with a line of bull, there'll be a day of reckoning one day when she finds out what you are really like. Then she'll be gone forever. You have to tell her what you stand for."

"I guess it's about time I decided that for myself," Dougal agreed. "Miss Sarah McLain is certainly worth the effort."

"I'll tell you what I'd do if I were you," Sam offered. "I think we will one day be sent north to join Lee's army. The losses at Gettysburg were too great for us not to be. The Yankees can't take Charleston and there ain't nothing happening south of here. It looks to me that we will go back through Florence at least one time. I would write to her and tell her about myself and see if she will see me whenever we pass through. If she won't, then it isn't meant to be and I would forget about her. You have a lot of other things to be concerned with such as staying alive."

"I guess you're right, Sam," Dougal admitted. "You always seem to have a plan for everything. I'll get started now on a letter."

"Now don't forget," Sam shouted after him as Dougal squeezed through the tent opening. "You have to be honest with this girl if you have any chance for this to be lasting."

Sam sat in the tent reflecting on his own courting experience which had certainly ended well and he was glad he didn't have to play the game any longer. If only this war would end and he could go home.

The white hot days of July and August ended on the Carolina coast and September arrived with some cooling breezes. At this time of the year, there is a distinctive weather change as the waterfowl and fish start migrating southward and the winds change directions. The Union Army had also changed its direction in its attempt to capture Battery Wagner. There would be no more frontal assaults, from now on, siege trenches would be dug nearer and nearer to the fort, bringing the big guns ever closer. The men of the 51st had to garrison the fort for one week a month and came to dread every minute of it. Soldiers on both sides would occasionally be killed, buried, and forgotten with very little ceremony.

Back at home, Betty and Susan were getting along as well as could be expected. There were definite shortages of anything which had to be brought in through the blockade such as tea, coffee and sugar. There was no cloth to be had for reasonable prices, but that was all right because there were no parties to attend. Betty received the Fayetteville Observer in the mail and read it eagerly for the war news which concerned the 51st. The news of Battery Wagner had arrived a few days after the battle. It was received with tears of joy when the two women did not find their husbands' names listed among the casualties.

One day, as they sat on the front porch mending some clothes while the children napped, Susan had a thought. "You know, Betty, I need to go over to the house and air it out. Its been shut up since the men left and there ain't no telling what kind of varment is holed up in there."

"You be careful of snakes," Betty warned. "They are looking for a place to spend the winter this time of year."

"I will," Susan assured her. "The mice will take over an empty house and the snakes will follow them in. I should have done something during the spring."

"You might want to take the shotgun in case you have to shoot something," Betty offered. "You know how to shoot it, don't you, just pull the hammer back and fire away."

"I won't need it today," Susan answered. "I won't be staying long. I'll just see what needs to be done. Betty, I certainly appreciate your concern for me. I don't know what I would have done if it hadn't been for your kindness when Thomas had to leave with me pregnant."

"Listen," Betty countered, "You have been a big help to me with my two children. You've been a lot more help than a hinderance."

The two friends stood up and hugged each other and Susan started down the steps of the porch to go to her house. "At least take a stick in case you see a snake," Betty said as she handed Susan a walking stick Sam had carved from a dogwood one Sunday while sitting and whittling.

"I will do that, thank you." Susan answered. She took the stick Betty handed her and walked across the field. As she walked through the grass, the grasshoppers flew up in front of her, fleeing from her approach and singing their fall song. As she walked along the road through the narrow swamp, she paused to watch a squirrel scurry up a cypress tree. She had not been here in more than a year and it seemed almost like a new experience. As she walked through the weeds, grown up in the yard, she thought of asking James to run a disc harrow over the area.

As she reached the house, a large black snake was sunning himself on the porch. The bulge in his belly indicated he had eaten recently, and there would be one less rodent for her to worry with. However, it made her glad when the reptile slithered off the porch and into the woods. She gingerly walked around a wasp nest at the eaves of the porch and opened the door. The musty smell she was expecting greeted her and she immediately began mentally cataloging the things she had to do to make the place livable again. There were no holes in the roof and a little airing out, sweeping, and a meal cooked in the fireplace would at least make the place smell like home again.

At that very moment in Charleston, Thomas was thinking of her and his home and wishing there was no war so he could be with his family at that very place.

The trenches pushed nearer and nearer to Battery Wagner and in early September it was not worth the cost to defend, so it was abandoned. The 51st was moved to Long Island where it could find deer and oysters. This improvement in diet also improved morale of the regiment very much. The morale of Dougal McKay was improved the most, however, when he received a perfumed letter from Florence, S.C. in late October. Sarah had answered his letter and had written that she was glad to hear he had survived the fight at Wagner, and she would be glad to receive him at her home when they next passed through. She had asked him to let her know when that would be even though she knew he wouldn't ever be given advance notice. This would be reason enough for Dougal to write her again and explain that. The game now had two players.

The strategy of the Union efforts to take Charleston changed somewhat with their occupation of Morris Island. Fort Sumter was battered into an unrecognizable pile of rubble, but all efforts to occupy it were thwarted by the Confederates. The Yankees then began shelling the city itself and destroyed the lower part. It had become evident to the Union high command that the capture of the city had lost much of its significance. It was not willing to waste the troops required to complete the effort which had now become largely symbolic.

It also became evident to the Confederate command that they could defend the city against any Federal attack from the sea. The troops who regularly garrisoned the city were sufficient for defeating any land assault. In late November, Clingman's Brigade was ordered to the railroad siding to board the troop carrying boxcars for the trip north to only God knows where.

All the men were glad to be leaving Charleston, but none was happier than Dougal. He had kept a clean uniform ready for this occasion and was able to get a bath before falling in formation to board the train. Dougal was able to get a seat near the door as the troop train started rolling west. The large smokestack of the wood burning locomotive belched heavy gray smoke which was quickly caught by the wind and spread back along the track. It was an overcast day and a coastal storm was moving into the area. The South Carolina low country was left behind as the train passed large fields of cotton, already picked, under the November clouds.

The water tank beside the railroad was the first feature of Florence to come into view. Dougal ran a comb through his hair and got ready to jump before the train even stopped rolling.

"You better let me keep that rifle for you," Thomas offered, "and wait till the dern train stops. There ain't no reason for you to break your fool neck."

"Oh, yeah. Thanks," Dougal replied. "It's just that this stop is timed and I aim to use every second of it."

Dougal handed Thomas the rifle and jumped to the ground as the train came to a stop. He trotted to Evans Street and started walking casually toward the big white house. He stepped up on the front porch, paused to straighten his clothes, and knocked on the front door.

He heard soft footsteps approaching the door. His heart was making a sound of its own as he waited in anticipation. The door opened and there she was. Sarah's hair was tied up with a bandanna and she was wearing an apron. She also had flour on her hands and a little on her face. "Oh!" she exclaimed. "Of all the times for you to stop by with me looking like this." As she spoke, she untied the bandanna and let her hair fall down her back. "We can sit out here on the porch swing and talk. How much time do you have?"

"That whistle is going to blow in about five or ten minutes and I'll have to run to catch the train," Dougal answered as he waited for her to sit down and then sat down beside her. "Sarah, I know this is a strange way to meet. This is only the second time we have seen each other, but I have tried to tell you about myself in my letters. Is there anything you want to know about me?"

"You never mentioned your religion. I'm Presbyterian. Do you attend church?" she asked.

"Why yes, I attend the oldest Presbyterian church in the

state of North Carolina. I mean, I go sometimes. After this battle I was in at Battery Wagner, you better know I talked to the Lord a whole lot," Dougal explained.

"I bet that was terrible. I was really glad you wrote me a letter soon after the battle. I have to confess I was a teeny bit worried about you," she said with a giggle.

"I'm really glad to hear that," he said. "It was getting to be where I was worried that nobody would care if anything happened to me."

"Now did I say I cared, or did I say I was worried about you ?" Sarah asked with a laugh, not resisting the chance to tease. "You might just have a big highfalutin opinion of yourself, Mister Dougal McKay."

"I reckon I do have a good opinion of myself, and it would honor me a great deal if you ever cared about me, even a little bit," he said with sincerity, looking her straight in the eyes.

They looked at each other for a few seconds with neither speaking. The tenderness of the moment was broken by a voice from upstairs. "Sarah, do we have a visitor? Are you cookin something?"

"It's all right, Mother. You just rest," Sarah called to her. "I need to check on my biscuits anyhow." She opened the door and went back into the house. She shortly returned with a sack. "These are some of my biscuits and a jar of grape jelly. It might be a little sour since I only had some honey to sweeten it with. We can't hardly ever get any sugar."

"Much obliged," Dougal said with his voice filled with gratitude. "Eating these will make it seem like we've died and gone to heaven. You can't even recognize some of the things they give us to eat." They sat back down on the swing and resumed their conversation.

"Is your Mama sick?" Dougal asked. "You ain't never told me about your family."

"My Daddy was a cotton trader. He built this house and kept us in fine style till he died from a heart attack right before the war started. When the war came, Mama and I couldn't keep the business going with the blockade and all. She's been poorly for the last year and the doctor keeps her in bed most of the time. He thinks she might also have heart trouble."

"Sarah, I'm sorry about your folks, but I've got to know something else. Is there somebody expecting you to be waiting for him when this war's over?" he asked.

"No, there's not," she answered, finding herself actually appreciating the question. "There was this one man from, you know, the right kind of family that my Mama liked more than I did. He joined the army and got shot near Richmond. The last I heard from him, he was in a hospital up there. I'm sorry he got hurt, but I never led him on."

"You've just told me you are a lady who is going to make up her own mind about her fellers. I'll tell you a lot more about myself in my letters if you'll write to me," he offered

"Oh, I would like for us to keep writing each other," she agreed. "I want to hear about all the excitement you get into."

"Sarah, that whistle is going to blow in a minute and I might have to leave and never come back," Dougal began. "Knights' ladies use to give them something to take with them into battle. Would you give me something?"

"Well," she said with a laugh, "you rode up here on a smoky ol' train instead of a white stallion, but I guess that'll have to do. Step into the foyer, please. I might have something for you."

Dougal stopped in the foyer as Sarah continued walking into the kitchen and quickly returned. She was carrying a clean blue plaid bandanna, like the one she had her hair done up in when she met Dougal at the door. "Lean forward and I'll tie it around your neck," she offered.

He bent down slightly as Sarah stood on her tiptoes to tie the cloth. Their faces were almost touching when they both made eye contact at the same time. Dougal instinctively put his arms around her waist, drew her to him, and kissed her. Sarah returned the kiss of the handsome soldier for a few seconds before growing tense, as if awaking from a dream, and pushed herself away.

"I guess I've proved myself to be a shameless hussy as you seem to have expected, Mr. McKay," she said sternly.

"No, you musn't say that. Don't you see, it was meant

76

to happen," Dougal quickly argued. "There has been no good come out of this war except that you and I have met. If I survive this war, you are going to have a hard time running me off."

The conversation was abruptly interrupted by the expected train whistle. "Keep writing to me. I want to know every thing you've ever done." Dougal said as he let himself out the door and jumped off the porch down to the ground.

"You know my address. Write to me and I promise I'll answer each letter," she answered. "Don't forget your biscuits. Now, run or you'll miss that train."

Dougal held the biscuits and jelly to his chest as he ran. When he turned to see Sarah for one last time, he stumbled and almost fell. He last saw her standing on the porch with her hands on her hips, laughing at his clumsiness.

He handed the biscuits up to Sam and jumped into the box car. "She must think I'm a fool," Dougal thought to himself as the train picked up speed. What he didn't know was that Sarah walked to an upstairs window and watched the train until it disappeared up the track into its own smoke and was lost from her sight.

"Help yourself to some biscuits, boys," Dougal said as he handed the jar of jelly to Thomas.

"It looks like you got a decent enough welcome," Thomas said.

"Who's got a clean knife?" Sam asked. "We need one to get this jelly out."

"I got one right here," Charles offered.

"Don't stick that knife in that good jelly," Uriah protested. "That thing ain't been washed since the flood."

"I got a spoon I washed before we left," Daniel said. "I know it's good and clean."

The biscuits were divided among the squad and each soldier got a healthy serving of the jelly to go with it. "You ought to marry that girl," Thomas said. "She sure can cook."

"You know," said Dougal thoughtfully, "that's just zackly what I'm going to do."

"I still don't see what was wrong with my knife," Charles said to no one in particular.

The train had up a full head of steam and was now rapidly taking these soldiers to their destinies in the North. Wilmington and Goldsboro were left behind and late that night Clingman's Brigade arrived at Camp Battle near Tarboro. This part of the state had not yet seen any invasion and the citizens of the area were very generous with food and clothing for the troops.

The Brigade rested there for three weeks, and as the year of 1864 dawned, it was to be part of a Confederate effort to retake the town of New Bern. This thirteen-thousand man army would be commanded by General George E. Pickett of Gettysburg fame.

Chapter 5
Pickett

In the early months of 1864, the Union Armies were preparing for the Spring offensives to which the Confederates would react accordingly. Since the Rebel response at this point in the war was defensive in nature, there were troops in Virginia which could be used elsewhere since no fighting was going on there. At the suggestion of Robert E. Lee, the Richmond government decided to recapture New Bern. The Yankees at New Bern had made no concentrated effort to cut the Wilmington-Weldon Railroad since General Foster's burning of the Goldsboro railroad bridge in December of 1862. Instead, they had made complete nuisances of themselves by destroying crops and burning houses within thirty miles of their base.

General Lee had suggested to Jefferson Davis that the expedition should be commanded by Brigadier General Robert F. Hoke. He was a North Carolinian by birth and had a talent for command.

The Confederate President thought that a higher ranking officer should lead the expedition and appointed Major General George E. Pickett to the command. Pickett had gained military immortality by leading the Confederate attack against the Union center on the third day at Gettysburg, but his military career had not been one of great accomplishments.

Clingman's Brigade had been sent to Kinston as part of a thirteen thousand man army to retake New Bern. Its capture would be significant in that it would open another port for the blockade runners, and allow a dozen eastern North Carolina counties to raise food for the army.

The 51st was marching with one file on either side of the road from Kinston to New Bern when General Pickett and his staff came riding down between their lines. There was no cheer for this commander since these troops didn't know what to expect from him. As the horsemen disappeared up the road, Uriah was the first to speak. "So that is the famous General Pickett. I wonder where he was during his famous charge?"

"Not up in the front, I'll wager," said Charles, who was marching behind Uriah.

"He wasn't supposed to be," Sam added. "Division commanders usually are not out in front."

"Now how do you know all that?" Thomas inquired. "You bucking for General or something?"

"I got a hold of a book on tactics by General Hardee one time," Sam answered. "I don't even remember where. I did learn enough to know you and I are always going to be among the ones to get fired at first."

"I've heard from some of the men sent down from Richmond who were at Gettysburg that Pettigrew's Division did just as much in that attack as Pickett's," Daniel said. " It don't seem right that they are calling it Pickett's charge."

"I got a letter from Neal right before we moved out, and that's what he says," Sam continued. "He got wounded in the leg on the first day and has been in a hospital for a right smart of time. The 20th was sent in without any pickets in front. Some Yankees hid behind a stone wall and fired down their lines. Almost wiped out the regiment."

"That's damn poor generalin if you ask me," Uriah snorted. "You got to know how to take care of yourselves or some highfalootin officer will git you killed."

"That's for sure!" Charles concurred.

"Anyway, Neal says the North Carolina regiments were in the thick of things and some of them got shot up pretty bad," Sam stated. "He said the wagon train of our wounded was more than fifteen miles long."

"I'm kinda glad I wasn't there," Thomas said. "How bout you Dougal?"

"Huh?" Dougal asked.

"I swear," Thomas laughed, "I ain't never seen nobody with his head in the clouds any more than that boy. You ain't heard a word we've been saying, have you?"

"I reckon I have," snorted Dougal, somewhat perplexed. "You've been talking about Gettysburg, but I've been looking up ahead. I think we'll be walking past some Yankee activity very shortly."

The land between Kinston and New Bern is very flat. The roads, through necessity, were built on the high ground which wound around the swamps and through the forests of long leaf pines, gums and oaks. The fields were hewed from the dry cultivatable soil where it was found, usually with a swamp on either side. As the troops marched further east, they noticed that more and more fields lay uncultivated. Dougal had been looking at a spot where several large trees had been scorched from a fire. As they walked past, it was obvious that this had once been a prosperous farm. The house had been burned, scorching the trees, and the fences had been torn down. The skeleton of a mule lay in the front yard, killed because it was no use to the raiders. There wasn't a man among the troops of the 51st who couldn't imagine his own house burned and his livestock killed. Lt. Garrison broke the silence of the march by an admonition, "Are there any of you who still have any doubts about why we must defeat this invader?" If there were any doubts, they were not made known at this time.

The Federal raids had created another situation which actually benefited the Rebel soldiers. The woods were scattered with chickens and hogs which had escaped the Yankee raiders. Uriah and Charles had begun to notice occasional hogs and chickens which didn't seem to belong to anybody. They were marching beside the horse of Captain George Sloan, the company commander, when Uriah made a request. "Sir, can me and Charles have your permission to forage in these woods a bit?"

"Granted," the captain replied. "Don't get left by the column and give anything you find to Mr. Mac so the whole company can have a share."

The two men went running into the woods to the front of the line of march. "There ought to be something holed up in this patch," Uriah said. "Here, load up with this," he said, handing Charles a small sack.

"What's this stuff?" Charles asked.

"It's some bird shot I brought from home. I thought it might come in handy," Uriah explained. "Cut your bullet out of a cartridge and ram it down. Then you can pour the shot in on top. Don't forget to ram down a patch so the shot won't roll out. We can get us some of those chickens with this."

The two soldiers spread out and advanced through the woods, walking parallel to the column's line of march. In a small clearing before them, they saw a group of chickens who were happily scratching away for the seeds and bugs in a patch of last year's wild peas. Two shots netted a rooster and a hen for supper. The loud reports startled a large hog which had a wallow nearby and sent him squealing through the woods.

"Reload with a minnie ball," Uriah shouted to Charles. "We might eat well tonight."

The hog had run a little more than a hundred feet when it stopped to see if the thing that had startled it was following. Charles and Uriah had loaded up and were stalking the animal. The unlucky animal had accidentally stopped and perked its ears up to listen where Charles had a clear line of sight. Just as he had done so many times hunting deer, a soft squeeze of his trigger finger put a bullet in the animal's brain and it dropped to its knees dead.

Uriah came walking up to Charles and put his hand on his shoulders. "Good shot. Just like I taught you," he kidded.

"Yeah," Charles responded. "If you ever make a shot that good, then you can teach somebody. Why don't you take these chickens to Mr. Mac and bring back some of his boys to help us move this carcass. I'll bleed it while you're gone."

Company I ate well that night. Other hogs and chickens along the line of march would suffer at the hands of this hungry Confederate Division.

New Bern had been captured by the Federal forces early in the war and the Confederates, since then, had been forced to maintain troops in the eastern part of North Carolina to protect Goldsboro and the rail line into Virginia. They now planned to put an end to this necessity.

The plan of attack was General Hoke's. The town of New Bern lies at the conjunction of the Neuse and Trent Rivers where the early Swiss settlers had founded it and named it after their capital in Europe. After its capture by Union forces, the Yankees had built forts across the rivers from the town to defend the channels from hostile ships. Two Confederate columns were to attack these forts while Hoke's men made the frontal assault against the defenses of the town. In addition, Confederate raiders, under the command of Commander John Wood, were sailing a small flotilla of boats down the Neuse River to take on any Yankee vessels they could find.

The enlisted men knew nothing of these plans and simply marched where they were told. In the predawn hours of February 1st, Hoke's men lined up in battle formation in an attempt to capture a bridge over Batchelder Creek, just beyond the outer defenses of New Bern. "I shore don't like sittin here in the dark, not knowing what's in front of us," Uriah complained.

Before anyone could reply, shots rang out near a bridge which crossed the creek and the bullets made a zinging sound as they passed overhead. "There must be Yankee's up ahead if nothing else," Sam concluded. "It looks like they have a bridge across the creek that we are trying to capture."

The crescendo of the firing up ahead was increasing as well as the number of bullets zinging overhead like death dealing hornets. Dougal made a quick decision and announced, "I think I'll dig me a hole and crawl in it till those bullets quit flying around. I have this fear of gettin kilt by something I can't see."

"Just stay low to the ground," Daniel advised. "These balls are flying high. I don't think they'll hit none of us."

There was some shouting down the Confederate line that soon died down, as did the firing. "I think we had better be ready to attack somebody in the morning," Thomas observed.

"Damn right! That's what I think too," Charles concurred.

The attempt to take the bridge failed because the attackers found it destroyed and withdrew. Batchelder Creek had to be crossed the hard way on this cool winter morning. "I sure hate gittin my feet wet in the wintertime," Thomas complained.

"Don't worry," Sam advised. "That Yankee fire is liable to be so hot, they'll dry right out."

Captain Sloan and Lieutenant Garrison walked up to take their positions for the attack just as the sun was coming up. "Good news, men," Sloan began. "Last night, during the attack on the bridge, a flotilla came down the Neuse and burnt the only ship the Yankees had. It was called the "Underwriter", and they captured and burnt it right under the guns of the forts. At least we won't get shelled from the water in this attack. The other news isn't so good," he continued. "One of those stray bullets that were going over our heads last night killed Colonel Shaw of the 8th."

The men responded with an audible groan because they knew of the Colonel's reputation as being a good officer. "We don't have time to mourn," Captain Sloan continued, "because we have to get this brigade across the creek after our artillery barrage lifts. We have to get ourselves in a position to attack the town's main defenses when we hear General Barton's attack across the Trent River. He is supposed to block the railroad and keep Yankees from getting reinforcements from Beaufort. Then he will attack the positions over there to keep them from firing on us." Just as he finished speaking, the Confederate artillery began bombarding the Union positions across Batchelder Creek. The ear splitting crash of the firing cannons was followed shortly by "Ka-whump" as the shells found their target.

There was nothing for the infantry to do but wait for the artillery to finish and hope they had weakened the Federal defenses so that casualties would be light in the attack. "Do you reckon we are going to git any breakfast this morning?" Charles wondered out loud .

"We might git some after the attack," Uriah answered. "You know it's better to not have a full stomach in case you git

84

gut shot."

"I ain't going to git shot, but I might starve," Charles replied. "Anyhow, that cannon fire is slacking off. They are about to send us in."

The shelling stopped and Captain Sloan stood up and shouted, "Forward, Company I." The company, in conjunction with the rest of the brigade splashed across the creek and formed a line of battle which rapidly advanced toward the forward rifle pits of the town's defenses. The Yankee pickets had no intention of trying to stop this force and fired a few harmless rounds at the advancing butternut ranks before retiring.

Clingman's Brigade swung into the main road and was rapidly marching toward a point where the road was crossed by a railroad. The purpose of this quick movement was to capture a train which brought relief troops and supplies to the forward Yankee positions. To the extreme disappointment of the Southerners, the train sped past the crossing just as the first units of Clingman's men arrived. The cars of the train were loaded with troops with a field piece on a car on the end. The gun fired a shell which landed harmlessly in the woods. Even though they had missed, the Union gunners let out a defiant cheer which riled one of the gun crews of Clingman's artillery. They had set up their gun to contest the train's passage and were just now getting ready to fire. The cannon fired and sent a projectile after the fleeing train. The shell exploded above the end car, possibly killing one of the Federal gun crew.

Suddenly, shots rang out back down the track. Another Confederate brigade had been advancing toward the railroad from the other side and had made contact with more than three hundred Yankee troops who were hurrying behind the train in an attempt to reach safety. The convergence of the two Confederate brigades surrounded and captured these unlucky men as if it were part of a plan. The Southern campaign against New Bern was off to a smashing start.

The captured Northern soldiers were in a sullen mood as would be expected. The very thoughts of spending time in a prison camp would cause deep depression. The Yankees were disarmed and sat by the railroad, waiting to be moved to the rear.

Sam was standing guard near some of the prisoners when he saw one looking at him. "Are you the troops that have been burning the houses and property of the folks around here?" he asked.

"We have been doing what's necessary to put down this rebellion," the man answered with a smirk.

"Does that include the destruction of a person's home?" Sam responded angrily. "Besides, we ain't exactly rebelling, we're trying to leave the Union."

"That can't be allowed by the National government," the man replied. "There is also the matter of freeing these slaves."

Thomas joined in at this point, "What are you going to do with 'em after you free 'em, take 'em back north with you to work in your factories?" he asked.

"What do you mean?" the Yankee asked. "I only know farming. I have a potato farm in New York and I don't use slaves."

Sam retorted, "I have a cotton farm in this state and I don't have slaves either, but some folks do and if you free 'em, what are you going to train them to do?"

"I don't know," the man replied. "I suppose someone in the government has a plan. It really is not my concern."

"Well, by damn, it ought to be somebody's concern," Sam said angrily. "The fact is, Ol' Abe wants us back in the Union so he can tax our cotton, and he's got you all down here thinking you're on some holy crusade."

Just then, Lieutenant Garrison walked up and barked an order. "Turn the prisoners over to this detachment and fall in." The prisoners left with the guards who started marching them back to the rear, and the 51st formed in marching order.

As the Confederates resumed their advance on New Bern, Sam broke the silence. "You know, I don't think those Yankee's know what this war is all about."

"Damn right," Charles concurred. "That's what I think too."

Clingman's Brigade formed the right of Hoke's attack as they took their positions from which to launch the assault. This area was heavily wooded in the section held by Company I. The tall trees shaded out the undergrowth and it looked like a good place to rest while waiting for orders to attack.

Lieutenant Garrison walked through the area where the men were resting on their arms and said to Sam. "Morgan, we have to furnish the pickets. Take your squad and advance them to the open area in front of these woods. You'll be able to see the Yankee artillery and they can see you, so keep your heads down."

Sam moved his men out, disregarding their groans and complaints. Pickets were the closest to the enemy, and the first to get shot at, and the first to die. "Why us?" Uriah complained.

"Yeah", Charles joined in. "We were out front at Battery Wagner and now this."

"My friends," Sam explained, "we have earned this honor by being such good shots."

"Yeah, Uriah," Thomas joked. "Why don't you miss some time?"

"I guess it's in my blood," Uriah answered. "Did I ever tell you that my mother's folks are kin to Daniel Boone?"

"Yes you did, and we still don't believe you." Daniel answered. "You might git a chance to prove it if them's Yankees I see up ahead."

"I believe you're right ," Thomas observed. "They might be trying to turn our flank."

Sam's squad had moved out of the forest and could now see the movement of the town's defenders over some open fields. The rapid advance of one group caught Sam's eye. It was cavalry.

"If those horse soldiers attack us, see if you can get off two shots before we fall back," Sam ordered. "Now, spread out and fire when you have a target."

The cavalry did plan to charge. The horsemen spread out in a wide attack formation and charged at the picket line to the left of Sam's position, giving his men good targets. Their first shots emptied three saddles, but the blue clad riders came on. As they neared the Confederate positions, their ranks were rapidly dwindling from the fire of the pickets. The second round from Sam and his squad had maximum effect as they fired down the line of charging horsemen and dropped six more riders. The Union commander, at this point, decided that his losses were not worth the slight gain he could make, since the main Rebel force waited for him in the woods. The Yankee cavalry wheeled and retreated back to the safety of New Bern.

The work of the pickets had been observed by the troops in the woods, who rewarded them with a lusty cheer. Almost on cue, the Union artillery opened up on these troops, who scrambled for cover as the shells began bursting in the tops of the pine trees. Fort Totten, the main Union position, joined in with its heavy caliber guns. The Rebels endured this bombardment for the rest of the day, but their casualties were very minor. Sam's squad was relieved in the picket lines and rejoined the regiment.

As the next day dawned, the 51st occupied the same defences and the troops were sprawled on the pine needles in all positions, getting what rest they could. The men were getting anxious to get on with whatever they had been sent here for. "When do you think we'll attack?" Daniel asked Sam.

"Well," Sam said jokingly, "I think it will be when the troops across the river begin their attack. Me and General Pickett were discussing this attack the other day and that's what we decided."

"The closest you ever been to the General was when he rode by the other day," Daniel countered. "You probably guessed right, though."

"I sure hope that's what we're waitin on," Thomas said. "I don't want those guns across the river to be firing down our lines while we're attackin'."

"That's right," Sam continued. "You see, being a General ain't so hard. I think that in the next war, I'll probably go in as a General."

"There's a railroad across the river which needs capturing so it can't be used to bring up more Yankees from the coast," Uriah added. "That's what the Captain said."

"See there," said Sam. "You could be a General too." Sam had been lying on his back with his hat pulled down over his eyes. He raised himself to an elbow and continued." How

88

hard can it be to take a brigade of troops and set them straddle of a railroad with their cannons so a train can't pass."

"Charles, you ain't had much to say. Don't you want to be a General too?" Daniel inquired.

"Shoot no," he replied. "I'm just trying to git some rest while I can. I figure this is the best duty we're going to git and some General has been up all night figuring out something for us to do that we won't like. That's too much thinking for me. I'll just stay a private." The men laughed and settled back to rest under the canopy of pine trees.

Late that afternoon, the sound of activity from the railroad south of New Bern indicated that it had not been cut and Yankee reinforcements were arriving. If fact, none of the Confederate forces north of the Neuse and south of the Trent Rivers had accomplished anything. General Pickett angrily called for a council with his Generals. Even though Clingman and Hoke wanted to attack, Pickett ordered a retreat back to Kinston. He was not about to send his unsupported troops against fortified defenses after his experience on the third day at Gettysburg. President Davis had picked the wrong man for the job. This was a mistake he made continuously throughout the war.

It was a sullen group of Southern soldiers who incredulously retraced their steps back to Kinston. They felt they could have taken the town if given a chance. Their mood was made even worse by a cold rain which fell upon them as they marched.

Several days later, back in Cumberland County, the newspaper arrived and was quickly scanned by Betty for news from the 51st. There was an account of the campaign against New Bern and the small casualty lists didn't include anyone she knew, much to her relief. Susan was busy mending some clothes and let out a sigh when Betty told her the news. "It certainly is terrible to have to read the newspaper to find out if you still have a husband," she said.

"I know it, but it's better than waiting and not knowing," Betty comforted. "After a while you start forgetting what it was like before our husbands left. The things mine did that got on my nerves don't seem to matter worth a hill of beans now." She got out her own needle and thread and sat down to help Susan. "You know," Betty continued, "all of Sam's work and money went to the farm or his family. The only thing he ever bought for himself was this gold watch I keep on the mantle."

"This will be the third crop we've had put in the ground since they left," Susan said wistfully. "I wonder where our husbands have been sent now?"

Their husbands were in Virginia. Clingman's Brigade was in winter quarters near Petersburg. They lived in shelters made of wood and chinked with mud with a fireplace for heating. These spartan structures were actually quite comfortable when compared to a tent or a single blanket on a cold night.

One night in early March, a heavy snow fell. The next morning, the men of the 51st decided it would be good training for them to attack the 8th Regiment with snowballs. In perfect attack formation, they advanced across the hollow which separated the two camps. The men of the 8th had observed their advance and were waiting with plenty of ammunition. The two lines surged forward and snowballs filled the air at point blank range. Every so often, the lines would meet and men would wrestle each other to the ground. The 8th was so determined to hold their ground that well aimed punches were thrown at the attackers, who gave as well as they received. The fight ended when the superior numbers of the 51st captured the camp of the 8th. The affair ended in a good spirit of friendship, despite there being a few bloody noses and loosened teeth.

Sam and his squad were on their way back to their own camp where they were ordered to report to Captain Sloan. They entered his tent and snapped to attention. "At ease, men," he said cheerfully. "That was an amusing bit of fun we just had, wasn't it?"

"Yes, Sir," Sam answered, "although Private Bass got punched in the jaw."

"No permanent damage, I hope," the Captain responded. "Private Bass is a stout fellow and should heal quickly." He continued, "The reason you were called here is to be given a chance to volunteer for an important mission. The 51st is going to remain in camp until needed here in Virginia. Colonel Murchison of the 8th has asked for sharpshooter volunteers to go with him on a decisive expedition. What do you say, men?"

"Well. Captain," Sam asked, "where will we be going? Will there be a chance for us to do some damage to the Yankees and win this war?"

"That I can assure you," Captain Sloan answered, "but, I'm afraid you can't get any details until you volunteer."

Sam made eye contact with the men in his squad and received an assuring nod from each one. "Count us in, Captain." Sam said. "We'll probably ask ourselves why we did this many times."

"Splendid!" Captain Sloan exclaimed. "Gather your gear and report to Colonel Murchison. You will be briefed by him when the time comes. You are now under his command, but I will tell you this much. The force you will be joining has an excellent chance of sweeping the Yankees out of North Carolina."

"We would all like to be part of that," Sam answered. "Will that be all, Sir?"

"Yes, good luck to all of you," the Captain replied.

Sam and his squad left somewhat amazed that they had volunteered for this unknown mission.

"We just got ourselves into a whole heap of trouble," Uriah said. "The first thing you need to learn in any army is to never volunteer."

"That is generally true," Sam countered. "But you heard what the Captain said about driving the Yankees clean out of the state. If we don't do it to them, they are going to do it to us."

"That's right," Thomas agreed. "Somebody's got to do it and it might as well be us. If this war keeps on lasting, all of us are going to git killed eventually."

"Just the same," Uriah added, "we might have just done a dumb thing."

"You just might be right," Charles said, concurring as usual with Uriah.

The squad made its way back to their camp to make arrangements for their departure. Sam and Dougal took the time to write letters. Sam wrote to Betty about the unsuccessful campaign against New Bern and the not unpleasant winter quarters in Virginia. He told of his love for her and the children and how anxious he was for the war to end. He didn't tell her he had volunteered for a dangerous mission in hopes of quickening that end.

Dougal's letter to Sarah was lengthy and detailed. She had said she wanted to hear of all his adventures and he meant to tell her as much of them as possible. He thought how much he was like one of the peddlers he had seen traveling through the country with a large bag of goods to sell, going from door to door. He was now trying to sell himself to a beautiful young girl hundreds of miles away. He really didn't know how successful he was being in this attempt.

He was actually doing quite well. Sarah looked forward to his letters and had kept them all in a stack tied with a blue ribbon. Occasionally, she would get them out and read them from first to last. She wondered what it would be like to actually be courted by Dougal. Could he have withstood the scrutiny of her Father who, before he died, had been suspicious of every suitor's intentions. Her mother would have certainly been interested in his family background. Sarah suspected that he almost certainly would have failed that test, but she didn't care. The young men from the "better" families her mother would have approved of were rapidly getting killed off trying to take or defend some hill in Virginia, Maryland, or Pennsylvania. Her Mother's heart trouble was getting worse and Sarah feared she would never get to meet the man her daughter would marry. Although Sarah was approaching the age most people considered unmarried girls to be spinsters, she was not going to marry some man she didn't love and become a baby factory.

Dougal had told her of his family's farm in North Carolina. While it wasn't huge, the family seemed to be prosperous and one would have to be industrious to manage it. While this in itself would not put Dougal very high in her Mother's ranking, it was good enough for Sarah and it just might be possible that she was falling in love with the writer of the letters she kept receiving.

In the evening of the day she received Dougal's letter, she went to bed wondering what he was doing in his camp in Virginia. Dougal was in fact no longer in Virginia. At that moment he was part of a Confederate force which was approaching the Albemarle region of northeastern North Carolina.

Chapter 6
The Albemarle

"We've volunteered to do what?" Uriah asked in disbelief. "I never said I wanted to be in the navy. You remember the size of the shells they were firing at us down at Battery Wagner. What in blazes is an ironclad anyhow?"

"It's an iron plated ram that will clear the Yankee ships out of the Roanoke River and the Albemarle Sound," Sam answered. "Our job is to protect it from being boarded during a fight. At least that's the way it was explained to me in the briefing."

"I thought we were volunteering to help out the 8th," Charles said almost whining.

"Colonel Murchinson said that the 8th didn't have enough replacements to do what we're being asked to do," Sam explained.

"Who are these other troops who are falling out of the column?" Thomas asked. "Are they volunteers like us?"

"They must be the crews for the heavy guns on the ram," Uriah speculated. "They have red trim on their caps, so they must be from the artillery."

"Ain't there any navy people to do this work?" Daniel asked. "It looks like they are just farm boys like we are."

"Our Captain is a good navy man named Cooke," Sam explained. "He'll show us what to do. Besides, shootin' at Yankees is what we've all been doing since we joined the army. Nothing has changed except we'll be riding to do it now. That's all I learned at the briefing. We will have to wait till we get to the landing to learn any more."

A Lieutenant rode up on his horse and addressed the men. "You volunteers form two lines and follow me to Hamilton's Landing. I believe we are going to be part of a great adventure. Good luck to us all."

The men had been part of a large Confederate column which was advancing on the town of Plymouth, North Carolina. They were under the command of General Robert F. Hoke and it was his intention to put an end to the Union Army's occupation of Eastern North Carolina once and for all. General Hoke had been the only Confederate General to enhance his reputation in Pickett's expedition against New Bern. When Pickett was recalled to Virginia, Hoke assumed the tactical command of the troops. He would now show what these soldiers could accomplish if properly led.

When Hoke was appointed to command this expedition, he immediately visited the town of Hamilton on the Roanoke River where the CSS Albemarle lay moored to the docks. His purpose was to get a commitment from Commander James Cooke that his ship would be ready for his assault on Plymouth. This iron clad ram had been designed by the man who had converted the USS Merimac into the CSS Virginia which met the USS Monitor at the famous battle in Hampton Roads. The Confederate Government had authorized the construction of five shallow draft ironclad rams to win back the sounds of North Carolina. The construction of these ships had been held up by bureaucratic inefficiency and bungling of material suppliers. Robert E. Lee had gotten behind the construction of the Albemarle, hoping it would be complete by the time Pickett made his effort to reclaim the land down east. This didn't happen, but Hoke made sure the ram was ready when he began his campaign.

Sam's squad, along with the rest of the volunteers for the Albemarle, left the long column and marched northward toward the Roanoke River. The land gradually sloped toward the river's flood plain through forests of oak and gum. The men talked very little on the way, somewhat apprehensive of what they might find when they reached the village of

Hamilton. The road made a bend and all of a sudden the broad expanse of the river was before them. Down below on the water lay the CSS <u>Albemarle</u>. It was 152 feet long and 45 feet wide with four inches of iron plating over its exterior. The iron covered oak bow of the ship was shaped to ram and sink its wooden hulled enemies and rode low just above the water. The main part of the vessel sloped upward on all four sides till it reached a flat roof. There were two gun ports in each side and one in each end. The reaction of the troops to the sight of this blockade buster was one of near surprise.

Uriah was, as usual, the first to voice an opinion. "That is the most ridiculous looking piece of floating garbage I have ever laid my eyes on!" he exclaimed.

"Before this trip is over, you will be glad that floating garbage has four inches of iron," the Lieutenant cautioned, somewhat perplexed at the remark. "That's thick enough to protect you from the hundred pound shells the Yankees are going to throw at you."

"How come it don't sink with all that iron on it?" Charles inquired.

"I can't explain it," the officer answered. "I just know that for the first time, Confederate infantry is going to have artillery support from the river in this part of the country."

"What is my squad going to be expected to do, Sir?" Sam asked the Lieutenant. "Are we going to have to be trained?"

"There is no time for that, unfortunately," the officer replied. "You and your men will function as Marines. You will keep us from being boarded and keep the Yankees from climbing up in their rigging and firing in our gunports."

"Where will we be firing from, Sir? There don't seem to be much room around the gun muzzles," inquired Uriah.

"When the action begins, you men will climb up to the top of the ship and fire from the topside," the lieutenant answered. "It should be quite safe from cannon fire since the sides of the ram are angled to deflect the shot. The iron plating does get kind of hot from the sun. Just remember to keep your heads down and lie as flat as possible. It looks like it will be some time before we cast off, so make camp over there in those woods and you will be called when the time comes."

Sam took his squad and made camp as ordered where they were presently joined by others who had volunteered for the same duty. There would be a dozen men assigned to the Albemarle who would serve as sharpshooters.

While Sam and his friends waited for their orders, the black clad congregation of the Presbyterian Church of Florence, South Carolina, gathered on a sunny April day to bury one of its members. The bright sunlight of the past several days had given life to the green grass and flowering things. It was a day like all Spring days should be.

Sarah stood with tear swollen eyes behind her black veil as her Mother's coffin was lowered into the grave. The words of the hymn the congregation sang gave a promise of eternal life and joyful reunions one day.

"On that resurrection morning when the dead in Christ shall rise, and the joys of his resurrection share. We will gather all together over on the other shore. When the roll is called up yonder I'll be there."

Most of the merchants of the town and their families were friends of the McLains. Many of them attended this funeral. While the young men of the town were absent, away with the military, Sarah was attracting the glances of many of the widowers in the crowd who were wondering if there was anything left of the once sizable McLain fortune.

Mrs. Grantham, the family friend Sarah had been visiting the day she met Dougal, had accompanied her home after the funeral. They sat in the drawing room talking.

"Sarah, what are you going to do to occupy your time now that your mother has passed away?" she asked. "I don't mean to pry into your affairs, but it helped me so much to do volunteer work at the hospital after my husband died."

"I am not going to have much time to do anything but earn a living," Sarah replied. "Mother's doctor bills have pretty much run through the finances. I am going to have to find a job to survive."

"Maybe we can join forces on a venture which will help us both," Mrs. Grantham offered. "I have twenty acres of newground that has just been cleared. If I can get some sweet potatoes for Malichi and his family to plant, will you help me market them? I'm sorry," she said suddenly. "This isn't the time for you to make any kind of decision like that."

"That's all right and it does sound interesting," Sarah admitted. "But, perhaps we can discuss it more clearly later."

"The main thing you have to be concerned with is the fortune hunters who are going to be knocking on your door," Mrs. Grantham continued. "They picture you as weak and actually needing them to run your affairs and to help you spend your inheritance. Would you believe I actually had some offers of marriage after my husband died?" Her melodious laughter indicated to Sarah that she might have appreciated the attention.

"Do you have any young man that you are interested in now, not that it is any of my business?" Mrs. Grantham asked.

"Oh, I don't mind you knowing," Sarah replied. "I do like a young private I met from one of the North Carolina Regiments that passed through on their way to the battle at Battery Wagner. I haven't even seen him but twice, but he is the handsomest thing you ever saw."

"I was kind of hoping you would find you a nice young man from Florence," Mrs. Grantham offered.

"I might have if any of them had been as sincere as Dougal," Sarah confessed. "He grew up on a farm near the South River up above Fayetteville and I can tell by his letters that he isn't lying to me about himself. I like sincerity in a person, but until this war ends, none of us can be certain of what tomorrow will bring and I'm not going to let myself get too involved with anyone."

"That is a very wise attitude, Sarah," Mrs. Grantham agreed. "We can at least send up a few prayers for the safety of your young man."

These prayers were very much needed at this time. It had been more than a week since Dougal and the rest of the sharpshooters had been sent into bivouac to wait for the completion of the Albemarle. It was not yet completed, but ready or not, the troops filed aboard on April 17th. Hoke's attack on Plymouth would begin the next day and it was now or never if the Confederate monster was ever to be of service.

Entry into the ironclad ship had to be made from an iron hatch in the top and as these soldiers turned sailors climbed inside, many of them wondered aloud if they were entering their tomb. The boilers had been fired up and the heat was already uncomfortable inside. "We're going to be boiled like a bunch of 'possums," Uriah said fearfully.

"You told that right," Charles agreed.

"If I ever volunteer for anything else, will somebody please kick me in the butt?" Daniel asked.

"I'll kick you if you'll kick me," Thomas agreed. "I still don't know what makes this thing float."

"Corporal Morgan," the Lieutenant shouted, "position your men near the entrance hatch. I'll give you orders when the time comes."

"Yes, Sir," Sam answered. "Hey, fellows, keep your weapons handy. We are going to be the first to go."

"That also means we are going to be near the escape hatch if this thing sinks," Dougal added. "I think that's probably a good trade."

Sam and his men took their positions along with the other squad to be ready for action as the ship moved out into the muddy water of the Roanoke River. Behind it trailed a smaller vessel with an iron forge to aid the workmen who were still banging and clanking on the iron covering. The huge beast moved downstream stern first, drawn as much by the current as it was by the power of its own engines.

At dark, the Albemarle dropped anchor three miles above Plymouth to examine some obstructions and torpedoes which had been placed in the river by the Yankees. It was determined that recent rains had raised the level of the river and the iron clad vessel would not be hindered.

Hoke's attack against the union forts which protected Plymouth had begun the day before. His artillery had pounded the defenses, but attacking infantry would be severely hurt by the fire from the Federal ships on the river. It would be the job of the <u>Albemarle</u> to eliminate this problem. As the Confederate warship passed the outer forts of the town's defenses, it didn't even bother to reply to the fire from the Yankee cannons. The iron shells merely made a sharp "Clang" sound as they bounced off the side.

Lieutenant Commander Charles Flusser of the U.S. Navy was the ranking officer of a gunboat squadron on the Roanoke River. His four ships, the <u>Miami,</u> <u>Southfield,</u> <u>Ceres,</u> and <u>Whitehead,</u> were sidewheelers, armed with rifled cannons and two 100 pounder Parrott guns. This artillery could make short work of anything the Confederates were known to have. The problem was that the Yankees were not certain about the size of the armament of the <u>Albemarle</u>. The intelligence received by Flusser had been very contradictory, but he was sure the ironclad would be a formidable day's work. As a precaution, he had evacuated the women and children along with sick and injured soldiers when it became evident that the Rebel ram was on its way down stream.

The Union skipper had devised a plan to help him combat the Rebel ironclad. Stationing his ships east of Plymouth where the river takes a northward turn, he lashed the <u>Southfield</u> and the <u>Miami</u> together with chains and spars. He hoped to get the <u>Albemarle</u> to sail between the two ships and become entangled. Then he could pound holes in the armor with his big Parrott Rifles.

The sun had just begun to burn the morning mists off the river when the <u>Albemarle</u> rounded the bend and chugged past the town of Plymouth with dark smoke bellowing from its smokestack and the Confederate naval ensign flying from its casemate. There before it lay the Yankee trap. Captain Cooke, on board the ironclad, quickly saw what Flusser had in mind. He swung the stern of the huge vessel around toward the south bank of the river and aimed the armored prow at the Union ship <u>Southfield</u>.

The Lieutenant yelled at Sam, "We're going to ram. Brace yourselves and get your men topside after we hit. Repel boarders at all costs."

The Federal sailors could only watch in horror as the ram sliced through the muddy waters, splintering the wooden hull of their doomed ship with a loud crash.

Sam and his squad were thrown to the floor by the force of the impact and had to scurry after their weapons. "Follow me," Sam shouted as he climbed out of the <u>Albemarle</u>

and up on the casemate. "Form along the front edge."

As the soldiers ran along the top of the ship, they were actually running downhill. Uriah was the first to notice that the Albemarle was going down with its victim. "That Yankee ship has got us so tangled up, we're going down too," he shouted.

"Fire at those Yankees on the other ship," Sam ordered, pointing at the decks of the Miami. Union sailors armed with cutlasses were going to board the Albemarle which was still held fast by the sinking Southfield. The sinking ship was pulling the Albemarle under and her forward deck was awash and water was pouring through the front gunports. Only the shallow river saved the ram, for when the Union ship touched bottom it turned on its side. The Albemarle popped free with a loud crash from splintering timbers and a huge geyser of water.

By now the Miami had pulled along beside the Albemarle and was getting ready to send a boarding party to capture the Rebel ship. Sam and his friends now numbered a dozen and from their commanding position poured a deadly fire into the Yankee sailors on the decks and in the rigging of the Union vessel. As a rifle was fired, it was passed below to be reloaded and quickly returned. The boarding party was defeated by their fire and several of it's members died by the railing of their ship.

The Miami was now directly abreast of the Albemarle and ready to slug it out. The Union skipper, Commander Flusser, was in the midst of the fray. He held the lanyard of his ship's most powerful gun, the ten inch 100-pounder Parrott rifle. The fuse for the projectile had been set while there was some distance between the two ships, but now the ten-second setting was much too short for this range. Flusser fired the gun point-blank into the side of the Rebel ship. The huge shell struck the iron plating of the Albemarle with a gigantic shower of sparks, bounced back to the gun that had fired it and landed on the deck. The unfortunate Commander Flusser could only watch as the shell exploded, blowing him to bits.

The cannons of the Confederate ship were now raking the Miami. The executive officer of the now crippled Union ship took over and steered it out of the fight, followed by the smaller Federal gunboats. The Rebel ironclad had done its job of clearing the Yankee guns off the river and General Hoke could now continue his conquest of Plymouth.

The <u>Albemarle</u> sailed triumphantly back to the town and began shelling the defenses with its eight inch guns. The sharpshooters had remained on the superstructure and were ready for any attack from the direction of the town. None would come.

"That was the durnedest thing I ever saw," Uriah said with disbelief. "That Yankee never figured he would get kilt by his own gun, but that shell shore bounced back and done it."

"Yeah, damn right," Charles agreed. "It almost makes you feel sorry for him, even if he was a Yankee."

"I don't reckon none of the Yankees would have cared if that had of happened to one of us," Thomas said. "You can look at the burned houses and killed livestock anywhere they go and tell that."

The conversation was interrupted by an occasional "whomb" of the report of the ship's guns. "I wish they would let us know before they do that," Daniel complained. "That scares the devil out of me if I'm not expecting it."

"I'll speak to the Captain next time he invites me to dinner," Sam said with a laugh.

The wet morning air began to resound with the sound of land based artillery and the concussions of the explosions could be felt on the <u>Albemarle</u>.

"Hey, listen!" Dougal exclaimed. "The infantry is going in. Hoke's starting his attack."

"I think that's only artillery," Sam observed. "I believe the General has moved his attack over to come in from the East. He couldn't do that before this floating iron chased the Yankees back down the river. Those big Naval guns would have fired right down our ranks. He can soften up the forts for the rest of the day and take them tomorrow when he gets ready. I would say that the <u>Albemarle</u> has done a decent day's work."

General Hoke could now completely envelope the town from the land side. He sent a brigade around to the east to cross Conaby Creek on a pontoon bridge while his artillery softened the Yankee defenses. The next day, April 20th 1864, Hoke ordered a general attack which completely crumbled the outer defenses of the town. Only the main position, Fort Williams, remained in Union hands. The 8th North Carolina regiment, flushed with victory, made an unsupported attack against the fort and was thrown back with heavy losses. This unnecessary action was the only blemish on an otherwise brilliant campaign, because the fort later surrendered, leaving the Confederates in control of Plymouth and the Roanoke.

Back on Sam's farm in Cumberland County, the fighting was still a long way off, but the effects of the war were being severely felt. Coffee and sugar were extremely rare commodities and most cloth was used for uniforms. In the rural Southern life-style, these were inconveniences which could be dealt with. All of the food was grown and consumed on the farm and the families could survive without things like lace and storebought clothes.

Susan had continued to keep her house neat and clean waiting for Thomas' return, even though she was not living in it. It now had a border of daffodils and jonquils that Betty had given her from the multiplication of her own bulbs. Susan's project for this year was two pink flowered rose bushes with running branches some folks call the Seven Sisters. By the time Thomas returned home, she hoped they would have grown into substantial bushes.

Her young son was over a year old now and was learning to walk into new adventures. She looked forward to the time when the war would end and she and Thomas could sit on their front porch, watching their son play and climb trees in his expanding world. On this day of a flawlessly blue sky, she and young Thomas had visited the house to chop weeds out of the new flower beds. Satisfied with her hour's work, Susan picked up young Thomas and started across the oak log bridge which Sam and her husband had laid when they built her the house. During the wet periods, the bridge was under water and you had to take the main road to Sam's long driveway. This way was much shorter. The same sassy squirrel chattered at her and the graceful motion of a cottonmouth in the water, swimming past the cypress knees, made her hurry her steps.

As Susan walked up the gradual slope from the swamp to Sam's house, she could see Betty, sitting on the front porch reading the newspaper. "There's some good news," Betty called out.

"Oh, tell me, tell me!" Susan exclaimed. "It isn't peace, is it?" Susan climbed the stairs to the porch and sat down in a rocking chair near Betty and began to rock young Thomas.

"No, not that good," Betty answered. "General Hoke has retaken Plymouth up near the Albemarle. They used an ironclad ram to sink the Yankee ships and they hope to retake all of the towns down east."

"Were our men involved?" Susan asked with alarm.

"I don't think so," Betty replied, unaware of her husband's part in the campaign. "The 8th and the 61st North Carolina from Clingman's Brigade were involved, but the 31st and the 51st were evidently not there."

"Thank the Lord.!" Susan said almost tearfully. "I pray every day for their safety."

"I do too," Betty concurred. "I feel so sorry for those who have lost their husbands or sons. There were a lot of casualties in the 8th. One of their companies is from over at Manchester."

"Betty, how much longer can this war last?" Susan asked. "There isn't much to buy in town anymore. All the men from around here are gone with the army. When will it all end?"

"It will last until one side is defeated or gives up," Betty replied. "The Yankees took Chattanooga and Vicksburg last year, but after three years of war, they are no closer to Richmond than they were at the beginning. If we can hold on for another year, some folks think that Lincoln will be defeated at the polls and the Yankees will make peace. General Hoke's taking back Plymouth shows we're still full of fight."

General Hoke's gray columns were at that moment leaving Plymouth to attack Washington, N.C. at the entrance to Pamlico Sound. From there, he would continue on to New Bern where its capture would extend Confederate control back into most of the sound area of North Carolina.

The success of the <u>Albemarle</u> had raised Rebel expectations extremely high for this venture. Hoke had asked Commander Cooke to furnish covering fire from the Neuse River when he attacked New Bern. To do this, the <u>Albemarle</u> would have to fight its way down the Albemarle Sound, past Roanoke Island, into the Pamlico Sound and up the Neuse River to the town. Even if it encountered no Union warships, this would be a journey of one hundred eighty miles. It had not been easy for Cooke to coax the ironclad the twenty miles down to Plymouth because of mechanical failures, but the Commander was game to give it a try. Confederate forces in this sector were now commanded by men who were looking for opportunities for victory, not excuses for failure.

General Hoke had Washington under siege by April 27th and captured it by the 30th. On their way out, the Union soldiers subjected the town to a savage looting and burned half of it, to the disgust of some of their own officers.

Hoke was now on his way to New Bern at the head of an army flushed with victory. Commander Cooke, on board the <u>Albemarle</u>, would do his best to meet him there.

Sam and his men had more than a week on dry land since their service aboard the ironclad. This welcome respite gave the sharpshooters opportunity to wash some clothes and write letters home. It was not a happy group of soldiers who were ordered back on board the ship and there was fear and apprehension among them as the <u>Albemarle</u> got under way.

"I still think this contraption could be an iron coffin," Uriah complained.

"Well, one thing's for certain," Sam countered. "We are safer here than anywhere else when the Yankees start throwing those hundred pound shells at us."

"That ain't what I'm talking about," Uriah continued. "We almost sunk when we rammed that Yankee ship and that's zackly what the Captain has in his mind headin down this river."

"Damn right!" Charles agreed, "He's going to ram another one."

"Isn't that what they built this thing for?" Thomas asked. "It looks to me like it did a mighty good job at Ply-

105

mouth."

"I don't think the Yankees are going to forget what we did to them at Plymouth," Daniel surmised. "If we are on our way to New Bern, you can bet they are going to try real hard to stop us."

"Yeah!" Dougal agreed. "As far as we have to go, they might even try several times."

The Union Navy was indeed taking the Confederate ironclad very seriously. They could not possibly maintain control of the North Carolina sounds with this monster roaming about uncontrolled. At the point where the Roanoke River flows into the Albemarle Sound, the Federals set up their first line of defense.

U.S.Navy Captain Melancton Smith had assembled four well armed, side wheeled steamers to block the Rebel ironclad's entry into the sound. These ships were powered by two steam boilers, each controlling a large side wheel. They were faster than the Albemarle and could move backwards as well as forward with ease. In addition to the Miami, which the Southerners had battled at Plymouth, the Union fleet consisted of the Matabesett, the Wyalusing, and the Sassacus. The Miami had been rigged with a torpedo on a long boom which they planned to detonate beneath the Confederate ship.

At 5:00 on the afternoon of May 5th, the Albemarle sighted the Union fleet and opened fire. Her second shot sheared off much of the Matabesett's rigging. The Sassacus closed with the ram and fired a broadside which bounced harmlessly off the armored sides with a loud "Clang".

"I hope our shells are having more effect on the Yankee ships," Sam said. "They might as well be throwing maypops at us."

Uriah was sitting where he could see the river at times through one of the gunports, as the gunners prepared for another shot. He stood up and cried out with alarm, "Here comes one that ain't going to throw no dang maypops."

The Sassacus had gotten some distance between itself and the Albemarle and stoked its boilers dangerously high in an attempt to ram the Confederate vessel. It had sprung forward and was heading to ram the ironclad between the iron casemate and the hull. The Lieutenant ran over to Uriah and looked over his shoulder through the gunport at the danger rapidly bearing down on them.

"Everybody lay down and brace yourselves," the Lieutenant shouted to anyone on board the Albemarle who could hear him. The officer, disobeying his own orders, remained in a squatting position and watched the approaching Union ship until it struck the Albemarle with a crash that knocked the sailors on both ships off their feet. The Lieutenant was hurled against the bulkhead and knocked unconscious. The impact also pushed the starboard gunports of the ram under water allowing water to come pouring in.

Commander Cooke, fearing the Albemarle was sinking, shouted, "Stand to your guns, and if we must sink let us go down like brave men."

Sam quickly sized up the situation and realized his job required him to get out just as fast as he could. "All sharpshooters topside to repel boarders," he shouted. Clamoring out onto the top, he could feel the ship slowly right itself. "Keep those Yankees out of the rigging," he ordered, pointing to the Union sailors who had climbed up and were trying to throw casks of gunpowder down the smokestack of the Albemarle.

The issue was decided when the grimy Confederate gunners sent a hundred pound shot through the starboard boiler of the Sassacus. The exploding steam from the over stoked boilers spread through the vessel and the screams of scalded Union sailors could be heard along with the gunfire. The Federal ship was jarred free from the ram by the very shot that crippled her. She drifted out of control downstream, still firing until carried out of range. No other Union ship came to challenge the Confederate Ram.

The Albemarle had also suffered some damage. The combined fire of the Union ships had been so severe that her steering had been damaged and her smokestack was so riddled with holes that it was difficult to maintain steam. Commander Cooke had no alternative but to return to Plymouth for repairs and even this was accomplished only by throwing lard, bacon and butter into the boiler.

Sam and the other sharpshooters returned to their

camp where they waited for the repairs on the <u>Albemarle</u> to be completed. They expected to one day board the <u>Albemarle</u> and set out to help General Hoke take New Bern. But Hoke now thought he could take the town without any help as his confident army swept aside the opposition and captured the protecting forts that previous commanders had thought to be so formidable. A frontal assault would now certainly retake New Bern, the second largest city in the State. This final, victorious attack would never be made.

Earlier in the year, Abraham Lincoln had appointed General Ulysses S. Grant to the command of all Union armies. Grant figured that if all the overwhelming might of the Union were applied at once, the Confederacy would not be able to defend itself.

On May 4th, 1864, the Army of the Potomac crossed the Rapidan River in northern Virginia where it soon became engaged with Lee's army in the Battle of the Wilderness. General William T. Sherman moved his army out of Chattanooga and began his drive on Atlanta. Both of these Federal Armies numbered well over 100,000 men. Another Union force of 30,000 men sailed up the James River and landed at Bermuda Hundred, Virginia. From there it could attack Richmond from the rear, or turn south and take Petersburg. Either move, if successful, would force Lee to abandon Virginia.

All Confederate forces in Eastern North Carolina were now needed to save the Confederate Capital. General Hoke received orders from Richmond to halt his attack, no matter how far it had progressed, and return as soon as possible. Reluctantly, he turned his bewildered army around and began a long march to the northwest, back to Virginia.

Chapter 7
Drewry's Bluff

The Confederate government had sent General Beauregard to gather an army and stop Butler's advance up the James River toward Richmond. As a result, General Hoke was ordered to assemble his forces at Goldsboro to begin the movement northward. Sam and his squad had remained in Plymouth and were there when the orders came. They made their way to a rail station near Tarboro where they were assigned transportation back to their regiment.

"Fall out over there in the shade and wait for the next train," Sam commanded the men. "The Captain said there would be another along directly."

The men lay down under some oak trees and began a much needed rest. "I bet this is going to be another one of them train rides to Hell," Thomas said. "I really do aim to finally ride a train to some place I want to go after this war is over."

"There's two ways to look at this train ridin," Dougal said from his reclining position. "We know there's going to be a fight up in Virginia and we're invited to it. We can either ride the train or walk. I'd rather ride and get shot sooner than to just get marched to death."

"Hey, ain't that smoke coming up the track?" Daniel asked. "We'll be riding soon."

A large cloud of gray smoke was coming up the track from the south. The men watched as the black shape of a locomotive came into view, then another, and finally a third.

These three engines were pulling a train of cars more than a mile long and were carrying the first contingent of troops from Goldsboro. There were passenger coaches for the officers, but the soldiers and horses filled the box cars. The artillery pieces were tied to the flat cars with the gun crews riding among the cannon wheels. Gray clad soldiers overflowed from the boxcars and rode on the tops. This was General Matt Ramsom's Brigade from Hoke's army and Sam and his squad would join the 24th North Carolina regiment for their ride north. These troops were used to victories, and expected more success wherever they were being sent.

The hissing of the steam and the grinding of the brakes announced the train's arrival as a huge cloud of smoke made by the three engines hung over the ground. The soldiers climbed off their cars and stretched, walking around to improve circulation and wandering over to the woods to relieve themselves. After taking on a supply of wood and water, the whistle sounded and the train resumed its journey north and continued through the night.

The next morning, three miles south of Petersburg, the troops had to leave the train because of a damaged railroad bridge, burned by Union Cavalry. The artillery crossed on a ford downstream while the infantry waded across the creek and climbed up the steep sides of the bank.

Soon, the city of Petersburg lay before them. The skyline of the city showed nice homes with many church steeples which were higher than their surroundings. The 24th North Carolina formed its companies and marched down the railroad tracks and into the city. Sam and his squad marched in the rear of Company H. As the dust covered ranks of lean soldiers turned down Sycamore Street, the populace flocked out in great numbers to cheer them.

Dougal set his cap at a jaunty angle on his head and straightened his rifle on his shoulder. He liked playing the conquering hero to cheering throngs. These were the first reenforcements to reach Petersburg from the south and the crowd welcomed them deliriously. Sometimes, in similar instances, a soldier would be handed some food or a cold drink as he marched past, but this crowd had been surprised by the

110

appearance of their deliverers and had only cheers to give. Dougal spotted two pretty young ladies standing beside the road waving their white handkerchiefs. He stepped out of the line of march just enough so he would pass close to them.

Suddenly, a stout middle aged woman broke from the crowd and walked beside him while asking, "How many of you soldiers are there."

"Thousands, Ma'am," Dougal answered. "With more right behind us, coming up fast."

"May heaven be praised!" She shouted and reached over, hugging Dougal around the neck and kissing him on the cheek without missing a stride, oblivious to the stench of the sweating, unwashed soldiers.

The woman released her embrace and the surprised Dougal marched on without looking back and forgetting about the two young girls. He could hear a chorus of snickers from his friends. As their march continued on to the Richmond and Petersburg turnpike, the cheering crowds were left behind and the friendly ribbing of Dougal began.

"Hey, boy," Sam inquired, "have you done gone and fell in love again?"

"She didn't make you forget about Florence already, did she?" Thomas added.

"Now you damn boys can cut that out," Dougal shot back angrily. "I can't help what that woman did. I ain't interested in nobody but Sarah right now."

"That might be a mistake," Uriah teased with a snicker. "That lady looked like she could keep you mighty warm at night."

"Damn right," Charles added. "We ain't got but one blanket apiece and that's all you would ever need."

"I ain't going to tell you idjuts again to shut up," Dougal retorted. "I just might come up side of somebody's ugly head."

"All right," Daniel said in conclusion of the kidding. "We were only trying to help. Anyhow, December ain't that long off."

The chorus of guffaws from Dougal's friends had just barely died away when firing was heard to the north. Orders

111

were given to double-time and as the regiment hurried toward the sounds of battle, the mood quickly became one of dead seriousness.

Night fell before Ransom's Brigade reached the battle scene, but the rest of the advance was made in battle formation with pickets far out in front in order to avoid an accidental firing on friendly troops or an ambush by the Yankees.

The advance stopped for the night at the banks of Swift Creek which crosses the turnpike just north of Petersburg. The men prepared to spend the night when more firing was heard to the northeast. The officer, who had given Sam and his men permission to board the train, was walking through the area making an inspection of his troops' deployment. Sam recognized him as he stood near a lamp outside one of the headquarter's tents. He walked over to the officer and stood at attention, not saluting under the battle conditions which existed.

"Capt'n," Sam began. "we are the men from the 51st. Is there any chance we can get back to our regiment at Camp Hill?"

The officer squinted at Sam and said, "Ah yes, Corporal. I had forgotten about you. You won't have to go to Camp Hill. That firing you hear is coming from General Clingman's area. Your unit is over there somewhere. Do you aim to try and find them in the dark?"

"Yes, Sir, if you have no objections," Sam answered. "This might be the closest we get to them. No telling where they might get sent off to after this fight."

"What you say could very well be true," the Captain replied. "From what I know, this battle could last a long time. Don't get yourself shot when you cross between the regiments. The password is "cotton" and the counter sign is "boll." Make sure the pickets can hear you coming and make sure you stay on the south side of Swift Creek. The Yankees are on the other side."

It was more than a mile through the woods, giving signs and countersign before a sentry offered a direct challenge. "Halt, who goes there?"

"Corporal Morgan and squad returning to the 51st,"

Sam answered.

"That you, Sam?" the sentry asked. "Advance and be recognized."

"Who's that?" Sam asked as he walked close enough to the sentry to recognize him. "Nathan? Nathan Deaver? What happened to the password?"

"Sam, nobody ain't told me no password. Anyhow, it's real good to see you," Deaver replied. "We were wondering if ya'll were ever coming back. When I get off guard duty, I want to hear all about Plymouth. That's Sergeant Geddie over there by that fire. He can take you to Cap'n Sloan."

Sam and his squad walked over to a small cooking fire where a large man was sitting on a log, drinking coffee. "Corporal Morgan and squad reporting back from Hell, Sergeant," Sam said.

"Sam, Thomas, Uriah, how are all you boys doing?" Sgt. Geddie exclaimed. "It's good to be getting some experienced soldiers back. I would offer you some coffee we just liberated from the Yankees, but it's all gone."

"That's all right," Sam replied. "We ain't seen any in so long we forgot what it tastes like."

Sergeant Geddie had a farm near Flea Hill Church not far from the Cape Fear River. The men had all known him before the war and respected his rank. He was a good natured person and did not insist on formality.

"What's been going on tonight, Mack?" Thomas inquired. "Have ya'll been in a big fight?"

"Not as big as there's fixing to be, I reckon," Geddie answered. "I hear tell the Yankees landed six divisions at Bermuda Hundred. They just been casting about here and there not seeming like they know where they are going. We just kept them from crossing Swift Creek and some of our regiment was out chasing them."

"If the Yankees wait much longer, they'll get a good welcome," Sam said. "We rode up here with some of Ransom's boys and there are more on the way. Have you heard that Beauregard has come up here to take command?"

"That's the rumor," the Sergeant answered. "By gosh, he'll fight with what he's got and it might be just us. Come on!

113

Let's us go check you in with the Captain." Before rising, Sergeant Geddie took a last slow sip of his coffee and savored it all the way down, enjoying that which he might not have again for some time.

The action Sam and his friends had just marched into was an attempt by Butler's forces to attack Petersburg from the north. The advance got as far as Swift Creek which the Union forces did not seem to take into account for they made no serious attempt to cross it. Butler's two corps commanders, Gilmore and Smith, who were both professional soldiers, suggested regrouping and making an attack on Petersburg from the east after building a pontoon bridge across the Appomattox River. Butler resented this suggestion and retorted that "he would build no bridge for West Pointers to retreat over when things got rough." This ended any meaningful command participation by the experienced commanders in the expedition. They would let Butler sink or swim of his own accord, and which one it was to be was becoming clearly evident by the hour.

Powerful Confederate reinforcements were pouring in from the west. It was now the eleventh of May and Butler's advantage, once forty to one, was now down to three to one. His reaction to his lack of success at Petersburg was to retire within his defenses and sulk for two days, thereby giving the Confederates more valuable time.

While Butler retired back to Bermuda Hundred, Clingman's Brigade was ordered north to get between the Yankee Army and Richmond. The Brigade was now part of General Robert Hoke's division. Hoke's new position would be at Fort Darling, a heavy gun position up high on Drewry's Bluff on the James River.

Upon returning back to the 51st, Sam had been promoted to Sergeant. His men would no longer function as a group of sharpshooters. Their duties would now be performed as regular infantry.

There were also two new replacements which had caught up with Company I. A new Conscription Act had drafted older and younger men than the previous one. Daniel McMillan was the teenaged son of the former company cook everyone had called Mr. Mack, who because of his age, had been transferred to the guard at the Fayetteville Arsenal. His son, just turned seventeen, was typical of the potential young men left back home between the rivers. At an age when he was becoming able to handle all the duties of the farm, he was sent off to war to kill or be killed.

His mother was the sister of Daniel Graham. The practice of raising military units and sending their replacements from the same community could have disastrous consequences on that community should that unit meet with tragedy on the battlefield.

J. D. Williams, on the other hand was typical of the older soldier who was now being called up. He was a farmer in his late forties who had a wife and family and a farm which he had time to plant just before leaving. He also had such a love for music that he brought his guitar with him.

Sam was being shown some of the new duties of his sergeant's rank. He had asked Uriah to help the replacements feel at home and give them a quick course in staying alive in combat. That instruction had to wait as Hoke's Division began its march north to Drewry's Bluff. The march continued as darkness fell. At one point along the turnpike, the Division passed close to the Union lines and could see the blinking of hundreds of campfires as the northern troops bedded down for the night. A refrain of a popular soldiers' song of the time came lilting over the trees in the warm May evening.

"You will not forget me, Mother, if I'm numbered with the slain."

"Hey, I know that one," J.D. Williams said with surprise. "Is that a Yankee song too?"

"Yeah it is," Uriah answered. "I don't know who wrote it, but, we both sing it."

"Yeah," Charles added. "We pray to the same God too. What do you think of that?"

"I think that if we're that much alike, what in the world are we fighting each other for?" J.D. asked. "Why didn't some body get together and talk things out before it got to this?"

"Oh, Lordy," Thomas said. "How many times have we tried to figure that one out? Don't you go trying to come up with some way to love them that's going to try to kill you tomorrow."

"That's right," Uriah said. "When we get to where we're going, I still got to show you how to stay alive. Don't let me forget."

"You can bet your hat I won't," J.D. said with a chuckle.

"Don't forget about me," Daniel McMillan chimed in from down the line.

"I'm going to make sure you get trained," Daniel Graham said. "If anything ever happened to you, your Ma would have my hide."

Fort Darling was reached the next day. Hoke's men were placed in line with the southward facing wall of the fort, which extended the defenses farther to the west. There were now significant Confederate troops between Butler and Richmond.

The men of Clingman's Brigade lay on their arms without much benefit of any kind of entrenchment. Malcolm McQorquedale, a farmer who lived near Uriah, was talking to his neighbor about the events of the week. "Yes, Sir," Malcolm said, "the Yankees came sailing up the river and landed where we didn't have nobody. If they had only guessed how few of us there were, they'd be in Richmond now."

"I don't think they'll walk in there now," Uriah said.

"No, we're in much better shape now than we were," Malcolm continued. "Still, some of the Yankees are armed with a new breech loading gun that shoots seven times without reloading."

"Is that so?" Uriah asked, propping himself up on one elbow. "Have you seen one?"

"Naw, but I talked to one of my friends who did," Malcolm went on. "He says they are carbine size and you load bullets down a tube in the stock. When you shoot, you pull a lever down and you're ready to shoot again."

"Have they got bayonets?" Uriah asked.

"I don't think so, but, I don't rightly know," Malcolm said. "What they do have is a coffee grinder in the stock of ever so many."

"Go on!" exclaimed Uriah. "Are you sure about that?"

"I ain't never seen one, but that's what I've heard tell," Malcolm said. "I reckon if a man can shoot seven times without reloading, he don't need to stick nobody and can sit around drinking coffee. That is if you are in the Yankee Army and can get coffee."

"I'll believe what you say about the rifle, but, I'll have to see one of those coffee grinders for myself," concluded Uriah. "Us talking about bayonets just reminded me of something Sam asked me to do that I ain't done yet. Hey, Williams! You and Mack come over here a minute."

The two newcomers obediently came forward and Uriah began their advanced training. "How much bayonet practice have ya'll had?" he inquired.

"Just a couple hours at Camp Mangum, then they sent us up here," J.D. answered. "We were shown the on guard position and how to make a thrust."

"That's about what I figured. I hope I'm wrong, but I think we are going into a full charge in the next day or two cause we ain't diggin' no trenches," Uriah surmised. "Let me just give you some advice if we do. It might help you stay alive."

Uriah now had the undivided attention of the two new soldiers and they listened intently. "First, when the attack has taken the position and the Yankees commence to runnin, don't shoot those who are runnin'. Only shoot those who are firing at you. Runnin' is what you want them all to do."

"Second, if you have to use your bayonet, stick him in some soft spot so's you can jerk it out quick. If you stick a Yankee in the chest, it will get stuck on some bone and you might have to shoot to blast it out."

"Third, don't quit runnin' and stand in one spot during a charge. You make too good a target. If you have to reload, lay on the ground," Uriah said, ending the quick advice.

"Why don't you shoot the enemy if he's runnin'?" Daniel McMillan asked.

"I'll tell you, Mack," Uriah answered. When we were advancing on New Bern, we overrun some rifle pits and I shot at a runnin' Yankee and missed. He stopped and aimed right between my eyes. I had to do some powerful scurrying around to get him to miss. I learned a lesson right then and there."

"Oh, one last thing," Uriah added. "Don't ever pick up the flag during a charge and try to be a hero. The whole regiment keys on the flag during an attack, and whoever picks up that flag after the color bearer's shot, is sure to get shot hisself. Every Yankee marksman will have you in his sights and they can shoot as good as we can. And you can bet that on the other side, some Yankee is telling his new troops the same thing I just told you"

Uriah and Charles kept up the training and discussions of staying alive till night fall. The rumor passing up the line predicted an attack on the Yankees the next day. Butler had finally decided to attack Richmond after all, and as General Beauregard had been inspecting part of the Confederate line near Drewry's Bluff, a Union shell had landed near him. The explosion knocked him down and covered him with dirt. He scrambled to his feet, shook his fist in the direction of the Federals, and said: "All I want you to do is stay right where you are till tomorrow morning." The rumor spread like wildfire and it was correct.

General Robert Ransom, the brother of Hoke's brigade commander, had brought his division down from Richmond and Beauregard now had twenty thousand troops. Although still outnumbered three to two, these were as good odds as any Confederate commander was likely to get. The plan was to hit the Federals hard from the north with Ransom's and Hoke's Divisions, and drive them away from the James River and their naval artillery support. Having done that, two brigades would advance from Petersburg and get between Butler and his base at Bermuda Hundred. This would surround the Federals and their destruction would be assured.

The morning of May 16th, 1864, was very foggy, but the Confederate camp began stirring at 3 A.M. Sam woke Thomas and said, "Pass the word to fix blanket rolls cause we won't come back here tonight."

"All right, Sam," Thomas replied. "I just hope we ain't in Hell instead." He proceeded to wake the rest of the squad and in a matter of minutes all the men had their belongings tied in their blanket rolls and swung over their left shoulders.

The attack was begun with Ransom's Division attacking the Federals nearest the James River. This general had a reputation for overrunning any enemy defensive position in his front, which he did again that morning. As the Union right began to give way, General Bushrod Johnson next attacked to secure the flanks of Ransom's men. That was the signal for General Hoke to send in his division.

"Fix bayonets! Guide to the center!" The commands came rapidly as Hoke's men crossed the protective ditch in their front.

"You new men, stick with me and you'll be all right," Uriah said to console Mack and J.D. "Them Yankees can't hit the side of a barn. I was just lying to you last night. Just remember the rest of what I told you."

As they neared the Union positions, an officer sprang forward in front of the ranks holding his hat in his hand and yelled at the top of his lungs, "Chaaaarge!" With a cheer from a thousand throats the Confederate ranks surged forward like an animal no longer restrained. The high pitched yip of a thousand Rebel Yells split the air, a sound many of the survivors would find to duplicate in the years to come.

The elbow-to-elbow ranks began to lose their alignment as the woods were reached. The trees and bushes were barely visible in the foggy dawn, but the advance continued. The Union lines were becoming more clearly defined in the fog by the muzzle flashes of the rapid firing Spencer carbines. Casualties among the attackers were becoming significant as these new rifles took their toll. Most bullets zinged by, but others made a sickening sound as they hit flesh and bone. A wounded soldier would fall screaming to the ground while those killed would collapse and hit the ground like a sack of potatoes. Sam kept repeating the same Bible verse over and over.

"A thousand shall fall at thy side, and ten thousand
at thy right hand, but it shall not come nigh thee.
A thousand shall fall at thy side ..."

Suddenly, the Union defenders were clearly visible to

the attacking Confederates. The Rebels in the front rank paused quickly to fire a volley into the ranks of the Yankees. Uriah saw that the Federal line was giving way, but one brave defender was desperately trying to reload his Spencer rifle. Just as the Yankee turned to fire at the attackers, Uriah fired and the man dropped. Uriah jumped into the trench and picked up the fully loaded Spencer, slung it over his shoulder and continued the charge without remorse. He had killed his enemy before his enemy could kill him. Groups of Union soldiers were surrendering all down the line, but there was still plenty of fight in others.

As Uriah continued to advance, he saw Mack and a young Yankee standing face to face to each other with rifles cocked, both frozen with indecision. "Don't make friends," Uriah shouted. "Kill him." As he spoke, he hit the Federal soldier beside the head with his rifle butt, knocking him unconscious. It was only then that he saw the youthfulness of his adversary. He was younger than Mack. "Are both sides going to finish this war fighting our children?" he thought as he continued on.

A general realignment of the Confederate lines was made after the Union troops retreated to their second line. Suddenly, a cannon boomed two hundred fifty yards away at the new Union position. An officer grabbed the colors of the 51st and charged toward the artillery battery. The butternut tide swept over the new position and the Rebels continued after the fleeing Yankees. This advance, made with the flush of victory caused them to outrun their support beside them. Suddenly, the 51st along with the 31st started taking fire from both flanks as well as the front.

Sam was reloading his rifle when a Yankee stood up from behind a split-rail fence and took steady aim at his chest. Sam heard a rifle fire beside him and saw the forearm of the man's weapon split and the piece go flying out of his hand. The soldier, now weaponless, beat a hasty retreat into the woods.

"Had to touch that one off a bit hasty or he might have got you for sure," Thomas said, rather matter-of-factly.

"Thomas!" Sam exclaimed. "You just saved my life.

That one had my name on it for certain."

"Look, we're falling back," Charles announced. "Let's get the heck out of here."

"Yeah," Daniel agreed, as the minnie balls zipped past his head. "I believe I can run out of this place faster than I ran in."

Clingman's Brigade had been too successful and had advanced too far. The men were now retreating out of the trap, firing as they fell back. Fortunately, for them, the Union troops were content to let the Rebels retreat back to the line of their original success.

Later in the afternoon, the Confederates again swept forward, driving the Federals before them. Butler was being soundly defeated, but Beauregard's plan called for his destruction. There were still two brigades of Confederate infantry and one of cavalry at Petersburg and the plan was for these troops to advance at the sound of the battle and cut Butler off from his base at Bermuda Hundred. However, the commander of the troops did not carry out his orders, and Butler was able to escape.

The sun began to set on a eerie landscape several miles wide and more than a mile deep, over which the attack had taken place. The wounded of both armies were being taken to the field hospitals and the dead were being collected for burial. Sam had sent Thomas and Uriah back over the battlefield to find any stragglers from Company I. More than half the company were casualties or lost their way in the confused fighting. This errand gave Uriah a chance to stock up on extra ammunition for his new Spencer rifle which he found in the abandoned Union positions and on the bodies of the dead. As night fell, they were able to find Dougal and J.D. and bring them back to the company area. The full extent of their losses would not be known till the next day. It was comforting to all the men to have J.D. play his guitar, so they could sit around a smoky campfire and sing the songs about home.

Butler continued his retreat to Bermuda Hundred and needed only one more attack from Beauregard to push him back to within his entrenchments. This attack was made on May 20th, 1864 and added the name of David Brock to those killed from Company I. Richmond and Petersburg were safe for the time being.

After hearing the news of Butler's failure, General Grant fumed that Butler's Army, "...was as completely shut off from further operations directly against Richmond as if it had been in a bottle strongly corked."

Richmond was indeed temporarily saved for a while, but Butler's Army had only been defeated, not destroyed. The fact that it was not destroyed would one day prove to be a problem for Clingman's Brigade.

Back at home, Betty and Susan were watching the third crop grow since Sam and Thomas had gone to war. They had spent the day chopping cotton and were enjoying a cool glass of well water as they sat, rocking on the front porch. It had been a week since the battle and Betty unfolded the newspaper which had arrived that day. There on the first page was the account of the Battle of Drewry's Bluff. "Oh, Lord, Susan!" she exclaimed. "The 51st has been in a big battle in Virginia. There's a long list of casualties."

"Oh, no," Susan gasped. "Are our husbands all right?"

"Thank God, they're not among the killed," Betty answered. She paused to continue reading before speaking again. "But Hiram Bunce from over at Bethany crossroads was. Oh, those poor children. Daniel Blue, John Guy, William Skipper, and John Tew, were also killed and I know them all," Betty said as tears formed in her eyes. She read on before continuing. "There are dozens of wounded, but our men and their friends from down on the river seem to have come out all right."

"Praise the Lord!" Susan exclaimed. "I'd just as soon be ruled by the Yankees than to lose my husband."

"I certainly hope it doesn't come to that, but I don't see how we can be winning. All the battles are being fought down here in the South and it doesn't seem to matter how many troops the Yankees lose," Betty surmised. "All we can do is keep these crops growing and pray real hard."

Chapter 8
Cold Harbor

Beauregard's force was now behind its own fortification opposite Butler at Bermuda Hundred. Sam and his men were settled into trenches so close to the enemy that a prudent man kept his head down, being careful to keep hidden from sharp-shooters. The Men of the 51st were in a somber mood because of the casualties they had suffered. Their previous battles had been fought on the regimental level and losses had been minimal. The Battle of Drewry's Bluff was fought with full Union and Confederate brigades and divisions fighting each other. The slaughter on both sides had been severe.

"This is the first time we have had several men killed that I have known all my life," Thomas said. "It sure makes you stop and think."

"We are all just penciled in this world for a certain amount of time and when that time is up, you'll go on to your reward," Daniel Graham added.

Sam entered the conversation by saying, "Daniel, you Scotch Presbyterians believe that way and you are entitled to believe what you want, but I don't see things like that. I could stick my head up over these logs and for certain would get killed, but, I ain't going to do that, so I'll live."

"That would be killing yourself," Charles said. "That don't count."

"All I know is that there is a God that made us and will call us home one day. While I am here, I am going to use my brains to do my dead level best to keep from gittin killed," Uriah said emphatically. "I ain't going to carry no flag and I ain't going to try to be no hero. I aim to give myself every advantage I can git. That's why I got me one of them new Spencer repeaters the Yankees are using and ya'll better get you one too."

"That repeatin rifle wouldn't have done Sergeant Geddie and young Mack any good. Did you hear what happened to them?" asked Charles.

"Naw, what happened?" Uriah inquired.

Sam answered the question. "I was informed by Capt'n Sloan that they were wounded in the attack, not bad I don't think. Anyhow, they went over to the field hospital and when the Yankees flanked us, they captured the hospital and all our wounded."

"Durn," Daniel swore. "He's my nephew and I'm going to have to write his mother about it. He's in for a rough time in a Yankee prison being wounded and all. He's their oldest son."

"Maybe the Yankees will parole him soon," Dougal said. "We can always hope for that. You can have some of my writing paper, Daniel. I'm getting a letter off to Sarah while I can."

"Much obliged," Daniel replied as he changed positions with Charles, being careful to keep his head down. "Hey, what's that you got around your neck?"

"That's a good luck scarf my lady gave me," Dougal answered. "I wear it into battle for protection."

"Protection," Daniel laughed. "That thing ain't going to stop no Yankee bullet. Good thing it's a blue plaid instead of red, else the Yankees would use it for an aiming point."

"That's all right," Dougal said as he took off the scarf and folded it neatly. "I didn't get shot, did I?" As he spoke, he put the scarf inside his shirt, next to his heart.

Two hundred fifty miles away, Sarah was hard at work in her kitchen. She was cleaning the fireplace where the cooking was done. Mrs. Grantham had sent Malichi and his two sons over the day before to knock the soot out of the chimney and Sarah was removing what was left. Her life was quite different now that her parents were gone. With no income and very little money left, she now had to do the jobs that someone else used to do. This was good in a way because she had little time to think about the death of her mother and the shortages the Southern population now faced.

She had entered into a partnership with Mrs. Grantham on the twenty acres of sweet potatoes planted on the Grantham farm. Sarah had even helped Malichi and his family peg out the tender shoots when they planted the crop. This had been her first taste of the back breaking labor of farming.

Her main responsibility in the arrangement was to market the crop, which she had done very successfully. Her beauty and dynamic personality had opened doors quickly for her and she had contracted with the Army to sell them the remainder of the crop in the fall after stocking their "tater hills" for their own use. However, anyone with food to feed the always hungry Confederate Army would have found doors quickly opened in 1864.

The kitchen was located in the rear of the house, built like an island in case of fire. Should fire occur, the rest of the house could be saved and a fire had been always kept going in the kitchen during more prosperous times. Sarah paused in her cleaning and listened for what sounded like someone knocking at the front door. There it was again, unmistakable this time. "Who in the world could be calling at this time of day?" she wondered. She quickly washed her hands and took off an outer dust coat she was wearing to protect her dress. She took off her head rag and let her hair fall down around her shoulders and after a few quick swipes with a wash rag to remove some soot from her face, she looked in the mirror and pronounced herself presentable to be seen. She walked back into the main part of the house, into the foyer and opened the door.

The sight of the man standing on the porch greatly surprised her. His name was Joshua Radnick, and in spite of his Biblical name, he was the owner of the "Palace" which was a prosperous saloon near the train station. He had appeared in Florence ten years before and bought the establishment he now operated. He was rich enough to be tolerated by the people of Florence, but not really accepted. His build was tall and slender and he had a thin gambler's mustache. His name certainly indicated he was "not from around these parts."

"Why Mr. Radnick," Sarah greeted. "To what do I owe this unexpected visit?"

"Good morning, Miss McLain," Radnick responded. "I didn't want to contact you too soon after the death of your mother, but may I come in to discuss a matter which might be of utmost importance to you?"

"Why yes, I suppose so," she replied, not totally certain if she should allow him in. "Have a seat in the foyer."

In Southern hospitality of the nineteenth century, there were varying degrees of status indicated by your acceptance at one's home. Workers and informal visitors came to the back door. Honored guests were shown into the formal living room. By inviting a guest into the foyer, the hostess, in this case, was politely telling the visitor to state his business quickly and then leave.

"Miss McLain," Radnick began, "I know how hard it must be to maintain a decent lifestyle with all the wartime shortages we are faced with. No matter how hard we work, we are simply doomed to failure through no fault of our own. Have you found this to be true?"

"I don't disagree with anything you have said so far, Mr. Radnick," Sarah answered.

"There are certain opportunities, however, which occur as a result of this terrible war," Radnick continued. "There are certain high ranking officers who frequent the "Palace" who would like nothing better than to enjoy the conversation of a refined lady such as yourself. They would pay well for a brief respite from this terrible war, and a beautiful lady could make herself a lot of money."

"If you are trying to appeal to my patriotism, Mr. Radnick, you have failed miserably," Sarah snapped. "You are only asking me to become one of your whores."

"No, you are wrong, I assure you, Miss McLain," Radnick said quickly. "There is nothing more expected than what I have just said."

"I'm sure that's the way it would begin. Please sit there

for a minute while I consider what you have said," Sarah said as she got up and started to the stairs to the bedrooms above. She had never been this insulted before and this affront to her virtue demanded an unmistakable answer. Reaching her bedroom, she walked over to her nightstand and picked up her Father's double-barreled Derringer pistol she kept there for protection at night. She checked to make sure both barrels were loaded and cocked the left hammer. She descended the staircase with the gun held behind her.

"I have an answer for you, Mr. Radnick," she said sweetly, causing her caller to sit up in anticipation.

"Just maybe," he thought to himself. "I might have struck gold. She might be more receptive than I thought."

His speculation was ended when he heard the loud report of the Derringer. Sarah had pulled the pistol from behind her back and fired a bullet into the wall which zinged past Radnick's ear and impacted with a loud smack. "If you ever make such a proposal again, I'll fire this other barrel right between your eyes!" she shouted emphatically.

Her caller might not have heard what she said because he immediately dived for the door, opened it and took one more step before leaping off the porch and running out to the street. He turned around and looked back toward the house as the color began returning to his cheeks. "You might not be so high and mighty if this war lasts much longer," he shouted.

"If we happen to pass on the street, Mr. Radnick," she countered, "don't bother to speak because I'll not respond." She watched as he hurried down the street, pausing to look back once before turning the corner and disappearing.

Sarah walked back in the house and toward the kitchen to continue her work. Passing by the mirror, she stopped to smile at herself, pleased with the stand she had just taken. She threw her shoulders back and turned a full revolution before the mirror. "Radnick might be a scoundrel," she thought, "but, he does have a good eye for beauty." She nodded at her reflection and walked back to the kitchen to continue her work.

In Virginia, Clingman's Brigade had manned the defenses opposite Butler's troops for more than a week. Neither army wanted to spend the number of troops it would take to defeat their opponent so the men became less likely to shoot at each other.

One day, Sam and his squad were deployed on the bank of a creek which flowed downhill into the James River. It was their turn for picket duty. Across the small stream, not more than thirty feet wide, some Indiana soldiers stood in groups as they watched the Confederates change their pickets. As soon as the officers left, one of the Hoosiers walked to the edge of the stream and said, "Hey, Johnnies! Those boys you just replaced and us had worked up a truce. They couldn't tell you about it with the officers around, but we would like to continue it."

"We're interested," Sam yelled back. "How does it work?"

"You can see behind us and we can see up the hill behind you," the Union soldier replied. "If we see your officer coming, we'll sing out and you do the same for us. Each side posts a guard and the others can relax. If either side gets orders to fire or attack, holler out a warning before you start shootin'."

Sam turned around to face his men and saw them all nodding approval. "Done," he said. "I've gotten a mite jumpy in the last week, having to keep my head down."

"You ain't telling us nothing we don't already know," the Yankee said with a laugh. "You fellers got any t'baccer you want to trade?"

"We always got t'baccer," Uriah said. "You need chawing or smokin?"

"Both," the Yankee replied. "And I know you Rebs always can use coffee. This stream ain't much over knee high so bring the t'baccer out in the middle and we'll bring our coffee out."

The traders met in the middle of the stream and completed their transactions without fear. Soon, the Yankees were enjoying the rich aroma of Southern tobacco while the Rebels were enjoying the taste of coffee once again. The lookouts were posted, not to warn of the enemy, but to warn of the approach of their own officers. If the men of a junior officer were caught fraternizing with the enemy by a senior officer, that junior officer could face a court-martial.

Soon, the adversaries began talking to each other across the stream. "Why don't you Rebs give up so we can all go home?" one of the Yankees asked.

"If ya'll would quit taxing our cotton, we might just do that," Sam replied. "I don't want to break my back growing the crop so some Northern mill owner can get richer."

"What are you talking about?" one of the Yankees asked.

"You know there is a tariff on our cotton if we sell it out of the country to some country like England, don't you ?" Sam questioned.

"I reckon I did, but I didn't know exactly how it worked," the Yankee replied. "My Pappy grows corn and wheat mostly."

"What if all the grist mills were in the South and you couldn't get flour ground nowhere else?" Sam asked. "You would have to sell us your crops and we would sell you back the flour. What if Canada would give you more for your corn and wheat, but because of a tariff put on your grain by the Southerners in Congress, the government taxed away your profits? That would force you to sell your grain to us at our price and we would sell you back the flour at our price. Wouldn't that get you riled up?"

"It durn shore would and I can see your point on that," the Yankee said. "What I'm fighting about is preserving the Union."

"The South would have never left the Union if these damned ol' tariffs had been abolished," Daniel added to the conversation. "Don't you see? It all goes back to taxation."

"What about slavery?" another Yankee asked. "I felt so strongly that slavery should be abolished that I joined up."

"None of us here own slaves, but even that might have been prolonged by these tariffs," Sam continued. "In order to keep the votes equal in the Senate, a slave state had to be admitted with each free state. All we wanted was voting power to defeat those cotton tariffs. Slave traders ain't zackly on top of the social ladder back home so we didn't really care what happened in the new territories."

"When this war is over," the second Yankee said, "slavery will be abolished. That's what the President's proclamation says and we are going to win."

"How do you figure that?" Dougal asked. "Here we are still fighting around Richmond like we were two years ago. We just came up from Charleston and you couldn't take that city neither."

A third Yankee spoke up, "We have just about all got all your seaports and the Mississippi River too. We got people coming into New York all the time who will fight for their pay."

"We have to fight for our pay sometimes," Charles said, causing the soldiers from both armies to enjoy a good laugh.

"You ain't helping us win this here argument, Charles," Thomas said. "Anyhow, I think slavery will end no matter who wins. General Lee has freed his slaves and Jackson did too before he was killed. I think men like that will be running our country after the war and I just don't think they will let it go on much longer."

"Hey," one of the Yankees said, "let's quit talking about these things and go swimmin'."

These men, who were enemies yesterday and who would be enemies tomorrow, all shed their clothes and enjoyed a dip in the swimming hole. The soldiers from the two armies could not help but remember the one back home and the hot summer days of fun with their friends. All too soon it was time to put back on their uniforms and continue the war.

"We're going to be relieved about dark by some troops who ain't as easy to get to know as we are," said the Yankee who had originally offered the truce. "I reckon you 'Johnnies' ought to keep your heads down after we leave. Hope you all make it through the war and if you are ever through Waynesboro, Indiana, look me up and we'll share a good jug of brandy."

"Sounds good, Yank," Sam replied. "If you make it through and are ever around South River in North Carolina, we'll show you what good corn squeezins taste like."

The friendly enemies then took up their picket positions

on their respective sides of the stream and both groups were soon relieved. Sam and his squad were all clean and refreshed from their swim and were looking forward to a good night's sleep. However, it was not to be.

Neither Lee nor Grant had any intention of leaving the troops of Butler and Beauregard to stare at each other over the defenses at Bermuda Hundred. Grant needed Butler's troops to make his thrust toward Richmond and Lee needed Beauregard's men to help block Grant's advance. Grant only had to give the command and 'Baldy' Smith's Corp was on its way to join him.

Robert E. Lee, on the other hand, had to request his reinforcements from President Davis and the War Department. Lee held a conference with Beauregard who felt he needed all of his troops to contain Butler. On May 30, 1864, Lee sent a telegram to Jefferson Davis stating:

> "Genl. Beauregard says the War Department
> must determine what troops for him to send...
> the result of his delay will be disaster...
> Hoke's Division at least should be with me
> by light tomorrow."

The President agreed and at two A.M. on the 31st of May, Sam was awakened by Captain Sloan who said, "Get your men up and have them pack their gear. We're moving north."

"What is happening, sir?" Sam asked. "Can you give me any details I can give the men?"

"I have nothing official, but if we are heading north, I reckon it will be to reinforce General Lee," Sloan replied.

Sam woke his surprised troops and had them formed and ready to move out very quickly. The word spread rapidly that they were moving north to become part of the Army of Northern Virginia. This would mean that they would take part in war at its deadliest. This was Lee against Grant, and these two would fight each other every day till one army could fight no more. Clingman's Brigade was now part of Hoke's Division and would now be a player on center stage for the remainder

131

of the war.

As Clingman's Brigade moved out in the predawn darkness, the mood of the 51st was one of excitement. They were now a confident regiment who had known mostly success.

"I told you we would get up here one day, didn't I Dougal?" Sam asked. "General Lee must think well of us after we kicked Butler in the seat of the pants. I read in the Richmond paper where Jefferson Davis himself spoke highly of the 31st and the 51st for our charge at Drewry's Bluff."

"I was kind of hoping we could finish the war in some back area and nobody would remember we were in the army," Dougal answered.

"I guess we're too good'a men to leave in the rear areas," Thomas added.

"Damn, right!" Charles exclaimed. "We ain't lost a battle yet."

"We didn't exactly win that first one at Goldsboro," Uriah offered. "We were outnumbered five to one."

"That's the only reason we didn't," Daniel added.

The march continued until they reached Chester Station where a train of the Richmond & Petersburg Railroad was waiting. The sun was starting to appear as Clingman's troops boarded the cars which would take them to Richmond. Thomas, as usual, was less than enthusiastic about riding another train to some unknown destination.

"I do believe that these boxcars are getting older and creakier," he complained. "I don't reckon they stay stopped long enough for anybody to fix a thing that breaks."

"Cheer up," Sam encouraged. "After we get with Lee's Army and whip Grant, we'll get to ride one home."

"Where do you think they are sending us, Sam?" Uriah asked. "Are they still fighting up at Spotsylvania?"

"I read they had moved on nearer to Richmond," Daniel said, answering the question. "Grant don't retreat after he gets whipped by Lee. He just swings around the flanks and keeps on coming."

"I think there is some real trouble up there or they wouldn't of got us up in the middle of the night to get started,"

Daniel surmised.

"Damn right," Charles agreed. "That's what I think too."

The apprehension of heading toward an ensuing battle limited the conversation as the train puffed and rattled toward Richmond. By mid morning, General Clingman and his troops had arrived in the Confederate Capital where they received orders to proceed northward to Mechanicsville and through Gaines Mill to Old Cold Harbor. There they would support General Fitzhugh Lee's cavalry who was moving up to meet Yankee troopers who were only twelve miles from Richmond.

The 51st was commanded by Colonel Hector McKeithan from Fayetteville and he positioned his men as ordered. General Clingman had advanced with the regiment since it would now be in the most dangerous part of the line. The attack upon its new position came quickly as dismounted Union Cavalry advanced, firing their Spencers as they came forward.

"Have you ever seen so many Yankees in all your life?" Uriah marveled. At that moment, the Regiment fired a volley which drowned out any answer. The frontal assault was slowed for a time, but mounted units were trying to flank the 51st on both sides. Colonel McKeithan was standing near Sam looking through his field glasses at a Union officer who seemed to be everywhere, directing his troops as if the Confederates weren't firing real bullets.

"Sergeant, see if you can put a sharpshooter on that officer," the Colonel ordered. "We'll have fewer problems if he can be taken out."

"Yes, Sir," Sam answered. "Dougal, see what you can do."

Dougal took careful aim and gently squeezed off a round at the exact instant the officer turned quickly and the round whizzed past his head. "The fool won't stay still," Dougal complained as he quickly reloaded. As Dougal took aim the second time, the Yankees began another advance which was met by another volley from the 51st. The shock of the concussion and cloud of smoke from the discharge of the black powder rifles occurred just before Dougal fired his sec-

133

ond shot. It also went whizzing past the Federal officer. By this time it was becoming obvious that the 51st was going to be flanked on both sides if it remained in its present position. The Rebels began a fighting withdrawal, firing as they retreated. Dougal could not get another good shot at his Yankee target and General George Armstrong Custer would live this day, only to meet his death years later in a more dramatic manner at The Little Big Horn.

Clingman's Brigade fell back to the edge of a field and began preparations to defend itself as night approached. The 61st regiment arrived from Bermuda Hundred during the night to bring Clingman's troops up to strength. Colquitt's Brigade, also part of Hoke's Division, arrived and took a position on Clingman's right.

The whole Confederate line was now positioned where the Battle of Cold Harbor would be fought. Hoke's Division was placed on the extreme right end of the line. Clingman's Brigade made up Hoke's left and connected with Kershaw from Lee's army at a heavily wooded branch. Expecting to be attacked after the morning's failure, the Rebels began to dig trenches with any tools they had including bayonets, tin cups and plates.

"This dirt here reminds me of what we plow at home," Charles said. "I sure wish I was back there choppin cotton right now."

"That's right," Daniel agreed. "I just never realized how much fun I was having when I was breakin my back on the farm."

"I'll never complain if I ever get a chance to do it again," Uriah added. "It's a durn sight better than gittin shot at by Yankees."

"I'll soon have a hole big enough to hide in if one of you can join your trench with mine," Thomas said. "Then we can pile some dirt on top of these fence rails."

"That's right," Sam commanded. "Make the trench deep enough to stand up in and put these fence rails at the edge so you can shoot over them."

"I always wanted to be taller," Dougal said. "Now I see that would just cause me to have to dig a bigger hole."

"Thank God for small favors," Daniel joked. "Maybe we can stay here long enough to grow some taters in this here good dirt."

"We'll probably be gone from here tomorrow," Sam said.

"Yeah," Uriah added. "Digging another hole some place else."

"I don't reckon this is too bad after all," Charles surmised. "Just so long as the holes we're digging ain't to put us in for good."

The conversation was disturbed by horses' hooves as General Clingman and his staff rode by to make sure his defenses met those of Kershaw. The General paused and looked at the trench. "Good work, men," he complimented. Looking over at Captain Sloan, who was standing nearby, he asked, "Have you seen any sign of Kershaw's men, Captain Sloan?"

"I haven't, Sir" Sloan answered. "Maybe Colonel Murchison on our left has."

"I expected them to extend their lines to link up with ours," Clingman stated. "I will have to extend the lines of the 8th to cover that branch over there if they do not. I will send orders to Colonel McKeithan if you need to move." The General turned his horse and headed down the left of his line past the 8th N.C., crossed the branch, and went looking for an officer from Kershaw's command.

Sam and his men had overheard the conversation and Uriah was the first to complain. "Oh, no, we're going to have to move and dig in all over again!"

"I don't think so," Captain Sloan comforted. "The General will extend the lines of the 8th to cross that branch and we will use their trenches."

No word ever came for such a movement as Clingman learned that Hoke had ordered Hagood's Brigade to protect that portion of the line. Around nine o'clock, the South Carolinians could be seen taking their positions one hundred fifty yards forward but across the creek. Clingman was now satisfied as the 8th and the 51st occupied the left of his line with the 31st and 61st on the right. His men now occupied a solid front with the rest of Lee's Army. The General made another inspection of the area at one o'clock, saw that it was protected to his satisfaction, and thought no more on it.

Robert E. Lee, however, was not satisfied with his right flank. There was a piece of high ground named Turkey Hill which overlooked the valley of the Chickahominy River. This hill had not been occupied in the previous day's fighting and Lee quickly saw its advantage. He ordered Hoke to extend his lines to cover this key position which was quickly done. This caused Hagood's Brigade to be moved to another point in the line. This movement was reported to all but General Thomas Clingman. The fifty-yard gap in the lines was again undefended.

As the Army of the Potomac approached Cold Harbor, the brigade of General Emory Upton moved into line opposite Clingman's troops. He had received a battlefield promotion after his innovative attack at Spotsylvania had penetrated the Mule's Shoe salient. This had been done by massing his troops on a narrow boxlike formation, making a penetration and then spreading out, thus expanding the breach. He would try to duplicate this success at Cold Harbor.

One regiment which would be part of the attack was the Second Connecticut Heavy Artillery under command of Colonel Elisha Kellogg. These "heavies" had been garrison troops at Washington until the severe losses in Grant's command had caused them to be sent to the front. They were easily distinguishable because of their unweathered dark blue uniforms and were the subject of teasing from the hardened veteran soldiers of the Union Army.

It was about 3:00 in the afternoon when artillery shells began to rain on the Confederate positions. "Now ain't you glad you dug that hole deep?" Uriah inquired to anyone who would listen.

"I just wish it was deeper now," Dougal cried out.

"As soon as this barrage lets up, they're going to be coming," Charles said, referring to the impending attack.

General Clingman had positioned himself on the left of the 51st. He still didn't know Hagood's Brigade had been ordered away. Suddenly, there was a sound of heavy firing across the branch, and then - silence. The shelling gradually

136

lifted and Clingman could see figures advancing from the location formerly occupied by the South Carolinians. "Hold your fire till our friends get in!" Clingman ordered. "Pass the word down the line."

As these "friends" got closer, Colonel McKeithan noticed they were in line of battle and said, "Sir, I believe those troops are Yankees." The Colonel's observation was indeed correct.

The Federals advancing toward Clingman's Brigade could see only the hats of the Rebels in their dug in positions. Part of the defensive line lay behind cleared fields and where there was woods, the undergrowth had been cut away twenty yards in front. Suddenly, the entire line lit up with what must have seemed to the attackers like a quarter mile of muzzle flashes which well marked the Confederate trenches. As one line of Union soldiers melted away from the terrific fire, another took its place. These heavy casualties were accomplishing nothing, so the attack was suspended.

"Sam, I don't think we are going to win this war," Thomas said while reloading his rifle. "We're going to run out of bullets before Grant runs out of troops."

"He's surely got a heap of 'em," Sam agreed. "Where are they all comin from?"

"Hey, there's the cease fire order," Daniel said. "Have we whipped 'em?"

"I don't know," Dougal answered. " One thing's for certain. We shore smoked up this place."

The smoke from the fighting hung low over the battlefield in the late afternoon doldrums. No wind was blowing and the smoke had to dissipate slowly. For a time, this haze shielded the approach of Colonel Kellogg's 2nd Connecticut Regiment as it moved up in front of the 51st, aligned in a boxlike formation. Its' movement had been hidden by a ravine until Captain Fred Blake, of Clingman's staff, raised up to get a better view. "Here they are, as thick as can be!" he exclaimed.

"Aim low and aim well!" came the command from General Clingman.

A sudden sheet of flame shot out from the 51st's defenses which knocked down the front ranks of the column.

137

Clingman later wrote about "a tall and uncommonly fine looking officer" who was shot down by a Rebel soldier beside him. This had to be Kellogg who was up front leading his troops and was quickly killed. The Confederates on the flanks of the attackers poured a deadly oblique fire into the massed Union ranks. The men in the column now lay down to escape their destruction, but General Upton had ordered this attack without waiting for support for his flanks and now there was no safe place to hide. The other Federal regiments which were moving up to exploit the breach Kellogg was expected to make had no place to go and were also ordered to lie down. This produced a large blue mass on the ground in front of the 51st and part of the 8th. Fifteen to twenty volleys were poured into the unlucky Federals, before Clingman ordered a cease fire. About one-tenth of the attackers then sprang up and fled for their lives.

While Upton's attack was being defeated, the 61st and the 31st on the right of Clingman's lines had also been repelling attacks. They had also inflicted heavy losses on the assaults. The enemy had been driven off everywhere along Clingman's front and a loud cheer went up from his men.

Just as the cheering ceased, a deadly fire came from the woods to the left and behind Clingman's position. Nearly an entire division of Federals had found the gap in the line that had occurred when Hagood was moved. The firing was heavy and the soldiers of the 8th were falling rapidly. The left of the 51st was being hit also, and this included Company I.

"Hey!" Sam exclaimed. "What the heck is going on?"

"Face about," ordered Captain Sloan. "We're being attacked from behind."

"How'd that happen?" Thomas asked as Yankee minnie balls zinged past. "Somebody on our left must of give way."

"It don't matter now, boys," Daniel answered. "We're fightin for our lives."

"I told you boys to git you one of these Spencers, "Uriah said. "We're outgunned sure as Hell."

The Southern officers were quick to react. The 8th was withdrawn by Colonel Murchison to the trenches of the 51st and the two regiments formed a line perpendicular to their original position. To hesitate was to be beaten and the 8th and the 51st, led by their Colonels prepared to immediately counter attack. General Clingman also ordered the 31st to file out of their entrenchments and join the assault.

The three regiments formed a battle line and quickly advanced against the attackers. The force of their attack regained the lost trenches in spite of fierce resistance. Colonel McKeithan was leading the 51st and quickly ordered pickets to be sent out as did the other regimental commanders. Colonel Murchison of the 8th was leading his regiment from a position in the front. A Federal volley shot him down as he advanced with his troops in this attack which regained the lost trenches. The pickets sent out by the regiments were feeling their way through the swampy creek bed to their front when they ran into a heavy Union counterattack. Some of them didn't have time to get off but one shot and all were quickly captured as the blue ranks surged through the thickly wooded branch and crashed into Clingman's ranks. Captain Sloan was on the right of the 51st which occupied a slight knoll. "Mark your target. Fire!" he ordered. The volley obliterated the front ranks of the attackers, but on they came.

Uriah and Charles found themselves on the left and to the rear of Sam and the rest of his squad after their advance. The Union ranks which had swept past to the left of his position had some gaps in it from the fire of his Spencer repeater. Suddenly, there were no troops to his front even though there were attackers still coming up in front of Sam and Thomas and their friends. As the smoke cleared on the far right of the position, he could see over the hill to the right and what he saw was disaster coming through the woods. There were no Confederates manning a defensive position in that direction, but there were hundreds of Yankees moving up behind the 51st.

"Look to your right," Uriah shouted in the direction of Captain Sloan. The Union troops were almost across their line of retreat. Sloan had not seen the danger and it was now too late for further warning. "Come on Charles, let's git," Uriah said as he cranked off two rounds at the advancing Northerners and ran through the woods as fast as he could with Charles right behind him. The two soldiers would later talk about whether they should have stayed and shared the fate of their friends, but, it would have done no good and a quick decision had to be made. Uriah remembered, as he ran, being bounced on his Grandmother's knee as she recited this rhyme from Revolutionary War days.

> He who fights and runs away,
> Will live to fight another day,
> But he who is in battle slain,
> Will never rise to fight again,

Uriah had become a survivor who indeed would live to fight again. But Uriah and Charles weren't the only ones who had beaten a swift retreat. Most of Company I had escaped the encirclement, but a full third of the Company was now surrounded. The Federals were now firing at them from all sides when a Union officer offered them mercy. "Give up, Johnnies," he shouted. "We have you surrounded and you don't have a chance."

Captain Sloan looked over the situation and saw it was true. He slowly and reluctantly turned his sword over and raised it handle first above his head. "He's right, men," he said. "Don't get killed for no reason. There's no dishonor in surrendering now." The remainder of the men turned their rifles up butt first indicating they would give no more resistance. The Yankees rushed in among the Rebels and started disarming them. Sam, Dougal, Daniel and Thomas looked at each other with disbelief that this was happening to them. Sam quickly took inventory of his friends who were now prisoners. There was Doc Pope, Bill Nunnery, Nathan Deaver, Duncan Monroe, and five of the Tew boys. Nearly forty men from Company I had just been captured, and Sam noted with some degree of relief that Uriah and Charles were not among them.

Clingman's troops with the aid of Colquit's Georgia Brigade and Hunton's Virginians would eventually seal the breach in the line. The day's fighting had ended in nothing but losses for all. The simple oversight of not communicating the movement of Hagood's troops away from their protecting position on Clingman's flank had cost him one-third of his brigade. Union General Upton called the attack "murderous" and said further, "Our losses were very heavy, and to no purpose."

Many good men on both sides had been killed at Cold Harbor and many more would die before the armies left this place. But, for those captured at Cold Harbor, new and different kinds of horrors were about to begin.

Chapter 9
Point Lookout

When a man's freedom is taken away, his sense of self-worth quickly becomes a casualty of his imprisonment. But, the unhappy group of Confederates from Clingman's Brigade who were herded to the rear were still full of spirit as darkness fell.

"Hurry it up, Rebs," one of the Yankee guards ordered. "We need to get you behind our lines while there's still light."

"Yeah, and you can go to Hell!" Sam shot back. "You might have us captured, but you ain't going to get me to take any orders from no damn Yankee."

"At ease, Sergeant!" Captain Sloan reprimanded. "The man is right. I suspect our artillery is getting ready to open up on this area as soon as it can."

Just as Sloan finished speaking, an artillery barrage began landing in the marshy creek area behind Hagood's abandoned lines where the Yankees had made their penetration. One shell was fired long over its target and went fizzing over the heads of the captured Rebels before exploding with a crash among the oaks and pines in the woods beyond.

"All right, you Johnnies, double quick," the guard commander ordered. This time the command was obeyed without hesitation and the prisoners ran at a slow trot to the Union rear area. The sounds of Clingman and Colquit's counter attack filled the night air as the lost trenches were again attacked.

The loud din of battle faded to a dull far away roar as

the prisoners were herded to a safe area more than a mile from where they had been captured. They had been allowed to fill their canteens at a creek and were given some hard tack to eat.

A Union sergeant walked up to the prisoners and made a chilling announcement. "You Reb's are under my care and are my responsibility. If any of you attempt to escape, you will be shot, buried and forgotten about. None of you will be allowed to do anything other than march to whatever prison camp you are going to. If you use what brains you have and follow all orders, some of you might even survive this war." Having made his statement, he turned and walked away. None of the prisoners said anything.

The captured Confederates remained in their field surrounded by their guards as the new day dawned. There was nothing for them to do but accept their fate and hope for the best. As the day wore on, the Rebels were amazed at the panorama of military might which passed before their eyes. General Grant had been encouraged by the near success of the previous day's attack which had resulted in the capture of Sam and his friends. He was massing his army for what he thought would be the final push through Lee's lines and the capture of Richmond only twelve miles beyond.

By mid-afternoon, what seemed to be an endless line of supply wagons began passing the captured Rebels along with infantry which seemed to have no number. The unlucky Southerners were watching General Winfield S. Hancock's II Corps, some of the best soldiers in the Union Army. Hancock's men had occupied Cemetery Hill at Gettysburg and had defeated the attack of Pickett and Pettigrew. However, these troops were sent down the wrong road in marching to this destination and were hours late getting into position.

"You Rebs are mighty lucky," one of the guards said to Sam. "Grant is going to be in Richmond this afternoon and there ain't a chance in Hell that Bobby Lee can stop him. You just might have got killed if you hadn't got captured."

"I reckon Grant had better hurry if he expects to get there today," Dougal shot back. "You don't have no idea what's waitin for you damn Yankees if you try."

"Is that so, Johnny?" the guard said with a smirk.

"Those troops there belong to Hancock and you ain't going to stop him." A late afternoon rain began to fall, ending their conversation. Dougal knew that his friends were soon going to be involved in a larger battle than the one he had fought in. He only wished he could be with them.

Grant fully intended to renew the attack on the morning of June 2nd, but Hancock's Corps did not all reach their position until late in the afternoon which made an attack impossible for that day. The commanding General would merely wait till the 3rd.

The extra day given to Robert E. Lee would prove disastrous for the Union assault. The Army of Northern Virginia was now in place and the defenses were being constructed to provide interlocking fields of fire. Clingman's Brigade had been pulled back to a reserve position because of their losses on June 1st and the men of the 51st lay around, cleaning their weapons and listening to the sound of axes as the Rebels cut trees to make barricades in front of their positions. By the evening of June 2nd, the defenses had been finished and now bristled with the guns of Lee's Army. The line at the swampy creek which had caused Clingman and Kershaw so much trouble was moved back to higher ground and strengthened.

The Union staff officer who was taking the orders for the next morning's attack noticed something peculiar. He was riding past one of the veteran regiments which had spent the day listening to sounds of the Confederates with axes strengthening their position. He noticed the soldiers had taken off their coats and were seemingly mending them. On closer examination he noticed these men were sewing on pieces of paper with their name, address and next of kin, feeling certain they would meet their fates in the impending attack.

In the predawn hours of June 3rd, Sam and his captured comrades were awakened by the sound of battle. The Union attack began at 4:30 and initially met with some success on the Confederate right by units of Hancock's II Corps. This success was short lived, however, but caused orders to press the attack to flow from the Union Army headquarters for most of the morning. The Confederates quickly recovered and began to do exactly what their defenses had been designed for them to do - thoroughly mangle all attacking units thrown at them.

"Listen, boys!" Sam exclaimed. "They're fighting like all Hell's broke loose."

"Yeah," agreed Thomas. "That's mostly rifle fire and it sounds like one big roar."

"All that's going on and it ain't quite light enough to see what you're shootin at," Daniel added.

"I wonder if the 51st is involved?" asked Dougal. "Somebody's shore catchin Hell."

As the day brightened and the morning wore on, the intensity of the battle increased. "The firing is shifting over to the right," Sam observed. "Grant must be attacking along the whole front."

The sounds of battle did tell what was going on. The movement back and forth of ambulances told the rest of the story. The Federal troops were being mowed down like wheat before the Confederate breastworks. It was over long before noon when the Union soldiers refused to take part in any more hopeless attacks. Once again, Grant had been unable to break through Lee's lines. General George Meade, the commander of The Army of the Potomac, noted that Grant was finding out that fighting Lee in Virginia was far different from fighting Bragg in Tennessee. Seven thousand Union soldiers had become casualties in less than an hour that morning.

There existed some controversy about what occurred at the Battle of Cold Harbor during the afternoon engagement of June 1st. After General James Longstreet was wounded at The Battle of the Wilderness, his corps came under the command of General Robert Anderson. Hoke's Division was also assigned to his command. This General had reported to the <u>Richmond Examiner</u> that it was Clingman's men who had "given way." This affront to the honor of the brigade could not go unchallenged so Clingman fired off a letter to the Richmond paper. A copy was sent to the Fayetteville paper..

The June 9th edition of the <u>Fayetteville Observer</u> had reached Betty on the next day. Susan was snapping some of the early beans from the garden as the two Morgan children helped. The two women enjoyed the front porch late in the day and some days could still feel a cooling breeze.

"Oh, listen!" Betty exclaimed. "Here is some news from Clingman's Brigade."

"Read it to me, please," Susan pleaded.

"It was written on June 5th," Betty began. " It says:

"To the editor of the Examiner: - My attention has been called to a statement in your paper that in the battle of the 1st instant, "Clingman's Brigade gave way for a time." As this statement does great injustice to the gallant and patriotic men under my command, I earnestly request you to publish, in your next issue, this note. My brigade was in line of battle on that occasion and was heavily attacked along its entire front from left to right. The enemy advanced not only in line of battle, but on the left wing also, in heavy columns masked by the line of battle in their front. This attack was repeatedly and signally repulsed with great loss to the enemy in my entire front. Near our left, where they came in columns, their dead were much thicker than I have ever seen them on any battlefield. Any force advancing in front would have been destroyed as fast as it could come up, for my men were regularly supplied with fresh ammunition and fought with utmost coolness, courage and cheerfulness.

There was, however, in the beginning of the engagement, a brigade from a state than my own was stationed on our left. This brigade did give way, and while the contest was going on in our front, the enemy in large force occupied the ground on our left and rear. After we had repelled the last attack in front, and the men were cheering along the line, the 8th regiment which formed my left, was suddenly attacked on its left flank and rear. The woods there being thick and the smoke dense, the enemy had approached within a few yards and opened a heavy fire on the rear of the 8th and its left. If this regiment had given way it might have escaped with much less loss; But, true to its reputation and its past conduct, it, by facing in two directions,

146

attempted to hold its position, and thus lost about two thirds of its number. The left wing of the 51st, next to it, suffered in the same manner-"

"Oh Lord!" Susan screamed. "It mustn't be true."
"There's more," Betty comforted. "Listen!"

"suffered in the same manner heavily, because it continued the fight by facing in two directions. They persevered in this even after the time when, seeing that the contest could not be maintained in this mode, I ordered them back, and with the aid of their officers, withdrew the survivors."

Betty began to read to herself silently, quickly scanning the column for more news while Susan cried silently. "There's no more news," Betty said. "The General closed with a statement."

"I earnestly request those editors whose papers have copied the articles referred, to publish this, remembering that next to his country the true soldier values the reputation and glory of his own good actions."

"I don't care about glory!" Susan sobbed. "I want my husband home."
"Don't dispare, Susan," Betty said. "They may have been among the survivors. I just knew that the men from around here weren't going to run." Betty buried her face in her apron and also began to cry softly.

As the wives of Sam and Thomas shed tears for their safety, more of the Confederates captured at Cold Harbor were added to their group and bivouaced in a field at White House Landing under heavy guard.

A week passed and the morning of June 10th dawned sunny, but a light fog on the Pamunky River bottom took a few hours to burn off. The Rebels saw the masts of ships docked at the landing, and as the day grew brighter noticed some strange happenings. The battles in Virginia had produced horrible casualties in the two armies, particularly Grant's. An organization called the U. S. Christian Commission had a crew at White House Landing to help with the gigantic stream of wounded who passed on their way to Washington hospitals. The men and women of this organization were standing and sitting in a group near their tents and ambulances.

"Hey, Yank, what are those people standing so still for?" Dougal inquired of one of the guards.

"They are being photographed," the guard replied. "See that square lookin wagon over there? That belongs to Mr. Matthew Brady. He is one of the men standing behind that box on stilts that is taking the picture."

"How long do they have to stand still?" Thomas asked. "You'd think some of them had gone and died."

"I don't rightly know," the guard replied. "They seemed to stand still for twenty or thirty seconds and then they change positions for another shot."

"Do you reckon he'll want to photograph us?" Sam inquired. "I doubt if Mr. Brady has ever been this close to real live soldiers of the Confederate States of America."

"I suppose he wouldn't pass up such a rare opportunity," the Yankee replied, sarcastically.

At this moment, one of Brady's assistants came over to the officer in charge of the guard and spoke briefly to him, then turned and walked away. The Union officer then spoke to Captain Sloan who nodded and turned to address his troops.

"Men," he began, "Mr. Matthew Brady has asked if he can take a photograph of our entire group. I think it is a splendid idea and have agreed. If any of you object, you may form in the rear where you can't be seen. We will all need to be very still and not move while he works." .

Nobody seemed to object to the idea so Brady and his staff came over and set up the camera. It was a large bulky box which sat on legs. While they were setting it up, Thomas sat down on the ground in a lackadaisical manner, facing the camera.

"Aren't you going to stand with me and look defiant?" Sam asked.

"I reckon I've been defiant long enough," Thomas replied. "I just want to be left alone."

Thomas remained sitting while Sam stood with his fists on his hips with his hat set at an angle. Brady set the primitive instrument to focus on the group of nearly eighty men while an assistant took the lens cap off and exposed the plate for five seconds. Although none of the Rebels would ever see the finished work, it would be identified as "View of Rebel Prisoners at White House Landing."

Later that day, all the Confederates captured at Cold Harbor and vicinity were combined in one group. The enlisted men were separated from their officers who were to be sent to another prison. The men were then loaded on the steamer S.R. Spaulding and shipped to the Union prison camp at Point Lookout, Maryland.

The prisoners were crammed into the hold of the vessel until it was full, then the remainder were allowed to stand on the deck under a heavy guard. The members of the 51st were lucky in that they were on the deck and didn't have to stand the stifling heat and odors of the hold. The route to the prison was down the Pamunkey River to the York River, down past Gloucester Point at Yorktown and out into the Chesapeake Bay. The steamer would then sail northward up to where the Potomac River flows into Chesapeake Bay and forms the cape on which the prison camp was built.

As the H. R. Spaulding entered the Chesapeake Bay the saltwater smell was new to some of the Rebel prisoners, but to most caused them to conjure up ideas of escape.

"How far do you reckon it is across this pond?" Dougal asked. "Reckon we could swim it?"

"Don't know," Sam answered. "I ain't aiming to swim across this thing anyhow. Home will be east and south."

"You Rebs hush that talking," one of the guards shouted. "If you can't swim ten miles, all you'll do is drown and then you get eaten by all these crabs in the water. There ain't any escape where you're going."

The new home for the prisoners was a low lying peninsula which was wet even during dry weather and covered with a maritime forest of short pines and scrub oaks. At the

149

very tip were the buildings of the original camp, long and narrow and arranged like spokes in a wheel. Nearby was the hospital and buildings to house the guard and their officers. The dirt streets in front were nearly always deep in mud. Like all prisoner of war camps at the time, this one held several thousand more men than it was designed to hold. This overflow of humanity was held in several tent cities surrounded by stockades.

The H. R. Spaulding docked at a wharf on the west side of the peninsula and unloaded its' human cargo. The Rebels were then lined up to be processed in.

"All right, Johnnies, empty your pockets out on the table!" an officer commanded.

Sam did as he was told and laid his belongings and a U. S. silver quarter on the table. He saw immediately how things were going to be when a guard picked up the money and put it in his pocket. All personal items were taken away and even their blankets were not returned.

The prisoners were assigned twenty to a bell shaped tent inside a stockade with walls sixteen feet high. There were no boards or even straw on the floors to keep the dampness out. The guards were black soldiers who had been recruited from captured areas of eastern North and South Carolina.

Sam, Thomas and Dougal walked around the enclosure to get oriented to the camp facilities such as the water supply. Dougal was drawing some water from one of the wells when a familiar voice said: "You might get sick if you drink from that one."

"Mack! Mack Geddie!" Sam exclaimed. "You sure are a sight for sore eyes."

"Ya'll too, Sam," Mack replied. "Where'd you boys get captured?"

"A place named Cold Harbor," Thomas answered.

"Yeah," Sam concurred. "A regiment on our left flank gave way and we didn't know about it till we got flanked by a division of Yankees."

"There are about three dozen men from Company I who are here with us," Dougal added.

"I'm truly sorry to hear that," said Geddie. There are

150

only so many of us going to make it back home. There's men dying here all the time. There is only one well of water fit to drink and it's not that one. You got to go over to Division 5 to get drinking water."

"What's that ditch between here and the stockade?" Sam asked.

"Nobody told you about that?" Geddie asked incredulously. "That's the dead line and all you got to do to get shot dead is to cross it. Some times you don't have to do even that. The other night, I heard that some of the guards shot into a tent and killed two men who were sleeping. The officers ain't done a blessed thing to 'em."

"Do they starve you here?" Sam asked.

"Yes," Geddie answered. "All they give you is some bread and pork each day and once a week some salt fish, and there ain't no cookin fires allowed."

It was in this hostile environment the captured men would attempt to survive. Meanwhile, the war continued. The Yankees were getting closer and closer to Atlanta. The Confederates under Johnston were being maneuvered out of one impregnable position after another by Sherman's numerically superior forces. In Virginia, Grant, now understanding he could not break Lee's lines at Cold Harbor, decided to go around them once again. On June 12th, the Federal troops left Cold Harbor and crossed not only the Chickahominy, but the James River as well. Grant's plan was to overwhelm Beauregard's small force and capture Petersburg before Lee's Army could come to its aid.

Back in Cumberland County, Betty and Susan were going through their summertime ritual of sitting on the front porch and preparing corn they had picked from the garden that morning. On this June day, there were a few white clouds in the light blue sky as a warm breeze blew, giving a foretaste of the approaching summer heat. The children played in the yard while Susan shucked corn. Betty had paused from her pea shelling to read the paper. Susan was shocked when, without a sound, tears started rolling down Betty's cheeks.

"What's the matter Betty?" Susan asked. "What have you read?"

"You remember when we read General Clingman's letter and feared some harm might have come to our husbands?" Susan replied. "They are missing. That almost certainly means they have been captured."

"Tell me all it says," Susan asked as she too began to cry softly.

"There are so many men from around here missing that they have to have been captured," Susan continued. "Listen to these names. Captain Sloan, Hall, Carroll, Deaver, Davis, Fisher, Graham, Jones, Jackson, Maner, Monroe, McDonald, McIntyre, McCorquedale, Norris, Nunnery, Pope, Smith, Strickland, Taylor, Tew, and Warren. There's over thirty in all. It says here that Company I only has twenty-nine men left for duty."

"Those names are from Flea Hill back between the rivers to Mingo Swamp," Susan observed. "What are all those families going to do?"

"Just what they are doin now," Betty replied. "Those men haven't been home for two years, so, I reckon us at home have to keep working and pray a lot harder."

"When I think about the filth and disease I've heard about in those Yankee prison camps, I just get a sick feeling," Susan lamented. "I almost wish they were still in battle."

"Grant has stopped the exchange of prisoners and there's no telling when they'll get out," Betty added.

At that very moment, the men of Hoke's Division were running toward a battle. "This is too rough for an old man," J. D. Williams complained. "We've been running for near a mile."

"I ain't never seen us get in this big a hurry," Uriah answered. "But you mustn't straggle."

"Let me tote your rifle for you. J.D.," Charles offered. "That might help some."

"I'll carry my own rifle, thank you," the older man replied. "I can make it somehow."

About that time, the welcomed order came to resume normal marching. Hoke's men had crossed the James River and were actually running south toward Petersburg. Since Grant had moved his army out of Cold Harbor and crossed the James River, there were not sufficient Confederate troops in the vicinity that could stop him. There were elaborate defenses around the city, but these were sparsely manned by local units of defense troops.

General "Baldy" Smith's soldiers were now south of the James and were moving against Petersburg with Hancock's splendid II Corps close behind. Had these two commanders worked together on the 15th of June, Petersburg would have fallen on that day. But nothing in Hancock's orders indicated to him that he was supposed to join in an attack. For one of the few times in the war, Robert E. Lee didn't know the whereabouts of his opponent. Grant had stolen a march on Lee and no Confederate General other than Beauregard seemed to be aware of that fact. Smith's Yankees were the first troops to arrive and since his command had suffered heavily at Cold Harbor, he was somewhat apprehensive about attacking entrenched Confederates.

General Beauregard looked through his field glasses toward the Yankees. "Why don't they attack?" he said to one of his aides. "The enemy has broken into our lines and surely their commander must know that Petersburg is his. He has but to advance."

Just then, the aide spotted a column of lean, gray clad soldiers advancing toward them at double-quick. "General!" he exclaimed. "It would appear our salvation is at hand. Hoke's Division has arrived."

Beauregard turned his glasses toward the advancing column. "Yes, by God!" he shouted. "It's not over yet."

General Johnson Hagood rode over to where Beauregard stood. He gave a salute and said, "Reporting as ordered, General."

"Thank God you're here," Beauregard greeted. "Who's with you?"

"Colquitt and Clingman are right behind me, but we've moved fast and there's been a lot of straggling," Hagood replied.

"I welcome all you brought. My aide will show you to your position, and you might well be attacked tonight," the Creole General stated.

Back in Clingman's column, the rapid march had

brought them to the Petersburg defenses as night fell. The double-quick marching was ended by the darkness and those who had straggled were able to catch up with their unit. "That you J.D.?" Uriah inquired, peering into the darkness.

"Yep, it's me," came the reply. "This dog-goned shoe has rubbed a raw place on my right foot."

"I didn't know if you'd be able to catch up as fast as we were moving," Charles said.

"Has anybody found out what the all-fired hurry was?" J. D. asked. "And why are we stopped if it was necessary for us to run down here to start with?"

"I heard that Grant crossed the James and is set to attack Petersburg. I heard from one of Hagood's men that all the troops we had in the trenches were old men," Uriah explained. "Some ain't got no teeth and can't even bite off the end of their cartridges so as to load their guns."

"Who'd you hear that from?" Charles inquired.

"That feller back side the road whose back had give out on him," Uriah replied. "I don't know who he heard it from."

On the morning of June 17th, Clingman's Brigade formed the right of Hoke's line supported by Wise's Brigade on his right. Among these Virginians were the boys and old men of the local defense force who had been thrown into the breech to defend the city. Their training, experience and equipment were not sufficient to prepare them for what was to happen that day.

Several probing attacks were made on Hoke's position that morning. Early that afternoon, Uriah, J. D. and Charles watched in disbelief as four lines of Union soldiers, spaced twenty paces apart, began advancing toward Wise's position.

"I shore hope those boys can hold," Charles said. "Those Yankees look like they mean business."

"I hope Wise's men are up to it," Uriah said. "They are in a good position. Look! Some of them are already startin' to run!"

Wise's Brigade was starting to retreat before the attack reached them. The untrained men panicked first as was feared. The officers of Clingman's Brigade were forced to quickly react and did just that. The guns of the Rebels were aimed to the right against the now unopposed Union attack. "Volley fire. Right oblique. Fire!" came the command. The fire had a tremendous effect on the front ranks. The second volley sent the attackers reeling back in confusion. A second Union attack captured the trenches.

Colonel McKeithan of the 51st took five companies of the regiment and formed with Ransoms' Brigade to attack the captured trenches. Uriah was running low on ammunition for his Spencer rifle and was happy to see an Enfield with a bayonet lying on the ground where it had been dropped by some militiaman as he fled in panic.

The Rebel line surged forward and in the gathering darkness jumped into the breastworks and engaged the Yankees in hand-to-hand fighting. Bayonets and rifle butts were in order this evening as there was not time to load and fire. This was combat at its worst since you could look into the face of your enemy as you killed him. Both sides were near exhaustion when the Federals began to retreat.

With the position secure, J. D. was almost sick on his stomach. "That's the first time I've had to kill somebody like that," he said. "Why is it that a grown man will cry out for his Mother when he's dying?"

Robert E. Lee would soon become convinced that Grant's Army was indeed south of the James. He would rapidly move his troops to join Beauregard and the war in the East would enter its final phase. But June 17th would be remembered as the day when Hoke's Division saved Petersburg.

Sarah McLain had wondered why the letters from Dougal had stopped arriving. He usually wrote every week without fail and she wrote just as faithfully. She had read about the terrible battles in Virginia and knew that whatever the reason for the lack of correspondence, it was probably bad.

The casualties from Lee's Army, while not equal to Grant's, were still significant. Many wounded soldiers were sent home, their injuries requiring long periods of recuperation. There was a definite need for medical attention for these men on their way home. A doctor in Florence set up a first aid station near the railroad to provide care for these soldiers.

Sarah's sweet potatoes had reached a point where there

was nothing more for her to do but watch the vines grow. Never one to live a life of idleness, she volunteered her services as a nurse and was soon at work. One day, after a busy day at the aid station she found a strange looking letter in her mailbox when she returned home. It was not the brown envelope so common in the South, but cream colored and of much finer texture and it had been addressed in Dougal's handwriting. It had a dull red stamp with a bust of George Washington and "U. S. Postage" across the top. Before she opened it, she already knew that Dougal was a prisoner of war.

Chapter 10
The Wreck at Shohola

The rapid movement of the Army of the Potomac had created the military situation General Robert E. Lee feared the most. He was backed up in a stationary defensive position at Petersburg and would have to counter each thrust by Grant with the troops he had on hand. The Union casualties had been brutal. Grant's Army had lost nearly 70,000 troops since he had crossed the Rapidan River on May 4th and began the Battle of the Wilderness. The Union losses had been quickly replaced among the wails in the North about "Butcher" Grant. Abraham Lincoln had at last found a General who knew how to use the overwhelming resources of the Federal Government and he would give him total support.

Another problem facing the Confederates, was a Yankee army advancing up the Shannandoah Valley as far as Lynchburg. Robert E. Lee, ever the gambler, dispatched one of his Army Corps under General Jubal Early to clear the Valley and threaten Washington itself.

The Southerners had devised a daring escape plan for the men at Point Lookout in conjunction with Early's raid if the Confederate cavalry could penetrate that far. The constant fighting in Virginia had produced thousands of new prisoners which made existing prisons extremely overcrowded. A new prison was opened at Elmira, New York, and even before Early's campaign against Washington, preparations were being made to transfer Confederate prisoners to this new camp.

Had the rescue effort been attempted, there would have been great excitement around Point Lookout on the 12th of July, 1864. As it was, preparations were now complete to move the fourth contingent of Confederate prisoners to the new camp at Elmira. This movement of prisoners included the Rebels who had been captured at Cold Harbor. These men had been processed through a battery of Union Army clerks to complete the paperwork for their transfer. They were in a small patch of woods on the west side of the peninsula waiting for a ship to transport them to their new prison.

"I can't say I'm going to be sad to leave this place," Sam rationalized. "It has an unpleasant feeling about it."

"Do you reckon the place we're going to will feel any more hospitable?" Daniel asked. "There is just plain something bad about keeping this many men in any place against their will."

"Where in the heck is Elmira, New York anyhow?" Dougal asked. "Is it cold all the time up there?"

"Naw, it can't be cold all the time," Thomas said. "It has to warm up sometimes for the Yankees to be able to grow food. Hey, look what I found." Thomas picked up a wing feather from a Pileated Woodpecker and stuck the black and white decoration in his hat. "We have these ol'birds at home," he said. "Maybe this will bring me good luck."

"Those things are first cousins to a Lordgod," Sam said. "But they don't fly nearly as fast."

"Yeah," Thomas agreed. "These woodpeckers kinda flap and then coast but a Lordgod flies so fast, dodging round the Cypress trees, you can hear the wind whishing off their wings. If I was a bird I reckon that's the kind I'd want to be."

"You'd be called an Ivorybilled Woodpecker then," Sam added. "I saw a drawing in a book one time and that's the real name for them."

"Lord, Sam," Thomas asked in amazement. "Is there any subject you don't know something about?"

"Yeah, there is," Sam answered. "That would be what's going to happen to us when we reach Elmira."

A large sidewheeler sailed into view and made a wide turn as it positioned itself on the wharf to receive its human cargo. It was the steamer <u>Crescent</u>, which was being used to transport the prisoners on the first leg of the journey to Elmira. All the men of Clingman's Brigade who had been captured on June 1st at Cold Harbor were kept together for administrative purposes. They were among the first to board the ship.

"You Rebs go all the way to the rear," the guard commanded as they climbed down into the hold. It was obvious to the prisoners that they were not the first to travel on this vessel. The dank insides of the ship reeked with the odor of human excrement and vomit.

"Good Lord!" Daniel exclaimed. "I'm going to be sick myself."

"If you're smart, you'll get a position over near one of those portholes," the guard advised. "At least you can get some fresh air once and a while. It's going to take about a day to get to New York City."

"There's a pile of fresh hay over there if you need to go or get seasick," the guard said. "This is the best we can do. **All right!**" he yelled to his fellow guards. "Send that next group down."

More than eight hundred Confederate prisoners were loaded and the <u>Crescent</u> began its passage down past the Virginia Capes into the Atlantic. The ocean was fairly calm on this day but the weather was hot. It took the ship slightly more than a day to make the trip and finally dock at the wharfs of New York. None of the prisoners or guards were sorry to be leaving the vessel.

The Southern soldiers looked in awe at size of New York City. The houses and buildings seemed to go on without end with the trade and commerce showing no signs that there even was a war. After the strangeness of their new surroundings wore off, their conversations returned to their own predicament.

"I hope I never have to travel like that again," Dougal complained. "That's the worst odor I can ever imagine. That smell is almost as bad as dead bodies on a battlefield."

"Maybe we won't," Sam said hopefully. "I don't exactly know where Elmira is located, but I think it's far enough inland so we don't have to cross any more seas."

159

"What's this water here at these wharfs?" Daniel asked. "It looks like we're going to have to cross it before we head west."

"That's the Hudson River," Sam explained. "Across the river is Jersey City. Most of New Jersey lies to the south, but some of it is west of New York City. I'll wager we are going to cross the river next."

"When we were standing guard duty at the docks in Wilmington, I bet none of us ever thought we'd be standing here before the war was over," Thomas said. "I reckon the nicer part of the city lies away from these docks."

"Yeah, and I doubt if our hosts are going to let us see very much of it," Sam concluded. "You know, they had some riots about the draft up here last summer. I read about them in the Charleston papers when we were down at Battery Wagner. A bunch of people got killed and they had to send in regular troops to put it down."

"They found enough from somewhere to send against us," Daniel allowed. "I never had any idea there were so many of them."

The eight-hundred and thirty-three Confederate prisoners were ferried across the Hudson River and loaded aboard a train of the Pennsylvania Railroad which took them to Jersey City. There they spent a restless night.

In the predawn hours of July 15th, Sam sat up from his uncomfortable position, glad it would soon be morning. "You awake, Thomas?" he asked softly.

"I durn shore am. There ain't nothing no harder to sleep on than the floor of a danged ol' boxcar," Thomas complained. "I think I'd rather have a mattress of cotton bolls."

"Aw, quit bellyaching," Sam chided. "I've seen you sleep in some mighty rough places. Remember that time we were coon hunting in the swamp? We lay down on the ground and went to sleep and it turned cold during the night. The next morning our pants legs were froze to the ground."

"Yeah, I do," Thomas answered. "That jug you brought sure made us sleep soundly. I came down with a bad case of the croup because of that too."

"You won't have a jug where we're going and you still

might come down with something," replied Sam. "Maybe you can boil that woodpecker feather in your hat for medicine. You might be glad to have it for dinner if they don't feed us up at Elmira any better than they did at Point Lookout."

The sounds of another train engine approaching in the distance became louder and louder. The lights of the locomotive came into view as a new train pulled into a siding beside the prison train with the puffing and screeching sounds that were becoming so familiar to the Rebels. "All aboard, Johnnies!" the nearest guard announced. "You are going to be guests of the Erie Railroad for the rest of the trip."

This new train was pulled by a wood burning locomotive with a large smokestack that angled upward until it was taller than the cab. The first three cars were boxcars with fifteen more passenger coaches behind. The lead boxcar was to be filled first and was over half full when the prisoners from the 51st began filing into the car.

"Wouldn't you know we'd get put in these dang boxcars," Dougal complained. "Just once I would like to ride in a coach."

The prisoners boarding the car were counted off and by a prearranged count or an arbitrary action, the guard stuck his arm between Thomas and Sam. "All right. Cut the line off here. The rest of you get on the next car," he ordered.

"Hey, let us ride together," Sam asked the guard while motioning toward Thomas.

Before the guard could answer, Thomas said, "That's all right Sam. I won't be very good company anyhow. I'll see you when we get to Hell."

Sometimes, lives are altered and fortunes changed by such seemingly insignificant events as the action of this guard. Sam would have reason to ponder on what had just happened in the months to come.

Sam, Daniel, and Dougal boarded the second box car and settled down in the rear to try to find a comfortable spot. Each box car held as many as thirty-eight Confederate prisoners and the five guards assigned to each car rode on landings between the cars. The coaches held sixty-two prisoners with the last three cars carrying the off duty guards with their

161

equipment. The train was scheduled to leave at 5 AM, but the Sun was making a red glow in the east and there was yet no movement.

One of the Union guards was standing outside the boxcar from Sam's position. He was looking down the track toward the end of the train, obviously interested in what was happening there. "Hey, Yank!" Sam called. "What's the hold up? When are we leavin'?"

"Three of you Johnnies have tried to escape," answered the guard. "That's the holdup. We were supposed to leave at five but this has made us an hour late. They've been caught now and everyone is getting on board."

The guard took his position with the other guard on the platform between the cars. The engine blew its whistle and began its chugging sound. The drive wheels squealed as they spun on the rails before gaining traction. Each car made a crashing sound as the couplers tightened to pull the cars behind and the train began to roll.

Engineer William Ingram and the fireman, Daniel Tuttle, soon got Engine #171 up to speed. It was not long, however, before they saw a red lantern up ahead, indicating they would have to stop. "We've caught the dang drawbridge open," Ingram said with a note of exasperation. "We're already an hour behind time."

The train ground to a stop and waited. Sam took this opportunity to converse with his talkative guard. "What's the matter now, Yank?" he asked.

"We've got a drawbridge open," the Northerner answered. "It don't seem that you Johnnies are meant to get to Elmira."

"What's the camp like at Elmira?" Sam asked. "Have you been there?"

"Sure have." the guard replied. "We took the first load of prisoners up there. There are barracks for everybody, at least for now. Not like Point Lookout where some of you had to stay in tents. It's going to be a darned sight colder in the wintertime."

"I can't say I'm looking forward to that," Sam stated. "You say you've been there before? Is this what you do-Guard

162

prisoners?"

"I'm part of what's called the Veteran Reserve Corps," the guard answered. "We served out enlistments under McClellan and most got wounded or have some problem that keeps them from being front line soldiers. We do things like this to free up men for front line duty. You probably have something like it in your army."

"Hell no we don't!" Sam exclaimed. "Back home, if you got a trigger finger, you're at the front totin a rifle."

The whistle of the locomotive sounded to signal the bridge was finally closed. The fireman had the firebox loaded with three foot lengths of cordwood to maintain a running speed of twenty to twenty-five miles per hour. The train moved out and the engineer was no doubt hoping to make up some of the time.

They were four hours behind schedule when the train pulled into the town of Port Jervis, New York, to take on water and replenish the supply of wood.

"What's all those people standing around for?" Daniel asked. "Is there a parade or something?"

"I don't know," said Dougal. "I just can't get over the number of able bodied men in the crowd who ain't in the Yankee Army. Everybody from home between seventeen and fifty is either fightin somewhere or deserted."

"Hey, Yank," Sam called out again. "What's the special occasion to draw such a crowd?"

"Haven't you figured it out?" the guard replied. "They've come to see you." It was true. The crowd had gathered to see these grizzled veterans from Lee's Army. The strangeness of the situation caused some comment from the prisoners.

"I guess I should've shaved," Sam retorted.

"I'd rather you'd a bathed," Daniel joked.

"Just how was I supposed to do that?" Sam asked. "I can't remember the last time I had me a tub of hot water and some lye soap."

"Is that why some of the ladies in the crowd are holding their hankys to their noses?" Dougal reasoned. "That sure is a pretty girl over there. I wonder what she's got in that

163

basket?"

The shriek of the train whistle warned that the stop was over and the locomotive began its slow acceleration, accompanied by loud chugs and puffs of smoke. Engineer Ingram hoped to make up for some of the lost time.

Soon the train had passed through New Jersey and New York and into the mountains of Eastern Pennsylvania. Many of the Southerners, from the eastern parts of the Carolinas and Georgia, had never seen mountains before. They amused themselves by admiring the beauty of the area and wondering what people did for a living in such unfarmable looking country

Thomas had ridden the first leg of the trip in thoughtful solitude. He was among friends as here were several members of Company I who were with him. Nathan Deaver had come from Bladen county to serve with friends in the 51st. Bill Nunnery, Travers Bryant, John Carroll, had served with him since the beginning along with John Davis who was just a boy. Malcolm McCorquadale and Duncan Munroe were descendants of the Scottish Highlanders who had flooded onto the Cape Fear Valley during the previous century. They had families back at home. They rode without speaking as the heat of the July day increased.

The next leg of the trip, twenty-three miles long, ran from Port Jervis to Lackawaxen, Pennsylvania. This single track had been laid along the rocky hills and curves beside the Delaware River, built only with great effort and cost. After an hour of traveling through this rough terrain, the village of Shohola, Pennsylvania was reached. As the troop train sped past, the telegraph operator telegraphed its passing to the agent at Lackawaxen Station.

Thomas' thoughts were hundreds of miles away with his family at that time. He was thinking about the year he spent with his new bride and the son he had never seen. He was thinking about all the fun things they would do after the war to make up for the two years that had been lost. Unfortunately, all the pleasant thoughts and dreams in the world can not change fate. There was no way of knowing that for Thomas and more than sixty other soldiers of the blue and the gray aboard this ill-fated train, death was approaching from the north at twelve miles per hour.

Four miles north of Shohola, the Hawley branch of the railroad merges with the main line at Lackawaxen Junction. Down this branch was sent the coal from the Pennsylvania mines for the hungry furnaces of New York City. The telegraph operator there was a man named Duff Kent. He had a severe drinking problem and had come to work that day with a "bad head" from the night before. He had been alerted that a special train was to be expected that day and it was his responsibility to hold all east bound trains until it had passed. The last train to pass his station had been flying flags that signaled an "extra" train was to follow. He had been heard wondering aloud why the troop train had not passed.

Somewhere around 2:30 PM, a coal train of fifty loaded cars screeched to a stop at Lackawaxen. The engineer was Sam Hoitt who, along with brakeman G.M. Boydon and fireman Philo Prentiss, worked the cab. The conductor, John Martin, jumped down from the caboose and walked to the station as the brakeman joined him. They found Duff Kent slouched over at his desk as the telegraph chattered away.

"Is the track clear to Shohola?" Martin asked.

"The track is clear," Kent replied. "All scheduled trains have passed."

Martin returned to the cab to inform the engineer that the track was clear as the brakeman walked up the track to open the main switch. The train swung onto the main track as Martin closed the switch behind his caboose. He made a signal to the engineer and climbed back on as the train picked up speed and was soon lost from sight.

Almost immediately, the telegraph began clacking with the message from the Shohola operator that the troop train had passed that station. At that point it became obvious, even to the alcohol muddled mind of Duff Kent, that he had just sealed the doom of the two trains.

The troop train was passing through an area called King and Fuller's Cut which had been blasted out of solid rock and ran through several blind curves. Only Engineer Hoitt of the coal train saw the approaching disaster and he only had time to jump as his engine headed toward a collision with the troop train.

Suddenly there was a terrific crash and all the men inside the cars were hurled forward without warning. Then came the secondary effects of the crash as the multiplied energy of the seventeen cars in the rear caused the sides and top of the car Sam was riding in to simply explode. The front of the trailing boxcar knifed into its rear and sent wooden and metal fragments slashing into the group of helpless prisoners. Something passed inches above Sam's head as he was being thrown to the floor and neatly decapitated an unfortunate man near him. Then, for a moment, all was quiet.

The brief calm was broken by the horrible screams and groans of the injured. There were men killed and hurt in all cars of the train, but it was much worse in the front. Captain Morris Church, the commander of the train, quickly reacted and threw a ring of guards around the scene. Despite his efforts, five prisoners escaped. Most of the Rebels entertained no such thoughts as they began trying to help their friends.

Sam was unhurt in the crash and quickly began looking to help others. "Dougal, are you all right?" he asked when he saw his friend lying with a group of injured.

"I think so, Sam," came his reply. "I'm a mite dazed. I must have hit my head on something."

Sam had been chatting with the talkative guard who was stationed just outside the boxcar on the landing. It was only then that Sam noticed the Union guard was still at his station, but a large pointed timber from the third car had been driven through his chest. He still clutched his rifle amid the debris, bleeding profusely from his mouth and gushing blood from the hole in his chest.

"Help me, Sam!" came a plea from Daniel. "I'm over here."

Sam cleared his way through the rubble and found Daniel with his right leg pinned down by debris. Dougal's head had now cleared and the two began digging out their friend.

"Can you move your leg at all?" Dougal asked.

"No, it hurts really bad," Daniel answered. "I'm afraid

it's broken."

"Get that piece of wood over there!" Sam commanded. "We can use it as a lever"

Several more men were now trying to dig their comrades out from the wreckage. Together they were able to free Daniel's leg. As they carried him down from the remains of the boxcar and laid him on the ground, it was obvious from the odd angle of his right foot that his leg had been crushed right above the ankle.

Suddenly, Sam remembered Thomas and for the first time looked at the front boxcar. This car had born the weight of the entire train as it crashed and the force of the impact had crushed the car into a mass not more that six feet wide. The tender of the locomotive had been forced upward and it fell back down on the crushed boxcar. One man had been thrown free, but for the others, all were dead. The effect of the crash on the thirty-six bodies inside the boxcar was similar to that on apples in a cider press. A huge amount of blood was pouring from the car and was running in a stream down the slope toward the Delaware River. From within, among the mostly unidentifiable remains of what had once been men, Sam could see a crushed, bloody hat with a woodpecker's feather still stuck through the side. He staggered back away from the scene and tried his best to wretch up what was left of the last meal he had eaten.

Dougal came over to where Sam was standing and together they stared in amazement at the wreckage of the first car. "Oh, God, not Thomas!" Dougal exclaimed.

"Not just Thomas, but three dozen more. About ten of the men are from around home," Sam said. "Most all of them have families."

When he finished the statement, Sam hung his head and began to cry. The hot, stinging tears of grief flowed profusely as he thought of his dead friend and their comrades and the effect this tragedy would have on their families back at home. As the initial shock of the disaster wore off, he began to notice the extent of the wreckage.

The fronts of the two engines had been raised high in the air by the impact and there they remained, like two large animals locked in combat. Large floor timbers had been snapped like twigs. The driving rods were bent like wire and the wheels and axles lay broken.

The wood from the tender of the locomotive had been thrown forward, killing Tuttle and pinning the unfortunate Ingram against the boiler where the escaping steam from a split plate slowly scalded him to death. Boyden and Printiss on board the coal train were killed in much the same way.

Sam's grief turned suddenly to rage as he shouted to a Union Sergeant nearby, "Don't you bastards know how to run a railroad? Are you still trying to kill us after we surrendered?"

"Easy, Reb," the Yankee replied in a calm voice. "We lost some men too. We don't know who's responsible for this, but we'll find out. You're a sergeant, so how bout getting some of your men to help look through the wreckage. We can work together and maybe save some lives."

"I guess that really is what needs to be done now, Yank," Sam answered. He saw a group of men from the 51st who had just laid some of their injured friends beside the track. "All right, boys," he ordered. "Let's work together and get this boxcar torn apart. There might be some more injured in there."

Those who had been injured by the wreck were found by their cries for help. As the soldiers tore the mangled wreckage apart, they uncovered more of the dead. The condition of the bodies was unimaginable. Most had been crushed, others mangled and impaled. Limbs had been severed and some bodies were decapitated.

The sound of the collision had been heard by the local people who flocked to the scene. John Vogt, a farmer whose fields lay beside the Erie track, was the first to arrive. As soon as he saw the extent of the tragedy, he and his family began cutting up sheets and blankets from their home to be used for bandages.

Other people from nearby began to arrive in small groups. They joined in with the Union guards and Confederate prisoners to help pull the injured from the wreckage in what must have been one of the most striking examples of cooperation between the two sides which occurred during the war.

Word of the wreck had been signaled all down the track and the Erie Railroad dispatched two relief trains from Port Jervis carrying railroad workers and doctors. These men were not prepared for the scene of carnage which greeted them at the wreck site. A group of Confederate dead, many crushed beyond recognition, lay on an embankment near the wrecked engines. A second group lay beside the wrecked cars. Many of the more gruesomely mangled bodies had been covered with grass and leaves to conceal the horrible sight. The dead Union soldiers of the Veteran Reserve Corps were wrapped in their blankets and laid at the edge of a field of rye beside the track. These unlucky men had been riding on platforms between the cars and all on duty had been killed or injured.

The soldiers had done all they could with their bare hands to free the dead and injured from the wreckage. A wrecking crane, sent up with the relief train, now began to pull the tangled mass apart.

"Nothing more we can do here, Reb," the Union Sergeant said to Sam. "It's time for the crane to do the heavy lifting. There are some of the local people coming with their wagons to move the injured. I could use a half-dozen of your men to help if you would promise me they wouldn't try to escape."

"All right," Sam agreed. "One of my best friends is hurt and I want to make sure he is taken care of." Sam walked over to where Dougal was standing beside the injured Daniel Graham.

"Dougal, that Yankee sergeant needs some help carrying the injured," Sam said. "I promised him we wouldn't try to escape. We need about four others who aren't hurt."

"Four of the Tew boys are over there," Dougal suggested. "Six of them got captured, but Daniel Tew has some ribs broke or something. It hurts him to breath. John thinks his left leg is broken. Alexander and Jack are all right. James Martin and Lemick were sort of dazed for a while, but they seem well now."

Sam walked over to the Tews and asked their help. "Sure, Sam," Jack answered. "We got some hurt kin over here we want to see get fixed up. Just tell us what to do."

169

The work of moving the wounded began and many were taken to the Shohola Glen Hotel where they were laid on the porch to await medical assistance. Others were taken to the railroad station. There were now six doctors on the scene treating anyone who needed it regardless of the uniform he wore.   The people from the Shohola area and Barryville, New York across the river, flocked to the wreck to offer assistance to the injured. The ladies of both villages worked round the clock in shifts to feed and help care for the casualties of both armies. They brought coffee and tea, pies, bread, crackers, jams, cold milk and soup, items the famished Rebels had not seen for some time. They not only fed the injured, but the other prisoners and guards as well.

Sam and Dougal sat with the Union Sergeant on the steps of the hotel porch drinking some cold milk. "This is the best milk I can ever remember drinking," Dougal announced.

"I can't rightly remember the last time I had milk of any kind," Sam added. "These folks are being mighty nice to us."

"Were you Rebs all captured together?" the Yankee asked. "What state are you from?"

"Yeah," said Sam, answering the first question. "There were about three dozen of us captured at Cold Harbor. We are from the 51st North Carolina and I can only guess how many of us are left after this train wreck."

"Hey, I spent some garrison time at New Bern," the Yankee said. "Right before I left, you Rebs sent an army against us but never did mount a full scale attack. You probably could have taken the place if you had."

"Yeah," Dougal replied. "That was Pickett and we was there too. It was in January so we missed the skeeters."

"You sure did," the sergeant agreed. "We got some new replacements in one day and sent them out near a swamp for picket duty. We told them the lightning bugs were skeeters with lanterns lookin for 'em."

"That's a funny story," Sam said. "I reckon we'll have a good laugh about it one day when we tell it. We just ain't too jolly after what happened today."

"That is a fact," said the Yankee. "Our friends died so far from the battlefields. It just don't make any sense at all."

He picked up a piece of wood from the ground, reached in his pocket and pulled out his whittling knife. He began to shape the piece of wood with short strokes of the knife. The men sat on the porch not saying much more of anything as the work on the railroad continued. The wrecking crane finished freeing the bodies. The heat of the mid July day made it necessary to begin immediate burial of the bodies. The railroad men, assisted by the Rebel prisoners, began digging a trench seventy-six feet long, eight feet wide and six feet deep. As night fell, the flames from huge bonfires, fed by wood from the wreckage, illuminated the eerie scene as rough coffins were fashioned out of other wood from the smashed cars.

In the light of the dancing shadows from the fires, the Confederates were buried four to a box with their names and units written on a piece of paper and pinned to their shirts. Shortly before midnight, a train arrived bringing individual coffins for the dead Union guards. Before the trench was covered, four more Southerners died and were buried beside their comrades.

Sam walked over to where Daniel was lying and said, "How're you feeling, boy?"

"Not too good, Sam," Daniel replied. "One of those Yankee doctors says they can't fix my leg. They have to at least take off my foot. Sam, I ain't going to be worth a damn for plowin."

"When are they going to do it?" Sam inquired.

"They say they want to wait till they get us to Elmira." Daniel answered. "One of the doctors there will do it."

"Maybe they will decide against it when you get there," Sam said, trying to be encouraging.

"Something has to be done," Daniel complained. "It hurts awful bad. Sam, did Thomas get killed? I saw the car he was in was smashed right bad."

"Not only Thomas, but about a dozen others from the 51st," Sam answered. "We got a lot of injured from our regiment."

"Lordy, Sam!" Daniel exclaimed. "This wreck has been worse for us than a big battle. Our regiment didn't lose that many killed at Battery Wagner or Cold Harbor."

"Maybe in our charge at Drewry's Bluff we had that many casualties," Sam added. "I reckon it can't be helped now. They 'bout have the track cleared so I reckon they'll move us out in the morning. See if you can get some rest."

With these words of encouragement, Sam walked back to the hotel and lay down on the porch with Dougal and the Tews. Several of the local shop keepers had stripped their stores of food, sheets and blankets. They helped the injured all through the night.

The track was cleared during the night and at 9:00 AM on the 16th, the first train since the wreck passed through. Duff Kent might possibly have been a passenger since it was reported that he boarded a west bound train and was never heard from again.

Another train pulled into the Shohola station later that morning, equipped to carry the survivors the rest of the way to Elmira. "The injured guards are going to ride in the first two boxcars, Reb," the Yankee Sergeant instructed Sam and his men. "Your hurt people will use the next four cars. There is hay on the floors to make it a little more comfortable. Let's start getting them aboard."

After the first two cars were filled, Sam and Dougal lifted Daniel's stretcher aboard the third car. "This is all we can do for you, Daniel," Sam said as he patted his friend's head to test for fever. "We'll be there to unload you at Elmira."

"Thank you and Dougal for all you've done," Daniel answered. "Maybe the Yankees can get us there without another wreck."

As Sam and his men boarded their car, Dougal asked, "What are you looking so worried about, Sam? Is it Daniel?"

"Yeah, it is," Sam answered. "He feels hot to the touch. I don't know what they can do for him at the prison".

At 11:00 AM, the new prison train left Shohola station bound for Elmira. More than sixty of the men who had left Point Lookout lay buried at Shohola. Captain Church, the train commander, wrote in his report: "Many of the prisoners killed were so disfigured that it was impossible to recognize them, and five escaping whose names are unknown, I am unable to give a correct list of killed."

The rest of the journey was uneventful and Elmira was reached around 9:30 PM. By the light of flickering torches, the prison train was unloaded and the unhappy procession of prisoners and their injured made its way up West Water Street to become residents of Elmira Prison. Of those who entered its gates, more than twenty-four per cent would never leave. Before a year had gone by, there would be more than three thousand graves in the cemetery. One third of the dead would be Confederate soldiers from North Carolina.

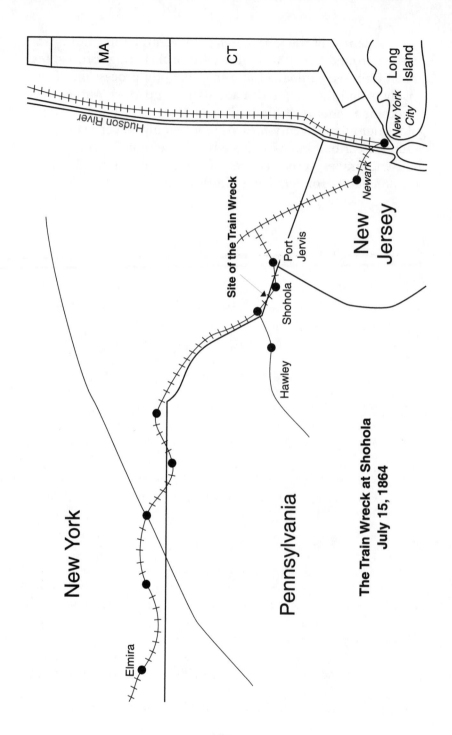

MA

CT

Long Island

New York City

Hudson River

Site of the Train Wreck

Newark

Port Jervis

Shohola

New Jersey

Hawley

New York

Pennsylvania

Elmira

The Train Wreck at Shohola
July 15, 1864

Chapter 11
Elmira

As the doors of Elmira Prison closed behind Sam and his friends, they entered a world completely foreign to the psyche of any independent person, whether Southerner or Northerner. There would be terrible times ahead and almost nothing a man could do to improve his individual situation.

Sam and Dougal carried Daniel over to the building which served as the hospital. "They'll take better care of you than we can," Sam said encouragingly. "Maybe these doctors can save that foot."

"The way it feels now, I don't think there's much hope," Daniel replied. "You boys come to see me if you can."

After all the injured were taken to the hospital, the prisoners were fed and then assigned to their barracks. These were a row of rectangular buildings which had previously been used to house Union soldiers. The first Rebel arrivals were fortunate enough to have rough wooden beds wide enough for two men and three tiers high. As Sam lay down to rest after the day's ordeal, he remembered that the first thing he would need to do in the morning would be to write home. He thought of the events of the past two days and how much he already missed Thomas.

At this point his emotions took over and he spent the remaining hours before dawn taking stock of his environment and remembering happier times as the hopelessness of his situation began to really sink in. He felt almost guilty for having survived the train wreck that had killed so many of his friends. If he had only insisted, would the Yankee guard have let Thomas ride in his box car? If he had, perhaps Thomas would have survived.

Early that next morning, after the final paperwork was completed on the prisoner's transfer, Sam was able to find some writing paper and began to write to Betty the account of the tragedy he had experienced in the last two days. He began:

"My Dearest Wife, It is my sad duty to take pen in hand to tell you of a tragic event which occurred on the 15th instant. It resulted in the death of my dear friend Thomas who I already miss very much. It is unfortunate that the heavy burden of telling Susan her husband will not be coming home has fallen upon your shoulders..."

Sam wrote three pages, telling in detail the death of Thomas and the final resting place of his friend. He tried to tell all the details that Susan could possibly want to know in order to make his wife's task as easy as possible.

Betty had become a good farm manager as the shortages caused by the Union Navy's blockade became more severe. The growing of cotton and tobacco had been replaced by food production. The labor needed to grow these crops was better used to help feed the armies and keep one alive at home. The losses of many of the more productive food producing areas had caused the Confederate Government to require some taxes paid by food to keep the soldiers in the field. The shortage of salt meant that not as much pork could be cured in the smokehouses to eat in the summer. There was much work for everyone in the household and Betty and Susan took their turns hoeing the crops and caring for the children. About three o'clock each day, whoever was in the field would come up to the house to get a cool drink of the water that tasted so good from the well in front of the house.

Every other day, the mail rider would make his rounds and bring the letters and newspapers, then the two friends would take a work break and discuss the news from the papers. In late July, there had been a disturbing article in The Fayetteville Observer concerning a wreck of a train of Confederate prisoners. Betty and Susan had been anxious about the tragedy but had decided they could not spend a lot of time worrying about it. About a week later, Betty had received the mail and sat down in her rocking chair on the front porch. As she sifted the paper she noticed a letter with a U.S. stamp. Her heart leaped when she recognized Sam's handwriting on the envelope and just as suddenly, a chill went up her back as she noticed something very disturbing. The letter was edged in black because it told of a death. Betty ripped open the letter and began reading rapidly. Sam's letter told of the wreck at Shohola and the many deaths of men from between the rivers. When she read that Thomas had been killed, her eyes quickly filled with tears and she lifted up her apron and cried into it.

Betty dreaded the arrival of Susan from the field and wondered how she would break the terrible news to her. She sat in her rocking chair on the front porch, trying to read the paper as Susan walked up and let the bucket down into the well by its chain pulley. The bucket made a distant splashing sound as it fell in the water and Susan pulled up her water with the squeaking chain and wheel. She sat the bucket on the edge of the well and dipped the community gourd into the water, pulled it up to her lips and began to drink deeply. She poured some of the cooling liquid over her wrists, then pulled a red bandanna from around her neck and wet it with the remaining water and washed her face.

Susan walked up on the porch, sat down in her rocking chair next to Betty and asked, "What's the news today? I hope it's good for a change."

"Susan," Betty said with a tearful voice." There is no easy way to tell you this."

Susan's face grew suddenly apprehensive as Betty continued. "You remember the train wreck we read about with the prisoners from Point Lookout? Our men and lots of others from around here were on it and many were killed."

"Thomas?" Susan asked with a trembling voice.

Betty couldn't bring herself to speak so she held up the black edged letter from Sam. Susan understood at once and buried her face in her hands and began to cry. Betty reached over and put her arms around her friend and helped her cry for several minutes.

Susan took the red bandanna and began wiping her eyes as Betty read Sam's letter to her. After the letter was read, Susan spoke. "I have been afraid something might have happened to Thomas," she said. "You see, even before we heard about the train wreck I've had this strange feeling. I couldn't figure out what it all meant. Now I think I know."

"Maybe you just need some rest," Betty offered. "We've all had about as much as we can bear."

"No," Susan objected. "I need to be alone and sort things out. If you will take care of little Thomas, I'll spend the night over at my house. I can't eat any supper."

"All right," Betty agreed. "I'll load up the double-barrel with buckshot. You don't know who you have coming down that road anymore."

Susan walked inside the house and looked at her year old son asleep in his cradle. She bent down and kissed him on his sweaty forehead. She brushed back the sweat matted red hair from around his ears and thought how much he favored his father. She gathered two sheets and a pillow to take with her and with the loaded shotgun walked down the steps of the porch and down the path through the swamp which led to her house. She was so engrossed with her thoughts that she paid no attention to the buzzing insects and the chattering squirrels in the tall cypress and gum trees.

Susan had been making periodic visits to the house to keep it clean and repaired for the day her husband would return. She opened the door and walked inside, noticing that the hinge squeaked a bit. She laid the gun on the table and lit the oil lamp which was in the same place she had left it. She shook her mattress to make sure there were no mice or black-snakes inside and made the bed. She walked over to the rocking chair, sat down and began rocking as the sun began to set and shadows lengthened.

Susan liked to be alone during times like these when she wanted to think clearly. Since today's mail had brought the most tragic and shocking news of her life, she was emotionally and physically exhausted. She stretched her arms and leaned back in the rocking chair and drifted off to sleep amid the serenade of the night time insects.

It must have been three hours later when Susan awoke. It seemed that in her sleep, she had subconsciously fretted over every disadvantage she had experienced in life. She had not been born into any privileged class that had money and education and had never known anything but hard work and sacrifice, but it had seemed that one day she and Thomas would accumulate more than the necessities of everyday life. The happiest year of her life had been the one they spent together in this little house. Now even the possibility of any more had been taken from her. "Why?" she felt like screaming at the top of her lungs.

She got up from her chair and walked over to the door, unlatched it and stepped outside. The sporadic buzzing of the katydids made a background for all sorts of night sounds. The bullfrogs in the swamp added their bass notes to the concert and far away, a screech owl made its ghostly wail. Susan looked up the path which led to the main road and remembered the day Thomas had kissed her and walked down that road to add his efforts to the War for Southern Independence. She had always thought of him as being so strong and indestructible and although she was fully aware of the dangers of war, she had always expected to see him walk back up that same road, embrace her with his burly arms and kiss her again as he had on that day which now seemed so long ago.

Susan walked back in the house and latched the door, adjusted the wick of the oil lamp and sat down in her rocking chair. She leaned back and closed her eyes as the hot, stinging tears of grief ran down her cheeks.

Two hours before dawn, Susan again awoke. It took her a moment to remember where she was and to recall her sadness which would not go away. This time, however, her bitterness was gone and she sensed a feeling of calmness and love. She looked around to make sure there was no one else in the room when suddenly she had a comforting thought. Some people live and die without leaving behind any evidence they had ever existed. Thomas had left a son and a house he had built. He had touched the lives of others in his thirty-four years and these people were better off for having known him. If the son of Thomas grew to manhood and fathered other sons, then

Thomas would never completely die. His values and ideals would live on for generations and even centuries. Many men might have lived for twice as long and not accomplished half as much.

It all suddenly became clear to her in this house where she had known such happiness and felt such love. That she was now a widow and there was not any more use in living in the temporary quarters at Sam and Betty's house. She would sleep till sunrise and then move back to this house where she could rear her young son among all her memories. Susan walked over to the bed and without undressing, lay down on the bed and pulled a sheet over herself and quickly fell into a deep restful sleep.

The prison camp at Elmira was located on a bend in the Chemung River and surrounded by a high, nearly rectangular board enclosure. Union sentinels patrolled from a walkway at the top, ready to shoot down any prisoner who ventured past the twenty foot "deadline" inside the walls. The original barracks occupied the center of the camp and a long narrow pond lay on the south side of the camp nearest the Chemung River. On the west side were six barracks which were increasingly to be used as hospitals. The injured from the wreck at Shohola were housed in the second building and once a day, visitors were allowed. Sam and Dougal took turns visiting their friend after the amputation of his foot and saw his strength slowly leave between visits. It had been more than a week since the train wreck and there was not much to talk about when Sam visited Daniel.

"Sam, you boys better do a heap of praying for me," Daniel requested. "I might not be able to make it much longer."

"Aw, shoot, Daniel," Sam would counter, "you're strong as an ox and will certainly lick this thing." That was the gist of the conversation and Sam had left, not believing the encouragement he had given his friend.

On July 24th when Sam made his visit, Daniel's bed was empty. "What happened to the man who was in this bed?" Sam asked to an orderly.

"He's over at the dead house," the orderly answered matter of factly. "He left us last night."

Sam turned around without responding and walked out into the bright sunshine of the summer morning. He pulled his hat down over his face to block the glare as he walked across the camp back to his barracks, stunned by the loss of yet another friend. He told Dougal about Daniel's death and the word quickly spread among the rest of his former comrades. Daniel would be one of three soldiers injured in the wreck at Shohola to die at Elmira. Sam sat down with his pen and paper and began to write a letter to Flora Graham who was now the newest widow in the land between the rivers.

The Confederate prisoners who died at Elmira Prison were buried at Woodlawn Cemetery under the care of the sexton, John Jones. Mr. Jones was an escaped slave who kept a meticulous record of the final resting places of the Southern soldiers he buried. Each grave was individually marked in contrast to many of the other prison camps during this war.

After Daniel's death, so close to the loss of Thomas, the hopeless realities of the prison environment began to have an effect on Sam. He had always been an independent, take charge sort of person who did not wait to be attacked by problems. He always met them head on with well planned solutions. For the first time in his life, he was unable to make any changes for the better in the situation in which he found himself. There was war in Virginia and his family back home had needs and there wasn't one dad-blasted thing he could do to effect either one.

The Confederate prisoners were fed in a mess hall twice a day where they received a small slice of bread and a piece of salt pork or pickled beef in the morning. The afternoon fare was another piece of bread and a tin of soup from the boiled beef. There were some camps which didn't feed the prisoners this well; however, almost every man who was there would, years later, complain of the constant hunger. As Sam's spirits continued to sink, he found that his appetite was satisfied by these near starvation rations.

He would walk from one end of the barracks to the other as if he were going somewhere. Then he would stop and dwell on the hopelessness of his situation and walk back to the other side from where he had begun. As night fell, Sam looked

181

forward to sleep when his mind would temporarily be free and he could rest. He usually would be able to fall asleep for an hour, then wake up and worry till dawn.

As July faded into August, Sam's friends could see the change which was occurring. One night before bedtime, Dougal felt the need to confront Sam. "You need to grab hold of yourself, Sam," he admonished. "This situation we're in ain't going to last forever. I can tell you are starting to go downhill."

"How can I stop being concerned?" Sam answered. "I'll confess that I'm worrying about a lot of things I can't control. How can I stop?"

"Do you remember pickin' cotton in September when it was still hot?" Dougal asked. "Your back's about to break and you can't see the end of the row."

"Sure," Sam answered. "Anyone who has done that will never forget it."

"Well," Dougal continued, "the way I got through that was telling myself I didn't have to pick but one more stalk and after I got done with that stalk, I told myself I didn't have to pick any more but the next one. After a time, I was at the end of the row and could rest."

"So you lied to yourself?" Sam countered. "How does that help us now?" Sam asked.

"No, you don't understand," Dougal continued. "It's more like making a promise to yourself. I'm going to live one day at a time and when I get out of here, I'm going to go down to Florence and marry the prettiest girl I ever saw."

"What if she ain't there? What if she didn't wait for you?" Sam questioned.

"She has to be waitin. That has to be part of the plan," Dougal shot back. "You see, Sam, there has to be an end of the row. There has to be some shade and some cool water to drink, waitin' for you. I have Sarah as a reward for me and I ain't going to let nothing get in my way. As much as you have to live for, Sam, it would be a shame for you to curl up here and die."

Dougal was right. Sam was suffering from a type of mental illness doctors in the future would come to know as "depression," an illness which can kill just as surely as any microbe caused disease.

One night after the lamps had been put out and the prisoners were sleeping, Sam remembered the God he had worshiped as a boy, but recently had only talked to him when bullets were flying. "Lord," he prayed, "I can't handle this imprisonment and I need your help. I turn my relief from this situation over to you. Thy will be done."

Sam drifted off to a restless state of consciousness where he was almost asleep, but not quite. He was transported in his mind back to the banks of South River and was walking past the huge cypress trees and moss draped oaks, always being aware that he was in cottonmouth country. The restfulness of his thoughts of this scene helped him drift off into the deep sleep he so desperately needed.

As he continued his walk down the river, he came to a bend and saw a man sitting on a log beside the water. Thinking this was a fisherman, Sam made ready to give the salutation all Southerners give to fellow fishermen: "Ketchenany?"

Before he could make a sound, he stopped cold, unable to utter a word. The man sitting on the log and whittling on a piece of wood was Thomas. "What's the matter with you, boy?" Thomas asked. "You got to get a hold of yourself."

Sam opened his mouth to speak, but he was interrupted by the figure before him. "Now just hold on, Sam." Thomas said with authority. "Most of the time you have things pretty well figured out, but this time you ain't, so just listen. You can't go on feelin sorry for yourself like this."

"But you're supposed to be...." Sam attempted to say.

"Don't you worry none about me," Thomas admonished. "I'm all right. Things happen a certain way for a reason. If you ever get to thinking nobody's in charge - well, somebody is. That's all I'm going to say about that."

Sam was spellbound as he waited for his friend to continue. "You got to get yourself a plan, Sam. You can still get out of this place alive if you work at it. You can't go on moping around like the dead lice is falling off of you. You need to lick this thing and you can't wait much longer to start. One other thing," Thomas continued. "Take care of my family when you can. They're liable to have it tough for a while without me."

Suddenly, Sam woke up with a start and sat up in his bunk. It took him a while to remember where he was because his dream had been so real. He could see out the window where the blue coated guards were walking their sentry duty on the walls. As reality came back to him, he marveled at what had just occurred. Had he just had a supernatural experience? Had his dear friend just spoken to him from beyond the grave? One thing was for certain, this had happened to him for a reason and he had to act on it. A peaceful feeling of relief swept over his fatigued body. He would begin planning his escape in the morning. He lay back down and slept soundly till dawn for the first time since he had arrived at this place.

Sam awoke to the new day with an enthusiasm which was immediately noticeable to Dougal. He even enjoyed the food in the morning feeding and for the first time in many days wanted more. "Let's walk out to Foster's Pond and see what's happening," Dougal invited Sam after the meal.

"What in the world could be happening out there?" Sam inquired.

Dougal laughed and replied, "You've been mopin around this place now for weeks and ain't seen half of what's going on. Man, there's some of the biggest rats out there you ever saw. Some of the men are catching and eating them."

"Durn!" Sam said emphatically. "I hope I never get that hungry."

"I saw one of them dressed the day before yesterday and it don't look no different from a squirrel," Dougal said. "We're liable to get pretty hungry before we leave this place."

The two men walked down to the long, narrow, stagnant pond which lay parallel the river on the camp's west side. There were several Rebels who were moving with long, slow steps beside the water like a hunting heron. They were stalking the rats. Sam watched with a bit of disgust. There was another figure who interested him more that the others. He wore no shoes and had waded out in the waters of the lake and was shaking his right leg ever so slightly. After the man had walked out of the water and made his way back toward the compound, Sam walked over to where the man had been and looked down in the dirty water. There was some dirt on the bottom which seemed foreign by its color. There were also several rocks which had been scattered carefully. Sam immediately came to a conclusion which gave him more hope than he had ever had about his situation here. The man was involved in digging a tunnel and was disposing of the dirt and rocks.

"Dougal!" Sam called. "Come over here."

"What is it, Sam?" Dougal asked as he approached. "You sick or something?"

"No, I've never felt better because of what I just saw," answered Sam. "Do you still see that man who was just here?"

"Yeah," Dougal replied. "That's him going yonder with the tan colored hat and no shoes."

"Well, you follow him and see where he goes," Sam instructed. "I'll go around the other side of the camp and meet him from the other direction in case you lose him."

"What's this all about, Sam?" Dougal asked. "What are we following him for?"

"He was dropping rocks and dirt into the pond," Sam replied. "He's digging a tunnel. I want to see if we can get in. Be sure not to let him know we are following him and for heavens sake, don't let anybody else know."

There were many prisoners walking around the camp after the morning meal and the chance of losing sight of the man was very real. The mess halls lay between Foster's Pond and the maze of barracks and tents which housed the prisoners. Dougal tried to catch up with the man but soon lost sight of his tan hat among the many others milling around in the camp. It was purely by chance that Sam caught sight of the man going in the fifth barracks from the end on the second row.

About an hour later, Dougal found Sam standing near the spot where he had last seen their quarry. "I lost him, Sam," Dougal admitted.

"Be quiet!" Sam ordered. "I know where he went. We've got to be ready when he comes out again."

In spite of their vigilance, the two friends didn't see the man   for several days. They did notice something consistent each day after breakfast. There would always be a different man without shoes wading in Foster's Pond among the rat

185

hunters. After he would leave, there would be a fresh deposit of stones and gravel.

There would periodically be the arrival of new prisoners from Point Lookout. Since no newspapers were allowed in the camp, the news of Lee's Army was always welcome, even if it was several weeks old. As the new arrivals were turned loose in the camp, the inmates who had arrived would seek out men from their old brigades and divisions.

One day, as a new group arrived, Sam yelled out, "Any of you men from Clingman's Brigade?"

"Yeah, I am," said a lanky, bearded soldier. "I'm Matthew Spence, 31st North Carolina."

"Hey," Sam greeted. "I'm Sam Morgan, 51st North Carolina and this here's Dougal McKay. When did you get captured? What's the army doing?"

"I got captured right after Cold Harbor," Spence began. "We were being run to death, trying to beat Grant to Petersburg so I know it's true that there's fightin down there."

"Yeah," Sam agreed. "That's the last we heard too. You got captured soon after we did. They got us at Cold Harbor."

"Not much has changed," Spence continued. "There's still a lot of fightin and dyin going on."

"There's some dying going on here too, Spence," Sam cautioned. "Take care of yourself."

The new arrivals moved out to get their assigned lodging and Sam and Dougal were left not knowing a whole lot more about the fighting in Virginia. They would, however, see Matthew Spence again.

One day after the morning meal, Sam was again walking near Foster's Pond when he saw the man with the tan hat, wading in the water. It had been a week since this particular man had been spotted, but each day a different man deposited rocks and dirt into the pond. This must be a sizable operation. Sam took off his shoes and walked out behind the person in the water. The man stopped his movements and stood motionless.

"Don't turn around," Sam ordered. "I know what you are doing, but I am your friend. I will not betray you and I don't even want to know your face. I want to join you, me and a friend. If you can use us, meet me under barracks number three, on the first row, at the northwest corner at eleven o'clock tonight." Sam turned and started walking out of the water to where his shoes lay.

"Wait," the man said. "You will know me by this."

Sam turned around and looked at the man who still faced the water. He had extended his left arm and Sam saw that he was missing his little finger.

As he walked back toward the prison compound, Sam saw his surroundings in a different perspective. There were huddles of men standing around doing nothing, with no hope and filled with aimless despair. He had made the first move in getting away from this unhappy place. It was like Thomas had told him in his dream, he needed to get himself a plan. Now he had one and he would defeat the circumstances which now held him in a viselike grip. Sam was beginning to feel good about himself once again. He now prayed daily and thanked the Lord in advance for his deliverance.

The hours dragged by slowly for the remainder of the day as Sam waited for his appointment. He had no watch and had meant for his contact to make for their rendezvous when he heard the guard call, "Eleven o'clock and all's well." He had not thought to be more specific on the meeting place at the time he had made his appointment and worried a little that he wouldn't be able to find the man with the tan hat in the dark.

Sam lay in his bunk until he heard the eleven o'clock cry of the guard. Without saying a word to anyone, he got out of his bunk and slipped quietly out of the window. He stealthily ran and crawled through the shadows until he reached barracks number three and crawled underneath. He was still on his hands and knees when he was grabbed around the head by someone and felt the point of a knife at his throat.

"Do you swear under penalty of death not to reveal anything you are told by us?" a raspy voice asked.

"Yes, I swear!" Sam said quickly, unable to do anything else.

"Then follow me," the voice said.

The hold on Sam's head was released and he could now see two figures who crawled on all fours out from under the barracks and out into the open area between the barracks and the wall of the camp.

"Stay flat of the ground and talk in a whisper," one of the men ordered. "The guards can't see us in this dark spot. Who are you and what do you know about us?"

"I'm Sgt. Sam Morgan, 51st North Carolina," Sam answered. "That's part of Clingman's Brigade in Hoke's Division."

"Where's your home?" Sam was asked.

"Cumberland County, near Fayetteville," he answered.

"What's the building in the center of the square in that town?" the second figure asked.

"The Market House," Sam answered. "The Cape Fear River runs by the town."

"What's the first tree to bloom in the spring on the river bank and what month does it bloom?" the man with the raspy voice asked.

"The redbud and it blooms in March," Sam replied.

"Well, if he's a Yankee spy, he at least knows something about North Carolina," the raspy voice said to the second man.

"I ain't no damned Yankee," Sam protested. "I just want to get out of here and go home."

"What tipped you off about us?" asked the raspy voice.

"The different colored dirt you left in the pond," Sam answered. "It had to be coming from a tunnel somewhere."

"See, I told you he was a sharp fellow," the second man told the man with the raspy voice. "Here's the sign I said you would know me by." the man said, extending his hand with a missing finger to Sam.

"We have made an oath that anyone who finds out about us must become one of us or die," said raspy voice. "Will you take the oath and enforce it?"

"I will take the oath to not betray you, but I'm not an executioner," Sam answered.

"Damn it, man!" raspy voice swore. "We are being killed a little at a time. They are slowly starving us to death and have you had any friends who went to the hospital?"

"One,' Sam answered.

"I'll wager he's in the graveyard now," said raspy voice.

"Why, yes," Sam said. "But I never thought..." his voice

188

trailed off.

"That graveyard is filling up mighty fast for the number of men who are here. We think one of them Yankee doctors is killin' our boys and we might all be too weak to escape one day. Damn it, man, are you in or not?" raspy voice demanded.

"I'm in and one friend will come with me," Sam answered emphatically

"How long have you known this friend?" asked raspy voice.

"All my life," Sam answered. "I grew up with him."

"Very well," missing finger said. "Meet us here at the same time tomorrow and we'll bring the Bible and give you the oath."

The Summer of 1864 was passing rapidly for Sarah McLain. Malichi had laid by the sweet potato crop and no more plowing and hoeing was necessary. Since she had quickly sold the entire crop, she had lots of time on her hands until the harvest in late summer. Freed from the everyday attention her mother had required, and since her livelihood was guaranteed for at least another year, Sarah was delighted to lend a hand when an aid station for wounded soldiers was set up in Florence.

The first aid station was the idea of Dr. T.P. Dargan who had served as the medical officer of the 21st South Carolina infantry. Many soldiers being furloughed home to the Gulf states, as well as deserters, traveled through Florence because there was no east to west railroad which ran the length of North Carolina.

By August of 1864, the stream of injured, sick and disabled soldiers was becoming substantial. The fighting in Virginia was almost without a stop. Just like the prison camps, the hospitals were overwhelmed by numbers they were incapable of handling. The space relinquished by one of the sick or injured was quickly filled by another. Many of the wounded were given minimum attention and then sent home to recuperate or die. These were the soldiers who came through the aid station at Florence, first as a trickle and then as a stream. Many left Florence enamored by a beautiful nurse who had merely changed a bandage or given a cool glass of water.

Chapter 12
Fort Harrison

J.D. Williams had taken Sam's place as the person who read the newspapers, when they could be obtained, and passed on the war news to the rest of the company. The Richmond papers had been complimentary of the work of Hoke's Division whose timely arrival had saved Petersburg on June 17th, but it was news from another front which worried J.D.

"It looks like General Johnston ain't going to stop Sherman this side of Atlanta," J.D. surmised. "Grant tried to bust through our lines before he swung around 'em, but Sherman just pecks away before he outflanks our army down there".

"That's why we've shot so many Yankees this summer," Uriah replied. "I wonder how long it's going to take before Grant realizes he can't whip us in frontal assaults?"

"Damn right!" Charles agreed. "But don't forget, we don't seem to be gittin' any replacements like we used to. Do you reckon we're losin' after all?"

"The papers don't seem to think so," J.D. answered. "It says here that if we can hold Richmond and Atlanta, Lincoln will be defeated in the election this November and the Democrats will make peace. This paper is six weeks old and a lot could have happened since then."

Much had happened very quickly, in fact. Jefferson Davis had relieved Johnston from command and replaced him with General John B. Hood, a Texan with a reputation for being a tough fighter on the division level. As an army commander, he quickly proved his appointment to be a mistake by sending his forces to assault an enemy twice his size. In six weeks, his army had sustained losses which now made it impossible for it to defend the city. Hood now had no choice but to withdraw or be trapped. On September 2, 1864, the Union Army occupied the city and General Sherman wired Lincoln: "Atlanta is ours and fairly won." This victory electrified the North and assured the re-election of Abraham Lincoln. A negotiated settlement was no longer a possibility. The war would now be fought out to the bitter end.

It was a warm September Sunday at Petersburg and there were many worship services being held for the soldiers of the Army of Northern Virginia. Hoke's Division had been pulled out of the line for a brief period of rest and refitting. Uriah, Charles and J.D. had attended a morning worship as a break from just lying around since their duty in the trenches at Petersburg had seldom allowed for such a luxury. A spirit of revival had swept the Confederate Army, no doubt spurred on by spectre of sudden death which hung over the heads of the combatants in this phase of the war. The chaplain preached on about the glories of the hereafter and laced his sermon with points outlining the correctness of the Southern position.

"There were eleven tribes who wanted only to leave Egypt but Pharaoh hardened his heart," the Chaplain preached. Thirty minutes later, he closed with, "Let us determine to bear whatever burden is required of us to rid ourselves from the tyrant's heel." The service closed with a hymn which promised eternal life.

"Amazing Grace, how sweet the sound, that saved a wretch like me. I once was lost, but now am found, was blind but now I see...
When we've been there ten thousand years, bright shining as the sun, we've no less days to sing God's praise than when we first begun."

The bass and baritone voices gave a creditable account of the hymn in the absence of any sopranos since the sincerity of the singers was very real. As Uriah and his friends walked back to their camp on this early fall morning, only the roar of distant cannons interrupted the peaceful scene.

"It's nice to be back where we don't have to do nothing but lay around," Charles said. "There ain't been many times in my life where I could do that."

"I'm about ready to go back to the trenches," Uriah said. "I never could stand to just do nothing."

"Did you boys get anything out of the sermon?" J.D. asked.

"The chaplain was telling us that God is on our side," Charles surmised.

"Do you reckon the Yankee chaplains are preaching the same thing to them?" Uriah asked.

"I suppose so," answered J.D. "Anyhow, I read where Napoleon said that God is usually on the side of the army with the best artillery."

"I ain't never been under our own artillery, but those Yankees can really shake the ground with theirs," Charles spoke with admiration.

"But, getting back to the sermon," J.D. persisted. "Is it not right for us to fight for our independence when the North seeks to force it's economic, and political will upon us?"

"What's all that mean?" Charles asked.

"Abraham Lincoln and the Republican Party wasn't even on the ballots in 1860 in the Southern states, yet he was elected and was supposed to be our President and dictate who we can sell our cotton to and even for how much." J.D. explained. "That's the main reason we left the Union and that's what the chaplain meant when he preached about us being under the heel of the tyrant if we lose."

Reaching their campsite, the soldiers lay about under the trees while J.D. strummed some songs on his guitar. This music had a positive effect on the soldiers and the sound of his music would always draw a crowd. The two week rest for Hoke's Division, however, was about to come to an end. This Division was ordered back to the defenses and had no sooner taken its place when an emergency arose north of the James River. The Federals had cut the Petersburg to Weldon Railroad the previous month and caused the Confederates to make a serious effort to recapture this vital supply line which ran all the way to the port of Wilmington. Clingman's Brigade along with those of Colquit and Hagood were used in the unsuccessful attempt to dislodge the Yankees. General Clingman was wounded in this effort and would be lost for the remainder of the war. The failure of the Confederates to recapture this lost ground caused them to extend their defensive lines further to the south.

Grant now decided to test the stretched defenses by sending Butler to attack two forts which protected Chaffin's Bluff, across the river from Drewry's Bluff. The Union attack on the Confederate defense line quickly overcame the small garrison at Fort Harrison, but Fort Gilmer was better prepared and resisted three attempts to capture it. The Yankees abandoned this effort and set to strengthening the rear of Fort Harrison against the expected attempt by the Rebels for its recapture. General Robert E. Lee had decided to do just that and had picked the divisions of Field and Hoke to make this attempt.

"What are they pulling us out of the lines for in the middle of the day for?" Charles asked as Clingman's Brigade formed in marching order and began heading north. "We just got here in time to be shelled yesterday and now we're going somewheres else."

"There must be some hot work to be done," Uriah answered. "It looks like Hagood and Colquit's Brigades are pulling out and going with us."

"I believe that's Kirkland's boys pulling out of their trenches off to our right," J.D. added. "This is a movement of Hoke's whole division."

"This looks like something big," Uriah said, apprehensively. "Ever since we fought at the Neuse River Bridge, when we've been moved quick like this, there's been some serious fightin' to be done."

"Damn right!" Charles agreed. "You can just smell it coming."

"It's a good thing we went through that farm where the horse soldiers had fought," Uriah said. "I was able to get me a good supply of bullets for this here repeatin' rifle of mine. I've been hoping I could find me one with a coffee grinder in the stock. I think it's a Sharpes rifle with the coffee grinder and this here's a Spencer I've got."

"I still don't know why, since we never have any coffee to grind," Charles lamented. "We don't get to trade with the Yankees here and it's been a long spell since we overran one of their camps where we could pick up any."

"If we ever do git holt of any coffee, we could carry it in J.D.'s guitar," Uriah kidded. "The way he carries it hanging from his blanket roll would shelter the coffee from the rain."

"I would never do any thing like that if it might harm the tone of this delicate instrument," J.D. answered with a chuckle. "Anyhow, I've about forgot what coffee tastes like. On second thought I might because that guitar keeps flapping around back there. Maybe a pound or two of coffee inside would make it tote a mite better."

The march took Hoke's Division north where it crossed the James River on a pontoon bridge and arrived at Chaffin's Bluff around ten o'clock that night. General Lee had hoped to be able to mount an attack that night before the Federals could strengthen the fort. Unfortunately, he was forced to wait for the arrival of all the troops until the early morning hours of September 30th. It was well up into the morning before Lee could explain his plan to General Field and General Hoke.

The Confederate commander had called the division generals and his artillery general to his headquarters to coordinate their duties in the attack. As the four generals and their staff looked through their field glasses at their objective, General Hoke could not believe what he was being instructed to attempt. Hoke's Division, according to Robert E. Lee's plan, would make a frontal assault against the strengthened fortifications. The advance would be across two hundred yards of open ground. Before the breastworks could be reached, a line of sharpened stakes had to be crossed under the fire of Fort Harrison's defenders.

"General Hoke," Lee asked after explaining his plan, "are your men in position for the assault?"

"Yes, Sir," Hoke answered. "All my brigades are in position. Colonel Hector McKethan is now in command of Clingman's Brigade and they will lead the assault supported by

Colquit's Brigade. However, Colonel McKethan has expressed his reservations as to the success of this attack. He feels we have little chance to even reach the fort and will undoubtedly sustain heavy casualties. I agree with his observation and implore you not to order this attack."

"General," Lee replied. "Our artillery will reduce the works with a thirty minute bombardment before you attack. General Field's division will attack from the north in order to support your assault. Are your troops ready, General Field?"

"They have all arrived and are formed for the attack, but I must concur with General Hoke's opinion. My men will have to advance five hundred yards to reach the fort. We have the word of prisoners captured yesterday that the Yankees are all armed with Spencer repeaters."

"Those people always have good equipment and more of it than we do," General Lee answered. "That doesn't mean we will not be successful. When your men have advanced to the point within two hundred yards of the fort, you will halt and wait for General Hoke to begin his attack. General Hoke, do not begin your advance too soon. Wait for General Field and both of you attack at two o'clock."

"Sir," Hoke pleaded again. "I still feel it would be wiser to fortify the position now held by my troops than to waste lives in this attempt."

"General Hoke," Lee replied, emphatically, "the attack will be made as planned. I feel that our soldiers are equal to this task. Please coordinate your efforts with the artillery."

Colonel Hector McKethan was also looking through his field glasses toward Fort Harrison at this time. This was the Fayetteville native's first major operation as commander of the brigade since General Clingman had been wounded and he was anxious for his troops to perform well. No matter how long he looked and thought, he could not see any way this attack could accomplish anything but to inflict severe losses upon the brigade. McKethan's troops were sheltered by a ravine some two hundred yards from their objective, but their advance would be over open ground. McKethan's thoughts were interrupted by a courier who arrived from Lee's head-quarters with orders from General Hoke. McKethan took the note from the messenger and eagerly read it, hoping it brought a cancellation of the attack. His hopeful anticipation was shattered when he read that Hoke had been unsuccessful in changing General Lee's mind and the attack would commence at two o'clock after Field's troops were in position. With a sinking feeling in his stomach, he relayed the orders to his regimental commanders.

Back at Lee's headquarters, General Hoke conferred with Lee's artillery General as the bombardment commenced. "General," Hoke began, "I had rather you not fire a shot from your guns, sir! You will demoralize my men more by your shells falling short among them than you will inflict damage on the enemy. If you will bring your guns up to my line and charge with my troops you may do some good, but not otherwise."

The General replied, "But my artillery horses will all be killed."

"Yes," responded General Hoke, angrily, "and my men are going to be killed. Are your horses of more value than the lives of my soldiers?"

"I will give the enemy's works a thirty-minute bombardment. That is all I can promise, General," the artillerist told Hoke.

As the cannons began to fire and the shells sailed toward Fort Harrison, the path of each projectile was marked by a thin trail of smoke. Charles shaded his eyes as he watched the pyrotechnic display while lying on the ground beside Uriah and J.D. "I heard them Yankees up there in that fort all have Spencers to shoot at us with. When we get up there, maybe you can get you one with a coffee grinder like you've been wanting, Uriah."

"Boys," Uriah responded, "I've been looking at this whole situation and I don't think we're ever going to git to that fort unless our artillery gits rid of more Yankees than they usually do."

"I heard we're going to get some support from another division," J.D. said. "Maybe there will be enough of us."

"If there ain't, and we git into some trouble, do you see that little hill-like place right in front of that third row of stakes?" Uriah asked. "I think we ought to head for that and lay down behind it if our alignment gits fouled up and it becomes every man for hisself."

"Damn right," Charles agreed. "That sounds like a good plan to me. J.D., are you going to make too big a target with that guitar on your back?"

"Not unless I get shot at from the side," he answered. "You can't see it from the front. Besides, there ain't no other place to keep it and we never come back to the same place. The problem I'm going to have is keeping up with you younger fellows if we have to run all the way up to that fort."

It was time for the attack to begin and Field's Division could be seen, beginning its advance from the north. Anderson's Brigade was in the lead and reached the appointed position where it was to wait for Hoke's Division to begin its attack at two o'clock. To the disbelief of Hoke's officers, Anderson's men moved up and passed by the point where they were supposed to stop and wait for Hoke. They began an unsupported assault on Fort Harrison.

Colonel McKethan looked on in horror as the Union artillery shells began to fall on Anderson's Brigade. Not only were they vulnerable without the support of Hoke's Division, but if this attack was defeated, then Hoke's attack would also have to go in without any support.

"Take this message to General Hoke," he instructed his courier. "He must give us permission to attack before Field is smashed."

There was not time to change the orders before the three brigades of Field's Division were broken in order by the bullets of the rapid firing Spencers. Then, it was the turn of Clingman's Brigade to advance across the open ground in front of the fort.

"You boys stay close on me when we charge," Uriah said as the brigade began its advance. "I got better fire power than you do and it will shorely come in handy. It scares my britches off to know that every one of those Yankees has one of these here repeaters."

The Union artillery began a bombardment of shrapnel shells which started to rain on the advancing Confederates.

After the first hundred yards were crossed, the command to charge was given and the brigade hurried forward at a dead run. The cannons were now firing grape shot at the Rebels and the parapets of Fort Harrison were flickering with the muzzle blasts of a thousand Spencer repeaters. As the grape shot in wooden cannisters was fired into the ground before advancing troops, it would bounce off the ground in a spread pattern like a giant shotgun blast. It would break rifles in half, sever limbs and crush the chest of the unfortunate soldier it hit.

To the three friends, the screams and groans of those being wounded seemed almost as numerous as the crashes of the guns.

"We're being cut to pieces!" Uriah yelled at the top of his voice. "Hit the dirt behind this bush."

Charles and J.D. gladly dived on their bellies beside of Uriah. They were nearing the fort and could see the multiple lines of Union soldiers, some firing and others loading the Spencers and passing them forward. The fort fairly sparkled as the seven-shot repeaters barked again and again.

" Look, We're pulling back," Charles shouted.

"Wait!" Uriah commanded. "I'll spray seven shots at those Yankees in our front and you run like the devil or else we'll git shot in the back. Then you stop and cover me. Is every body loaded up?"

"Yeah, we are," J.D. answered.

"Then, go!" Uriah shouted as he emptied his seven rounds into the crowded ranks of the Federals to cause some diversion. After seeing his two friends pause among the retreating Confederates, Uriah leaped up and ran as fast as he could in a zigzag pattern toward them. "Let's go!" he shouted as he reached them. Soon, the survivors of the attack had retreated back to where the attack had begun, leaving the ground in front of Fort Harrison covered with dead and wounded.

Back at their safe position, the defeated Rebels thought their work for the day was done, but Robert E. Lee, astride his gray horse, Traveler, rode up to the retreating soldiers and implored them to make another attempt to take the fort. He still felt that a coordinated attack by Field and Hoke could yet be successful. A loud cheer went up from the Confederate troops as they reformed their lines for another assault. General Lee had the utmost confidence in his Confederate infantry and these soldiers always tried to do what he ordered them to do.

Uriah had joined in the cheer for their commander, but had serious misgivings about the chances of success in this second attack. "General Lee," he said aloud to himself, "What are you putting us back into this for?"

"Can you make it again, J.D.?" Charles asked his older friend.

"It might take me a little longer to get there, but I'll be right behind you," J. D. replied.

Once more the gray and butternut ranks moved out into the open and the Union artillery immediately began its deadly work. The shrapnel shells burst over McKethan's advancing brigade, taking their toll at long range. As the fort was neared, the charges of grape-shot made swooshing sounds as they sped past and dull smacking sounds when steel shot met flesh and bone.

Uriah was nearing the row of sharpened wooden stakes in the fort's front when, looking back, he noticed that Charles and J.D. were no longer with him. "We need to tear a hole in these stakes," he shouted to anyone near.

Before the line reached the stakes, a volley of fire from the fort sent bullets zinging past his ear and kicking up the dirt around him. He saw several men near him go down. Suddenly, there was a loud explosion which threw him up in the air and then - darkness.

When Uriah awoke, he was somewhat confused about where he was. What was that weight on top of him? He lay still as he tried to clear his head. "Is this what it's like to be dead?" he thought.

He continued to lie still as his head cleared and perspective slowly returned. He was aware of people moving around nearby so he remained still. "Look at this pile," he heard a voice say. "We mowed 'em down like grass. None of 'em are alive here." Then he understood. The battle was over and the second Confederate attack had been smashed like the first. The Yankees were scouring the field for survivors and taking the wounded to hospitals and the uninjured to prison camps.

Night was falling and he could still make an escape if he remained calm, but there was something under him which was uncomfortable. He reached down and felt his Spencer rifle. It was pure luck that he had fallen back down on top of his valued weapon since it had to have been blown out of his hands by the explosion. There was still a ringing in his ears from the explosion, but he didn't hurt anywhere else.

He now realized that a body of a man was on top of him and the blood of this man had colored his shirt. That's why the Yankees had thought he was dead. He didn't want to know the dead man's identity, for mere hours before, the man had been a fellow soldier, maybe a friend, but at least a comrade who had grown up near Uriah's home. He rolled the body off his back and looked around. It was dark now and the Union search parties had lit flaming torches to aid them in finding those still alive among the hundreds of bodies on the field. Uriah held his weapon in his right hand as he started crawling back down the slope, keeping his distance from the search party and their torches.

After an hour, Uriah knew he was nearing his own lines. He had to be certain he would not be shot by his own troops. He had now reached a position he recognized as being near the ravine where the ill-fated attack had begun. He whistled to make the pickets aware of his approach and was immediately challenged and welcomed back to his lines.

"Uriah!" Charles shouted with excitement as he saw his friend approach the camp fire. "I thought you were dead. Are you hit? You're all bloody."

"It's not my blood and I would like to git a fresh shirt as soon as I can." Uriah replied. "Are you all right? What happened to your head?"

"I got creased on the scalp by a bullet early in the attack. Knocked me colder than a cucumber," Charles explained.

"It probably saved your life," Uriah said. "It was a slaughter out there. Where's J.D.? Did he make it back?"

"I ain't seen him yet. Maybe he'll come draggin' in like you did," Charles said, hopefully.

But J. D. Williams would not come back. Somewhere on

the field before Fort Harrison lay a guitar, shattered by grapeshot, among the piles of dead. Two weeks later, J. D.'s wife would receive a letter from Lt. James H. Taylor of the 51st which read:

Mrs. Williams,

It is my painful duty to inform you that your husband Pvt J.D. Williams was captured in the charge on Fort Harrison near Chaffin's Bluff, Va. on the 30th Sept. I think he was unhurt and no doubt you will hear from him soon...

Several wives of the soldiers of Company I received similar letters. Neither their husbands nor J.D. Williams were ever heard from again. Although accounts of casualties suffered by Clingman's Brigade vary, it is obvious that of the more than nine hundred men led forward by Colonel McKethan that afternoon, there were fewer than four hundred remaining to answer roll call that night. There is no record of any casualties among the artillery horses.

Up in Elmira, the work on the tunnel was progressing slowly. Sam and Dougal had been accepted into the tunnel society and had quickly become respected members. In order to insure there would be no betrayal in this venture, no one went by his real name. In the event someone was caught, it would be hard to identify his accomplices. Raspy Voice named Sam, "Hawkeye", for spotting the operation and Dougal was simply called, "Kid." The tunnel began under barracks number five and ran through an area where the prisoners were housed in tents. This route was not the nearest to the wall, but the need for ventilation holes for the tunnel was met by sending up air shafts under the tents.

There were more than two dozen men who were working in shifts to dig and get rid of the dirt. As each man would fill his box with dirt, he would crawl out of the tunnel and spread it over the compound. Sam quickly saw the inefficiency of this method and made the suggestion that cords should be tied to each end of the box and when it was filled, it could be pulled out of the tunnel and emptied into another container. Then the man doing the digging could pull it back to be filled again. This single change greatly increased the speed of the digging because it eliminated so much crawling back and forth.

There were several tunnels under construction at the same time at the Elmira Prison and the Union guards were constantly looking for any signs of digging. Occasionally, a tunnel would be found and the diggers would be placed in solitary confinement for several days. Sometimes, tunnelers would dig into someone else's tunnel not knowing it was there. Every prisoner was aware that when a tunnel was completed and escapes were made, the guards would scour every inch of the prison and probably find any remaining tunnels, thereby dooming all their hard work.

This happened on the morning of October 7th when the morning roll call indicated ten prisoners had tunneled out of the prison. There was much excitement as cavalry patrols were sent out to try to find the escapees. None of the ten were ever captured, and several like Sgt. Berry Benson, Fox Maull, and Wash Traweek became famous because of their success.

The success of these men doomed others to failure as the Union guards, in a thorough search of the grounds, uncovered five more tunnels. Sam's tunnel was not discovered since it had been carefully concealed from the beginning by Raspy Voice and Missing Finger and could be quickly hidden when the need arose. However, as a precaution, Raspy Voice suspended digging operations for two weeks.

By early December, the need to finish the tunnel became critical due to the approaching winter. The ground was becoming frozen and if the frost line in the ground became as deep as the diggings, it would make completion of the tunnel much more difficult. On December 6th, as the first major snow of the season was falling, it was Sam's turn to dig. The previous digger had run into a large rock which barred the way and Sam was working slightly under it. Too much dirt had been removed and the boulder suddenly broke loose from the roof of the tunnel and fell on Sam's left arm. There was a sharp stab of pain as part of the roof fell on his head, putting out the candle

202

and leaving him in total darkness.

Sam held his breath as he waited for the rest of the roof to fall. In the pitch black darkness, he tried to figure out what had happened. He could still breathe and could move every-thing but his left arm. In this awkward position, he pushed at the boulder with all his strength and moved it enough to free his arm. He backed out of the tunnel with each bit of pressure on his left arm causing a sharp pain. As he stuck his dirt cov-ered head up through the entrance, Missing Finger was there to help him out. "What happened, Hawkeye?" he asked.

"Cave in!" Sam answered. "A big rock dropped down from the roof. I think my arm's broken and it's starting to swell already. I'd better get over to the hospital."

"Not unless you got a death wish, boy." Raspy Voice said as he brushed the dirt from Sam's head. "Haven't you noticed that you Tar Heel boys don't fare too well over there?"

"Maybe not, but I've got to get this thing set," Sam said. "It's really hurtin' now."

"You've got to come up with a way this happened before you go over," said Missing Finger.

"That ain't no problem. I'll slip on the ice over there in front of the barracks. Kid," Sam said, nodding at Dougal. "If I don't come back tonight, hide my blanket so the guards won't take it. I'll see you as soon as I can."

All of the diggers wore their clothes inside out when working to avoid having them stained with dirt of a foreign color. Sam went inside one of the tents and shook out the dirt and, in spite of the pain in his arm, turned his clothes right side out and combed the dirt from his hair. He then walked to in front of the barracks where he slipped on the ice and acted out his charade. Entering the hospital, he walked up to the front desk and spoke to a Corporal who was writing in a journal and failed to acknowledge his presence.

"I've broken my arm," Sam said as the Yankee finally looked up.

"Corporal, I'll see that man." a Union Army doctor said from across the room. Sam was puzzled at the doctor's interest as he took off his coat to reveal his swollen arm.

"We need to set this arm and keep it in a splint," the

doctor said after examining it. "You need to stay here for a few days so I can keep an eye on it." As the man worked on the arm, he kept asking Sam questions about his home, his family, even the names of his parents and grandparents. Sam was still puzzled by this attention, but it was warmer in the hospital than in his barracks. The sick in the hospital were given more food and it had to be better than what he was used to. He would have no objection to the doctor's unexpected orders. Besides, the temperature outside was dropping and it was snowing very hard.

Chapter 13
Fort Fisher

The men of Clingman's Brigade were kept in the Richmond defenses after the debacle at Fort Harrison. However, the brigade was never at full strength after that battle because it could never find enough recruits to replace its losses. The fighting men from between the rivers and the rest of the South had simply been used up. Since Grant began his offensive in May, he had lost more men than Lee had in his entire army. The Union Army could replace these losses many times over and the Confederates could not. As the siege of Petersburg continued, the Yankees kept extending their lines south and west around the city. Each move had to be countered by Lee and after the attack on Fort Harrison, he had two thousand fewer troops with which to do it.

It was now mid-December and down in Savannah, Lewis Hobson stood by his artillery piece as he watched the line of small dark specks appear out of the woods and start advancing across the marshy ground in his front. Sherman had arrived and this was a probing advance which was designed to draw artillery fire, thus giving away the fortified position of each piece. This attack would not amount to much, but it didn't matter. Sherman's Army of sixty thousand would soon envelop the city and try to trap General Hardee's seventeen thousand Confederates. When that city fell, Wilmington would be the only port remaining in the South where the blockade runners could bring in a meaningful amount of the vital supplies from outside. Charleston was now effectively sealed by the blockade and any advance into South Carolina by Sherman would cause the city to be evacuated. One night, Hardee led his troops out of Savannah on a bridge of lashed together rice flats, leaving the city to Sherman

Earlier that year in October of 1864, the Confederate government became concerned about a possible Union attack on Fort Fisher at the mouth of the Cape Fear River. Nearly all of the supplies used for sustaining Lee's army now came through Wilmington and to guard this vital supply line, a formidable defense system had been built along the lower Cape Fear with Fort Fisher as its key. The architect of this elaborate defense was General W. H. C. Whiting who was the mentor of Colonel William Lamb, the commander of Fort Fisher. These two had teamed up to build a system of earthworks which could withstand anything contemporary naval artillery could throw at it.

In spite of these reasons for not doing so, Jefferson Davis chose to replace Whiting with his old friend Braxton Bragg in October of 1864. This officer was one of the most disliked Generals in the Southern Army, one whose fellow commanders described as having a talent for "snatching defeat from the jaws of victory." Bragg's undistinguished record was such that the <u>Richmond</u> <u>Examiner</u> published an editorial concerning his appointment. "Bragg has been sent to Wilmington," it read. "Good-bye Wilmington!"

Fort Fisher was called the Gibraltar of the Confederacy because of its strategic location and imposing defenses. However, its garrison was too small and some of its long range breech loading cannons had been taken to other locations, but it still mounted at least forty-four heavy guns as well as numerous fortifications and batteries along the Cape Fear River. A Union attack on the lower Cape Fear area would cause a need for reinforcements to be sent to defend this vital supply line. With Hood's smashed army now licking its wounds in Tennessee and disorganization prevailing most everywhere else, the only source of troops was Lee's army.

If Richmond was the head of the Confederacy, Wilmington was now its heart. The Cape Fear River acted as an artery to bring the life sustaining supplies to Lee's Army and Fort Fisher kept this artery open. Without it, the supplies could not flow up the artery and the heart would die. This fact was well understood by General Grant and on December 18, 1864, a Union invasion fleet gathered some twenty miles offshore from Fort Fisher.

Robert E. Lee knew he could not hold Richmond if Fort Fisher fell, so he immediately gave orders to detach Hoke's Division from Longstreet's Corps and send them to Wilmington. A coastal storm had sent the invasion fleet to seek shelter at Beaufort and bought some time for the defenders, but the cold front which followed it brought some of the coldest weather felt during the entire war. It was snowing as Clingman's men left their winter quarters and marched through the Confederate Capital for the last time.

"I always did like walking in the snow," Charles said almost cheerfully. "Uriah, you think we can maybe track some rabbits like we used to do back home?"

"Who knows when we'll slow down long enough," Uriah answered. "Since the Yankees have cut the railroad to Weldon, I hear we've got to go around by Danville and Greensboro and Raleigh to get to Smithfield. We'll hit the old line there and go through Goldsboro on the way to Wilmington. We need to be down there now and we ain't even left here yet."

"You know, it'll shore be good to be back in the Old North State for a spell," Charles said. "It's sad to think of all the good men we came up here with who ain't going back with us."

"We can't git too caught up in that," Uriah answered. "Is that our train up there?"

"Oh, Lord!" Charles exclaimed. "I shore hope not. It don't have no coaches, just flat cars and box cars."

The men from Clingman's Brigade were loading on the railroad cars when Uriah looked toward the woods and noticed the shape of a rotting log rapidly being covered by the falling snow. He walked over to the log and kicked away the snow and leaves with his foot and then found what he was looking for. The tree was a pine and beneath the rotting humus were many solid pieces, lightard knots, oozing with pitch. He gathered an arm load of the fire-starting material and walked back to his squad.

"Hey, boys," he announced! "Go over yonder to that tree and git yourself some lightard knots. We can have us some heat on this here train ride."

The men of Company I knew exactly what Uriah was talking about and very shortly had thoroughly stripped the woods of any of the easy burning material. As the train carrying Clingman's Brigade gained speed and headed toward Danville, many parts of it appeared to be ablaze from the fires the shivering Rebels had built on the floors of their box cars.

The need for all able bodied men in the South to be in the army had caused the railroad system to be in dire need of repairs, so the movement of the division toward Greensboro was at a very slow pace. The soldiers had to cut wood for the fire boxes of the locomotives and sometimes ran along side the train to keep warm. Several soldiers actually froze to death in the near zero weather prompting their generals to order "stimulants" to be ready for the troops as they passed through the stations on the way. When North Carolina was reached, the progress was faster even though the cold continued. The men of Hoke's division were met by cheering crowds at each stop with the local populace sharing what meager food they now possessed. It was felt that all would be well when these men reached Fort Fisher. Even though General Hoke was still between Danville and Greensboro, the lead elements of Kirkland's Brigade began arriving at Wilmington on Christmas Eve of 1864. On that same day, the largest invasion fleet ever assembled in the Western Hemisphere reappeared offshore from Fort Fisher and began bombarding the Confederate stronghold.

The fleet was commanded by Admiral David Porter who had been with Farragut at New Orleans when he sailed past the defending forts on the Mississippi River and captured the city. Wilmington would be a different situation. Any attempt to send a flotilla up the Cape Fear River would be bound to get ships stuck on the shifting sand bars and have them blasted to bits by the Confederate guns at the mouth of the river. Fort Fisher would have to be taken by a land assault.

The commander of this assault would be General Ben Butler who had failed miserably to perform the task given to him below Drewry's Bluff. This politician turned soldier had managed to get command of the troops heading for the Lower Cape Fear with the hope of a well publicized success. A victory here, he hoped, would catapult him into the presidency one day.

Fort Fisher would be a very formidable obstacle to overcome. The fort was in the shape of an inverted L and the north part, or landface, of the fort stretched across the peninsula to guard against a land attack from the north. Where the L bent southward was located the Northeast Bastion, one of the most heavily fortified parts of the fort. From there, the parapets of the seaface stretched for more than a mile down to the Mound Battery. This part of the fort had been built up to a height of sixty feet and was armed with two heavy artillery pieces which could sweep hostile ships from New Inlet, located due south. The Mound Battery could be seen for several miles out at sea and a beacon was added to the top to signal blockade runners. Forty-four heavy guns defended Fort Fisher, but it was soon to be attacked by a Naval force which out-gunned it ten to one.

The Union command had developed a unique plan for the destruction of Fort Fisher. An aging flat bottomed blockader named the Louisiana was filled with two-hundred tons of gun powder and ignited in the surf near the fort in the night. The explosion was heard very clearly in Wilmington, but did no damage at all to Fort Fisher. When General Whiting telegraphed Colonel Lamb inquiring what had occurred, Lamb could only imagine a Federal blockader had run aground and blown up.

The Union fleet had taken its bombardment positions the morning of the 24th and began to throw every thing they had at the fort. The day dawned mild and sunny and Colonel Lamb, inside Fort Fisher, watched the first shell making its arching approach toward him and gave the command to return the fire. For the rest of the day and through Christmas, the churchgoing citizens of Wilmington heard the continuous roar of artillery being fired a little more than twenty miles away.

The lead brigade of Hoke's Division had reached Wilmington and had a twenty mile forced march to reach the Confederate positions at Sugar Loaf, a high, fortified area of sand dunes five miles north of Fort Fisher. It was commanded by General William Kirkland who had served in the U.S. Marines before the war and knew about amphibious landings and how to defend against them. As Kirkland positioned his troops from Sugar Loaf overlooking the Cape Fear River to Battery Gatlin at the end of Masonboro Sound, he heard the cheering of some Union sailors who had just captured Battery Anderson, north of Fort Fisher's landface. Skirmishers were quickly sent through the sandy maritime forest of scrub oaks and pine trees to contest the Yankees, now advancing from the ocean. The staccato sound of musket fire was heard all through Christmas Day. Kirkland quickly saw that his one brigade was facing three Federal brigades and more would soon land. The fate of Fort Fisher might well depend on how fast the rest of Hoke's soldiers arrived to aid his efforts.

Clingman's troops had been some of the last to leave Richmond and were just getting ready to leave Greensboro on Christmas day. Their train was taking on water and a fresh supply of wood and the remainder of the trip would be on a better maintained and therefore faster track.

"This has been our worst train ride yet in my opinion," Charles complained. "If we can march as fast as the train can go, I'd just as soon march all the way."

"That's probably what's going to happen when we reach Wilmington," Uriah answered. "I figure we'll stay there now that the Yankees have Georgia. We'll walk wherever we go."

The "all aboard" sounded and the train lurched forward and picked up speed as it swung onto the main track to the east. "Uriah, do you really think it's true that the Yankees have taken Savannah?" Charles asked.

"I don't have any reason to doubt it. They seem to be going wherever they want to these days," answered Uriah. "If they are, the Confederate States of America stretches from Richmond to the Georgia border and that's all." The train built

210

up speed and the troops settled into as comfortable position as they could find for the long journey. "It seems to be warming up a bit," Uriah added. "I don't know about you, but I'm going to wrap up in my blanket and sleep all the way to Wilmington." He very nearly did.

Wilmington was reached on the evening of the 28th and the troop train crossed the Cape Fear River and pulled into a siding near the docks. Clingman's men found the people there in a euphoric state. As the soldiers were unloading, a man staggered by with a bottle of whisky in his hand, obviously celebrating something. "What's happening?" Uriah asked him. "What's all the fuss about?"

"The Yankees have left," the reveller responded. "We've whipped them. You boys won't be needed tonight."

"I'll settle for that!" Charles exclaimed. "Do you think it's really true, Uriah?"

"We'll soon know," he answered. "Usually when we git to the place where we've been sent, it ain't long before we're in a scrap."

To the delight of Clingman's men, they were not hurried into action. Instead, they were sent to one of their old camp sites where they stayed for a week.

It was true that the Yankees had left, but it was not true that they had been whipped. The Union Navy had fired twenty thousand shells at Fort Fisher and had wrecked several of the fort's heavy guns. The pine buildings inside the enclosure had been burned, but damage to the fort's ability to defend itself had been light. General Butler had landed one third of his assault forces but never got up the nerve to attack. After learning from a captured Confederate of the approach of Hoke's Division, he feared being trapped during an attack thus causing a disaster to his army and his political career. He ordered the troops that had been landed to be withdrawn, much to their displeasure. Admiral Porter was so displeased that he sent a steaming letter to Washington stating that "the fort can be taken any time they want to send a real soldier to do it." It would not take Grant long to do just that.

One night when Charles and Uriah were standing guard where Market Street became the road to Fort Fisher, a man on horseback was challenged by the pair.

"I am Frank Vizetelly of the <u>London Illustrated News</u>," the heavy set man announced. "I have a pass from your government to go to Fort Fisher and make sketches and reports of the coming battle for my newspaper."

"What makes you think there's going to be another battle?" Charles asked as Uriah looked at the pass the man handed him.

"There has to be," the man replied. "My sources tell me the Yankees are getting ready for another attempt."

"Maybe you should take this information to General Bragg," Uriah suggested. "He might need to know this."

"No need for that," the Englishman replied. "This is the most important city you have left and I'm sure your General is well aware of the consequences should it fall."

"I need to let the officer of the day look at this pass," Uriah stated as he turned and disappeared into the darkness to find Lieutenant McArthur, leaving Charles alone with the man.

"Are you the same reporter I saw down at Battery Wagner?" Charles asked. "There was a Britisher there."

"I very well might have been. I was certainly there." the man answered. "I submitted a sketch and a report of the battle to my newspaper and it was well received."

Just then Uriah and the Lieutenant joined the pair. "Your pass is in order and you may proceed," the Lieutenant said.

"Thank you. I look forward to sketching another smashing victory by you chaps." With that, Vizetelly clucked to his horse and proceeded toward Fort Fisher, leaving the three soldiers discussing the sanity of a man whose job required him to look for the hottest battles and then place himself in the midst.

With the Federal Government obviously winning the war, General Butler's performance at Fort Fisher had spelled the end of his army career. Since Lincoln had been re-elected, General Grant had no reason to coddle to a political general and immediately relieved him of his command. He was replaced with General Alfred H. Terry. On the second day of

1865 Terry visited General Grant at his City Point, Virginia headquarters and received sealed orders to lead an amphibious operation. Terry and his eight-thousand man army put to sea on the fifth of January bound for Beaufort. There he would meet Admiral Porter and his powerful fleet and proceed immediately to Fort Fisher.

"Why are we staying here at Wilmington?" Charles wanted to know. "If we were going to lay around when we got here, why didn't we wait until it warmed up before we left Richmond?"

"I guess somebody's plans got changed," Uriah guessed. "I just heard we might be going back to New Bern again."

"I shore hope not," Charles complained. "We walked down there once and didn't get to do nothing."

"We ain't going no where," Uriah replied. "We were sent down here to keep the Yankees from taking Fort Fisher and that's what we're going to wind up doing, but we can't do it from here."

"I know it," Charles agreed. "We should at least be digging some rifle pits or some kind of works where the Yankees will probably land. It don't make no sense our just hanging around Wilmington. It ain't going to be attacked."

"I just know you are going to make a fine general some day, boy," Uriah kidded Charles. "I heard that's just what General Hoke wants us to do but General Bragg has other plans for us."

"That's another thing," Charles added. "General Hoke took Plymouth and coulda captured New Bern if he hadn't been ordered back to Virginia. Then we whipped the Yankees at Cold Harbor, but I ain't never heard no tell of General Bragg winning a battle nowhere. So why does General Hoke have to take orders from General Bragg?"

"I reckon President Davis is the only one who knows the answer to that." Uriah said thoughtfully.

The two weeks after the unsuccessful attempt by the Union forces to take Fort Fisher was looked upon as merely a brief respite to Colonel Lamb, the fort commander. He repaired his defences and sent out constant requests for General Bragg to send more troops and to replenish ammunition and torpedoes. Lamb's requests were basically denied or ignored.

General Hoke shared this view and recommended that one of his brigades be sent down between Fort Fisher and Sugar Loaf to be ready to contest any future amphibious attack while it was still in the surf. Hoke knew what he had been sent down there to do and knew how it should be done. This request was also denied by Bragg.

There was only one of the key players in this unfolding drama who saw no danger to the lower Cape Fear. Unfortunately, that player was the area commander, General Braxton Bragg. Why he thought that a still intact Federal fleet with an army that could call on unlimited numbers of troops would not make another attempt to capture Fort Fisher is inconceivable. That, however was his mindset. Bragg was so confident that the Lower Cape Fear was safe that he was planning to use Hoke's Division in an attempt to retake New Bern.

On the afternoon of January 12, 1865, Bragg was staging a grand review for the citizens of Wilmington. Dressed in a new uniform, presented to him by the grateful people of that city, the General reviewed his troops. Just like Belshazzer in the Biblical Book of Daniel, he revelled in his position and power, oblivious of the force that was bearing down upon him. At that very moment, a larger and more powerful Union invasion fleet was steaming past Topsail Island heading south toward Fort Fisher.

It was midnight before Bragg learned of the impending attack. He immediately ordered Hoke to take his division and proceed to Fort Fisher where he was to "make every effort to prevent a landing of the enemy." Hoke's men were not in carefully designed and protected works near the fort which he had asked General Bragg to allow him to construct and place his troops at the possible landing sites. Instead, his soldiers were scattered around Wilmington twenty miles from where they were desperately needed.

It was eight A.M. on the thirteenth when Hoke and his leading brigade reached the Confederate positions at Sugar Loaf, five miles from Fort Fisher. Even as Hoke arrived, two-hundred boats filled with Union soldiers were approaching the beach. One hundred yards off the beach, sixteen gunboats provided a protective fire which blew great holes in the forest of scrub oaks and stunted pine trees from the surf all the way to the Cape Fear River. For the second time, the Confederates had lost the race to the invasion beach and were unable to contest the landing of the Union troops.

Kirkland's Brigade had traveled by boat to the Sugar Loaf defences and quickly settled in. Clingman's, Colquit's and Hagood's Brigades rapidly followed on land. It was early afternoon and the men of the 51st were within five miles of their destination.

"This has to be the hardest marching I've ever done," Charles complained. "When you put your foot down, it just sinks up to your ankle in the sand."

"That's right!" Uriah agreed. "But it shore is purty. I'm just glad I don't have to grow anything on it. Look at all these short scrub oaks. They won't give us much protection where we're going."

"Nothing except digging in the ground like a mole can save us from those guns." Charles replied. "Listen at that racket."

The sound of the six hundred Naval guns made a continuous roar as they bombarded Fort Fisher. The roar grew louder as the long column of gray and butternut clad troops finally approached Sugar Loaf. From the top of this dune of white sand, the troops could see the masts and spars of some of the ships from this gigantic fleet.

"Good Lord!" Uriah exclaimed. "Have you ever in your life seen anything like that? Those Yankee ships cover the whole ocean as far as you can see."

"Damn right!" Charles agreed. "All those masts look like the dead pine trees in that slough near the river that the beavers dammed up."

"Yeah!" another soldier agreed. "Those guns firing look like hundreds of lightnin' bugs. Listen to those shells hit the fort. How can anything live under that?"

"We lived under it at Battery Wagner," Uriah recalled. "You can bet the Yankees will git a warm reception when they attack."

The first line of ships, assigned to cover the landings, had stopped firing to prevent a shell with an insufficient powder charge from landing among the boatloads of Union soldiers. In the distance, a large cloud of smoke was rising from both the ships firing the guns and the fort where the shells were landing. Due to a lack of timely orders by General Bragg and indeed a lack of understanding of the tactical situation, eight thousand Federal troops were soon landed without a shot being fired at them.

Before midnight, this force had extended its lines across the peninsula to face Hoke with an extended front. At night, without the protection of the guns of the fleet, this force was vulnerable and possibly could have been defeated and captured by a night assault. Bragg ordered Hoke to maintain his position in the Sugar Loaf defences even though Colonel Lamb had prepared his command to attack simultaneously from the fort, thus sandwiching the Federals between their forces. Bragg never even bothered to reply to Lamb's request for this joint operation.

Back in Wilmington, General Whiting was still second in command of the lower Cape Fear defences and wanted to be used. He asked for permission from Bragg to take command and use Hoke's Division to drive the Union forces away from Fort Fisher and was refused. After a day of watching Bragg make plans for possible withdrawal, it became clear to Whiting that the Confederate commander was already defeated. Without any orders, Whiting walked down to the docks and boarded a motor launch to take him to Fort Fisher. Arriving there, he walked from Battery Buchanan, at the southern end of the fort, to Colonel Lamb's headquarters through the Union Navy's bombardment. Whiting had graduated first in his class at West Point and his engineering genius had created this fort which was known and admired all over the English speaking world. His years of toil in this lonely post would be for nought, he was convinced. Giving command of such defences to Braxton Bragg was like throwing pearls to swine, he must have thought.

Lamb was surprised at Whiting's appearance and was even more surprised by his greeting. "Lamb, My boy," he said.

216

"I have come to share your fate. You and your garrison are to be sacrificed."

"Don't say so, General," Lamb argued. "We shall certainly whip the enemy again."

Whiting told of what he had seen at Bragg's headquarters. There would be no supporting attack on the Yankees attacking the land face of the fort. It was now clear that Fort Fisher would stand or fall on its own.

The morning of January 15, 1865, dawned clear and cold with a light surf running. The shelling of the fort resumed with the same intensity. Bragg finally sent one thousand men in three boats from Hagood's Brigade to reinforce the garrison of Fort Fisher, but their ships kept getting stuck on river sandbars and only three hundred and fifty finally arrived, exhausted and almost useless. Whiting had sent Bragg several messages urging him to allow Hoke to attack the Federal rear, but around three o'clock he sent his most urgent one. It read: "The enemy are about to assault. They outnumber us heavily. Nearly all guns disabled. Attack! Attack! It is all I can say, and all you can do."

The shelling by the Federal fleet had been steady since daylight, but stopped abruptly when Admiral Porter signaled from his flagship <u>Malvern</u>. Almost immediately the steam whistle of each vessel united to give the signal to charge. The ships then resumed fire, shifting their aim to the seaface. Porter had armed sixteen-hundred sailors with pistols and cutlasses and without waiting for the supporting army troops, they sprang forward. Perhaps Porter mistakenly thought his guns had left no one in the fort to defend it, or maybe it was a case of inter-service rivalry, but every officer in the attack tried to be the first up the walls. The assault was aimed at the point called the Northeast Bastion where the L shaped fort made its turn south. Marine sharpshooters armed with Spencer repeaters tried to cover the attacking sailors.

The sailors and marines had to cover twelve hundred yards against canister shot and the fire from the only Colombiad still operating on the landface. At one-hundred fifty yards, the Confederates in Fort Fisher fired a volley which slowed the advance. Fresh rifles were handed up to be fired into the dense blue mass as it approached, littering dead and wounded men along the route the charge had taken. Confederate gunners at the Mound Battery turned their pieces on the Naval assault as did those manning the bronze Napoleons in the center sallyport. Though there were individual acts of heroism, the attack was soon spent. The bluejackets looked for safety and since there were no officers in the rear to rally them, they ran for their lives back the way they had come.

While it was not meant to be, the attack by the Sailors and Marines became a diversion for the Union Army's simultaneous assault of the fort's land face. After cheering the defeat of the Naval column, Lamb and Whiting looked with disbelief as Union Army banners appeared upon the northern walls of the fort.

General Terry had to be pleased with the leap-frog advance of his troops. They had moved ever closer to the walls by sending sharpshooters armed with Spencers forward at a run. Then, by digging rifle pits into the soft beach sand they provided covering fire for the advancing brigades. The Army troops reached the fort and obtained a foothold in a lightly defended part of the landface wall. Hand-to-hand fighting quickly began for its posession.

The Confederates were also bringing up troops. Hoke had finally been allowed by Bragg to send Clingman's Brigade as well as that of Kirkland to make contact with the Yankee land defences. This they did and quickly chased in the pickets and occupied the rifle pits of one of the Union Brigades protecting the rear of the attacking Yankees. These were all North Carolina troops and they were confident of success and anxious to go to the aid of their fellow Carolinians in the fort. Their officers felt these veteran soldiers could roll up the Federal defense line which stretched from the ocean to the Cape Fear River. They would then hit the Union attack from the rear at the time it would be most vulnerable and win the first Confederate victory since Cold Harbor. Hoke's men were ready. Their weapons were loaded. All they needed was the order to attack.

The sounds from the fort indicated a terrible battle was being fought. The roar of rifle fire and screams of the artillery shells intermingled with the cheers, shouts and curses of soldiers who were fighting for their lives.

Uriah and Charles lay flat on the ground as they awaited the orders to charge. The Union attack had now been going on for two hours and the inactivity felt strange to them. Hoke's Division was the largest and most experienced remaining in Confederate service. They had a good fighting record and a reputation respected in both armies and the word of Hoke's approach had been enough to cause General Butler to cancel his attack and withdraw at Christmas. Even now, General Terry's attacking Union troops were looking over their shoulders, expecting the attack which had to come.

"You ready to go, Charles?" Uriah asked. "Got your piece all loaded up?"

"Sure have," Charles answered. "Did you know those are black troops in our front? I wonder if they're the same ones we whipped at Battery Wagner?"

"It don't matter none," Uriah replied. "We're going to cut through 'em like they ain't even there. They've got to be a little jumpy here in the dark and they'll run like hell when we hit 'em."

General Hoke had ridden up to the lines of the 51st to converse with its acting commander, Captain Lippert, and was standing near some ancient oak trees talking with Lippert and his staff when a courier from Bragg's headquarters rode up. Uriah had observed the actions of commanders long enough to know they would soon be going into action. He saw General Hoke read the dispatch, wad it up in his hand and explain something to one of his staff officers who kicked the ground in disgust. Orders were given and instead of attacking, Hoke's Division began a withdrawal back to Sugar Loaf.

Instead of using the best division left in the Confederate Army to inflict a crushing defeat upon the Yankees, Bragg chose to abandon the piece of real estate most vital to the survival of the Confederacy. At ten o'clock that night, six and a half hours after the attack commenced, flares and signal rockets from the Federal fleet celebrated the capture of Fort Fisher.

The lights and explosions from the flares and rockets were clearly visable to the men of Hoke's Division who realized their meaning with stunned disbelief.

"That celebration can only mean one thing," Uriah said sadly. "The Yankees have overwhelmed our troops in the fort."

"How in the heck was that allowed to happen?" Charles inquired. "We could have pushed through those black troops like a hot knife through butter and saved the fort."

"We ain't got no way of being supplied from the sea now," Uriah lamented. "This could be our worse defeat of the war." The Rebel soldiers had very little more to say as they watched the flares and rockets shining through the smoke still hanging over the captured parapets of Fort Fisher. If the Confederacy had not before been mortally wounded, there was no doubt that this new wound would prove to be fatal.

Hoke's Division occupied the positions around Sugar Loaf for several weeks without much effort from the Federals to assault their position. However, there was some activity on the Cape Fear River. Braxton Bragg had further weakened the defenses of the Lower Cape Fear by ordering the fort on Smith Island to be abandoned and Fort Caswell destroyed. With a blast heard as far away as Fayetteville, one-hundred tons of gunpowder were blown up. Instead of contesting these areas, Bragg handed the Union command a landing site on the west bank of the Cape Fear from where they could mass their troops and work their gunboats over the bar at their leisure.

The Confederates fell back to Fort Anderson, built on the ruins of the old town of Brunswick, a colonial port which once rivaled Wilmington for the trade of the Cape Fear. Cornwallis had burned the town in 1776 and it never recovered. It was directly across the river from Sugar Loaf.

A week after the fall of Fort Fisher, the 51st occupied a campsite near a lake with moss covered oak trees. One night, the men of Company I were huddled around their fires when some replacements walked into the camp.

"Is this Company I?" one of the new men asked as he walked up to the fire.

"What's left of it," Uriah replied. "Who wants to know?"

"Private Daniel A. McMillan," came the reply. "How have you been, Uriah?"

"Well I'll be dang!" exclaimed Uriah. "It's Little Mac

come back to help us win this war. You got captured at Drewry's Bluff, didn't you? How'd you escape from the Yankees?"

"The Yankees sent me home," Daniel answered. "I got wounded in the right shoulder at the battle and they came along and captured the field hospital I was at. I was in one of their hospitals for a spell and then they swapped me and some other wounded for some of theirs. I got a sixty day furlough and went home and got well.

"We're glad to have you back," Charles added. "We lost a right smart of good men this past year and we ain't got many left."

"I heard about the big battles the regiment was in. They told me about them when I got home," Daniel continued. "It was bad so many got captured at Cold Harbor. You knew my uncle Daniel Graham got hurt in that train wreck and died at Elmira, didn't you?"

"Yeah," Uriah replied. "Bad news always spreads fast. We heard about it. You just remember what I told you about how to stay alive back in Virginia."

Daniel McMillan quickly settled in with the 51st. By February 1st, 1865, he was fully aware of the activities around him and wrote a letter to his father.

Near Shooger Loaf
Camp 51 Reg
Feb. 1, 1865

Dear Father, I now set myself to drop you a few lines in answer to your kind and welcome letter which came to hand this morning, which gave me much pleasure to hear from you once more. ...This leaves me well and hearty hoping that these few lines may early reach you and find all the family well. The Yankees shell more or less every day. One man was killed by a shell near the beach yesterday. He was getting out oysters. We had a skirmish the day before yesterday. Skirmished with two lines of Yankees. Two of Colquitt's men got wounded. The Yankees came up the river in a wood boat and shelled Fort Anderson. The shells fell a mite short. Fort Anderson fired back and shot a ball through the boat. Two Yankees deserted their army. They said our shot went through their boat and they expected us to charge them with a heavy force.

I have more hope of peace now than I have since the war commenced. A man from Richmond said that the white flags is up all over and the Yankee commisioners are going to Richmond. The Vice President is going to Washington with two other commisioners. When I first came to Wilmington, I thought Wilmington would have surrendered before now. But now I don't think they will give up till they are obliged to. ... Our rashons is sorry but they are better than the Yankees give. The Yankees commenced shelling Fort Anderson again today. The sand here looks like shooger. Company I draws thirty rashings. Officers all furnishes three pickets a day and knight. I have no news that would prove further interesting to you so I must come to a close by requesting you to write as soon as this comes to hand and give me all the news.

I remain yours truly,

Daniel A. McMillan

To Neil McMillan

The peace commissioners Daniel wrote about to his father were actually meeting with Abraham Lincoln aboard the steamer <u>River Queen</u> at Fortress Monroe, Virginia. Hopes were high among the ground troops of both armies that peace was finally at hand. With Fort Fisher captured and the blockade now complete, the only terms Lincoln discussed sounded like unconditional surrender to Southern leaders. The meeting would come to nought and the war would continue into its final phase.

Chapter 14
Sherman's March

Union General John W. Geary was getting ready to leave Savannah. He commanded the Second Division of Twentieth Corps and his troops had been assigned by General Sherman to garrison the town. Geary had served two terms as mayor of San Francisco before the war and showed aptitude for administration as well as command. Under his leadership, Savannah had been treated well by the invaders. He kept local officials doing their jobs, hauled in firewood, and encouraged public meetings. A vote of thanks was extended at one of these meetings and a resolution was adopted urging the Georgia governor to call a state convention to discuss peace with the Union.

On the same day Daniel McMillan wrote the letter to his father, General Geary and the rest of Sherman's Army moved out of Georgia and headed north into South Carolina. Sherman and his men blamed South Carolina for the war and without a major Confederate Army to contest this advance, the people in the state had reason to expect the worst.

The fall of Fort Fisher was big news on both sides of the Atlantic. The Union Army at Petersburg fired its guns in salute of the feat. British investors and blockade runners working out of Nassau and Bermuda quickly understood that this was the end of the rich, profitable trade with the South.

Sam and Dougal had heard the news as their captors allowed them to have it. Any news with a Union slant was mistrusted. One day in February, there arrived a large group of prisoners with the red trim on their collars and sleeves denoting a heavy artillery unit. Sam walked out of his barracks and joined the gathering crowd of prisoners hoping to learn some war news and news from home.

"What outfit you fellows from?" Sam asked, using the same greeting he had used many times.

"We were the Thirty-sixth North Carolina till the Yankees captured us," the new prisoner replied.

"Good Lord!" Sam exclaimed. "Then it's true. You were the defenders at Fort Fisher. We were hoping the Yankees were lying to us." Sam paused for a moment, staring at the ground, now that the crushing defeat had been confirmed. When he looked up, the man had moved on.

"Hey," Sam shouted after the man. "I might know somebody in Second Company B." Where're they at?"

"I'm one of what's left," a voice behind him said. "My name is Vann."

Sam turned around and extended his hand. "I'm Sam Morgan, 51st North Carolina from Clingman's Brigade. My old outfit is in Hoke's Division, Do you know of it?" Sam asked.

'Yes, we do," Vann said with disgust. "Hoke's Division stayed in their trenches while Fort Fisher was captured. Never lifted a finger to help us. We were out numbered five to one and Hoke could have hit the Yankees from the rear and saved the fort."

"That don't sound like the General I fought with," Sam countered. "Have the Yankees taken Wilmington?"

"Not that I know of," Vann answered. "But, they probably will when they take a notion to."

"I want to talk with you some more later," Sam said. "Your Company is from Sampson County, isn't it?"

"Why, yes, it is" the newcomer replied. "How did you know?"

"My farm is across the river in Cumberland County and I had heard some of you boys were at Fort Fisher. I bet we know some of the same folks," Sam answered.

"Yeah, and some of them might be right here with us," Vann said as he moved on to be processed.

It might have been the sudden change of winter climate or the results of the shelling they had endured or just plain despair over their hopeless situation, but the members of the 36th North Carolina Heavy Artillery Regiment were destined to sicken and die at an alarming rate while at Elmira.

General Bragg had ordered Fort Anderson abandoned even though it was still a good position to defend. This move provided the Union gunboats with a field of fire into the rear of the Sugar Loaf defenses so it too was abandoned. On February 22nd, the Union Army occupied Wilmington. The elaborate defenses of the lower Cape Fear had been wasted in the hands of Braxton Bragg. General Whiting called for an investigation into Bragg's conduct. He wrote from his prison death bed, "That I am here and that Wilmington and Fort Fisher are gone, is due wholly and solely to the incompetency, the imbecility and the pusillanimity (cowardice) of Braxton Bragg..." Meanwhile, Hoke's Division retreated from Wilmington north toward Goldsboro.

As prisoners from other fields of battle were added to the numbers at Elmira, they carried with them many unwelcome visitors in the form of diseases. It was only a matter of time before the most dreaded one of all arrived - smallpox. It was carried by some prisoners transferred in from another prison. It soon spread rapidly and a special quarantined hospital was set up for care of the inmates.

A mild childhood illness had made Sam immune to this disease, but no one knew it among those with medical knowledge of the time. Dougal had no such immunity and one day came down with aches and a high fever. The rash on his face told every one around him that any contact with him would be almost equivalent to a death sentence. Dougal made his way to the smallpox ward and was admitted. Sam would not see him again at Elmira.

Sam had been asked by the doctor to continue wearing a sling for his broken arm even though the arm seemed completely healed. One day the doctor sent a messenger for Sam to report to his office. Sam was puzzled by the call but trudged through the snow to the hospital. He always liked to see it snow back home, but soon afterward it would melt when the

225

southerly winds blew again after the cold front had passed. Here, no southerly winds blew and one snow fell on top of the last one. There was now three feet of snow on either side of the path to the hospital. Sam walked up the steps and was shown to the doctor's office. He stood at attention in the doorway as was required. "You wanted to see me, Captain Mitchell?" Sam inquired.

"Yes, Sergeant Morgan," the doctor replied. "Come forward and stand easy, please." Sam did as ordered without speaking and waited for the doctor to speak. "Morgan, General Grant has reopened the exchange of wounded and sick prisoners. There will be a shipment of men from this camp within a week. I have put your name on the list because of your arm."

"I don't understand, doctor," Sam said half in protest. "There are men much worse off than I am."

"Damn it, Man," the doctor swore. "You can have a ticket out of this hell hole if you keep your mouth shut. Nobody will question my decision."

"I'm much obliged, Sir, but why are you doing this for me?" Sam asked.

"A father's whim, perhaps," the doctor answered. "You are the spittin' image of my son. You look like him, you walk like him, and even your voice sounds like his."

"Is he in the army too, Sir?" Sam asked.

"He was till he was killed at Shiloh, nearly three years ago," responded the doctor.

Sam was stunned. His grandfather had told him years ago that everybody has a double somewhere, but he didn't really believe him. Now the love of a father for a lost son he happened to look like would get him out of this place where many would die. Sam snapped to attention, saluted and responded, "God bless you, Sir." Captain Mitchell acknowledged the salute with a nod of his head and Sam left the building and walked back out into the snow. He had to contact Dougal before he left Elmira.

One of the prisoners who had been ill with smallpox was Matthew Spence, whom Sam had met briefly in the late summer. If anyone would know how to contact Dougal it would be Spence. Sam approached him the next day and asked questions about the contagious aspects of smallpox.

"I don't really know nothing more than what I've gone through," explained Spence. "They told me it was dangerous to breathe on anybody else while I had it and after I got well I couldn't give it to nobody else or catch it again. While I was in the hospital I know that each morning when I woke up they would be hauling out some soldier who had died the night before who wasn't nearly as sick as I was."

"Then it wouldn't be dangerous for you to get a message to Dougal for me?" Sam asked.

"I don't think they would let me back in because I might bring something out to you on my clothes or somethin'," Spence offered. "Maybe some of the guards and orderlies I know would help."

"That would be great!" Sam exclaimed. "I just need to let him know that I got a chance to leave and see if I can do anything for him before I do."

"I'll go see what I can do right now, Sam," Spence said. He stood up and wrapped his blanket around him and walked out in the lightly falling snow toward the smallpox hospital.

Within an hour, Matthew Spence returned. "I got one of the orderlies to carry your message to your friend, Dougal. He says for God's sake, get out of here if you can. He can't send letters out, so he wants you to write his lady friend for him and tell her that he was all right when you saw him last. He said you would know where she lived. He says to tell her he will come to see her just as quick as he gets out. I guess that makes sense to you."

"Yeah, it does," Sam answered. "Only problem is, he might die here and never get out."

"That's not in our hands, is it?" Spence countered. "The boys in his ward says he's fightin' real hard. He just might make it."

"Thanks a lot, Spence," Sam said, appreciatively. "Maybe I can do something for you sometime."

It was not snowing in Florence, South Carolina that February afternoon, but there was a disturbing black cloud in the western sky. Sarah stood with Mrs. Grantham and Malichi on the front porch of the Grantham house watching the cloud

227

growing larger. The letters from Dougal had stopped coming and she feared the worst. Sarah spent more and more time in the evenings with Mrs. Grantham, discussing the events of the day.

"Malichi, are you planning to leave when the Yankees get here?" Mrs. Grantham asked.

"They ain't goin to make me leave, are they?" he asked. "I've got too much work to do to go traipsin off some where else."

"No, they won't make you leave, but Lincoln's proclamation frees the slaves in the areas the Yankees conquer," Mrs. Grantham explained.

"Right now there doesn't seem to be any way of stopping this bunch of Sherman's from going anywhere they want to go," Sarah added. "I've heard there are thousands of blacks trailing along behind them."

"I know all about that, too," Malichi stated. "I done some thinking about what I would do when freedom came. Freedom don't mean freedom from work, does it?"

"No, indeed not," Mrs. Grantham replied. "We all still have to make a living somehow."

"Are you still going to need some help on your farm and are you still going to grow your sweet potatoes?" he asked.

"That I am," Mrs. Grantham answered. "I reckon if we can't sell 'em then we can eat 'em."

"Then if you're going to need some help on your place, I'd like to stay here and work," Malachi said. "You kept my family together even when you had some hard times and I'll always be obliged for that. Me and my family, we're good for this land."

"Malichi, I don't know why we didn't have this talk years ago after my husband died," Mrs. Grantham said. "I'll draw up the papers tomorrow making you and your family free. You can stay in the house you're living in and I will supply the plants and fertilizer if we can find any. I'll give you enough of the crop so you and your family can live good."

"I don't reckon I can git that good a deal any place else!" he exclaimed happily. "I need to go home and tell my wife and boys!" With his freedom promised, he stepped off the

228

porch and walked off into the lengthening shadows.

As the sun set and the stars came out, the two women continued to watch as the black cloud in the western sky turned to a dancing red glow. Sherman's forces had penetrated into the middle of the state and Columbia was burning.

Moses Hawkins was ready to go home. He had risen to the rank of Sergeant in the 54th Massachusetts Regiment and his three year enlistment was up. The regiment had remained in the South Carolina low country after taking substantial losses in the attack on Battery Wagner, and he still bore the scar that Thomas had caused with his rifle butt atop the Battery Wagner defenses. Moses bore no resentment for the incident because he knew being knocked off the parapet certainly saved his life. The war was obviously winding down and he thought Sherman would certainly head into the middle of North Carolina in an attempt to link up with Grant. He would join the thousands of "contrabands" who were following the Union Army and leave it when he got close to home.

Moses said his good-byes with his army buddies and set off cross country to intersect with Sherman's forces near Winnsborough, north of Columbia. He knew the dangers a black man faced traveling by himself and used the main roads mostly at night. The second night on the road he slept soundly in a grove of pines growing in a larger forest near the main road from Winnsborough to Cheraw.

He was up at dawn and had traveled several miles down the main road, ducking into the woods when he saw traffic approaching. It was getting late in the afternoon when he saw a plantation up ahead. The work day was over and he would stop by the slave cabins and see if he could find some supper. Moses' arrival coincided with the arrival of the lead elements of Sherman's forces.

Moses had obtained a piece of cornbread from a large black woman when a group of blue clad mounted foragers burst into the front yard of the plantation house. The woman noted the arrival of the Yankee troopers and raised her hands toward the sky and shouted, "Praise de Lawd! We is all free!"

The first troops to dismount burst through the doors of the house ignoring the displeasure and pleas of the owners.

This "army of liberation" sought first to liberate gold watches and silverware. One soldier pulled out his pistol and held it to the head of the plantation owner in an attempt to extract the hiding place of these valuables. Furniture was thrown out the windows, followed by clothes from the wardrobes. The china was taken outside and thrown against a tree where it lay broken in a pile. Livestock was quickly rounded up and herded off. More Yankees arrived and quickly cleaned all meat out of the smoke house. The horses and mules were bridled and loaded up as pack animals for the stolen wealth of the plantation.

The slave quarters were not immune from plunder. One of the Yankee foragers rode down to the cabins and entered each house, looking for food or valuables. The cheering of the occupants soon turned to concern as their few animals were killed and added to the Union larder. "If you want us to free you, then we have to be fed," one Yankee shouted out to anyone within listening distance.

"Don't take my old goose," the woman who had fed Moses pleaded. "He's too tough for the table and eats the bugs in my garden."

The old bird spread his wings and bowed his neck as he prepared to defend his territory. He hissed as a warning to the Yankee approaching him with a cavalry saber sharpened for just such work. A quick swing of the weapon laid the bird's head on the ground and its still twitching body was tied by the feet to the Yankee's saddle. Without a word to anyone, he rode back to the front yard which was now full of blue clad soldiers. Rail fences, fruit and shade trees quickly became fuel for the evening camp fires as the horrified owners watched the work of generations disappear in one evening.

Moses noted that discipline seemed to be lacking in this army. There didn't seem to be any penalties for what in peace time would be crimes. The arrival of officers didn't stop the searching for valuables as groups of soldiers stuck swords, bayonets and ramrods into the ground, searching for buried heirlooms. The destruction of this plantation had been the work of a powerful army with some of its parts out of control. The foragers, or "bummers" as they were called, preceded the advance of the Army in search of food and were now nothing much more than bands of robbers that would soon be crossing into North Carolina.

The string of Confederate disasters finally forced the appointment of Robert E. Lee as Commander in Chief of all the Confederate forces, a rank enjoyed by Grant for over a year. General Lee quickly tried to collect a force to face Sherman's hoards. His first act was to restore Joseph E. Johnston to command what was left of the Army of Tennessee. This army, once commanded by Johnston, now rested in Mississippi. General Hardee had now reached Cheraw with the garrison of Savannah, which included Lewis Hobson, and the troops from now abandoned Charleston. Most other Confederate forces were far removed from the events which were rapidly deciding the fate of the Confederacy. The task assigned to General Joseph E. Johnston was to gather together these forces and defeat Sherman somewhere in North Carolina.

Sam Morgan was also on his way back to the Tar Heel state. He was one of the prisoners to be exchanged and was on board a train retracing the route he had traveled back in July. He remembered the heat and odors of that fateful day which contrasted with the now freezing temperatures. As the train neared Shohola, the snow-covered graves of Thomas and his comrades were visible from his coach window. He said a prayer for his fallen friend as the train sped past, somehow knowing he would never pass this way again.

The trip from Jersey City to Virginia was made by steamer and the two-day passage to freedom ended when Sam and his comrades landed on a wharf on the James River. Sam was back in the Confederate States of America. After a quick examination in the hospital, he was again on board a train heading through Danville on his way to Greensboro. Since the cutting of the Petersburg to Weldon Railroad, the rerouting of rail traffic through this Piedmont town had made it a supply center for North Carolina troops.

Sam was sent to the quartermaster to be issued a new uniform with extra trousers and socks. He had not been this well outfitted at any time during the war. "Would you like to have a sidearm, Sergeant?" the quartermaster asked.

"Certainly!" Sam replied, expectantly. "What do you have?"

"How about a nice Navy Colt revolver?" the man asked. "It's got to the place where we have plenty of weapons and not enough soldiers to use 'em. It's single action and you have to cock it before you fire it. I'll add it to your receipt for these uniforms. Sign right there," he said, pointing to a line on the receipt.

Sam signed the paper and retired to a side room where he dressed in his new uniform and boarded the train for Raleigh. His orders were for him to report to Goldsboro and from there he would be sent to where ever Hoke's Division had been sent.

As Sam's train pulled into Raleigh, the city was buzzing with apprehension. Sherman had occupied Cheraw, South Carolina, and was poised to invade North Carolina. Sam exited his coach and walked down the streets of the capital to stretch his legs. In the distance, he could make out the buildings where the business of the State of North Carolina was transacted. He wondered if Governor Zeb Vance was home and what it would be like to meet him. He returned to the train and sat down. His orders didn't allow him time for any leave to go home and see Betty and his family for the first time in nearly three years. A few days shouldn't matter very much to anyone, he was beginning to think. As the coach filled up, a man Sam's age walked up beside him. "Is this seat taken, Sergeant?" he asked.

"No, not at all. Please sit down," Sam offered.

"I'm Nathan Smith on my way to Goldsboro," the man said.

"Glad to meet you, Smith. I'm Sam Morgan and I'm heading there too," Sam said, returning the greeting. "How close are the Yankees to Goldsboro?"

"They're still at New Bern and Wilmington as far as I know, but that's close enough for me to be concerned about the safety of my slaves I've hired out to the government," Smith said.

"How do you get to do that and if you don't mind me inquiring, and how much do they pay you for them?" Sam asked.

"I get to do it because I own twenty slaves. That is enough to keep me out of the army to look after them, and some of them are needed to build defenses and repair the railroads," Smith explained.

"And you get paid for their services?" Sam asked.

"I get at least five hundred dollars apiece for them, but if the Yankees get too close they'll slip away and I'll lose them," Smith continued.

"Isn't that worth the risk?" Sam questioned. "The army needs fortification to defend against the Yankees and railroads to bring supplies."

"I just feel I've done my part for the war effort," Smith said as he opened a newspaper and began to read, effectively bringing the conversation to a close.

Sam was fuming. Here was a man who had stayed safe at home making money hiring his slaves out to the government. A Confederate soldier made about one hundred and fifteen dollars a year if he was lucky enough to get paid. Now, with Union forces closing in on all sides, this man was more worried about keeping his slaves than the survival of his nation. Sam sat in silence as the train covered the miles of flat farm land between Raleigh and Smithfield. The train was approaching the station at Smithfield when he made a decision. The welfare of his family was more important than any further contribution he could make to the army with its diminishing chance of success. The idea of Smith being excused from military service because of his wealth made the decision that much easier to make.

The train screeched to a stop at the station as Smith folded up his newspaper and stood up. "Let's take a walk and stretch our legs," he offered.

"No," Sam said without looking. "I'll be getting off here."

"I thought you were going to Goldsboro," the puzzled Smith questioned.

"I was but I've changed my mind," Sam said as he turned and exited the train. The warm March sun was refreshing as he stepped on to the ground and he didn't miss the

233

snows of Elmira one bit. He threw his bag of belongings over his shoulder and began the twenty-five mile walk to his home. Sam enjoyed his walk for the first five miles. He had forgotten the smells of the pine forests and the newly plowed fields. He was glad to see the bluebirds and cardinals in their mating flights and listening to the cooing doves. The horrors of war were left far behind as he was reintroduced to the beauty of nature and bounty of the land that was his home. He was so engrossed in his thoughts that he almost didn't hear the horse and buggy approaching from behind. The horse gave a bubbly snort which alerted Sam that he wasn't alone.

"Can I give you a lift, soldier?" the driver asked. "I'm going to Fayetteville."

"You certainly can, sir," Sam responded. "I live near Graham's Bridge and I'm going home for the first time in three years. I was beginning to wonder if I could make it before dark."

"You can now, Sergeant," the man said, noticing Sam's rank. "The name's Beasley. I travel these parts and it won't be much out of the way for me to take you to your doorsteps."

"I'll be much obliged for that," Sam said, appreciatively.

"No, it is us who are obliged to you soldiers," Beasley said. "I travel from Raleigh to Wilmington selling farm tools. Used to sell a whole heap of plow points before the Navy started building ironclads and used up all the iron. We were at economic war with the North for years trying to get a decent price for our cotton. Then, we had to go to war for our state's rights and it looks like we'll lose them both."

"What's the latest about Sherman?" Sam asked. "Where's he at now?"

"He's all the way up to Cheraw ready to cross the Pee Dee River and plunder this state too," Beasley said. "He might head for Greensboro and Danville to attack General Lee from the south or he might head for Goldsboro and tear up this part of the country, according to the papers. There'll be the Devil to pay whichever he does."

Sam was nearing home and didn't really want to talk about the war which seemed so far away. He was now in Sampson County and near the land he had grown up farming just across the river. The sights which had at one time seemed so familiar to him were now almost foreign and strange. The horse traveled at a steady gait along the road through the sandy loam and the miles quickly melted away. There could be no mistaking the tall juniper and cypress trees up ahead marking the flood plain of South River. Looking straight down the road, the structure of Graham's Bridge came into view. He was now less than two miles from home and he could smell the distinctive odors of the cypress-covered river bottom.

"Mister Beasley, you don't know what a service you've done for me," Sam offered when they neared the road to his house. "Would you like to stop at my house and get a drink of the best tasting water around? My well is famous around these parts."

"Thank you, Sergeant, but I want to cross the Big Creek Swamp and make it to the plank road at the nine mile post before dark. I can make it on to Fayetteville easy after that," Beasley explained.

Nothing more was said until Sam saw the road to his house up ahead. "This is where I'll get off, Mr. Beasley, and thanks again."

"Maybe I'll stop for a drink of that water one day. You take care of yourself," Beasley answered, and with a cluck to his horse, he left Sam standing on his own property once again and disappeared down the road.

Sam started up the road which led to his house. He was anxious, yet a little nervous at the thought of seeing his wife for the first time in three years. The sun was setting behind the pine trees when Sam's son William walked out on the front porch. Betty had put on an apron and was in the kitchen making some biscuits from the small amount of flour that remained.

"Mama, there's a soldier coming up the road," William said as a warning as well as an announcement.

Betty quickly wiped her hands on her apron, walked over to the fireplace and grabbed the shotgun from above the mantle piece. She walked to the front door and looked at the figure walking up the road. Her heart started beating rapidly as she blinked her eyes and looked again at the approaching figure. "I believe it's your father, William," Betty announced. She ran back to the fire place and placed the gun back where she got it. She knew her hair was a mess but it didn't matter. She walked down the porch steps and stopped once more to look at the approaching figure in the gray uniform. There could be no mistake: it was Sam. She ruffled her hair with her finger tips and began a fast walk toward her approaching husband.

Sam had seen his wife walk out the door and began a slow trot in her direction. They met in a hard embrace each had been anticipating for three years. "I had no idea," Betty sobbed.

"Not now, darling, not now," Sam said as he squeezed his wife, with tears running down his face. "There'll be time to talk later."

The couple walked back to the house arm in arm to begin Sam's reintroduction to his family. It would last for several days as they talked about what had happened to them during their three years of separation. Sam's oldest son, William, was now eight years old and could barely remember his father. Rufus, now four, still stood behind his mother's skirts, not knowing what to make of this intruder. In the days to follow, William would start to know and admire this lean figure from his past. He followed him over the fields and saw where the corners of the farm were marked. He walked with him down to the houses of James and Lonnie to see the sincere joy of these black neighbors as they welcomed him home. Sam also treasured these days and soon made another decision.

"Betty, I'm not going back to the army," he announced one morning at breakfast. "I'm going to stay here and raise my crops. Take the stripes off my uniform shirt and I'll use it to work in."

"What made you decide that?" Betty asked, quite surprised.

"I have nothing to gain by fightin' anymore," he answered. "Poor ol' Thomas is in his grave and all he ever wanted was a decent price for his cotton. I rode on the train with a man who owned twenty slaves and rented each one to the government for three times what we made as soldiers and that kept him from servin' in the army. I ain't fightin' for his benefit any more.

"Won't the Marshalls eventually come after you?" Betty asked apprehensively.

"Let'em come," Sam said adamantly. "I've got my weapons and I've probably killed more men than they have. If I see I can be of help to the army and we can accomplish something, I might go back, but it'll be of my own choosing." He finished his breakfast and walked toward the stable to hitch up his mule and start breaking land for the spring planting. On that same day, General Sherman's Army of sixty-thousand soldiers crossed the Pee Dee River and entered North Carolina.

Lewis Hobson had not been accustomed to the rapid marching that was now being required of him. He was part of the Tenth North Carolina Battalion of Artillery which had briefly contested Sherman outside of Savannah. These troops had become part of General Hardee's Corps and had retreated by rail through Columbia and up to Cheraw. The railroad ended there and Hardee continued his rapid retreat into North Carolina.

On March 8th, Sherman had crossed over the State line and into the vast pine forests which grew in the sandhills of North Carolina. His bummers soon learned that the huge resin filled trees, which had been tapped for turpentine, had large, pitch covered scars which burned fiercely and made good beacons with which to guide the invading army. The advance was begun with a vast column of fire and smoke with which to mark its passing. The Union Army turned almost due-east in its march which quickly told the Confederates what its next objective would be - Fayetteville, with its arsenal. Beyond this town would lie the rail junction of Goldsboro and the supplies brought in from the coast that Sherman's men now desperately needed. Joseph E. Johnston now ordered the Confederate forces to concentrate at Smithfield where he would attempt to take advantage if the invader should show any strategic weakness.

The Union cavalry, commanded by General Kilpatrick, scouted along the left flank of Sherman's advance. This command grew careless due to the lack of any meaningful opposition and early one morning it was surprised by an equal number of Confederate cavalrymen under Hampton and Wheeler at Monroe's Crossroads. While the fighting ended in a tactical draw, the Union General was never able to live down the fact he had been rousted from his bed before dawn and had retreated to the woods before he had time to dress in what was called "Kilpatrick's Shirttail Skedadle."

There actually was some tactical advantage gained by the Confederates in that they now could rejoin Hardee's command at Fayetteville. Lewis Hobson rested under a tree near the arsenal he had marched so hard to reach as the 8th Texas Cavalry Regiment rode by. Some of the troopers stopped to water their horses in a large trough in front of the government buildings.

"Is it true that you fellers whipped ol' Kilpatrick?" Lewis asked.

"Whipped him good," came the reply from one of the westerners. "We'll do it again if we git a chance to."

"We'll all git a chance to," Lewis responded. "I've heard Sherman ain't more than a day's march behind us. If we don't make a stand soon, the army will just about all go home."

"We'll still be here," said the Texan. "Good luck to you." The man mounted his horse and clopped on down the hill into town.

The ladies of Fayetteville spent the day cooking for the Confederate soldiers as they marched through the town. Lewis ate his first home cooked meal in months while stopped on the parklike lawn of the arsenal, enjoying the peacefulness and serenity of the majestic buildings. Later that day he would retreat past the very buildings where he used to work. As for the Armory buildings, in less than a week it would be hard for anyone to tell what had once been there.

General Johnston and General Hardee met at the Fayetteville Hotel to discuss future plans for the army. The rapid advance of Sherman had made it impossible for the Confederates to concentrate enough troops there to give him a battle. Hardee would fall back along the Northern Plank Road toward Raleigh in order to determine if Sherman was heading to the Capital or to Goldsboro. Johnston hoped to be able to strike him whichever he did.

Hardee's Corps marched through Fayetteville on the night of the 10th and camped two miles east of the Cape Fear River. Confederate General Wade Hampton was eating breakfast the following morning at the hotel with two of his aides when a scout galloped up with the news that the Yankees were in the town. The general quickly learned that he could not reach the stable where his horse was quartered. He grabbed the first one he could find and gathered a small force to charge the approaching Federals.

It was a pistol firing, saber swinging clash in the middle of the town that occurred next, a fight that left bullet holes in the Market House and bodies lying in the streets. The Rebel cavalry fought off the Federal's attempts to cut them off from the bridge and soon had all their men across the Cape Fear River and the Clarendon Bridge in flames. The army that had captured Atlanta, Savannah and Columbia was now in possession of Fayetteville and was poised to ravage the farms and villages in the land between the rivers which now lay in its path.

Chapter 15
Averasboro

General Wade Hampton and his staff reined in their horses at Flea Hill Church and looked through their field glasses to the southwest in the direction of Fayetteville. The General stood up on his stirrups to watch as the huge column of black smoke billowed up from a turpentine distillery on the west bank of the Cape Fear River which had been set ablaze by the Federals. There were numerous other smaller blazes as the fires from cotton mills and the destroyed arsenal covered the horizon with smoke.

"If we didn't know it was Sherman, we might think the Devil was moving Hell this morning," Hampton remarked to his staff. "He's either advancing on Raleigh or more likely Goldsboro and we have to find out which it is for General Johnston."

Just then, two scouts rode up to Hampton and saluted. "General, the Yankees are crossing the Cape Fear on two pontoon bridges. There is one there at the bridge we burnt and another about three or four miles south. One of their regiments has advanced about five miles to where the creek crosses the plank road about a mile or two from here. They have stopped and are digging in."

"They are setting up a perimeter so the rest of their troops and wagons can fill in behind them after they cross," Hampton reasoned. "Whose troops are they? Did you see any Corps flags?"

"Yes, Sir!" the scout answered. "I think it's 14th and 20th corps. One of their flags had an acorn on it."

"That's Slocum then!" Hampton exclaimed. "What about General Howard? Do you know where he's heading with the 15th and 17th corps?"

"We sent some men down there," the scout replied "Here they come now."

Two Confederate cavalrymen came galloping into the church yard, their horses' necks foamy with sweat. A corporal saluted General Hampton and gave his report.

"Sir! The Yankees crossing on the south bridge seem to be heading down the Blockersville road. There is another bunch that is taking the Wilmington road. They've got all the slaves that followed Sherman out of South Carolina. He must be sending them to Wilmington or some place else. A boat came up the river and blew its whistle several times and the Yankees got all excited about that."

"Sherman must have made contact with General Terry at Wilmington," Hampton surmised. "With Howard's wing of Sherman's Army heading east, they have to be aiming at Goldsboro. They could turn north at any time, but they are too far south for this to be just be a deception. They're headin for Goldsboro." Hampton said to his staff who nodded in agreement.

Another rider galloped up to the group and saluted. "Colonel Lipscomb, Second South Carolina Cavalry, sends his compliments to General Hampton," the scout reported. "He has been ordered by headquarters to take a position where the road from Fayetteville to Goldsboro crosses the South River at Graham's Bridge. He is also covering the New Bridge to the south. He wishes to make his orders known to you."

"I thank the Colonel," Hampton replied. "Were those all of his orders?"

"He is to report the approach of the enemy from the direction of Fayetteville," the scout answered.

"They are definitely approaching," Hampton said. "Look at this map over here." The General dismounted, followed by his aides and the scout and unfolded a map. The map was laid on the front steps of the church. "I suggest the

Colonel dig some entrenchments at intervals along the Goldsboro road, starting at the nine mile post. Give the Yankees enough fire to slow them down. If your regiment is large enough, send some men to this bridge near Gainey's Mill and do the same. Does the bridge have a name?"

"It's Maxwell's Bridge, General," one of the aides announced.

"I predict there will be plenty of Yankees at both these bridges to report on in about two days," Hampton said. "Take this information back to your Colonel." The scout saluted without comment and headed back toward Graham's Bridge.

Hampton then gave further orders to his officers. "Send a squadron of cavalry around to the road by the river and see if we can capture some Yankee foragers. I don't want any of Kilpatrick's horsemen to slip behind us at Wade's crossing there at Kyle's Landing. Scout up this middle road between the river road and the plank road. "We have to let General Hardee know when the Yankee's head his way."

The General turned back to observing the smoke from Fayetteville. He cursed silently to himself as he thought of all the rivers Sherman had been allowed to cross. The Confederates could not muster enough troops to even annoy him, much less strike him at this most vulnerable time. He thought of what he could do right now with just half the men Sherman had at his command. However, a plan was starting to take shape in Hampton's mind. If enough distance occurred between the two wings of Sherman's forces, the opportunity General Johnston was seeking might well present itself. A lot would depend on Hardee, who was now camped near the Bluff Church.

Sam had worked hard since his release and had prepared much of his farm for planting. His horse had died in his absence and now he and the mule spent several hours a day plowing and it seemed strange for Thomas not to drop by for a chat occasionally. The day after his return, Sam and Betty had visited Susan to talk about the train wreck at Shohola. The only consolation he could give to Susan was that Thomas'end had come swiftly and without pain. They made plans to help Susan with her spring planting. He also took care of another chore he had promised to do. He wrote a letter to Sarah McLain and told her Dougal had been well when he saw him last, but he felt like he was lying to the girl because he didn't expect to see his friend alive again.

Sam was getting used to not being in the army, but one thing caused him concern. He had noticed that the traffic up and down the road these days appeared to be Confederate Cavalry, which always seemed to be in a hurry.

By the Twelfth of March the ground was getting too wet for Sam to plow because each day brought more rain. The rivers were rising and low places in the roads became nearly impassable swamps. One afternoon, Sam and Betty were sitting on their porch watching the rain. There was no newspaper since Sherman had occupied Fayetteville and had burned the newspaper office. Sam squinted his eyes as he watched two mounted figures approaching up the road to his house. As they drew closer, he could see they were soldiers.

"Step up here on the porch after you get a drink from the well," Sam shouted at the approaching figures.

"I don't reckon we need any water," one of the men said as they dismounted and tied their horses to the hitching post. "We just need to get in out of the rain. How're you doing, Sergeant Morgan? I didn't expect to find you home . You got captured up near Richmond, didn't you?"

Sam didn't answer, but looked intently as the two drenched visitors walked up on the porch, keeping on their hats and coats. "You might not know us. We're from Company K, 51st Regiment. We knew who you were when you were a Sergeant in Company I. I'm Mike Barefoot and this here is Henry Pope."

The men shook hands with Sam and tipped their hats to Betty. "Sit down and rest yourselves," Sam offered. "What brings you fellows back down this way? Are you still in the army."

"Yes, we're up here on a mission," Pope explained. "Hoke just whipped the Yankees at Wyse's Fork near Kinston and now is somewhere near Goldsboro. A lot of our troops are concentrating at Smithfield and we might try to stop Sherman somewhere."

"If we can't try to stop him before he gets here, I ain't

243

really interested," Sam said emphatically. "I've been fighting for three years including time in a Yankee prison camp and ain't got a single thing out it. I'm not going back.

"Morgan, we need experienced leaders like you for this coming battle. General Johnston wants everybody that can fight to come back," Pope stated. "You still have some friends with the 51st and you might make a difference as to whether they live or die if you're there. Anyhow, when the Yankees find a soldier at home they send him to some prison, so your family is in more danger with you here than with you gone."

"I don't know." Sam replied. "I just don't know."

"Well," Barefoot said as the pair stood up to leave, "We've got other men to visit. We'll stop by your road at dawn the day after tomorrow. Hope you'll be there."

The two men stepped off the porch and mounted their horses and disappeared down the road.

"You don't suppose that was a threat, do you?" Betty asked.

"I don't care if it was. I got this Navy Colt and my mind's made up unless something happens. I don't know what else I can do," Sam replied. The rain had stopped and the blue skies indicated a dry day tomorrow. With the ground soft, it might be a good day for taking the mule and pulling those pesky stumps out of the newground he was trying to plow. The couple sat on the porch, rocking and talking about the approach of Sherman's Army and what they could do to survive its coming.

Lewis Hobson couldn't believe the irony of his situation. He had joined the "Black River Tigers" which had become Company B of the Tenth Battalion N.C. Heavy Artillery and had spent most of the war around Wilmington. In the fall of 1864, the unit had been sent to Savannah to help contest Sherman's advance on that city. Since then, there had been nothing but retreat in front of the Union invaders until now. Lewis was working to help set up an artillery piece in what looked like a formidable defensive position. He had been assigned to help the with the artillery supporting McLaw's Division. The rest of his unit had been issued rifles and now functioned as infantry. The thing which caused him concern was the fact it was only two miles from his home. He had obtained leave the previous afternoon to visit his family and help them to prepare for the invasion which was certain to come. He had helped his father bury the valuables and hide the meat from the smoke house deep in the woods. Now he was helping to set an artillery piece and getting ready to contest the advance of the Federals who would soon be coming up that road.

The area where the South River rises and flows through Black Mingo Swamp forms a neck of land with the Cape Fear River which is only two miles wide. It would be the best position to defend in this area with its flat, swampy ground. General Hardee had to fight a battle soon or his army would continue to waste away. The thirteen thousand troops he had taken out of Savannah had diminished to less than seven thousand mostly because of desertions of soldiers who left to protect their families in the path of Sherman's march. If the Yankees pushed toward Raleigh, any officer from either army who had a map could see there would be a battle at this spot near Averasboro.

The Union Army took the better part of two days to get across the Cape Fear River. As Sherman's troops consolidated their positions on the east side of the river, reconnaissance parties were sent out to scout out the next day's advance. Lt. Colonel Philo Buckingham with a brigade of Connecticut, Massachusetts, and Illinois regiments began a push down the Northern Plank Road and made contact with Confederate skirmishers around the eleven mile post near Wade's crossing. The Yankees advanced until they were met by increasing numbers of Rebel Cavalry in a prepared defensive position with three pieces of artillery. The resulting skirmish had the makings of a real battle as the Yankees tried to flank the Confederate position.

Sam had spent the morning with his mule pulling the stumps from the newground and after lunch had continued on into the afternoon. He stopped suddenly when he heard an unmistakable sound he had not heard since Cold Harbor - artillery fire. Betty had stepped onto the porch to hang some wet dust rags out to dry when she heard the same sound.

"Oh, Lord!" she hollered to Sam across the field. "Is that cannon fire?" knowing it could be nothing else.

"It certainly is," Sam replied. "It's coming from the direction of Kyles Landing and the Bluff Church. There seems to be a lively scrap going on."

For the rest of the afternoon, Sam tried to work, but he would occasionally stop and listen to the sound of the distant guns. Betty watched him through the window as he seemed to be held by an unseen force. It was then that she realized her husband was still a warrior and he would be leaving her tomorrow when Pope and Barefoot came by. Even though the chances to stop the invading hoards were almost nonexistent, his duty to his country and his personal honor required that he try. Betty walked over to the closet and took out Sam's gray uniform shirt. She sat down beside the window and began sewing the sergeant's stripes back on the shirt, crying as she worked.

In the middle of the afternoon, sounds of rifles firing were added to the noise of the distant artillery fire. The South Carolina troopers had dug defensive positions across the Goldsboro road as General Hampton had ordered. A party of Yankee foragers had been ambushed and forced back not over two miles from Sam's house.

Sam unhitched the mule and led him up to the trough near the well to drink. He walked up on the porch and shouted to his wife in the house who was still sewing. "Betty, the Yankees aren't far off and I'm going to get James and Lonnie to hide the mule and the cow."

Sam led his mule down the path to where his black neighbors were all standing outside their small houses listening to the sounds of battle in the distance. James was the first to speak. "Mistuh Sam, do you think the war is coming this way?"

"I think it's certain the Yankees will be here tomorrow," Sam answered. "Would you take this old mule and the cow down to the swamps and hide 'em for me? The river is high and you can leave 'em on the island that forms near the back fields when the water rises. Just leave 'em there with some hay and hope the Yankees don't find 'em."

"Yas, suh, I'll do it," James replied.

"I'll sneak over and milk the cow so she won't beller none," Lonnie volunteered.

"That's good." Sam agreed. "Don't take any milk up to my house like you usually do until the Yankees leave. They won't be here but a day or two."

"What are you going to do, Mistuh Sam?" Lonnie asked.

"I've got to leave," Sam answered. "The Yankees would send me back to prison if they captured me. Do what you can for my family while I'm gone."

"Yas, suh, we'll do what we did for Miz Betty when you was gone the fust time," James said. "It seems a shame a man can't stay on his own property though."

"Well, that's just the way it is right now. I'll see you when I get back," Sam answered.

"Don't you go off gittin' yourself kilt, Mistuh Sam," James shouted as Sam turned and headed back home. "You take care of yourself."

Sam thought of the irony as he walked back to his house. His black neighbors would joyfully welcome the end of slavery for their friends and relatives on other farms, but they had a sincere concern for his safety as he went back to war as a Confederate. The two races depended upon and needed each other in this agricultural society between the rivers. The war would alter the relationship, but basically the means of making a living would not be changed all that much.

As night fell, Sam spent some time with his children, reading to them and discussing the values he would teach them if fate should prove kind enough to give him the chance. He wanted to give his boys something to remember him by if he never came back.

After the boys were in bed, he spent some time showing his wife how to use the single action Navy Colt revolver. "If you think your life is in danger," he told her, "cock back the hammer and aim straight. If you don't kill your attacker, he'll probably kill you. If you think you can survive without the pistol, then don't use it."

After the weapon instruction, Betty heated a large pan

of hot water on the stove which Sam carried to the back porch and took the last hot bath he was liable to have for a long time. Sam and Betty blew out the oil lamps and climbed into bed where they lay snuggled in a loving embrace, waiting for the dawn they knew must come but hoped would not.

Sam suddenly sat up in the bed. He had not remembered going to sleep, but a light was beginning to show in the east. He was usually awakened by the crowing of the rooster, but had not heard him this morning. He turned up the oil lamp and read his watch. It was almost time for him to leave. Sam wakened Betty who fixed his breakfast while he dressed. After eating, he looked at his sleeping sons for what might well be the last time, and wondered what might happen to them if he didn't return.

He turned around and saw Betty looking at him as he said his good-byes. There was time for one last lingering kiss. Arm in arm, they walked out on the front porch. "My gold watch is on the mantle. Hide it and keep it safe for me," Sam said as they stood there, arms around each other while the dawn broke and the morning mist rose. Suddenly, they could see two men on horseback stopped near the main road.

"I'll love you forever," Sam said as he kissed his wife for what might be the last time.

"I'll love you till I die," Betty said as her grip slipped from his coat sleeve and she watched him walk down the steps and past the well to join the gray figures gathering near the main road.

Her heart was so full it felt like it was about to burst and she had something else to say to her husband. "Wait, Sam!" she shouted and ran as fast as she could through the mist to embrace him once more. "Please listen to me," she shouted.

"Promise me you won't take any unnecessary chances with your life," she pleaded through her tears as she wrapped her arms around his neck.

"Promise me you won't be among the last to die in the final battle of a lost war. I don't want you dying gallantly like the paper says about dead men who led a charge. The places where our granddaddies fought the British are now just piles of rocks and dirt in the woods. Nobody knows who died there and how they died. I want you to come home to me. Promise me you will."

Betty had tried to be strong throughout the war and she would have to be strong again, but this time she let her emotions flow freely. Her tears soaked into Sam's chest as he held his sobbing wife. "I want to come home to you more than anything else in the world," he comforted. "I promise you I'll do exactly what you say."

"We'll look after him, Mrs. Morgan" a voice said from atop one of the horses. Betty saw through her tears that it was Henry Pope and he was wearing a Captain's uniform. Mike Barefoot was also there astride his horse. He was a Lieutenant.

"It's time for us to leave now, Ma'am," Barefoot said.

Sam kissed Betty once more and squeezed her hand and then turned and took a place in the line. He was immediately greeted by several of his old comrades from the 51st. Betty recognized most of the men in the column. They were the walking wounded and the sick who were being gathered in a last ditch effort to stop Sherman.

"You men take care of yourselves," she encouraged. "Your families are going to need you bad after this" The men responded by a nod of their head or a tip of the hat to Betty and then disappeared down the road toward Graham's Bridge and into the mist rising off South River. It was only then she noticed the chill of the March morning and that she was shivering.

As the Southern soldiers approached Graham's Bridge, they saw that the work of getting it ready for destruction had begun. Several soldiers had buckets of turpentine and were coating the undersides of the bridge near the swirling water turned brown by the recent rains. A Lieutenant stood at the entrance to the bridge and saluted the approaching officers. "Good Morning, Sir" he greeted. "Are you Capt'n Pope?"

"That's right," Pope responded. "These are all the men that will be coming with me."

"We were told you would be the last to cross so I reckon the next soldiers we see after the rest of our men get back here will be Yankees," the Lieutenant responded. "I guess our work's almost finished here."

"Don't tarry too long," Pope Cautioned. "I figure they'll be along bright and early." With a nod of his head, the Captain led his men across the bridge and over into Sampson County.

The sun was rising and the clouds were giving way to the morning sky when Pope's small column stopped for a rest. Now Sam was able to carry on a conversation with some of his old comrades. "Mister Mack," he said to Neil McMillan, "I haven't seen you since Charleston. Have you been stationed near home?"

"It's good to see you again, Sam," the older man responded. "They let me come home and help guard the Arsenal since I was elected to the Court of Pleas and Quarter Sessions at Fayetteville. I'd rather be fightin' than in a prison camp some where. The day before Sherman came, ol' John C. Monroe locked the front door to the Arsenal, stuck the key in his pocket and went home to Eagle Springs. He's probably safe at his home right now, but I couldn't stay at mine since the Yankees are going to come through."

"You're exactly right," Sam agreed. "I'm one who knows about prisons. I reckon John Monroe can stay at his home since Sherman ain't headin' north, but we can't cause he's shore comin' our way."

"We were hoping to pick up more men from the 51st, Sam" Captain Pope said. "Some of the men got leave to look after their families and were supposed to come back with us. Two of the Boulton boys got captured near their homes and I heard the Yankees were chasing Bob Melvin, trying to capture him. I also heard they shot Archibald Murphy. They just shot him because he was too sick to keep up. There's a lot of them camped near the Holmes house near Murphy's Mill. The bastards burned the furniture from the house and made one of the small boys throw his shoes in the fire. One man can't do anything, but if we can gather enough men together, we might just be able to give ol' Sherman a bloody nose some where up this road."

Reveille had also sounded early in the Union Army camps. The right wing under General O.O. Howard consisted of the Fifteenth and Seventeenth Corps and would march nearly due east for a time before a planned swing to the north toward Goldsboro. General Henry Slocum led the left wing which was comprised of the Fourteenth and Twentieth Corps. It would move north on the Plank road toward Raleigh and then swing quickly toward Goldsboro. Sherman's Army would pass down every road heading in the direction of Goldsboro and leave near starvation in eastern Cumberland County.

The "bummers" were the first to leave camp, since their main duty was to find food for the Army by any means necessary. Occasionally, some of them would fall into the hands of Wheeler's Rebel Cavalry, a band almost as undisciplined as themselves, and meet a fate some of their own troops described as "well deserved."

It was mid-morning when a small group of Confederate horsemen rode up to the well in front of the Morgan's porch and began filling their canteens. "Thank you for this good water, Ma'am," their Captain said to Betty as she walked out the front door. "We most likely won't be by this way again cause the Yankees ain't far behind."

"Will there be a battle?" she asked apprehensively.

The Captain shook his head. "No, Ma'am," he answered. "There ain't enough of us to give 'em a battle, but there might be a fight down at the bridge. Stay behind the chimney if you hear firing cause there might be some stray bullets come over this way. "The troopers mounted and with a touch of his hat, the officer led his men off toward Graham's Bridge. Betty stood on the porch for a minute watching the horsemen disappear up the road and knowing the next men she saw would be the Yankees.

Susan had also been up since dawn on this particular day. Her cabin was hidden by trees and didn't have an inviting road up to its front door so it was never visited by the travelers along the road. She got an early start on hoeing the garden as Thomas played by the edge of the field. The rain had actually stopped and the sun shown brightly. It was past mid-morning when she walked over to the blanket she had laid for little Thomas' nap under a large oak tree and drank some water from a jar she had brought with her.

Her son was playing near the path which crossed the

251

cypress swamp on the way to the Morgan house. She had not heard the horse and lone rider which had quietly approached her house. The snort of the animal startled Susan and she wheeled around to see a soldier in a faded blue uniform and a worn black hat slide down from the saddle.

The Yankee approached with a smirk on his face and his right hand on his holstered pistol. "I don't have very much food," Susan said, unable to think of anything else to say.

"Well, what do we have here?" the soldier said. "I found myself a Secesh wench all by herself in this out of the way place."

"Take what you will from the house," Susan offered.

"Oh, I aim to take what I want all right," the man said. "That man of yours has been away a long time from the looks of this place. You're going to be glad a real man like me came along."

Susan turned to run but the man grabbed her and pushed her down on the wet ground. "Thomas, run to Betty's," she shouted to the toddler as she tried to fight off her attacker.

The soldier fell on top of her and started ripping at her clothes as she continued to struggle. He was straddling her waist holding her down when a dark figure unexpectedly stood over the pair, making a shadow. The Yankee looked back over his shoulder and squinted into the sun, trying to see who was interfering with his evil intentions. With his head twisted at this odd angle, his neck snapped like a match stick when the heavy stock of a Springfield rifle smashed into his jaw.

"You all right, Miz Susan?" the tall dark figure inquired.

"Moses? Moses Hawkins? Is that You?" Susan asked, pulling together her torn dress.

"It sho is, and just in time I'd say," Moses answered.

Susan suddenly thought of her son. "Get Thomas. He ran toward the swamp," she yelled.

Moses ran toward the creek crossing which was now under water because of the recent heavy rains, dropping the rifle as he ran. Thomas had run to the waters edge and had slipped in the mud and was now clinging to a cypress knee. He was screaming at the top of his lungs, frightened at the approach of the large black man who was unknown to him. "Let me git you out of here before you git snakebit," Moses said as he picked up the screaming youngster and handed him to his mother.

"Moses, I can't thank you enough," Susan said as she calmed down her frightened child. "But we're going to have some trouble when the Yankees find one of their soldiers dead, aren't we?"

"Naw," Moses quickly replied. "I'll just put him under that low limb and it'll look like his horse reared and he hit his head. I'll turn his horse loose and keep this rifle. You and the boy need to go up to the Morgan house for your own safety. There's a whole division of Yankees coming up that road and some of them are out of control. I know cause I followed them for two hundred miles."

"You're not going to shoot at them with that rifle are you?" Susan asked.

"Oh no!" Moses answered. "Where that blue army goes, the slaves is free. I know that too 'cause I was in that army for three years and I ain't going to do nothing to git in the way of that. I'll just stay in the woods and watch over things and not let things git out of hand."

Susan led Thomas around by the main road to take refuge in the Morgan home. They were welcomed as always and Betty felt better with her company as the two families awaited the arrival of the Yankees.

Union General John W. Geary was not particularly happy with the task which had been give him this day. His administrative talents had been known and appreciated by General Sherman, so Geary would not accompany the left wing down the Raleigh road toward Averasboro. Instead, his Second Division of 20th Corps would advance on the road between the two wings of Sherman's Army and would escort the army's wagons. This was not the duty an ambitious politician would be able to use to his advantage in the campaigns of the postwar North. There would likely be action down the plank road, he thought, as the 14th Corps and the remainder of 20th Corps marched past the Second Division which waited

253

beside the road for them to pass. After they had marched past, Geary's troops turned right at the nine mile post of the Northern Plank Road and slogged down the Goldsboro road toward Graham's Bridge.

The soldier Moses had killed on the morning of fifteenth had been a mounted forager who moved out several hours before Geary's division. But there were two dozen others who had the same task and around midday four of them came whooping and shouting into the yard of the Morgan house. The first two rode out behind the house and began shooting the hogs, startling the women and children inside. When they had finished, one of them shouted, "Where are the chickens? See if you can find 'em. Everybody's got chickens."

A burly sergeant and a much smaller Yankee private dismounted and approached the front porch where Betty was standing, her hands holding her rolled up apron at her waist. The Sergeant spoke first. "As payment for your sin of secession, the U.S. Government requires me to commandeer all of your treasonous livestock for consumption by President Lincoln's Army. My fee for this hazardous work will be all the food you got cooked in your kitchen and your silverware to eat it with."

"There isn't any food cooked and there isn't any silverware," Betty answered, which was technically correct since Sam had buried the silver under an oak tree in the woods before he left.

"Have you ever heard such treasonous talk, Emil?" the Sergeant asked his diminutive companion. "We sure have found ourselves a hotbed of secession."

Earlier that morning, Betty had tied Sam's watch around her neck and it hung down between her breasts in a pouch called a "bosom buddy". This device was used by ladies of the time for safekeeping their valuables. Unfortunately, the watches' ticking was very loud and the Yankees could hear it.

"I do think there is something we need to confiscate, Emil,' the sergeant said. "I order you to reach in there between them bosoms and capture that gold watch."

"I'll gladly obey that order," Emil stated with a smirk and started up the steps to the porch.

Betty had brought another belonging of Sam's with her

out on the porch. She quickly drew the Navy Colt pistol from her apron and cocked the hammer back. She aimed the barrel between the little Yankee's eyes and said, "You do and you'll shake hands with the devil in less than a minute."

"Careful, Emil!" the sergeant said. He had not expected his stealing to be challenged since it usually wasn't. He reached to draw his own weapon and at the same moment, in the woods across the field from the house, Moses Hawkins pulled back the hammer of the Springfield and aimed for the Sergeant's chest. "It looks like we're going to have to burn this place after all."

Just then, a clatter of hooves interrupted the confrontation as a column of blue clad horsemen galloped into the yard led by a Captain. Seeing this, Moses released the hammer of the rifle and watched as the officer took charge of the situation.

"Capt'n," the burly sergeant began, "this woman just pulled a gun on one of my men. We ought to burn this place down."

"That's a perfectly natural reaction for someone trying to protect their home," the captain responded curtly. "Your duties are ended here."

"But Sir," the sergeant said, trying to explain, "we've been nearly shot..."

"That will be all," the Captain said firmly. "We had hoped to surprise the Rebels at the bridge and capture it intact, but with all the shooting and racket you're making there's no hope of that now. Round up your men and leave."

Turning to Betty, the officer said, "I'm Captain Voorhees, Pennsylvania Light Artillery at your service, Ma'am. This war forces us to sometimes do things some of us hate to do."

"But some of you seem to relish in thievery," Betty countered.

"That may well be true, but you and your family are in no danger while my men are here," Voorhees replied. "I will have to confiscate your weapon because General Geary and his staff will be along directly and will need some of the rooms in your house."

"Do I dare to expect rent from the United States Army

for turning me out of my own home?" Betty said sarcastically.

"No, but there will be an advantage to you," Voorhees said. "You and your family will remain and no soldier in our army would dare bother you with the General in the same house. Will you please surrender your weapon?"

"May I have it back when you leave?" Betty asked. "Yankees aren't the only ones I need protection from."

"I'll see to it personally," the Captain promised. He rode his horse over to the porch and Betty handed the pistol to him. Captain Voorhees looked into the eyes of what he considered to be the type of woman he would want for a wife when this war ended. He was impressed by this beautiful lady defending her home and honor against odds she couldn't hope to match. It would be safe to say that the occurrences of the last few minutes would have a lasting effect on the Captain. He stuck the pistol in his belt and touched the brim of his hat as a gesture of courtesy to Betty.

He rode out behind the house about one hundred yards and looked at the terrain through his field glasses. He was looking for a bluff or knoll where he could post his artillery to cover Graham's Bridge. He didn't find what he was looking for and rode back toward the main road speaking again to Betty who had been joined by Susan and the children on the front porch.

"I'm going to post a Corporal's guard here till the General arrives. These men will have to search your house for other weapons, I'm afraid." Leaving the Corporal and four men at the house, the Captain and his troops rode off toward the river.

Two regiments of Union infantry were already in position for the assault on the bridge and soon the sounds of war were heard along South River. Since the river was very high at this time, the Confederate position could not be flanked by the Yankees and a direct charge across the bridge would be suicidal. The action became little more than an artillery duel and after a time, Colonel Lipscomb of the Second South Carolina cavalry decided that honor had been served and withdrew, leaving Graham's Bridge furiously burning.

The remainder of the left wing of Sherman's Army had

continued up the plank road and had camped for the night at the Bluff Church and up at Taylor's Hole Creek. On March 16th, as the Union advance was resumed, scouts of General Kilpatrick's cavalry encountered something they had seldom seen since leaving Savannah - Confederate infantry and artillery behind three lines of entrenchments they didn't plan to give up without a fight.

Lewis Hobson waited beside his field piece in the rear of McLaws Division on the Confederate third line. He could hear the rifle fire from the action at the front line and knew that today he would fire his gun in anger.

· The Confederate first line was a brigade under the command of Colonel Alfred Rhett who lately had been the commander of Fort Sumter. The initial skirmishing in the Battle of Averasboro had begun on the afternoon of March 15th between intermittent downpours of rain. In the dark, foggy conditions of the thick pine woods, Colonel Rhett ran into some Yankee scouts and was captured. The mortified officer dined with General Sherman and his staff that night in an old cooper shop near the post office at Kyles Landing. Since he had spent some time in prewar Charleston and knew the family, Sherman thought the incident significant enough to be mentioned the next day in a dispatch sent from Kyles Landing.

Infantry from General Slocum's two corps moved up in the rainy night to begin the assault early on the 16th. Rhett's Brigade, now under the command of Colonel William Butler, was attacked and held for five hours before being flanked by cavalry and pulverized by twelve Union artillery pieces, set up near the Smith house. The South Carolinians, after some heavy losses, fell back to the second line manned by Taliaferro's Division.

General Joseph Wheeler and his cavalry had crossed South River the day before after a slight skirmish near Smith's Mill. Hearing of the conflict at Averasboro, Wheeler asked for and received permission from Wade Hampton to go to Hardee's assistance. The Rebel commander led over a thousand of his troopers through the pine woods and past the fertile fields east of South River, galloping toward the sound of the guns.

Wheeler's arrival brought Hardee's troop total up to nearly eight thousand and enabled the Confederate line to be extended all the way to the Cape Fear River. This help arrived in the nick of time as five regiments of Federal troops were at that moment crossing the deep ravines near the river in preparation to attack the Confederate flank. By this time, the second line had given way and when both divisions of Fourteenth Corps arrived, the Yankees would have more than twenty thousand men to send against Hardee's third line.

Now that the might of both armies faced each other, neither side wanted a pitched battle. General Johnston had sent orders to Hardee to withdraw toward Bentonville earlier that day, but the battle had already begun and it would be dangerous to disengage. Sherman on the other hand thought that Hardee would retire during the night and spare his troops from making a frontal assault with the multitude of wounded that would cause. Hardee did withdraw during the night, leaving Wheeler's cavalry to act as his rear guard.

General Wheeler retreated in front of the advancing Yankees to the village of Averasboro. Wheeler's horse soldiers maintained contact with the Federal advance until it turned toward Goldsboro. It now became certain to the Confederates, that Johnston and Sherman, the two antagonists who had fought each other in the red clay hills of Georgia on the road to Atlanta, would fight once again. This time the battle would occur in the flat fields and tall pine forests of eastern North Carolina.

When Sherman later wrote his memoirs, he called the four hundred seventy-seven wounded suffered at Averasboro "a serious loss," since every wounded man had to be carried in an ambulance. This shows that had Sherman been confronted by a major Confederate army in the low country of South Carolina, the march through the Carolinas probably could not have occurred. Jefferson Davis' decision to replace Joseph E. Johnston with Hood before Atlanta, and General Hood's subsequent wasting the army in Tennessee at the battles of Franklin and Nashville was proving to be disastrous for the people of the South.

Chapter 16
Bentonville

The sounds of the cannons at Averasboro could be distinctly heard at the Morgan house, but the main activity on the 16th of March on the Goldsboro Road was the construction of a new bridge across South River. Four companies of the First Michigan Engineers immediately began work on the bridge and had it repaired by eleven o'clock. In spite of all the other things the people of the South said about Sherman's Army, they had to grudgingly admit that it was very efficient.

General Geary had arrived during the night and had slept on a couch in the sitting room and left before dawn. Betty and Susan saw very little of the bearded, future two time governor of Pennsylvania.

It had rained heavily again during the night and the sound of axes echoed in the woods as the Yankees cut trees to "corduroy" the road up to and on the other side of South River. For the rest of the day, a Union Army Division and five hundred wagons passed in front of the Morgan house and across the newly reconstructed Graham's Bridge.

Most of the wagons were drawn by mules taken from the farms and plantations in the path of the advance of Sherman from Savannah. A mule is an animal who seems to actually understand the English language, but only if it is liberally sprinkled with oaths and curses. The language of the Yankee "mule skinners" almost turned the air blue as the unfortunate animals pulled their loads over the unaccustomed corduroy roads and bridges.

In the middle of the afternoon, a lone rider trotted up the road to the Morgan house. It was Captain Voorhees who had come to return the pistol to Betty. "I promised to return this personally, ma'am, and here it is. I hope you will never have to use it for protection." Without waiting for a reply the Captain spoke to the guard he had left at the house, "Corporal, we'll be moving out now."

Betty recognized that this officer had saved her and her home from much grief and she had nothing to give him in return. "Captain, I appreciate what you've done for us and I'd be glad if you would at least let me fill your canteen before you leave." she offered. "We have mighty good tasting water in our well."

"I'd be grateful, ma'am." the Captain replied.

Betty walked over to the well and dropped the bucket into the water with a splash. She pulled up the bucket with the rope around the squeaking wheel pulley and swung the bucket up where she balanced it on the wall of the well. She filled the officer's canteen and said, "Have your men give me their canteens and I'll give them some fresh water too." Captain Voorhees waited till Betty finished and then with a tip of his hat rode out of the yard and down the road to the rebuilt Graham's Bridge. General Geary's Division and his five hundred wagons would spend the next night in Sampson County, camped at the farm of H.T. Jackson. The Captain had never inquired on the marital status of the lady who had exchanged a simple kindness with him, an enemy, in a wartime situation. But, over the coming weeks, it would be hard for him to get her out of his mind.

Sarah McLain could tell by the type of soldiers coming through the aid station in Florence that the war was lost. These were not always sick and wounded men, but now included able bodied soldiers who had given as much as they had to give. They were now just on their way home to see if home was still there.

Sherman's advance had been to the west of Florence leaving the town untouched, but the South Carolina countryside had still been stripped of food by the shortages of war and the needs of the returning soldiers were not always met. The aid station became not just a place which extended medical care but a place where a hungry soldier could find nourishment. The buildings of the complex soon proved too small for the needs of the men passing through. Tents and makeshift lean-to's were soon added to the aid station. The close proximity to the cooking fires of some of this flimsy construction was a recipe for disaster.

On the day of the fight at Averasboro, the wind was blowing in strong gusts at Florence. Sarah was helping Dr. Dargan change some bandages before lunch and the men who could walk were lining up for their meal. Malichi was bringing a few of the smaller sweet potatoes that Mrs. Grantham sent for the soldiers ever so often and had almost reached the aid station. A strange smell of smoke drifted over the area which was not that of like that of the cooking fires. One of the tents in the rear of the station was on fire.

Sarah ran down to the tent where the front half was ablaze. Sick men were crawling out on all fours along the sides of the tent, saving themselves as the flames advanced. She saw that most of the men were safe but there was one she didn't see. "Where is that Corporal from Alabama that had the fever?" she shouted.

Without waiting for an answer, she darted inside the burning tent through the thick smoke. She could see the Corporal desperately trying to stand but unable to do so because of his weakened state. Suddenly, a blazing piece of fabric separated from the burning tent and fell across Sarah's left shoulder. She screamed from the pain and tore at the burning cloth, coughing from the smoke and at the same time smelling her own hair burning. All at once a figure came bursting through the smoke and pulled the burning tent from on top of her. It was Malichi. He picked her up and threw her across his shoulder like she was a sack of cotton seed and started out of the tent which was now near collapse.

"Get the Corporal!" she screamed just before she fainted. Malichi reached with his right hand and grabbed the sick soldier by the shirt and pulled the two to safety just in the nick of time as the tent collapsed in a mass of flames.

Help was waiting as two soldiers had gotten buckets of water which they immediately threw on the three just as soon as they reached safety. Malichi had rescued the two so quickly, he hadn't received any severe burns, but the Corporal was gasping for breath as two nurses immediately began attending to him. Sarah was placed on a blanket and Dr. Dargan quickly saw she had burns of her neck and shoulder. "Get some of that lard from the cook!" he ordered.

The fresh air quickly revived Sarah but the doctor instructed her to remain still as he applied the lard to her neck and shoulder. She would survive if her burns didn't get infected, but dozens of soldiers looked on in horror as the doctor worked hurriedly on what moments before had been the most beautiful woman most of them had ever seen.

General Wade Hampton and his troops were up early on the morning of March 17th headed for Bentonville. The road from Averasboro to Goldsboro led through this small hamlet and the General's forces would spend this day delaying the advance of the Federals and studying the terrain. Confederate Army units which had once been widely dispersed were now gathering in sufficient numbers at Smithfield to give Slocum's wing of Sherman's Army a severe thrashing if enough of them could reach this spot before the rapidly advancing Yankees.

The General liked the terrain of the forests and fields along the Goldsboro Road. Here at Bentonville, a trap could be set for the overconfident Federals which could duplicate the Confederate victory on the first day at Gettysburg. Hoke's Division was coming from Goldsboro to the east while the Army of Tennessee and Hardee's Corps would be arriving from the north via Smithfield. The arrival of these forces on the field at the right time would be crucial. Hampton was satisfied with what he had seen and when he got back to Smithfield, he would present his plan to General Johnston that night.

Charles and Uriah were very talkative as they marched through the pine forests which reminded them so much of home. "It's hard to believe we're going to fight some Yankees this close to home," Charles said.

"Yeah, it is," Uriah agreed. "I want to find out what

happened at Averasboro. That's a lot closer to home than we are now."

"Do you ever think we'll see home again?" Charles asked. "We fought down at Charleston and we fought against Grant in Virginia. Now we're going to fight against Sherman. We ain't seen home in three years and now home seems like a dream of some far off place to me."

"You ain't gittin' that feeling that you ain't going to make it, are you?" Uriah asked. "It's dangerous to think like that."

"It's just that after we fought at Kinston, we stopped the Yankees," Charles related. "Then we marched on to Goldsboro and left it wide open for the same Yankees we whipped to walk right in when they git ready to, even if they ain't done it yet. If we do whip Sherman, we probably got to turn around and take Goldsboro again. That ain't even counting the Yankees coming up from Wilmington. There's too dang many of them and not enough of us, I figure. I think I just rather go on home."

"You might be right," Uriah responded. "But I figure 'ol Joe Johnston's got himself a plan and I want to stick around long enough to see if it works."

General Joseph E. Johnston did indeed have a plan. He had managed to gather from all sources an army of twenty-one thousand men and he had adopted Wade Hampton's plan to surprise Slocum's wing of Sherman's Army which numbered thirty thousand. When Slocum was routed, Johnston would then deal with the other Union forces.

Hoke's Division was digging in along the Goldsboro Road, awaiting the advance of Slocum's troops. As the sun rose on the morning of March 19th, a group of figures approached the position of the 51st. Charles and Uriah were trying to warm themselves by stretching and walking around after a night on the wet ground with no fires. Uriah noticed something familiar about the walk of one of the approaching men. "Charles!" he exclaimed. "I'll be dang if one of these men don't look like Sam."

"The Devil you say," Charles answered. "Where?"

"The one in front," Uriah answered. "Ain't that him?"

"It shore is!" Charles shouted. The two friends grabbed their rifles and ran toward the approaching group giving the Rebel yell and jumping and leaping.

Sam immediately recognized the two former comrades and began running toward them. "I never expected to see you two rascals again!" Sam said happily.

"You shore are a sight for sore eyes, Sam," Uriah said as he hugged his long lost friend.

"You boys look good, too," Sam said. "They must be feedin' you lots of hard tack and salt pork."

"Only when they capture some from the Yankees," Charles said. "Most of the time it's only parched corn."

The three friends were now reunited and since the replacements had already drawn weapons, they stood around their positions in the piney woods and caught each other up on what had happened since Sam's capture.

"I reckon ya'll heard about Thomas and Daniel Graham gettin' killed 'cause of that train wreck," Sam began. "There's something else ya'll need to know. When I left Elmira, Dougal had smallpox so bad I never expect to see him again. He might be dead already."

"I'm downright sorry to hear that," Uriah said.

"Damn Right!" Charles added. " Six of us left together and now there's only three left alive and there's still some more fightin' to be done."

Just then a soldier walked up in front of where the replacements had dug in. "Sergeant Morgan. Major Garrison wants to see you," he announced.

Sam returned in just a few minutes with a stunned look on his face. "I've just been made a Lieutenant in I Company," he announced, followed by the yells and whoops of congratulation from his friends.

From up the Averasboro Road to the west came the sound of distant rifle fire. The Yankee foragers of 14th Corps had run into Dibrell's Confederate cavalry division of Wheeler's Corps. The Rebels would grudgingly give ground before retiring when they reached Wade Hampton's barricades and Hoke's entrenchments behind that.

Hoke had his veteran troops dug in, forming a position

south of where the Goldsboro-Bentonville road forks. The brigade of Junior Reserves was placed on the right along the Bentonville Road near the Willis Cole Plantation.

The leading Union division on that day was that of General William P. Carlin. These soldiers advanced against the increasing fire of the Confederate cavalrymen and as the advance became more and more difficult, word was sent back to the Federal commander to the effect that these Rebels "don't drive worth a damn." This was a phrase not used since the Atlanta Campaign.

It was almost ten o'clock when the Yankees came into view of Hoke's troops. Sam and his men watched from behind their fortified positions as the firing drew closer. The dismounted cavalrymen kept firing as they retreated across the fields in front of the Cole house. They formed a unified front and fired a volley toward the approaching Federals before passing through the waiting lines of Hoke's Division. "I reckon their work is done for the day," Uriah surmised.

"Our's shore ain't," Charles said as the Federal skirmishers advanced toward the dug in Confederates. As the advance portions of Carlin's leading brigades joined the attack, Hoke's artillery began to fire, momentarily halting the attackers.

The Yankees were still under the impression they were facing only cavalry and Slocum sent word to General Sherman that whatever was in their front would be brushed aside. The red-haired General had picked this day to ride over to O.O. Howard's Corps and accompany them in a triumphal entry the next day into Goldsboro. He was well on his way when the battle started and was able to hear the sound of the guns. When he received Slocum's message, he considered the situation under control.

Sam was now in command of Company I. Not used to being an officer, he soon had an Enfield rifle and was firing along beside his comrades. "Mark your target and aim low!" was his only command as sheets of flame lashed out at the surprised Yankees. More and more Federals were being sent against Hoke. Morgan's Division of Slocum's Corps attacked and after a healthy encounter was driven back where it dug in south of the Goldsboro road.

In the past, when the troops of Sherman had met Joseph E. Johnston, the Federals had enjoyed a two to one advantage in numbers. The only strategy necessary was to send a brigade or two around the Confederate flank and force them to abandon one strong position after another. Carlin employed the same strategy when he ordered the brigades of Buell and Hobart to swing around to the left of Hoke. Hobart made some headway, but Buell's men ran into a meat-grinder among the tall pines and swampy ravines and was forced to hug the ground where they were. Hobart went forward far enough to create a gap in the Union Lines. General Slocum, realizing his opponents were larger than first thought, now sent a request to Sherman for reinforcements.

The Confederate line resembled a giant sickle with Hoke as the handle and the Army of Tennessee under Stewart and Hardee's Corps as the blade. An attack now would send 14th Corps reeling back in confusion and place Slocum's entire wing in serious trouble. However, there were two factors, unknown to the Yankees, which were going to save them from total defeat.

First, Hardee's Corps was now just arriving from Averasboro and taking its place in Johnston's attack. Because of faulty North Carolina maps, Hardee's men had to travel at a forced march pace since the map had shown their last camp was six miles closer to Bentonville than it actually was. They were fatigued and in need of rest when they arrived.

Secondly, Braxton Bragg was one of the Confederate commanders on the field. Hardee's arrival coincided with a heavy attack on Hoke's position which caused the jittery Bragg to call for help. General Johnston, in a move he would always regret, detached McLaw's Division to reinforce Hoke. This move weakened the force of attack and cost valuable time. By the time McLaws reached Hoke's position, the Union attack had been beaten off and McLaws was left with nothing to do.

"Ya Hoo!" Charles shouted as the blue backs of the attackers disappeared in the pine woods. "The Yankees are falling back again. They can't drive us out of here in a million years."

"These pine logs shore make a difference, don't they?" Uriah said. "They make it a lot less costly to defend than to attack."

"Aren't you sorry you complained so much when you had to chop them down?" Sam asked. "Hey, look to your right! I heard the Army of Tennessee was here, but this is the first I've seen of them."

The attack of Johnston's sickle shaped formation was under way at last. It was nearly three o'clock and what was left of the Western Army marched out of the woods and in perfect alignment, headed for the exposed Union flank.

"Look at that!" Uriah exclaimed. "That's downright beautiful."

The gray and butternut line, five thousand strong, advanced across an open field with officers on horseback leading from their assigned positions and the red battle flags flapping in the gentle breeze of the spring day. The Junior Reserves who formed the right of Hoke's line stood up and cheered as the last offensive assault ever to be made by a Confederate army passed to their right.

"It sort of makes you sad to see how close together their flags are," Uriah observed.

"Damn right!" Charles agreed. "Their regiments are the size of companies and the divisions look like regiments."

"Just think what they could do if they were full strength," Charles wondered. "Just think of what we could do if we had Thomas and Daniel and the Tew boys and all the others we've lost back with us."

"Yeah," Uriah agreed. "As long as you are raisin the dead, how about gittin ol' Stonewall to command us."

This attack paused momentarily when it hit Carlin's defenses and then surged forward again. Carlin had not straightened his lines as ordered and now General D. H. Hill's Division charged through the gap. The Yankee defenders who saw they were in danger of being flanked and surrounded gave way in panic. One of these young soldiers later wrote: "We showed the Rebs as well as our side some of the best running we ever did...."

Carlin's Division crumbled quickly and fell back in

confusion through the tall pines, thickets and fields of the Union left. Hoke's Division was supposed to advance with this attack, but General Bragg either misunderstood or disobeyed his orders and held them back. In addition, McLaws Division, which Bragg had begged for earlier in the day, was given no orders at all and saw no action for most of the day.

General Jeff Davis, the Union commander of 14th Corps, ordered his reserve division of General Fearing to advance north from Morgan's position on the Goldsboro road and hit the Rebel breakthrough in the left flank. This it did with great determination but in doing so was hit in the flank by other advancing Confederates and was forced to pull back some three hundred yards to save itself. This withdrawal opened another gap in the Union lines which three of D. H. Hill's brigades immediately found and rushed through, heading for the rear of Morgan's position on the Goldsboro road.

General Hoke liked what he saw through his field glasses. If he could support Hill's division's breakthrough with an attack of his own, Morgan would be forced to withdraw and the 14th Corps rout would be complete. The Confederates were on the verge of a shocking victory at Bentonville.

But once again, Braxton Bragg was able to snatch defeat from the jaws of victory. Hoke implored his superior to let him attack the breach in the Union lines Hill had created. "Sounds too risky," was his answer. "Better make a frontal assault to keep Morgan occupied." He just didn't seem to understand the opportunities like the one Hill was presenting had to be quickly and firmly exploited by an army which was always outnumbered. There was no way an attack against fortifications like these, which the Federals had ample time to prepare, was going to be successful.

Hoke's soldiers walked slowly through the thick pine forest. They were formed in two lines of battle which seemed to have no end. "Wait for my command," Sam ordered as the dug in Yankees were now visible through the trees. The command Sam gave was drowned out by a volley of fire from the Yankees behind their pine log barricades. The minnie balls clipped the pine branches and felled small trees around the Rebels who sprang forward in their attack.

Uriah fixed his sights on a Yankee when he heard a "thwack" beside him as a bullet struck Charles in the leg above the knee. "Oh, Lordy, I'm hit," his friend screamed as he fell to the pine needle covered ground.

"Put your belt around it and stop the bleeding," Uriah shouted. "I'll be back for you directly."

The attack pressed forward and became a face to face slugging match at Morgan's line as Hoke attacked his front and Hill's three brigades attacked from the rear. This part of the battle would later be compared to Cold Harbor and Gettysburg by soldiers who fought at both places, and Sam thought of Betty and the promise he had made that he would come back to her. As he fought for his life against the desperate Federals who were fighting for theirs, he realized this was as good a place for getting killed that he had ever seen. He could hear the "zing" of the minnie balls as they went by his head and into the pines, but he kept firing his pistol into the massed Federals behind the logs. Morgan's Yankees were almost surrounded and the outcome of the contest would be decided here and now. Among the screams of the wounded and the shouts and curses of the men who were not, the troops of Hoke and Morgan attempted to annihilate each other.

It was at this point the squandered time of the early afternoon came back to haunt the Confederates. The 20th Corps of General Alpheus Williams reached the battlefield and immediately sent the brigade of General William Cogswell to the aid of the beleaguered troops of Morgan. This advance came in on the rear of Hill and forced him to withdraw. Hoke also had to suspend his attack and retreated back to his lines.

"Sam, help me find Charles!" Uriah pleaded. "He was hit when we first attacked."

Sam hadn't known that Charles had been hit until he saw him on the ground, weak from the loss of blood in spite of the belt wrapped around the leg. "Here he is!" Sam yelled to Uriah. "Grab his other arm." The two ran with their friend through the pines to the ambulances which were waiting in the rear.

They laid Charles on the straw floor and tried to make him comfortable. "They'll take care of that leg at the hospital and you'll be good as new," Sam comforted.

"Damn right," Charles said only slightly above a whisper. "Uriah, I'll see you fellers later." Uriah couldn't bring himself to speak. He had seen the bullet had shattered the bone and the leg would have to be amputated. He squeezed his friend's hand and sent up a prayer in his behalf.

Hoke's casualties had been substantial in the frontal assault. Instead of exploiting a general breakthrough, Hoke's troops attacked a fixed defensive position which had been prepared to defeat just such an attack. General Hagood was unforgiving of Braxton Bragg when he wrote: "The loss in our division at least would have been inconsiderable and our success eminent had it not been for Bragg's undertaking to give a tactical order upon a field that he had not seen."

All of Union 20th Corps had now reached Bentonville and was digging in behind pine log barricades. The numerically superior Yankees knew they only had to defend themselves and wait for reinforcements. The attacking Rebels could not afford for that to happen. Five separate attacks from the Army of Tennessee were beaten back by the Federals and their massed artillery. By nightfall, the Confederates had suspended their attacks and had fallen back to the lines they had held at the beginning of the battle. Slocum's wing of Sherman's Army had narrowly escaped disaster on this day, but now it was safe. Nothing that was going to happen in the last days of the war would be changed because of the fighting on March 19th, but it was only the first phase of the battle that had ended.

General O. O. Howard, the commander of Sherman's right wing, had been concerned about the sounds of the distant battle he heard on the 19th. He had started a division marching to Slocum's support. Sherman countermanded the order when he arrived since his last communication with his left wing indicated there was only cavalry in his front. Slocum's second dispatch, asking for help, reached Sherman late in the evening.

The General was in his tent and clad in only a red night shirt when the dispatch was brought to him. He came charging out of the tent chewing on a cigar, and with his hands clasped behind him, issued the necessary orders which started the right wing toward Bentonville. The first troops of Howard's wing began arriving there around dawn of March 20th.

Since the 15th Corps and the 17th Corps were approaching Goldsboro, the Union advance was coming from the east down the Goldsboro-Fayetteville road. This movement would threaten the rear of Hoke's position.

"We've been facing west with our backs toward Goldsboro," Sam explained to his regiment. "Now there are more Yankees coming at us from that direction, we've got to take up positions along side the road and swing it down beside that branch over there."

This movement of Hoke's brigades caused the Confederate lines to be shaped like a giant horseshoe. The curved part of this position was manned by Kirkland's battle scarred command and by three companies and one battalion of the North Carolina Junior Reserves. These boys, most of them seventeen and under, were an unknown quantity. More than two hundred had surrendered at the first battle of Fort Fisher and they had downright refused to charge with Hoke's division at Wyse's Fork near Kinston. As fate would have it, they were now located at one of the most crucial parts of the Confederate line. There was only one route of escape for Johnston's army and that was a bridge over Mill Creek which was flooded and nearly unfordable with wagons and cannons. The new Confederate position now invited disaster.

"Cut those scrub oaks down so we can have a field of fire to our front," Sam commanded as the 51st started to prepare its position. "Sharpen them short logs up and place them in the ground to help break up a Yankee attack. We need to dig some rifle pits down the slope. You six," he said to a corporal and five of his men, "take these shovels and make them pits large enough for four men."

The rain was still falling in intermittent downpours and everybody was wet. Colonel William Devane had become the brigade commander after Hector McKethan had been hospitalized at Wilmington about the time Fort Fisher fell. Colonel Devane and his staff came riding by as the sound of cannon fire was heard from the direction of the Junior Reserve's position.

The Colonel observed the preparations for battle made by the 51st and nodded at Sam. "Lieutenant," he said, "your defenses are superb. I think you can defend yourself against any attack. General Hoke is concerned that the boys are in harm's way and might need some aid. I might need every third man from your command. Give me a runner to take with me and I will send him back if I need your help."

"Uriah, that sounds like you," Sam said. "Go with the Colonel and keep your head down."

The firing was coming from the place where Kirkland's Brigade and the Juniors defended. The 14th Michigan and the 16th Illinois from Morgan's command had advanced over Hoke's abandoned lines and attacked before Kirkland's men had finished fortifying their new position. General D. H. Hill had seen that the Confederate rear guard was being attacked and directed Colonel Starr's six gun battery to fire into the Federals as they dashed across the Goldsboro Road. This fire halted the advance and gave Kirkland's Tar Heels time to deploy into their positions. Part of the attack fell on the Junior Reserves who coolly aimed and fired behind their pine logs and sent their attackers running for cover.

"The boys did well!" the Colonel exclaimed. "They might be able to hold their own.

This question would be immediately answered. The two Federal regiments advanced through the pine trees and charged forward once again, this time determined to take the artillery pieces. The teenaged Reserves again stopped the assault and sent Sherman's veterans hurrying back to safety. Kirkland's men at the same time were leaving piles of Union casualties in front of their position.

"I think this part of our line can take care of itself," Colonel Devane shouted over the roar of the gunfire. "You men can return to your positions. Tell your commanders we won't need any of their troops after all."

General Johnston had remained at Bentonville hoping Sherman would make a frontal assault as he had at Kenesaw Mountain, but the Union commander had no intention of doing so. This attack on parts of Hoke's Division was the heaviest fighting on the 20th.

Uriah didn't immediately return to his regiment as night fell. It began raining very hard as he made his way toward the field hospital. He had not had time to check on the condition of Charles, but he walked past Hagood's brigade and he knew the hospital was not far away. He walked past a pile of arms and legs outside the first hospital tent and heard the screams and moans of the amputees. It was then Uriah was hit with a feeling of dread that Charles' chances of recovery were not going to be good.

"Pardon me sir," Uriah said to a doctor with a blood covered apron. "I'm looking for a friend who was brought here late yesterday. His name is Charles...."

"We don't have time to learn names, soldier," the doctor spat out. "They come to us and we try to patch them up the best we can. You can find him in one of the last two tents if he lived and if he didn't, they're diggin' a big hole somewhere for them."

Uriah didn't find Charles in any of the tents which housed the living and he didn't see the need to look any farther. The tears running down his cheeks were quickly washed away by the pouring rain as he walked back to the position of the 51st. His boyhood friend was gone. The companion of countless squirrel hunts would never accompany him again. He was just another casualty in the last battle for Southern independence and there would be more tomorrow. Uriah reached the 51st's position and sunk down in the trench where he would try to rest till morning in the wet and cold.

The morning of March 21st was wet and drizzly. The soldiers under Sam's command were stirring and wringing out their wet clothes. "Did you get any sleep last night, Uriah?" Sam asked.

"Heck, no!" Uriah replied. "I was wet and cold and halfway expectin the Yankees to attack. Course, I really don't remember it ever being any other way."

"That's right!" Sam said. "It just seems like a long ago dream when we used to go squirrel hunting and catfishin'. Do you reckon we'll ever get to do it again?"

"We might, but ol' Charles won't," Uriah said sadly. "I went by the hospital before I came back last night and he wasn't there. There was some bodies laying in a pile in the back, but I didn't try to see if one of them was him."

"I was afraid of that," Sam replied softly. "That wound looked pretty serious. The worst of it is, he just might be one of the last to die in the last battle."

"It surely will be if Sherman attacks us all along the line," Uriah said apprehensively. "Sam, I saw the creek in our rear and now it ain't a creek no more. It's a river out of its banks. His whole army is here now and if he breaks through and gits to that bridge first, we're trapped. Have you been told any different?"

"I haven't been told anything," Sam replied.

Suddenly, the notes of a bugle rang out, calling the men of the 51st to yet another fight. The Yankees were advancing through the pines and threatening the Confederate rifle pits at the base of the ravine. Entrenched on the ground overlooking the branch, Sam's company poured a deadly fire at the advancing Federals who advanced one pine tree at a time.

The actions of one particular Yankee caught the eye of Uriah. He dashed from tree to tree, being careful not to expose himself to the Confederate fire. "He moves a lot like Charles," Uriah thought to himself as he marked the man in his rifle sights. The thoughts of his dead friend kept him from squeezing the trigger. The Federal sighted his rifle to fire, but Uriah fired first, purposely ricocheting a bullet off the pine tree just inches above the Yankee's head, causing him to dive for the ground. At that moment, the attack was ordered back and Uriah never saw the soldier again. Months later in Illinois, there would be a joyous homecoming for the Union soldier. He and his family would never know that his life had been spared by Uriah in a strange moment of compassion, as a tribute for his fallen friend.

Sherman had hoped that Johnston would slip away during the night but he did not. Sporadic skirmishing and sniping continued for most of the day. In the middle of the afternoon, General Joseph A. Mower led two of his brigades around the left flank of the Confederate positions. They pushed through the swamps in a pouring rain and overran two lines of rifle pits and were advancing toward the bridge over Mill

Creek - the Confederate's only avenue of retreat. One regiment, the 64th Illinois, broke through into General Johnston's headquarters and captured some of the horses of the staff officers.

The Rebels were slow to react to this major threat, but when the did it was with great vigor. First, Cumming's Brigade of the Confederate Army of Tennessee stopped the Illinois soldier's advance just as the Yankee pickets entered the village of Bentonville. General Frank Cheatam's troops were not all present, but the general was and led one of his hard fighting divisions against Mower's breakthrough. In addition, two cavalry regiments from Tennessee and Texas joined in the attack.

The 8th Texas, known as Terry's Texas Rangers, rode into the fray holding their horses reins in their teeth and firing their Navy Colt pistols. General Hardee's sixteen year old son Willie took part in this attack and was mortally wounded.

Sherman would later admit in his memoirs that he should have supported Mower's attack but failed to do so because he wanted to avoid a general engagement before being resupplied. The Union commander gave orders for Mower to end this attack, but it had been countered by the Confederates before the orders were received.

There was nothing more General Johnston could accomplish at Bentonville. As night fell, what was left of once formidable Confederate armies withdrew from their positions, followed their artillery across the Mill Creek Bridge, and marched off into history.

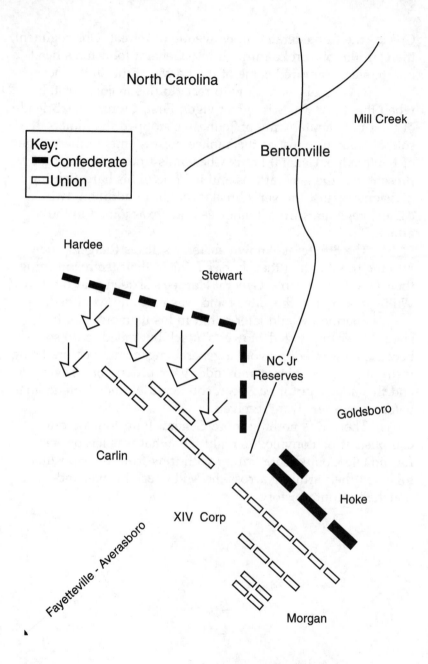

North Carolina

Mill Creek

Bentonville

Key:
Confederate
Union

Hardee

Stewart

NC Jr
Reserves

Goldsboro

Carlin

Hoke

XIV Corp

Fayetteville - Averasboro

Morgan

**Battle of Bentonville
First Phase
March 19, 1865**

© Mari Jones 2000

276

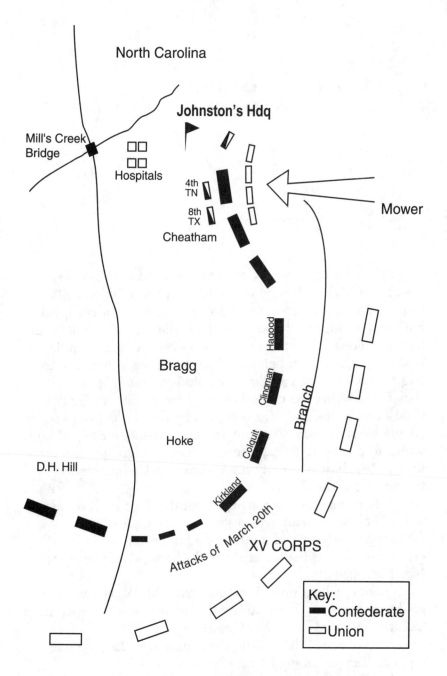

North Carolina

Johnston's Hdq

Mill's Creek
Bridge

Hospitals

4th
TN

8th
TX

Cheatham

Mower

Bragg

Hagood

Clingman

Branch

Hoke

Colquit

D.H. Hill

Kirkland

Attacks of March 20th

XV CORPS

Key:
■ Confederate
□ Union

© Mari Jones 2000

**Mower's Charge, Bentonville
March 21, 1865**

Chapter 17
Greensboro

The Federals would be united at Goldsboro because on the 21st of March, the day of the last fighting at Bentonville, General Schofield had advanced from Kinston and occupied the town. If this event had occurred earlier in the war, it would have been one of the most significant events of that conflict. It would have cut the supply line from Wilmington to Lee's Army and forced it out of Virginia. It would have made great changes in where the major battles of the conflict took place. Goldsboro, in the end, was occupied by the Union troops simply because there were not any Confederate forces left with which to defend it. Its capture now had no consequences other than to be a base of supply for a victorious Union army advancing from the south.

Johnston's Army rested at Smithfield for several days while Sherman's Army was rested and resupplied at Goldsboro. Sam noticed on the morning of March 23rd that one man was packing his gear up like he was leaving. It was Neil McMillan.

Sam walked up to him and said, "Mr. Mack, we were glad to have you with us during the battle. Have you men from the arsenal guard been reassigned?"

"No, Sam," the middle-aged man with the long hair replied. "I'm just going home when it gets dark."

"Things have happened so quick here lately that I don't have any written orders assigning you to Company I," Sam responded. "I won't try to stop you."

"Things is so confused around here that I'd eventually leave," Mister Mack responded. "Anyhow, I don't think I have any more to give to the Confederate States of America. I just fought in a battle where you could walk for a mile on the bodies of the dead. My oldest son James died of typhoid shortly after Fort Fisher. I left a wife and three teenaged daughters in the path of Sherman's thieving Yankees. I don't know what I'll find when I get home. My other son, Daniel, is goin to stay with you till the end so take care of him."

"I can't say I blame you," Sam replied. "How are you going to keep from runnin' in to some Yankees?"

"I aim to make it to Averasboro and stay on the west side of South River," Mister Mack said. "I reckon the Yankees are all gone from that side."

"Let me ask you two favors," Sam said. "Don't let anybody from my regiment know you're leaving."

"All right," the older man agreed. "Daniel already knows, but he won't reveal it if I tell him not to. What's the other thing?"

"Let my wife know that I survived the fight at Bentonville. She knows who you are and that you'll tell her the truth," Sam explained.

"I'll do it," Mister Mack promised. "Take care of my boy if there are any other battles. " Sam nodded to the older man and then walked away.

Sam's command duties kept him occupied for most of the time at Smithfield. There were letters to be written to the next of kin of those who had been killed at Bentonville. The platoons of Company I were equalized by number soldiers remaining. Feeding and supplying the troops took more and more of his time.

One day he noticed Uriah sitting on a log in the woods outside the camp. He had his back toward the encampment, but as Sam approached him, he could tell his friend was sobbing uncontrollably.

Sam sat down on the log beside Uriah and waited for his friend to speak if he wanted to. "Why'd we do it, Sam?" he asked. Sam didn't respond.

279

"Why did we fight that last battle where Charles got killed?" Uriah asked. "We didn't have a chance of winning. We should have all left and gone home. I think Charles wanted to do that, but I wanted to stay around and see what would happen."

"Don't blame yourself, Uriah," Sam comforted. "Each man made his decision on his own. Anyhow, we might not be whipped yet. You know they ain't going to whip General Lee and if we can link up with him, our army will be hard to beat."

"We'll still be outnumbered right bad and out of supplies. And you know our rations can't git much worse," Uriah argued.

"They never have been real good for a long amount of time," Sam said.

You're right!" Uriah agreed. "I guess the fact of Charles death has caught up with me. I just don't feel very good right now."

"We all thought a lot of that ol' boy," Sam comforted. "But we just can't give up and quit just yet."

"We ain't givin' up," Uriah said. "Sam, have you heard what happened with the troops from Magnolia on our move to Kinston before you joined us?"

"Don't believe I have," Sam replied.

"It was after Wilmington had fallen and we were being moved up to Kinston to stop the Yankee advance on Goldsboro and we had to go through Magnolia," Uriah began. "There was guards posted on the box cars because some of the 51st's men who were from Magnolia were ridin' in them. You see, they were to keep men from desertin' when they got so close to home."

"I understand," Sam said.

"Well, those ol' boys from down there at Magnolia politely told their officers that they were going home to see their families and they would all be along the next day. The officers didn't have the heart to arrest 'em, so they all went home. You know what? They all showed up at Kinston in a day or two, just like they said they would, and rejoined their companies. That's what kind of men we got in this army."

"Our troops have proven their worth time after time,"

Sam said. "We just never seem to have enough of 'em. Maybe when we get back in Lee's Army things will be different."

Sam's opinion of Robert E. Lee and his army was shared by most American's in the North and the South. The strategy of both Johnston and Sherman was still predicated on what was occurring in Virginia. On April 6th, Sherman issued an order putting his army in motion for a possible link up with Grant "somewhere near Petersburg." The next day the stunning news came that Lee had pulled out of Richmond and Petersburg. Sherman immediately amended his orders and now made the capture of Raleigh the next objective of his army.

On that same day, a train carrying Jefferson Davis and his cabinet arrived in Greensboro and parked on a siding off of Elm Street. The day before, the Confederate President had sent a telegram to General Johnston ordering him to that town for a Council of War to be held on the 13th. This telegram also informed Johnston that General Lee had surrendered to Grant on April the 9th. The Army of Northern Virginia was no more. That fabled band, upon which all loyal Confederates had rested their hopes for eventual victory, had succumbed to overwhelming force. Johnston did not pass on this information because he knew it would cause the immediate disintegration of his forces. He immediately headed for Greensboro and the meeting with his Commander in Chief.

When Johnston arrived at Greensboro on the morning of April 12th, he was met by General Beauregard who was the commander of what there was of the city's defenses. The generals spent two hours discussing the military situation of the rapidly shrinking Confederacy. There had been times in the past when they had not agreed, but this time they did. There was nothing else the South could give militarily and it was hopeless to even try.

The meeting the next day began with Jefferson Davis revealing the extent of the dream world in which he now lived. He spoke of the latest setbacks as being terrible, but not necessarily fatal. He thought victory could still be achieved if the people would turn out. Eventually, he asked the views of General Johnston.

The general was brief and to the point: "My views are, sir, that our people are tired of the war, feel themselves whipped, and will not fight" he said. "Our country is overrun, its military resources greatly diminished, while the enemy's military power and resources were never greater, and may be increased to any extent desired," he continued. "We can not place another large army in the field, and cut off as we are from foreign intercourse, I don't see how we could maintain it in fighting condition if we had it."

"My men are daily deserting in large numbers, and are stealing my artillery teams to aid their escape to their homes. Since Lee's defeat, they regard the war as at an end. If I march out of North Carolina, her people will leave my ranks. It will be the same as I proceed through South Carolina and Georgia.... I shall expect to retain no man beyond the bye road or cow path that leads to his home. My small force is melting away like snow before the sun...."

There was a period of silence when the General finished speaking. Jefferson Davis had been sitting with his head down, listening intently to the man he had removed from command at Atlanta less than nine months before. Eventually, he began polling the other Confederate leaders. "What do you say, General Beauregard?"

"I concur with all that General Johnston has said," Beauregard answered.

"Well, General Johnston, what do you propose?" the Confederate President asked.

Johnston proposed that peace efforts should be started at once. Davis again polled his cabinet and all but Judah Benjamin, the Secretary of State, agreed with the Generals. Very reluctantly, President Davis gave General Johnston permission to contact General Sherman about a cease fire and eventually a negotiated surrender. So it was that the final planning toward ending the terrible struggle of the past four years was begun that day in Greensboro.

Hoke's Division had left Raleigh as Sherman resumed his march and drew closer to the city. The red-haired Union General had received the word of Lee's surrender and now made the destruction or capture of Johnston's Army his main objective. The civilian officials of Raleigh contacted Sherman to ask that the State buildings and shops along Fayetteville Street not be looted. They received assurances from the Federals to this end, but it is not clear whether they meant to keep their promise because undisciplined Confederate cavalry cleaned out the town before the Yankees arrived. Many of the Southern soldiers, after hearing of the fall of Richmond, considered the war over and started for home in ever increasing numbers.

On April 13th, the day of Jefferson Davis and Joseph E. Johnston's historic meeting at Greensboro, Hoke's Division resumed its march westward and camped near Chapel Hill. Acting as Johnston's rear guard, the Division, along with Wheeler's cavalry skirmished with Sherman's advance at Morrisville and New Hope Creek where Yankees and Rebels would continue to die.

A Union artillery piece on the east side of the creek fired a round which burst near where Lewis Hobson was manning his gun. All of his gun crew was wounded - except him. He helped his friends to an ambulance and returned to shoot the wounded horses. There was one frightened, unhurt animal remaining which Lewis calmed and unhitched from his harness. He looked at the artillery piece and saw it was beyond repair and knew there were no replacements. It was here that the war ended for Lewis Hobson as he mounted the animal and headed him south - toward home.

The rains had resumed and each camp site was wet and uncomfortable. It was during one of these showers that Major Garrison ordered Sam to report to him at his tent.

"You sent for me, Sir?" Sam asked as he entered.

"Yes, Morgan, have a seat," the Major said, motioning with his head to a camp stool. "I have a mission for you that might be dangerous."

"The Yankees ain't hit me yet," Sam replied.

"This danger might not come from just the Yankees," the Major replied. "There is a good possibility that the rumors of Lee's surrender are true. If they are, we should start seeing his troops drifting down this way on their way home. They will be desperate and hungry which will make your job more dangerous. I want you to take a dozen wagons we have gathered up and go to Greensboro and load them with food at the warehouses there. Get shoes if you can find any there. I have all the requisition orders in this pouch. You might have to defend this food with your lives, so take a driver and two guards for each wagon from Company I.

"May I ask why the supplies are all in Greensboro, Sir?" Sam inquired. "Aren't there any closer than that?"

"No, there are not," the Major answered. "Many of these supplies were being sent to Lee's Army. The railroad from Greensboro to Danville wasn't that good, so supplies backed up. Then, when Sherman entered the state, Governor Vance directed most of the State's stores to be sent there if Lee and Johnston could join forces somewhere near Greensboro and then turn on Sherman. You can imagine what would happen to this army if that rumor of Lee's surrender proves to be true."

"Yes, Sir!" Sam exclaimed. "We would cease to be an army, but, I don't believe that for a minute. General Lee will never surrender."

"I don't believe it either," Major Garrison agreed. "Until we know for sure, you have an important job to do."

"Where will I bring the supplies to, Sir?" Sam asked.

"As you are aware, we are now part of Hardee's Corps and we have marching orders which will take us south of Greensboro through Red Cross and Bush Hill in Randolph County," Major Garrison explained pointing to a map on the table. "Meet us at Red Cross near Providence Church with the supplies in three days. If you're not there, the men will wander off looking for food and our army will disintegrate. That's why you need to take enough rifles with you to fight off any attack. Shoot anybody who interferes with you. Is that clear?"

"Yes, Sir!" Sam replied. "You can count on me and my men!"

"That's why I picked you," the Major agreed. "That food and those supplies have to be there."

"Will there be any cavalry to escort us, Major?" Sam asked.

"I'm not sure we have any cavalry left that wouldn't rob you themselves," the Major replied. "You're on your own."

It took all the men who remained with Company I to

drive and guard the wagons. Nevertheless, Sam had his caravan on the move at daybreak the next day, passing through Chapel Hill. The early risers in the University town, while friendly and supportive of their own soldiers, could not help noticing that military traffic invariably headed westward. There were others who were also considering the strategic importance of Chapel Hill.

On that same day, Sherman sent this dispatch to his cavalry chief:

In the Field, Raleigh, April 14, 1865.
Major-General Kilpatrick,
Commanding Cavalry:

General: I sent you orders today, but now enclose a copy. You will see I am to put my army where, if Johnston tries to pass out by Charlotte, I can strike him in the flank, but if he remains in Greensboro I shall capture the whole. All I expect of you is to keep up a delusion that we are following him via the University and Hillsborough until I get my infantry heads of column across the Haw River. Next day, all move by separate roads for Asheboro.... I want you to cross also and feel out toward Greensboro till I get to Asheboro, ... if he remains at Greensboro, I can approach him from the south and force him to battle, to surrender, or disperse.... I am very anxious to prevent his escape toward Georgia. General Howard tomorrow will have one corps at Jones' Station and one at Morrison's Station. If you reach the University, do not disturb its library, buildings, or specific property.

Yours truly,
W. T. Sherman,
Major-General, Commanding.

The two armies began their advance into the rolling hills of the Piedmont section of North Carolina. Since crossing the fault line which separates this section from the Coastal

Plains, the flat, sandy, loamy soil gradually changed to rock filled deep ruts which meandered through the clay hills. Sam rode at the head of his column beside the lead wagon which Uriah was driving. Two riders traveled in front of the column to guard against any ambush. Chapel Hill was left behind and the wagon train pushed further into the Piedmont.

"I never knew how pretty the dogwoods are in this part of the state," Uriah said. "You can see a whole hillside full of them as you pass by."

"Yeah," Sam answered. "You could almost think we were in some other state."

"Which way are we takin' to git to Greensboro, Sam?" Uriah asked, as a fork in the road approached.

"Take the left fork. We're going to pass through Chatham County to get to Red Cross and then up to Greensboro," Sam explained. "I think there's less chance of us running into any trouble going that way."

"I've heared tell some of the folks in the center of the state didn't support the Confederate government like we did," Uriah said.

"You can guess the reason for that being true," Sam answered. "There are a lot of Quakers who live up here who didn't support the war because of their religion, but just look at the ground we're traveling over. It's rough and rocky and ain't worth a flip for growing cotton. It just seems like the more a man had to do with cotton, the more of a Confederate he became. The unfair Yankee taxes were aimed at cotton more than any thing else."

"All the Quakers I've ever met didn't believe in fightin' nobody. Is that true for all of them, Sam?" Uriah asked.

"Most of 'em, I guess," Sam replied. "I don't think you can say anything is one-hundred per cent true about this war."

By the afternoon of the second day, Red Cross was reached and the caravan turned northward toward Greensboro. As the city drew closer, Sam and his command began to see Rebel soldiers, individually and in small groups, who obviously had left their units and were on their way to their homes.

As night fell, Sam noticed some excitement in the camp

286

of one of the lead elements of Johnston's Army which had
already reached Greensboro. "He's a lying Yankee spy!" a
soldier shouted. "Git some rope and we'll string up the lying
dog." A group of soldiers had another man by the arms and
was dragging him toward a tree. The victim was fighting hard
and was getting in some well placed punches and kicks.

Sam halted his column and rode over into the group.
Drawing his Navy Colt, he fired a shot into the air. "What's
going on here!" he demanded.

"This lying dog has told us Lee's surrendered, Lieutenant," one of the men shouted. "We all know that's a lie."

"Do you have a signed parole?" Sam asked. "You
would if your outfit surrendered."

"That's what I've been trying to tell these here idjuts,"
the man said. "It's right here in my pocket, Lieutenant."

"Turn him loose!" Sam ordered. "Let's see what he's
got."

The man reached into his pocket and pulled a folded
paper which he handed to Sam, who unfolded it and began to
read.

"This parole is signed by an officer of the Army of the
Potomac," Sam said. "It appears there has been a surrender.
What outfit are you from, soldier?" he asked the man.

"I'm in the 20th North Carolina and we've fought
under Stonewall Jackson and General Lee from beginning to
the end," he answered. "I got three Yankee bullets in me and I
ain't 'bout to git hanged by idjuts who should know better."

"Hey, I've got a cousin in the 20th. Do you know Neil
Morgan?" Sam asked.

"Shore do!" exclaimed the soldier. "He's probably not
more that a half a day behind me."

Suddenly, the clatter of horses hooves interrupted the
meeting as two Confederate officers, a major and a captain,
rode up to see what was happening. "What's the trouble here,
Lieutenant?"

"No trouble, Sir!" Sam answered. "The men were
discussing a rumor that General Lee has surrendered. Is there
any truth to it?"

"And who might you be, Lieutenant? I don't recall you

in this outfit," the major asked?

"I'm Lieutenant Morgan, 51st North Carolina, from Hoke's Division." Sam replied. "I'm in charge of this wagon train heading for Greensboro for supplies. There was some commotion here about the question of General Lee's surrender and I stopped to help. Do you know if it's true?"

"A pleasure to meet you," the major said, ignoring Sam's question. "You are part of a splendid Division. I'm Major Hollowell of the 4th Arkansas. We're part of Pat Cleburne's old division."

"The pleasure's mine, Sir," Sam said. "Your division's reputation and accomplishment's are well known even here in the East, but do you have any knowledge of General Lee?"

The major looked up in the air as if to collect his thoughts. "I had planned to call my men together to inform them of what I've just learned at General Cheatham's head-quarters. I guess the news will spread before I can do that. Yes, it's true! We have been officially informed that General Lee was forced to surrender on April the ninth."

An audible gasp was heard from the group of men. "It's all over then... I'm going home... I'll not surrender"... were some of the shouts from the assembled mass.

"Men!" the Major shouted. "I urge you to get a good night's sleep. Things will be clearer in the morning. This is not the time to lose our heads."

"Lieutenant," he continued, turning to Sam, "if I were you, I'd get my supplies tonight and be out of town by morning. I honestly don't know if we'll still be an army tomorrow or just an armed mob."

"I'll do that, Sir," Sam acknowledged. He turned and mounted his horse and started his wagon train toward Greensboro, still three miles away, leaving the man he had rescued with the Arkansas men who now pressed him with questions about Lee's surrender.

The town of Greensboro had become a madhouse. In early March, the wounded from the battles around Petersburg had arrived. Next came the wounded from Bentonville which quickly overflowed to Greensboro after filling the hospitals of Raleigh. Jefferson Davis and his Cabinet was the next to arrive and the streets of the town hosted the highest ranking civilian and military officers who remained in the Confederacy. Refugees from Sherman's advance preceded the arrival of the army of General Joseph E. Johnston. The normal Greensboro population of two thousand had swelled to one hundred thousand by the latter part of April. Many of the Confederate soldiers in Johnston's army since Lee's surrender, now saw no need in fighting any more and would take no more orders. The fact that these men were still armed made the situation quite dangerous.

It was dark when Sam led his wagons down the muddy streets of Greensboro, illuminated by the flickering flames of the street lamps. As Sam rechecked his map to the supply depot in the dim light, he heard the sounds and shouts of an angry group of people coming from the direction he was heading. A detachment of Confederate soldiers, with their bayonets fixed on their rifles, were approaching at the double time from the rear of the column. They were led by an officer on foot who shouted at Sam. "Let us by! There's a riot at the storage depot. You'd better get those horses off to a side street till we get things calmed down."

Sam complied with the officer's advice and pulled his column off of Elm Street and approached the depot from a side street. From his vantage point, he could hear the noise of the approaching mob. "Fix bayonets and protect these horses," Sam ordered. "Uriah! Get two other men and follow me. Let's get closer and see how we can approach this place."

The party moved through the shadows, taking care not to be seen and moved toward the depot. From across the street, Sam and his men witnessed the advance of the mob. It was composed equally of civilians and soldiers who no longer obeyed orders. The soldiers who had rushed through the street past Sam's column were now positioned in a double line with fixed bayonets to block the front of the building.

Uriah's sharp eyes noticed something familiar about one of the soldiers in the angry crowd. "Sam!," he exclaimed. "Ain't that Neil with them Corporal's stripes?"

Sam looked in the direction Uriah was pointing and immediately recognized his cousin Neil Morgan. "Stay here and cover me if anyone gets in my way," he said, drawing his pistol.

Sam ran out into the street and up to the edge of the crowd and grabbed Neil by the arm. "Don't ask questions and come with me!" he commanded.

"Sam!" Neil exclaimed. "Where did you come from? How..."

"I'll explain later," Sam shouted above the noise of the crowd. "You with any friends?"

"No. I'm by myself," Neil answered. "But how....?"

"No time to explain!" Sam said emphatically. "Let's get out of this crowd before somebody gets killed."

Sam led his cousin to the safety of the side street as the crowd cursed the guards and shouted for the food in the warehouse to be distributed. The officer in charge explained that the supplies were for the army and in a loud voice ordered his men to fire on anyone who tried to break their line. Still angry and sullen, the mob began to disperse, convinced that the officer meant what he had said. This confrontation was ended, but in other parts of town at commissary depots, shots were fired and several people were killed.

"That was a near thing, Sam," Uriah said as the mob wandered back down the street the way they had come. "It would be bad to have to shoot our own soldiers who have given so much."

"Is that Uriah Bass?" Neil asked, squinting through the darkness. "Hell's bells! It shore is somethin' runnin' in to ya'll in this here confusion."

"What's all this riotin' about?" Uriah asked Neil. "Is it about food? Has General Lee really surrendered?"

"Yes! It's true. There's thousands of us on all the roads," replied Neil. "I ran out of rations yesterday and don't know when I'll eat again. Some of Lee's best soldiers are going to starve before they can git home."

"There probably won't be nothing for them to eat there after the Yankees have been through," added Sam. "All the men in our army have to be concerned about their families."

"Do you still have an army?" Neil asked. "I've heard tell that Johnston is going to surrender."

"I haven't heard that," Sam said. "But it has been two days since we left our camp. A lot could have happened since then." Sam walked out in the street and made sure the mob was gone. "Pull those wagons up to the depot and head 'em south," he commanded. He walked up to the commissary office and gave his requisitions to the officer in charge. The officer immediately put his men to work gathering the items.

"That was a dangerous thing with that hungry mob," Sam said.

"Yes it was," the depot officer agreed. "I hope enough requisitions from Johnston's army come in to clean this place out so we won't have to kill anybody."

"Well, we'll do our part," Sam offered. "Can you fill all these requisitions?"

"We can do better than that," the officer answered. "We've got thousands of uniforms we've had for months with no way to get them up to General Lee. Do you need any?"

"Not unless it's on our order," Sam said. "I don't reckon we got much extra wagon space. Just don't forget the shoes."

"Here's one thing I hope you'll take with you," the officer said. "This is a keg of whiskey belonging to the "Medicinal Department" of the Confederate Government. I don't want any crazed mob getting hold of that."

"Hey, there's a lot of 'ol boys in our regiment who ain't had a good drink in a long time," Sam said thoughtfully. "We might just be able to make room for that. We can make some toddies if you've got some brown sugar."

"There in the corner," the officer said, nodding in the direction of the sugar. "I can let you have those two bags."

"Men," Sam commanded. "Stash this keg and sugar in the middle of one of the wagons and cover it with supplies where it can't be seen. If we're going to surrender, we'll at least have one last party."

"Did you know that the President is here with all his Cabinet?" the commissary officer asked. "I understand they have a good supply of whiskey too. I understand you can get a drink over at their railroad coach just for asking."

"That means that Greensboro is the Capitol of the Confederate States as long as we can hold it," Sam added.

"Have you seen any of them?"

"Oh, yes!" the officer replied. "President Davis goes for lots of long walks around the town, even at all times of night. Sometimes, Vice-President Breckinridge is with him. He wears his General's uniform and is something to see. Other times there are well dressed civilians with him that I reckon are Cabinet members like Judah Benjamin, but I can't identify any of them. Maybe ya'll will see 'em as you leave."

"Probably not." Sam answered. "I hope to be out of town by sunup."

The loading was completed in a couple of hours and the wagon train prepared to leave. "Neil, you can throw in with us till we find out what's going on," Sam offered. "At least we'll have something to eat for a while." The wagons pulled out on the main thoroughfare and headed south through predawn Greensboro, while Neil answered questions about Lee's surrender.

On Sunday, April 16th, the last of Wheelers cavalry rode out of the college town in the morning and in the afternoon, Union cavalry quietly rode in. On that same day, General Johnston finally received a reply from Sherman, agreeing to a peace conference and promising that during the talks, all troops would remain in place where they were. Chapel Hill would be the last town occupied by Sherman on his advance through the South.

The wagon train, now loaded with supplies, moved slowly through the red clay ruts of southern Guilford County and into Randolph. At midday, Red Cross came into view and Sam was glad to see the lines of troops from Hardee's Corps that had already reached the area. There were other wagon trains on the road which had made the same trip to Greensboro and now had supplies for their respective brigades.

An officer who seemed to know what he was doing rode up to Sam and the two men exchanged salutes. "What division are you with?" the officer asked.

"We're with Hoke's Division," Sam replied.

"Hoke will camp east of the crossroads," the officer said. "Turn left for a half a mile and then wait for him on the side of the road," Without waiting for a reply, the man wheeled his horse and rode off to give instructions to other wagon masters.

Sam followed his instructions and found a hillside where they parked the wagons and the horses were fed some corn and were watered. "You men can get some rest now, since we've been up all night," Sam said to his troops.

"I want one man from each wagon to stay awake while the other two sleep. I don't want anybody taking any of these supplies until we turn them over to Major Garrison."

Hoke's Division had served as the rear guard of Hardee's Corps and were the last troops to reach Red Cross. It was late in the afternoon when Major Garrison came riding up to the parked wagons with an obviously delighted look on his face. "Well done, Lieutenant Morgan," he said. "You've done a good job," he said as he eyed the parked wagons which were bulging with supplies. "This should feed our brigade for some time."

"I've been able to get something else, Sir." Sam reported, uncovering the keg of whisky and the brown sugar. "We were almost forced to take it with us," he said with a grin.

"I'll take personal charge of these goods," the Major said, also grinning. "This will be a good way to reward the men if this army ever has anything more to celebrate. Anyhow, we're only going to stay here for the night. We'll be moving on in the morning."

Sam and Uriah were glad to be back with their regiment and settled into camp for the coming night. All of Sam's men had been well fed for a change and settled down early with their blankets. As the sky darkened and the sun went down behind orange clouds, the white dogwoods stood as silent sentinels around the Confederate Camp. Sam lay on his back and watched the stars appear, thinking of his family and home. The orders for tomorrow were to break camp and march just as they had done on a hundred other mornings. "This war can't last much longer because we ain't got a whole lot left to defend," he thought to himself. Meanwhile, in Washington, Abraham Lincoln boarded his carriage for the ride to Ford's Theater where he would keep his rendezvous with destiny. It was April 16th, 1865.

Before Sam could doze off to sleep, a messenger arrived from Major Garrison. "The Major sends word that our orders to move tomorrow have been countermanded, Lieutenant Morgan," the soldier reported. "He's dividing the spirits you brought and asks that you send a man with a small bucket for your share."

"What has happened?" asked Sam. "What has brought on this change"

"I wasn't told by the Major," the messenger answered, "but General Johnston is going to talk to General Sherman tomorrow. This just might be our last night in this here army."

"So it is this close to being over," Sam thought to himself as he put back on his well worn boots. "Uriah, I've got one more mission for you," he shouted to his friend, sending him for the whisky. "Sergeant Buie, wake the men and have them stoke that fire and make a pot of hot water," he ordered. "We have some news to discuss this night."

The weary men of Company I gradually assembled around the fire as Uriah arrived with the whisky and brown sugar and began cooking up the hot toddies. The company numbered only around thirty men now out of the one hundred and seventy-nine who had served in its ranks since the beginning.

"Anyone who wants one, help yourself," Sam said, aware that some of the men were teetotalers. "We have some things to talk about."

The cups were filled and the soldiers looked toward Sam for the announcements they knew were coming. "Men," he began. "We have all been to Greensboro and have seen the conditions of our government. I have been told that we will not move tomorrow because General Johnston will meet with General Sherman to discuss the conditions for the surrender of this army."

There were rumblings of agreement and disagreement among the men which Sam quickly addressed. "Control of the situation is out of our hands," he pointed out. "You might have met my cousin Neil. He was with General Lee's army and has been given a parole to return to his home. I believe we can expect the same treatment. In what may possibly be our last night together, I propose we drink a toast to all of our comrades who have been lost during the past four years."

The men raised their tin cups and clanked them in unison to the memory of their fallen friends and drank deeply from the warm liquid. They stood around the fire for the next few hours reminiscing about their lost buddies in other times and other places. At this same moment, in Washington, John Wilkes Booth checked again to make sure his derringer pistol was loaded and entered the theater box where Abraham Lincoln was watching the play.

Chapter 18
The End of the Road

General Joseph E. Johnston and General Sherman were approaching each other under a flag of truce that morning. Their advance scouts met each other between Hillsborough and Durham and arranged with a farmer named Bennett to use his house for their negotiations. As the two Generals sat down to begin their discussion, Sherman showed Johnston a telegram he had received that morning informing him of the death of Abraham Lincoln. Johnston read the dispatch in disbelief. He told Sherman he took no pleasure in the news and he was certain no one in the Confederate Army had anything to do with the assassination. Sherman agreed with Johnston and the negotiations began.

The Confederates remained in their camp as the day wore on, pondering the fate that awaited them if they surrendered. "Do you think the Yankees will send us to prison camps if General Johnston surrenders?" Daniel MacMillan asked Sam. "I think I'd just as soon keep fightin' as to go back to a Yankee prison."

"I think we will be paroled back to our homes just like Lee's men were," Sam answered. "The war will be over when this army is gone."

"We should just leave now," Neil said. "We can be home in a few days."

"You have your parole and we don't," Uriah answered. "That might an important item to have in the days to come.

Anyhow, I will have some satisfaction in the years to come just by being able to say I fought all the way."

"I have some responsibilities I can't walk away from," Sam added. "I've been told that General Johnston expects better terms if the army stays together than if everybody leaves. But, if anybody wants to leave now, I can get him a pass from Division headquarters."

"I guess I ain't in any real big hurry," Uriah concluded. "I ain't got no wife to git home to. Although, maybe that's what I ought to do when I git home, find me a wife. I wonder if the Johnson girls are all married off?"

"Probably not," Sam replied. "I was just thinking last night when we were toasting. There's been nearly a whole generation of men wiped out by this war in our neck of the woods. That's probably true everywhere. There'll be lots of young girls wantin' husbands and lots of widows too."

The day passed slowly for the soldiers in Johnston's Army while he negotiated with Sherman. In the afternoon, there was a commotion in the camp as a group of cavalrymen rode through, announcing that they were leaving. "There's some food in those wagons, let's git it," Sam heard one of the horsemen say.

"Get your weapons!" he ordered. "Form a skirmish line around those wagons. We can't let our food be stolen."

Sam's command reacted quickly and were in place when the horsemen galloped up to the wagons. "Git out of the way," one of the cavalrymen ordered. "We're goin' out and we need some supplies!"

"What you're goin' to get is some empty saddles if you try to steal our supplies!" Sam shot back. "Each of my men will drop one of you."

The horsemen thought better of the confrontation and began to withdraw. "Why are you leavin'?" Sam asked one of them. "This army can be attacked without warning if we don't have a cavalry screen."

"This army is bein surrendered and a smart man will git out while the gittin's good," one of the retreating cavalrymen hollered back.

Behind the horsemen came panicked infantrymen who

were leaving with the cavalrymen. "Every third man, fall out and extend this line around our camp," Sam ordered. "This mob will steal our personal gear too if we ain't careful."

Sam's quick action avoided any confrontation with the deserting soldiers, but until they left, any food or horse which could not be defended by its owner was sure to be lost. Sam and his men were watching an army die before their eyes. Men who, only a month before at Bentonville, had charged Union cannons loaded with double loads of grapeshot would fight no more. Their only thoughts were now of going home.

As the drama played out at the camp, the next few days brought serious negotiations between Johnston and Sherman. The Union General now realized he could possibly could have trapped the Confederates at Bentonville, but let them elude his grasp. The last thing he wanted was for the Rebels to break up into small groups and continue the war indefinitely from the mountains of North Carolina, so he was prepared to be magnanimous. Sherman not only offered Johnston the same terms Lee's Army had received, but also recognized the right of the state governments to continue to operate until they were replaced by Washington.

The new government of Andrew Johnston rejected this part of the treaty and told Sherman to negotiate another one or renew the war. This was done and the surrender remained an accomplished fact. It took several days to complete these negotiations as the Confederate army continued to dwindle away. Men who now only had thoughts of getting home and taking care of their families continued to leave in ever increasing numbers, usually without telling their officers. For those Rebel soldiers who did remain, their food supplies were rapidly being used up and provisions promised at the surrender never completely arrived. All of these procedures took the rest of the month of April to complete and as May arrived, the few remaining Confederates received orders to march.

"Where are we going, Sam?" the ever inquisitive Uriah asked, as the Army marched to the west.

"We're going to stack arms and then go get paid before we head for home," Sam answered. "It's all just about over."

The Rebels marched into a large field and were ordered

to ground their arms. The first three men in each column hooked their Enfield Rifles in a triangular configuration and the soldiers behind rested theirs against it as they filed past.

"I feel like I'm saying good-bye to an old friend," Uriah lamented as he stood his beloved Spencer carbine against the stack. Then he and his comrades simply marched away.

The now unarmed Confederates marched to Jamestown where they were to be paid for the last time in Confederate service. Part of the Confederate treasury which had been moving through Greensboro with the now nomad-like Confederate government was under the control of the army. President Jefferson Davis, who was now in Charlotte and would finally be captured in Georgia, ordered the money sent south to him. General Johnston saw the futility in this action and decided to divide it among the troops. Each soldier, regardless of rank, received one dollar and twenty-five cents in silver, one of the coins being a silver dollar minted in Mexico.

Sam called his company to attention and read to them statements of appreciation from their commanders. He had his own advice to give. "Men, we will travel as a group down the railroad track toward Raleigh. I am ordered to give you your paroles on down the road and get you on your way home. I figure it will take the better part of a week to get back to South River and you need to make your rations last."

Sam and his friends followed the railroad track from Jamestown and soon were approaching Greensboro. As they crossed Elm Street and continued on their way, they were aware that these rail sidings they passed had just weeks before held the train of Jefferson Davis and his Cabinet and many of the decisions which now effected their lives were made there.

East of the town, a wood burning locomotive coupled to a long line of cars was building up steam on the railroad. Many of them were flat cars which were loaded with artillery pieces. There were Union soldiers stationed four to each car. As Sam and his party filed down the tracks, a tough looking Yankee Sergeant spoke to them. "Would you Johnnies be needin' a ride toward Raleigh?" he asked. "We've been ordered to help you git home if we can."

"That would sure help us a right smart," Sam agreed.

"That's where we're going."

"Then climb aboard!" the Yankee shouted. "We're about to roll."

Sam and his friends gladly boarded the train and took their seats around the artillery. The engineer gave a loud squeal on his whistle and the train lurched forward with the usual crashing sounds as the couplers engaged. "I reckon you fellers were in that fight at Bentonville," the Sergeant said."

"We sure were," Sam replied. "Were you?"

"No, we're part of Schofield's Corps," the Yankee answered. "We were advancing on Goldsboro while that battle was goin' on. We heard you boys made 14th Corps skedaddle like all git out. You know their Corps badge is an acorn so the boys in 20th Corps call Bentonville the Battle of Acorn Run."

"Is that a fact?" Sam asked with a hearty laugh. "We're part of Hoke's Division, and from where we were on the battlefield I didn't see nobody on either side run. We just stood toe to toe and slugged it out."

"A lot of good men were lost on both sides," said the Sergeant. "Yes sir, a lot of good men."

"Damn right," Uriah said, remembering his friend Charles. "Damn right."

"Hey, I think this is the artillery from Hoke's Division we're haulin'," the Union Sergeant said. "I suspect you've traveled with it like this before."

Sam didn't answer the question as the noise of the railroad was now so loud it was hard to hear and carry on a conversation. He thought about how they had ridden with some of this same artillery after Hoke's attack on New Bern was canceled. They had arrived in time to save Petersburg, at least for a time. Only he and Uriah were left from that squad. Thomas Strickland, Daniel Graham, and Charles were dead, maybe Dougal too. Hiram Bunce, Duncan Autry and some of the Tew boys were also gone. "And for what purpose?" Sam wondered to himself. They had fought all the way, but it was now clear they had been doomed from the start. Engrossed in these thoughts, Sam settled into as comfortable position as he could find against the spoked wheels of the cannons and drifted off to sleep as night fell.

Sometime in the night, the train began to slow for a stop to take on wood and water at Company Shops. This refueling station on the rail line would one day become the town of Burlington. "Time for a stretch," the Yankee Sergeant announced as the train ground to its usual screeching halt.

Sam hopped off the train and suddenly remembered one last duty he needed to perform. "All men from Company I form over by this bank!" he ordered. The men did as instructed, even though Sam didn't have any authority over them since the Confederate Army no longer existed. He unfolded the paroles he had carried in his coat pockets and began handing them out. The men stayed in their ranks until Sam finished, waiting for him to speak.

"Men, from this point on you are free to make your way to your homes the best way you can," he began. "I know how little food all of you have with you, but I urge you to obey the law on the way home. You should always be proud of your performance in the service of your country even if all you have to show for it is a few silver coins. The South will never be the independent nation so many of us wanted, but think on this. I don't remember fearing the laws of the United States before the war and I don't expect it to be any different now that the war is over. Go home and be good citizens and may God go with you. It has been a privilege to command you. Dismissed!"

The men gave a cheer and gathered around their former commander and said their good-byes with back slaps and hand shakes. Sam was somewhat misty-eyed by the show of affection, but now he would have a singular focus as he climbed back aboard the flat car. He no longer had his command to be concerned with and from now on his only thoughts would be of his wife, family and of home. He felt as if a heavy load had been lifted from his shoulders as the train chugged down the track.

The sun was coming up when the train approached Raleigh. The smoke from countless Union Army campfires made a haze over the town. When the news of Abraham Lincoln's death had reached these soldiers, they had marched on the Tar Heel capital intending to burn it down. Union General Logan had posted armed troops to protect the city while he convinced the mob that no one in Raleigh could have had any part in Lincoln's assassination. He had thus spared North Carolina's capital from the fate of Columbia.

The train screeched to a halt and the soldiers jumped to the ground. "Thanks for the ride, Yank," Sam called out.

"You Johnnies take care of yourselves and good luck on the way home," the Sergeant said with a wave and a grin.

Men who would have killed each other less than a month ago were now sincerely wishing each other well. It was like the soldiers recognized the merit of their former adversaries and considered them part of the same military fraternity as themselves. "Maybe the wounds of this war will heal quickly after all," he thought to himself as he turned to leave.

Sam announced, "Since the rations we were promised by the Yankees didn't reach us before we left, I ain't goin' to go beggin' no Yankee for 'em now. My stomach is already rubbin' against my backbone and we ain't got nothin' to eat. I bought some fishhooks when we last came through Raleigh. We can reach the Cape Fear at Averasboro by tomorrow night, catch some of them blue tailed Channel Cats and have the strength for the last leg home to South River."

"Once again Sam has it all figured out," Neil said.

"It's just out of habit," Uriah agreed. "Havin' some sort of plan for the last three years just might have kept some of us alive."

"I'm glad to be travelin' with men who know what they're doin'," Daniel McMillan added. "I'm just ready to hit the road for home."

"That won't be long," Sam said. "Another mile and we'll be turnin south down the Averasboro Road. Each step after that will take us that much closer to home."

The friends walked around the south side of Raleigh, past the near endless camps of Sherman's troops. General Grant was in town to confer with Sherman, but the four homesick soldiers could not have cared less. There was nothing any of them could do from now on to help determine the direction of state and national policies and the only ground they would attack or defend from now on would be their bottom land farms near South River.

Down in Florence, South Carolina, the stream of returning soldiers passing through the town had become a flood. Doctor Dargan and his helpers did what they could to help these men in spite of their meager resources. Sarah Mclain had recovered from her burns and had resumed her volunteer work with the Doctor. She now had scars on her left shoulder and beneath her ear which hurt when she walked in the sun. Her wardrobe of off the shoulder dresses were no longer used and she had let her hair grow to help hide her disfigurement.

She had not heard from Dougal in over four months even though she had received that strange letter from Sam which merely said Dougal was alive when he last saw him at Elmira. She wondered if he was dead. She now often regretted why it had been her fate to live in such terrible times when the men of her generation had been so determined to kill each other off. How nice it would have been if she could have been properly courted by the handsome young soldier who had appeared in her life so briefly and continued to profess his love for her in his letters until they stopped coming. One day, she thought to herself, the soldiers would all be home and she could start sorting out her life.

As Sam and his friends made their way along the road from Raleigh to Averasboro, it began to appear they were to become victims of their own pride in not asking for supplies. Hardly any of the homes Sam's party passed by had any food to spare since they had already been visited by parties of foraging soldiers. All too often, the friends were saddened by the memories of a pale woman with children hiding behind her frock tails, waiting in vain for a husband or father who had already found a final resting place in Virginia. It was during this final march back home that many ex-Confederate would tell of eating some rather repulsive things merely to stay alive.

In the afternoon of the second day after leaving Raleigh, the smells of the Cape Fear River began drifting in on a southernly breeze. "I know I'm near home when I start sniffing those river smells," Neil said. "You can't imagine the times in the last three years when I thought I'd never git back here."

"I always thought I'd make it back," countered Uriah. "Those old catfish are out there waitin' for us, I'll bet."

What's that roarin' sound?" Sam asked. "I don't re-member there being any rapids on this stretch of the Cape Fear."

"Look, you can see the water already," Daniel said. "I ain't never seen it that high before. You can see the water line on the trees where its been still higher."

"How stupid of me!" Sam said disgustedly. "All that rain that's been fallin' on us since early March had to go some-where. The river's in flood stage and we ain't got a jackasses chance of catchin' any cats out there.

"I reckon that means we're goin' to sleep without supper again tonight," Neil said dejectedly.

"I saw a sassafras bush a little ways back and I'll go back and git it," Uriah said. "We can use the good water in our canteens and make us some tea. We got one more day before we make home and it will just have to last."

The disappointed soldiers had seen the Cape Fear River in a flood stage seen once a century. This one would be remem-bered by the locals as "Sherman's Freshet" and had already washed many of the bridges left in the ravished land. The men boiled and drank their tea and then went to sleep thinking of their homes they would reach tomorrow.

Betty Morgan awoke at dawn the next day and walked out on the front porch to watch the sun rise over the cypress and gum trees in the river bottom in the distance across the fields. This had become her habit since Sam went off to war three years ago. It was almost as if her faithfulness was a guarantee that one day her husband would walk down that road again and everything would be wonderful forever. The road was still empty and she turned and went back into the house to begin the chores of the day. There was nothing in the house to eat except eggs and she was one of the few people between the rivers to have that.

On the day Sam went back to the war with Pope and Barefoot, they had almost slept too late because the rooster had not crowed. The wise old bird had taken the hens and hid in the swamps the same day the Yankees came and devoured all the other chickens for miles around. After the uninvited troops had left, the rooster led his flock back home they now provided eggs for the destitute family. Betty had been amazed at the old bird's action and though she would never know why he had done what he did, she knew he would never wind up in the stew pot. She would at least show her appreciation in that way.

If Sam and his friends had possessed the rooster that morning, there is no doubt what would have happened to him. They had survived the last three days on what was left of their meager rations in anticipation of a catfish dinner. When that didn't occur, the men now felt severe hunger pangs and weakness from lack of food. The fact they were only a day from home would supply them the energy for the final push.

The soldiers struggled on as the sun rose higher in the May sky. "It's just a matter of putting one foot in front of the other for the rest of the day. Just figure each step is a cotton stalk you have to pick," Sam said. "The end of the row is in sight."

"It sure will be good to git to the end of this road," Uriah agreed. "I'm goin' to lay down and rest for a month when I git home."

"I'm goin' to eat every thing I can find to eat for the next month," Neil said. "I don't ever plan to be this hungry again."

"I think I'll find me a wife so I'll never be cold again at night," Uriah added. "I never want to go to sleep in the rain no more. I wonder if any of the Johnson girls are still single?" Uriah was beginning to remember one in particular.

As the day progressed, the party increasingly passed evidence of Sherman's march. Almost no rail fences remained. Barns had been burned for fire wood or wantonly destroyed. An occasional house had been burned with its furniture strewed about the yard.

"When we went up to Gettysburg with General Lee," Neil related, "he posted armed guards around private homes in Maryland and Pennsylvania to keep them from bein' bothered. We didn't git the same treatment from Billy Sherman, it don't look like."

"General Lee was too much of a gentlemen than to make war on civilians," Sam concluded. "When I see some-

305

thing like that burned house back there it makes me more worried about what I'm goin' to find when I get home."

"We ought to know in just a few hours," Daniel said. "There's cypress trees up ahead so that means South River can't be far."

Betty had just finished hoeing her garden. The cucumbers ought to start bearing soon now. She had picked some dandelion greens to supplement the eggs and milk diet she and her sons had lived on for the past six weeks. She walked into her kitchen to begin preparation for the evening meal.

Suddenly, her oldest son, William, came bounding up the steps of the front porch and rushed through the house and into the kitchen. "Mama!, he yelled. "There's four gray soldiers coming up the road and I think one of them is Daddy."

Betty grabbed the Navy Colt pistol and wrapped it in her apron as she repeated a ritual developed in case any of the men stopping by her well proved dangerous. "Oh Lord! Let it be true!" she prayed as she stepped out on the porch and saw the approaching figures. One of them had an unmistakable gait in his walk she had been hoping to see for several weeks now. This time she completely forgot about her appearance and ran toward the men. Sam saw her coming and even in his weakened condition, rushed forward to embrace his rapidly approaching wife. When they met, they locked in an embrace and a kiss which meant to both of them that everything was going be all right from now on.

Sam swung Betty around as they kissed even though a loaded Colt pistol was still in her right hand . "Let me hold this while ya'll finish saying hello," Uriah said after grabbing the gun to prevent an accidental discharge.

Suddenly, Sam and Betty remembered that they weren't the only two people left in the world. The two sons, William and Rufus, had caught up with their parents and Sam lifted them up in his arms while Betty hugged his friends. "Oh, Neil!" she exclaimed. "It's so good to see you after four years. Your Mama has been praying hard all that time."

"Uriah Bass!" she continued. "Thank you for helping Sam through this terrible war."

"We helped each other, Miz Betty," Uriah answered.

"And Daniel McMillan," She said while hugging him around the shoulders. "I'm so glad you're all right. When you see your daddy, please tell him again how much I appreciated his stopping to tell me that Sam was all right after Bentonville."

"I hope you have some food," Sam said hopefully.

"We have some eggs," she answered. "You boys are probably starved. I picked some greens and Lonnie milks the cow twice a day and brings us milk every night."

"So the old cow escaped the Yankees!" Sam declared. "How did any chickens survive?"

"That was the beatenest thing," Betty answered. "I'll tell you about it on the way to the house.

While the men were being fed, Lonnie came up to the back door with the bucket of milk he brought each day to the Morgan house. He and James took turns milking the cow and feeding their mule in return for half of the cow's milk and occasional use of the mule. Lonnie knocked on the back door to announce his arrival and Betty left the kitchen to get the milk.

"Was dat Mistuh Sam I saw coming up the road with them soldiers?" he asked.

"Yes!" Betty answered. "I can't be any happier than I am right now."

"Praise de Lawd he's all right!" Lonnie agreed. "We was all prayin' for him." He paused a moment to be sure he relayed a particular message correctly. "You know Moses Hawkins came home and him and Spicey can git married now, don't you?

"Yes we certainly do," Betty replied. "He was like a guardian angel to Susan and myself while the Yankees were here."

"Well, he wants to talk to Mistuh Sam about some of dat land across the creek," Lonnie explained. "He wants to see if he can buy some."

"Tell him to come up sometime and talk to Sam then," she answered. "He would come out and speak, but he's been starved and I'm feedin him now. You brought this milk just in time. Give him a chance to get settled down and rested up. Moses will see Sam in the field with the mule when it's time."

It took three days of rest, nourishment and love before

307

Sam was ready to start rebuilding his farm. He was plowing some ground to plant some field peas in when Moses Hawkins walked across the furrows to where Sam had stopped to adjust the animals harness. They exchanged greetings and Sam noticed a deep scar on Moses' left cheek bone.

"So it was you that Thomas saw at Battery Wagner the night of the attack?" Sam said.

"Yes it was," Moses replied. "That lick probably saved my life. I would have been kilt up on the fort if Thomas hadn't knocked me off. I was bleedin' like a stuck hog and there was some white soldiers who wouldn't let any blacks retreat that weren't wounded. Anyway, it's all over and I'm glad."

"I don't miss the war at all, that's for sure," Sam agreed. "Betty said you wanted to talk about some land across the creek."

"That's right!" said Moses. "I want to git married now that blacks can and I need a place to build a house and grow some food. That land across the creek from James and Lonnie's place would do real good. I'll give you ten dollars in Yankee gold pieces for it."

"That land's kind of low, ain't it?" asked Sam. "Is there a good place for a house? It would take a lot of work to clear it.

"Yes, there's one good site and I could use the timber to build with," Moses answered. "Would you sell it?"

"I sure need some money to get this farm goin' again," Sam answered. "If you've got gold, I'll sell you ten acres for ten dollars. Come up to the house tomorrow and I'll give you a contract. I'll take five dollars then and five when I give you the deed. I reckon that's still how we'll do things when the Yankees get through with our government."

"Done!" Moses said. "There is one more thing I'd like to ask. I want to stay around here and I don't know if the white people will take it too kindly if they knew I fought for the Union."

"I'll keep it under my hat," Sam answered. "We all did what we had to do and there's nobody who was at Wagmer that night that's still alive who knows you. You can count on me."

"I'm obliged, Sam," Moses said. "I'll see you tomorrow

afternoon."

Moses Hawkins wasn't the only visitor to the Morgan farm that day. Sam finished his plowing and put the mule in the stable for the night. Betty had finished washing Sam's dirty uniform and hung it out to dry. They both had decided to get a drink from the well at the same time and stood there drinking the water and enjoying the presence of each other.

The clatter of the hooves of a large body of cavalry interrupted their solitude. At least two companies of blue coated horsemen stopped along the Goldsboro Road and three riders pealed off from the column and approached the house at a brisk trot. It was Captain Voorhees who had come to see for himself if the dark haired lady whose beauty still haunted him was all right-and perhaps if she was a widow.

"Good afternoon, Ma'am," he greeted Betty. Noticing the officer's coat on the line he nodded to Sam," Lieutenant."

"Why, Captain," Betty said, breaking the awkwardness of the situation. "I hadn't expected you to come back this way."

"We are taking some wagons of food to Averasboro to set up a commissary and I remembered you asked if you would get any rent for General Geary's visit," the Captain explained. "I've brought you two sacks of corn meal in payment for your hospitality. This is the best I can do."

"You aren't obligated to even do that, but we're might grateful just the same," Betty answered.

"We're much obliged, Captain," Sam said. "My wife has told me about the incident where you saved our house. I wish we had something to give you in return."

"I'm glad to have been of service," the Captain said. "Good luck to you both." Voorhees wheeled his horse around to speak to his men. "Put the sacks on the porch," he ordered his troopers. Turning to Sam and Betty, he touched the front of his hat in a salute. "Good-bye!" he added. Then the three horsemen galloped back to the road to continue their journey. The Captain would soon return home to his victory parades and a successful postwar life. However, a small portion of his heart would remain behind between the rivers in North Carolina.

"I've just thought of something," Sam said. "If the Captain was near Goldsboro and heading toward Averasboro, this ain't the shortest way. He came to see you and if I hadn't been here, he might have stayed awhile."

"Well," Betty said with a tease, "He was certainly handsome and very dashing."

"No more than me," Sam said as he gave his wife a playful pat. As they walked up the steps and into the house, Sam felt a deep appreciation for his wife and knew he was a fortunate man.

The scarcity of food was so severe that Sam no longer cared where it came from, but what there was of it had to be shared. He would send William down to tell James and Lonnie to take one of the sacks of cornmeal. They had certainly helped his family while he was away at war.

The days passed and only an occasional returning soldier now stopped by the Morgan well. It was early June when a lone figure made his way up the road and walked right past the well. Sam was at the far end of the field and noticed something familiar about this man. He started the mule back toward the house as the figure walked up on the porch and knocked on the door. Sam let out an audible gasp when his wife opened the door and threw her arms around the man. He tied his mule up at the stable and rushed to the house. "You never thought you'd have to worry about me again, did you, Sam?" the man said.

There stood a thin man with carefully combed hair and a face marred with scars. "Dougal!" Sam exclaimed. "Dougal McKay. Sam leaped up on the porch and embraced his friend just like his wife had done a few moments before. "I've counted you among the dead for the last few months. I don't know when I've been happier to see a person. Sit down here in one of these chairs on the porch." The two comrades sat in the two rocking chairs while Betty went to the well and came back with two glasses of water.

"I truthfully don't know how I made it either," Dougal confessed. "A lot of our men are in the ground at Elmira."

"It's like you taught me when I was so down in the dumps at Elmira, you have to take it one stalk at a time and not be overwhelmed by the total length of the row," Sam remembered.

"I kept seein' Sarah when I was out of my head," Dougal recalled. "It was like she was going to be there when I licked that smallpox."

"Do you know if she is?" Sam asked. "I mailed her that letter just like you said."

"I don't know," Dougal replied. "Some letters from her piled up at Elmira while I was sick and in late March, they stopped. She never did have my home address."

"What are you going to do?" asked Sam.

"Why I'm goin' right down there after her!" Dougal said emphatically. "If I can find some money, I'll ride the train and if I can't, I'll walk."

"Are you strong enough for a trip like that?" Sam asked.

"Lord, yes!" Dougal said. "After there was so much fuss made about Andersonville Prison in Georgia, well, some of us in Yankee prisons looked like them. I think they kept us longer to fatten us up cause the food shore got a lot better. I could help you plow if I have to."

"Dougal, I've got some money you can have," Sam announced. "Betty, can we spare Dougal enough to get to Florence? Two dollars ought to do it."

"Sakes alive, it'll cost that much for him to get there and then he has to eat and maybe pay a preacher," Betty argued. "Give him one of those five dollar gold pieces you got paid for the land."

"I don't know when I'll be able to pay you back," Dougal said. "I ain't never even seen that much gold."

"You won't have to if you marry that girl," Sam offered. "That will be our wedding present to you."

"I don't know of any better friend I could have had," Dougal said. "I never expected anything like this."

Betty went back in the house and came back with the gold coin. "Don't you lose this," she admonished him. "And you'd better get on the road. If that girl is as pretty as I've been told, she might not wait too long."

"Thank you again," Dougal said. "I'll do something for

you sometime." He shook hands again with Sam and walked out of the house. His fast gait down the road left no doubt he would be in Florence as soon as he possibly could.

Dougal spent most of the next day wishing the train could go faster. He had plenty of time to think of the wishes of Thomas and how he wanted to one day ride in a coach instead of a boxcar and the coach would be taking him some place he really wanted to go. That was what he was doing now and poor Thomas was dead in Pennsylvania. That chapter in his life was closed, another chapter was about to begin.

When Dougal reached Florence, he had no trouble finding out where Sarah was working. The story of her sacrifice was well known and she was something of a heroine for saving the soldier. He quickly found the aid station and was directed to the tent where he saw Sarah, sitting with her back to the door, mending a worn out shirt for some soldier.

Dougal walked up to within three paces of Sarah before he spoke. "Sarah, I've come for you," he said.

She turned around and stood up with her mouth open in disbelief, dropping her sewing as she did and said, "I thought you were..."

"I'm not!" Dougal interrupted.

Sarah noticed the smallpox scars on his face and could only think of one thing to say, "You sure do look funny."

Dougal understood what she was trying to say and responded. "You sure do look beautiful," he said.

It was as if these words were a signal for them to leap into each other's arms. They embraced and kissed a kiss they both had only imagined for the past two years.

"I thought you were dead when your letters stopped coming," she said.

"I had smallpox," he explained. "I might have sent the disease to you somehow in my letters."

"I didn't realize how much I loved you until those letters stopped," she said as they looked into each others face.

"I always knew how much I loved you from the first time I saw you," Dougal answered as they kissed again.

Back at South River, William, the oldest Morgan son was expanding his world. He occasionally would go down to where their land bordered James' and Lonnie's place. He had made friends with Pete, James' son who was about his age. On this day, the two boys were mastering the manly art of tall tale telling.

"What you done today, Pete?" William asked.

"I took me a good runnin' start and jumped over the house," Pete answered.

"Naw you didn't. Let me see you do it," William insisted.

"I done it once today and dat's enough," Pete said.

"Shoot, that ain't nothin," William countered. "I went down in the woods and took my fist and knocked down a big tree,"

"Let me see you knock down that one," Pete said, pointing at a big Chinaberry tree near the house.

"Naw, knocking down a tree takes a lot of work and I've done it once today. Maybe I'll show you tomorrow," William said.

James walked over to the two boys and spoke to William. "Tell your Daddy we'se much obliged for the corn meal. The river's down and I've found some good catfish holes I can show him if he wants. Some catfish would taste mighty good with dem hushpuppies. I'll be by your house near three o'clock."

"I'll run tell him," William shouted, dashing off to find his father

William thought three o'clock would never come, but at the appointed time, James and Pete came up to the Morgan house where Sam and William were rigging their fishing poles in the back yard. "So you've got some good catfish holes for us to fish, do you?" Sam asked.

"I ain't failed to git a nice'en yet," James greeted. "I dug us plenty of worms for bait."

"I've got some new hooks if you need one and I just cut up two minnie balls to use for sinkers," Sam offered "I haven't fished since I joined the army, so my poles need riggin'."

"I figure these boys can fish at a bream bed I'se found and we won't have to worry about dem fallin' in no deep water," James said.

"That sounds good to me, Sam replied. "I'm ready to go."

The South River bends and curves its way through low land forests before it enters the Cape Fear near the coast. Each curve bites into the bank of one side while depositing sand and gravel on the opposite side. Here the bream make their spawning beds in the Spring. They are fiercely protective and attack anything which violates their nest. You will always catch fish at a bream bed during their Spring spawn.

The fishermen followed the river about a mile. "We'll leave the boys here to catch bream while I fish dat hole near dat stump," James said. "I'll be able to keep an eye on 'em. Dere's a log by the bank around the bend, Mistuh Sam. You can sit on it and fish on the bottom straight out and catch some nice cats."

"All right, that's what I'll do," Sam replied and walked on down the river as James had indicated. He had not been on this part of the river for several years and was enjoying the beauty of the huge cypresses and the moss covered oaks and gums. As he rounded the bend in the river and saw the log that James had told him about, he suddenly stopped and a chill ran up his back. He was looking at the very log he had seen in his dream at Elmira when Thomas had appeared to him.

Being careful not to tangle his fishing line in the low bushes, he walked over to the log and sat down as James had suggested. He reached in his pocket and found a lead minnie ball and whittled off some shavings with his knife. He fastened these on the line a foot up from the hook, put on some worms and cast out in the middle of the stream. He soon had a nice bullhead catfish flapping around on the bank. The excited shouts from up the river told him that the boys were being successful at the bream bed and supper would be guaranteed for the evening.

He baited up and cast out again, hoping nothing would bite for a while so he could do some thinking. The dream at Elmira had saved his life. Was that dream the work of the heavenly father that he prayed to and sang about at church but didn't really know until shot and shell was zinging past his ear? He had seen this very spot in his dream. Did that mean it was predestined for him to survive the war and one day come to this spot so he could understand that a higher power was really in control? Sam decided then and there that he would mend his ways and establish a closer relationship with his God in the future.

For the first time since coming home, he was now completely relaxed with his thoughts. Fishing will do that for a person. He remembered his lifelong friendship with Thomas and felt a deep void now that his friend was gone. He and William would take some of the fish to Susan. In the time to come he would teach young Thomas the things a boy should learn from an older man. Sam felt a trembling tug at the end of his line and soon had a second catfish on the bank. He baited up and cast out again. He was finally, really and truly home from the war.

Suddenly, Sam was startled by the "swoosh, swoosh, swoosh" of the wing beat of two large birds. A pair of Ivorybilled Woodpeckers flew right down the middle of the river and passed not more than twenty feet from where Sam was fishing. He could distinctly see the yellow eyes and whitish beaks of these magnificent duck sized birds as they flew by. They pitched on the side of a huge cypress tree that had lived since the time of Christ and began probing the bark for grubs.

He remembered that Thomas had admired the speed with which these birds with their constant, duck-like wingbeat flew through the trees of the cypress lined river bottom. Sam would think of Thomas and the woodpecker's feather he had worn in his hat the day of his death whenever he saw one from now on. But, the same war which killed his friend had also doomed the Ivorybill. Wooden hulled ships were now obsolete and the tar and pitch for these hulls would no longer be needed from the Carolina forests. Large sawmills would soon devour the pines and cypress trees of the uplands and bottoms. With their habitat gone, the trumpetlike call of these woodpeckers would one day no longer be heard in the forests of the South. Sam watched with admiration as the pair flew from their perch and headed down the river toward another feeding place, dodging through the trees and limbs until they disappeared from sight.

Chapter 19
Epilogue

It was April of 1904. On this glorious spring day, the brilliant sunshine highlighted the white dogwoods which paint the hills of Piedmont North Carolina at this time of year. A lone horse and buggy was traveling the eight miles from Durham to Chapel Hill. Its two occupants were James Hunter and Polly Fulton, two members of the newly formed North Carolina Civil War Commission. Private individuals had appointed the members of the organization and had funded it to compile histories of the North Carolina regiments which had served in the Confederate Army. James and Polly had agreed to serve as volunteers for this effort.

James Hunter was an official of a Durham tobacco company and had an eye for detail as his job required. Polly was a legal secretary for a Durham law firm and took the notes of the interviews. Her occupation required the same attention to detail as did Hunter's. On this day they were to interview Sam Morgan, former Lieutenant of the 51st Regiment, North Carolina State Troops, Confederate States Army. Sam and Betty now lived in a new house they had recently built in the popular gingerbread style of the time. It was located on Franklin Street in Chapel Hill.

Sam had been drawn into local politics after the war. He had fought against the carpetbagger rule during the Reconstruction, and his need for knowledge of the law had led to the study of law and then to a legal practice. He had been a well respected professor of law at the state university for the past two decades. He was confident in his knowledge and opinions and now had a slight touch of the crankiness that advancing age sometimes brings.

Betty had been the perfect wife for Sam. She was always supportive of his ambitions but could bring him down to earth when the need arose. She had some wrinkles and her hair was almost gray. She still possessed the beauty, and grace which had kept Sam beguiled for the past forty years.

Sam and Betty were expecting the visit from the commission members and were waiting for them on the front porch. James Hunter stopped the buggy at the hitching post and after tying the horse, helped Polly down. Sam met them at the gate, carefully stepping on the flagstones of the walkway recently joined together by mortar.

"Am I addressing Mr. Sam Morgan, former Lieutenant of the 51st North Carolina Regiment?" Hunter asked.

"Yes sir," Sam replied, "and I did have that honor."

"It's a pleasure to finally meet you sir after all of our correspondence. May I introduce my associate, Miss Polly Fulton," Hunter responded.

The guests were led up on the front porch where they were introduced to Betty who took over as hostess of the occasion. She showed the guests into the large drawing room where there awaited cakes and tall cool glasses of lemonade.

After a brief period of the usual small talk which begins the conversation at social calls in the South, the talk turned to the reason for the visit - Sam's recollection of the Civil War. His memory was unfailing as he described the events that had occurred nearly forty years before. He told of the hardships, forced marches, and short rations endured by the 51st. He discussed heroic victories and crushing defeats. He gave vivid descriptions of naval bombardments, advances, retreats, and train rides to Hell.

Sam had to pause ever so often when he became choked up and misty-eyed as he recalled the friends he lost in the war. He had never forgotten the train wreck at Shohola and the bloody hat with the woodpecker's feather that Thomas had worn. The memory of the constant hunger at Elmira was

317

still very painful after forty years as was the last desperate effort at Bentonville. After nearly four hours, Polly Fulton had taken enough notes to be able to write the Regimental History of the 51st North Carolina Regiment as Sam Morgan remembered it. She also had questions about some of the women in Sam's account.

"Mr. Morgan," she asked. "Did Dougal and Sarah ever get married?"

"Yes!" Sam answered. "Indeed they did. Sarah made him stay and help with the sweet potato crop. She insisted that he court her properly and they were married that fall in Florence."

"Good for her," Polly said with delight. "This part of your story has a happy ending."

"There's more," Sam said with a chuckle. "They came back to South River that winter after selling her mother's house and bought some land over across the river in Sampson County and became very prosperous. They had six of the prettiest children you ever saw. I guess you could use the old story book phrase that 'they lived happily ever after'."

"Good!" exclaimed Polly. "What happened to Susan? Did she ever remarry?"

"She never did," Sam answered, "She lived there in the house she and Thomas had built 'til she died ten or fifteen years ago. I taught her son all I could about farming and he became a good one. He's bought his own place and the last I heard he was doin' rather well. He was hired out to me as an apprentice when I was cuttin' timber. Me and Tom and my boys would make rafts out of the logs and float 'em to Wilmington. Sometimes James' and Lonnie's boys would go with us if we had a lot of trees. We'd float 'em down the river and then ride the train back. I could really tell you some stories if we had the time."

"What ever happened to Uriah?" Polly inquired. "Did he ever marry one of the Johnson girls?"

"Yes he did," answered Sam. "He actually married two. His first wife died suddenly after they had been married about ten years. It wasn't long before he married her younger sister. I lost track of how many children he has, but he certainly did his

318

part to repopulate our part of the country after the war. Moses Hawkins did too. He was always building on to the house on that land he bought. Some of his children went to school up in Boston."

Satisfied with Sam's account of the 51st's part in the war, Hunter began to pose broader questions.

"Mr. Morgan, what in your opinion were the major causes of the war," he asked ?

Sam thought for a minute before answering. "Well, the Yankees would have you believe it was a holy crusade against slavery. It is probably true that if it had not been for slavery there would have been no war, but I believe that if there had been only slavery there would have been no war. Wars are fought for economic reasons," Sam snorted, "Don't you forget it. The large Southern planters were the last to make a profit out of slavery and now all Southerners take the blame for it. The African blacks themselves sold the prisoners they captured in their tribal wars to slavers. They have done that for centuries and perhaps still do. The sea captains who brought them to this shore were Yankees. I defy you to find a Southern ship engaged in transporting slaves to America."

"Anyhow, the Yankees found it was more profitable to work European immigrants and their children for long hours at starvation wages. They didn't have to feed them or nothing when they left their sweatshop factories. These conditions in their factories are the reasons for the rise of the trade unions which is occurring today."

"No Sir," Sam continued, "the cotton tariffs caused the war more than anything else. The South believed in free trade. That was necessary since we had to import or buy from the North nearly all our manufactured goods. Our main export was, of course, cotton. The Northerners controlled Congress and passed tariffs to tax our cotton as it left for Europe and then taxed the manufactured goods as they were imported by Southerners back from Europe. These unfair tariffs were meant to force the South to sell its cotton to northern mills at prices set by the mill owners. These prices were below what the British mills would have paid if it were not for these tariffs.

"One solution to this problem was to build cotton mills

in the South and this was done to a certain extent. There were not nearly the number of mills in places like piedmont North Carolina as there are now. When the Yankee armies passed through any part of the South, they always burned the cotton mills. What does that tell you?" Sam rose from his chair, stretched, and walked over to the window where he looked out at the virgin greenness of the trees with their new Spring growth. He continued, "Since the population of the North was much greater than that of the South there was no chance of winning any votes in the House of Representatives since House membership is determined by the population of each state. As I'm sure you know, each state has two Senators. Do you follow me so far?" asked Sam.

"I do indeed, Sir. Your logic is perfectly clear," responded Hunter. He continued, "It remains that a Southern controlled Senate would defeat the tariffs and shift the taxes to the manufacturers."

"Precisely," said Sam, almost shouting. "When the Republicans and Lincoln won the election in 1860, one of the planks in their platform was not the abolishment of slavery, but that no new slave states could be added to the Union. That eliminated any chance that the cotton tariffs could be stopped by the Southern states, so South Carolina chose to secede. Why else would the average citizen of any Southern state care if slavery existed anywhere else in the country?"

"These facts have been conveniently forgotten by the Yankees," added Hunter.

"There is no doubt about that." Sam continued. "As for slavery, it could have been maintained more easily by the slave states remaining in the Union than by seceding. Most all of the Supreme Court decisions concerning slavery had been decided in favor of the pro-slavery forces. The Dred Scott decision is the most famous of the court cases. To secede from the Union meant war with Lincoln as President, yet, South Carolina did it."

Hunter interrupted, "If I may summarize, the points you have made are in effect saying that the Southern States seceded from the Union for the same reason our grandfathers declared their independence from Great Britain. Both were rebelling against illegal taxation."

"We Southerners have never said anything else." said Sam. "Practically none of the men in the ranks I served with in the army owned slaves and would not have benefited if slavery had spread into the territories or was abolished all together. By the time my group joined up, the Yankees had burned towns in the eastern part of the state and were to loot Southern cities. Yes sir, we were fighting for the rights of our state and to save our homes. In all of the diaries I have read from the war, I have never found where an average Confederate soldier wrote that he was fighting to preserve slavery."

"It is well known General Lee freed his slaves before the war while General Grant and his family owned slaves who were not freed till after Appomattox. Lincoln's Emancipation Proclamation only freed those slaves in areas still separated from the Union on January 1, 1863. Also, slavery wasn't ended in Maryland or Kentucky by that Proclamation. It was only meant to force the seceding states back in the Union or to keep them from getting foreign recognition if they kept on fighting. It took the Thirteenth Amendment to the Constitution which was passed after the war to free all the slaves. Now tell me who was fighting for what?" Sam fumed.

"When we decided in 1776 that we wanted to be free from the King, there was a Declaration of Independence which left no doubt what we were fighting about. If the War for Southern Independence was fought to end slavery, why wasn't there some declaration made by the Yankees at the beginning which said so?" Sam continued. "Also, after we gained our independence from Great Britain, we experimented with government for six years before we finally ratified the Constitution. The Confederate States of America never got a chance to correct the weaknesses of its government. It will always be remembered as it existed for four and a half years as it tried to establish a government and fight a war at the same time."

"I have told you to remember that wars are fought for economic reasons," he continued. "You would do well to also remember that the winners of a war will write the history."

"No matter how you look at it, slavery was a millstone around the neck of the South. Without it, many thought, the

321

agricultural economy of the region could not be sustained. With it, the Confederate States could not get the foreign recognition which was critical to our achieving independence."

Hunter interrupted, "Do you think the Confederacy could have won the war if foreign recognition could have been achieved?"

"Probably," responded Sam. "If that recognition had come from England, her navy could have broken the blockade. If she could have supplied us with war ships to defend our coast, we would not have needed any ground troops."

"You are talking about actual intervention in the war by England after she recognized the Confederacy. Would one have followed the other?" questioned Hunter.

"I think so," answered Sam. "England's need for cotton by late 1862 could not be met. Her cotton mills went through some rough times until other sources of supply were found. Her economy would not have had to suffer if she could have solved this problem by recognizing the Confederacy. This action would have been very unpopular with the British working class as long as slavery existed in the South. I think that England would have found the possibility of naval war worth the risk if she could have solved her economic problems."

"That is a very interesting speculation," said Hunter, "although it is one not many people consider."

"Don't forget," continued Sam, "during the Revolutionary War the Continental Army wasn't very successful militarily. It was only with the help of the French that victory was achieved at Yorktown. The Confederate armies were much more successful in the field and lacked only help from Europe to have ultimately won the war."

"What do you see as the most significant and lasting effects of the war," asked Hunter?

Sam was quick with his answer. "The authority of the Federal Government was established once and for all to be greater than that of the individual states. Differences of opinion on this question was one of the major causes of the war and it was finally laid to rest by the victory of the Federal forces. No states will ever try to secede again. This is actually good when you consider we will need to be united to face the problems of this new century. It is bad when you consider the probability that the Federal Government will gradually take over the duties of the states as well as do away with many of our individual liberties."

"Doesn't our Constitution protect us from that?" interrupted Hunter. "It specifically states that all rights not given to the Federal government are reserved for the states."

"You are referring to the tenth amendment and I predict that part of the Constitution will one day be conveniently forgotten, "Sam continued. "Even now there is talk of a Federal tax on a person's income, as if all the other sources of revenue were not sufficient."

"The American people will never stand for that," Hunter fumed. "Such a thing would cause armed revolt."

"No it won't," countered Sam. "You have missed my point. The Confederate States rebelled and were defeated. Armed rebellion against the Federal Government will never happen again. Washington will one day be all powerful."

"Besides," Sam continued, "our attention will now be focused on the development of our new colonies. Since we fought the war with Spain in '98 and won it, we have become an international power. Britain, France, Germany and Italy have gobbled up colonies right and left in the last century. They are on a collision course for the greatest war in history. I don't know where it will be, but it will happen because of economic competition. We might also be involved in it because we now have an army in the Philippine Islands."

"I can see our national interest in controlling Cuba and Puerto Rico. I don't even disagree with President Theodore Roosevelt wanting to build a canal through Central America so our ships can go from the Atlantic to the Pacific a lot faster. But, for the life of me, I don't think we should have a colony in Asia. If we stay in the Philippine Islands, we will one day have to fight a war simply because we are there."

"Who do you think we will fight?" asked Hunter?

"I don't know at this point," responded Sam. "But mark my words, some other country will one day want the raw materials of these islands and we will be forced to defend them. Don't forget what I said earlier in this interview that wars are fought for economic reasons."

"You keep making that point," said Hunter, "but we are digressing from my original question about the lasting effects of the Civil War.

"Oh yes," laughed Sam. "I do have a tendency to get on my soapbox. In addition to the Federal government becoming all powerful, the economy of the South was ruined for generations to come. While the industry in the Northern states boomed because of the war, the industry in the South was destroyed. Even now the agricultural exports, such as your tobacco, Mr. Hunter, are still our main reasons for trade. A few manufacturing plants have been built to take advantage of our cotton crop, but our industries are not nearly as diverse as they need to be. Our labor force is untrained."

"Oh, I suppose we are industrious enough in our agriculture and timbering, but that won't last forever. After the war I made some good money cutting cypress and pine logs and floating them down the Cape Fear River to the mills at Wilmington. That couldn't go on forever, so I turned to other things. We simply have to diversify our economy so that we manufacture a multitude of finished products and trade them with the rest of the world."

"The end of slavery was the other of the lasting effects of the war," Sam continued. "Lincoln started the war to keep the Union together, but as it progressed, it eventually became a means for him to end slavery."

"Hold on," Hunter interrupted. "Are you saying that Abraham Lincoln deliberately started the war?"

"Figure it out for yourself," Sam challenged. "There were many other forts in the seceding states which the troops of these states occupied without a fight. He stopped that practice when he became President. Why did he make such an issue over Fort Sumter? If he hadn't of tried to send re-enforcements to the garrison, the fort wouldn't have been fired on. I think he knew that with South Carolina, Georgia and the Gulf states already gone, he was president of half a country. Starting a war was the only way to bring the Union back together. He knew with a little pushing those fools in Charleston would make it happen and they did. If they had only waited a few days more, the garrison would have left Fort Sumter because they were running out of supplies. After he called for troops to put down the rebellion, Virginia seceded and North Carolina had no choice but to leave also."

"Incredible," exclaimed Hunter. "I have never in my life considered such a thing and I have never read where anyone else has. I wonder why? The facts certainly point in that direction."

Sam quickly answered, "Remember that I said the winners of a war will write the history. Consider this also. If it hadn't been for Fort Sumter, and first states to secede remained a separate nation, there would be national border down at the South Carolina line. The Confederate Constitution banned tariffs on trade with other countries, so exports through the Gulf ports and Charleston would have boomed and smuggling would have been rampant through the ports of Wilmington and Memphis. Remember, North Carolina and Tennessee would still have been part of the United States and trade exports would have been sucked out of the country like bees flying out of a turned over bee hive. The trade gained by the Southern ports would have been at the expense of Northern ports like Boston, New York and Philadelphia. How long do you expect the Yankees would put up with that?"

"I have read that more than half of the Federal revenues were raised by taxing cotton before the war. Do you think the Yankees were going to stand by and let that money get away? Not on your life! Lincoln had to get the flag fired on so he could use force to bring the seceding states back in the Union. We need to guard against that in this century. Be suspicious of a President who gets the flag fired on to make war on another country, Mister Hunter".

Suddenly, Sam stopped and said apologetically, "I was making a point about the end of slavery and got sidetracked."

"Please continue," invited Hunter. "You are making some good points with which I most heartily concur."

"Does it make any sense that a country would fight a terrible war for four years, lose four-hundred thousand soldiers and then go home and not provide any kind of training for the freed blacks to earn a living. No it doesn't," emphasized Sam, answering his own question. "That such a thing did happen makes hypocrites out of the Abolitionists and all other people who would have you believe the war was fought to free the slaves alone. There has been no educational help for them of any consequence for nigh on to forty years since the war ended."

"Most blacks have traded legalized slavery for an economic slavery from which there is no escape except education. Poor blacks and whites who are engaged in agriculture and don't own their own land are sharecroppers. They supply the labor to work the fields for a share of the crops barely large enough to feed and clothe them and their families. So I ask you, what has changed since the days of slavery?"

Sam was now in his university lecture mode and continued making his points. "There is glimmer of hope on the horizon, Mr. Hunter. This year the state of North Carolina will make it compulsory for the children of this state to attend a public school. Think of it, man! We are making a step which can mean the end of illiteracy one day. Only it has to be available for all people of all races, and the people must be willing to take advantage of this opportunity."

James Hunter had not spoken for some time. He had been overwhelmed by the rapid-fire words of Sam Morgan, the ex-Confederate soldier, politician, farmer, lumberman and now professor of law. Hunter's tobacco factory employed lots of unskilled laborers. He had a low opinion of these people, both white and black, who worked for the wages he and others like him could afford to pay in the post war economy. "I don't think the people who work for me would benefit from several decades of schooling." Hunter said. "It's hard enough to get an honest days work out of any of them."

"But who is to say what even some of these people could have accomplished if they had been taught to read and write at an early age. Education has to be the answer or else this region of the country will suffer from the effects of the war for many generations to come. Since we either thrive or suffer together, education and equality of opportunity must be afforded to all people regardless of race. You and I will not live to see it, but it has to happen."

Hunter disagreed with these ideas of Sam's but chose not to argue his points. It was getting late and he had a very good first hand account about the 51st Regiment's part in the war. This, after all, had been the reason for the visit. However, Sam had made some interesting statements on the causes and effects of the war and Hunter now wanted his opinions on its leaders.

"What is your final opinion about Abraham Lincoln, Mr. Morgan?"

"His place in history is secure regardless of my opinion, Mr. Hunter," Sam answered. "After all, his portrait is on our currency and his bust is on our postage stamps. But, he had to know that his efforts immediately after his election would lead to war, and it might well have been that our sectional differences had become so great that war was the only answer."

"Do you recall, Mr. Hunter, that Lincoln ordered a blockade of all Southern ports while North Carolina was still part of the Union? That was a strange thing to do if the President really cared about our remaining in the United States. It was early decisions by Lincoln from Washington which changed a rebellion of Southern coastal states, which were geographically indefensible, to a full scale war which lasted four years. North Carolina contributed one-hundred and twenty-five thousand troops to the Confederate Army as well as providing an unguardable coast line and the port of Wilmington. Take that away from the Confederacy as well as the leadership of Lee and Jackson and the rebellion couldn't have lasted very long, not even counting the soldiers from Virginia, Tennessee, and Arkansas."

"The North would not allow free trade and the South was angry about the tariffs on cotton. We believed in the rights of the individual states and Lincoln believed in the Union at all costs. It might have been that his real greatness lay in the fact that he saw what had to be done and set the nation on the course to do it. Four years later, all the questions I just mentioned had been answered. When he was shot by that damn fool Booth, it was a disaster for the South."

"How can you be sure of that, Mr. Morgan?" Hunter asked. "Would things have been all that different if Lincoln had lived?"

"We need only to look at what actually happened to see the change of attitude in Washington," Sam answered. "Lincoln fought the war on the premise that no state could leave the Union. After his death, each Southern state that had seceded had to be "readmitted" to the Union. Now if a state never left, it shouldn't have to do anything to get back in, should it?"

"I can give you no argument to your logic, Mr. Morgan," Hunter answered. "That is a very good point. But I would like to change the subject and get your opinion on some of the Generals. How would you compare Grant and Sherman to the Confederate Generals?" Hunter asked.

"It's almost impossible to do so," Sam countered. "Grant and Sherman knew how to use the overwhelming forces of the North which had existed all along. To be a successful Confederate general, you had to deal with shortages and be successful with half the troops your opponent commanded. Lee could very well have been the only general in the war who was able to do that, except maybe Stonewall Jackson."

"General Lee's place in history is just as secure as Lincoln's, is it not?" Hunter asked.

"Yes, it is!" Sam answered. "Many of my colleagues in the North are of the opinion that the war would have lasted not more than a year if Lee had accepted the command of the Union army when it was offered."

"Do you think that could be true?" asked Hunter.

"It's very likely," Sam responded. "It was Lee's victories in Virginia which almost brought us recognition from Europe and kept the Yankees out of Richmond for three years. If Jefferson Davis had given General Lee command of all the Confederate forces, he might have found a good general for the western army who wouldn't have gotten run out of Tennessee. If we could have kept a stalemate goin' there like Lee had in Virginia, Lincoln might not have been re-elected. If he had been defeated in the election of 1864, the Democrats would have made peace. But Sherman took Atlanta and Lincoln won a second term."

"You know," Sam continued. "The last memories we have of that conflict are of victorious Yankee armies and the defeated South, and it is easy to forget how danged close we came to winning that war. Not only on the battlefield, you see, but politically. There were a lot of people in the North who were tired of the heavy casualties by the time Lincoln's first term ended. I suppose we should thank the Almighty for his wisdom in directing that we should forever be one nation. I will confess, however, Mister Hunter, I still have a hard time doing that."

"Hear! Hear! That is a good place to conclude our discussion, Mr. Morgan," Hunter said appreciatively. "You have been most gracious."

The interview completed, he and Polly said their good-byes and mounted the buggy to begin the trip back to Durham. As the horse plodded along the muddy, rutted road the two historians traveled in silence. They had interviewed many Confederate veterans, but Sam alone had seemed to understand the cause of the events he had lived through and the repercussions caused by these events. It was Sam's seeming ability to predict the coming together of social, political and economic forces which intrigued Polly. His statement concerning racial equality was harder to grasp in these times than his prediction of war between the colonial powers.

"Do you suppose," Polly began, "that Mr. Morgan is correct that there will be war among the great powers and that blacks in this country will one day have equal status with whites."

Hunter made a grunting sound before answering as if to emphasize the sureness of his response. "The war might well occur," he scoffed, "but equality has no chance of happening if I have anything to do about it." The winds of change which would reach hurricane proportions by the latter half of the twentieth century had not yet begun to blow.

Bibliography

Baltz, Louis J., III. The Battle of Cold Harbor
H. E. Howard, Inc., Lynchburg, Va. 1994

Barefoot, Daniel W. General Robert F. Hoke, Lee' Modest
Warrior, John F. Blair, Publisher. Winston-Salem,
1996

Boyd, Joseph C. The Chemung Historical Journal,
"Shohola Train Wreck", Vol. 9, Number 4, PP
1253-1260. Elmira, New York, June 1964

Bradly, Mark L. The Battle of Bentonvile, Last Stand in
the Carolinas. Savas Woodbury Publishers
Campbell, Ca. 95008, 1996

Clark, Walter (Editor). Histories of the Several
Regiments and Battalions from North Carolina in
the Great War, 1861-65, Published by the State of
North Carolina, Goldsboro, 1901 (four volumes)

Foote, Shelby. The Civil War, A Narrative by Volumes
1,2,3. Random House, New York 1958

Frassanito, William A. Grant and Lee, The Virginia
Campaigns, 1864-1865; Charles Scribner's Sons,
1983

Freeman, Douglas Southall, edited by. Lee's Dispatches
to Jefferson Davis. G.P. Putnam's Son's, New
York, 1957

Gragg, Rod. Confederate Goliath, The Battle of Fort
Fisher. HarperColins Publishers, New York, 1991

Harmon, N. F. Confederate Veteran, "Prison Experiences
at Point Lookout". Vol. XV, Number 10, P.400
September 1907

Holmes, Clay A. The Elmira Prison Camp, A History of
the Military Prison at Elmira, N.Y. July 6, 1864,
to July 10, 1865. G.P.Putnam's Sons, New York
and London. The Knickerbocker Press, 1912

Luvaas, Jay. Johnston's Last Stand - Bentonville, North
Carolina Historical Review 33, 1956. PP. 332-58

Michie, Peter S. The Life and Letters of Emory Upton

D. Appleton and Company, New York, 1885

Trotter, William R., Silk Flags and Cold Steel, The Civil War in North Carolina: The Piedmont. John F. Blair, Publisher. Winston-Salem, North Carolina, 1988

Trotter, William R., Ironclads and Columbiads, The Civil War in North Carolina: The Coast. John F. Blair, Publisher. Winston-Salem, North Carolina, 1989

Thompson, Mangus S. Confederate Veteran, "Plan to Release Our Men at Point Lookout", Vol. XX, Number 2, PP. 69-70. February 1912

Vizetelly, Frank. Illustrated London News, March 18, 1865; Hoole, pp132-33. Historical Times Illustrated Encyclopedia, p.789, Vol VI